Charles A. Wiley

Wiley's Elocution and Oratory

Charles A. Wiley

Wiley's Elocution and Oratory

ISBN/EAN: 9783337375409

Printed in Europe, USA, Canada, Australia, Japan

Cover: Foto ©Andreas Hilbeck / pixelio.de

More available books at **www.hansebooks.com**

WILEY'S

ELOCUTION AND ORATORY:

GIVING A THOROUGH TREATISE ON THE ART OF

READING AND SPEAKING.

CONTAINING

NUMEROUS AND CHOICE SELECTIONS OF

DIDACTIC, HUMOROUS, AND DRAMATIC STYLES,

FROM THE MOST CELEBRATED AUTHORS.

FOR COLLEGES, ACADEMIES, AND SEMINARIES, AND A GUIDE FOR
TEACHERS, CLERGYMEN, AND PUBLIC SPEAKERS.

By CHARLES A. WILEY,

TEACHER OF ELOCUTION.

NEW YORK:
CLARK & MAYNARD, 5 BARCLAY STREET.
CHICAGO: S. C. GRIGGS & CO.
1869.

PREFACE.

THE primary object in the preparation of this work, was to arrange in a single volume, the principles of VOCAL CULTURE, and STYLE OF DELIVERY now used by the best elocutionists of the day; and, at the same time, to present a work for reading and for practice, that would contain the choicest gems of both ancient and modern literature.

These selections, containing the highest order of elocutionary merit—many of them of a purely patriotic spirit—the compiler, at the expense of much time and labor, has arranged or adapted, in a manner eminently fitted for the use of teachers and students in our colleges and schools.

That to which special attention is directed in this volume, is the *systematic arrangement*, unlike any thing that has yet appeared, both of the PRINCIPLES OF VOCAL CULTURE, and the RULES FOR DELIVERY, carefully and suitably prepared, for students of Elocution whether in schools, or colleges, or for private learners.

So completely in keeping with the advancing spirit of the art of Elocution will the rules and exercises in this volume be found, that no student who thoroughly conquers them can fail to become a master of Elocution.

CHARLES A. WILEY.

CONTENTS.

DEFINITIONS AND DIRECTIONS.

SELECTIONS.

DIDACTIC AND MORAL.

NARRATIVE AND DESCRIPTIVE.

SENATORIAL AND NATIONAL.

CONTENTS.

ELOCUTION AND ORATORY.

I. ELOCUTION.

ELOCUTION is the art of delivering with ease and propriety, written or extemporaneous composition.

Good reading or speaking, therefore, may be considered not only as uttering the words of a sentence so that they may be distinctly heard, but also, giving them all that beauty, force and variety, of which they are susceptible.

The prime qualification of an orator, is a pure and cultivated voice; therefore, a knowledge of the right use of the breathing apparatus, together with the proper manner of disciplining and using the voice, is the first subject the student should notice.

"Ignorance of the right way of using the lungs and the larynx, in speaking, reading, and singing, has caused more cases of bronchitis and pulmonary consumption among students, vocalists, clergymen, and other public speakers, than all other causes combined."—KIDD.

II. BREATHING.

Stand in a perfectly erect, but easy posture, with the weight of the body resting on one foot; the feet at the proper angle and distance from each other.

1. EFFUSIVE OR TRANQUIL BREATHING.

Draw in slowly, a full breath, and send it forth very

slowly in a prolonged sound of the breathing *h*, or *a-h* in a whisper.

2. EXPULSIVE OR FORCIBLE BREATHING.

Draw in, somewhat quicker than in Effusive, a full breath, and emit it with a lively, expulsive force; the sound of the *h* but little prolonged.

3. EXPLOSIVE OR ABRUPT BREATHING.

Draw in a full breath, faster than in Expulsive, and emit it very quickly in a very brief sound of the *h*.

This exercise in Breathing is an admirable one; as it not only gives command and strength to the organs of breathing, but it tends to allay the irritation of the fibers, that cause much of the harshness heard in many voices.

III. WHISPERING.

For students accustomed to articulate poorly, practice in whispering is one of the best remedies. For in speaking we may be understood if we do not articulate distinctly, but in whispering it is impossible. Let, then, the exercises under this head be confined exclusively to whispering.

1. EFFUSIVE WHISPERING.

Let the breath pass from the mouth in as gentle a manner as possible; so that, at first, a person at the distance of about ten feet would understand.

Examples.

STILLNESS OF NIGHT.—*Byron.*

All heaven and earth are still,—though not in sleep,
But breathless, as we grow when feeling most;
And silent, as we stand in thought too deep :—
All heaven and earth are still: From the high host
Of stars to the lulled lake, and mountain coast,
All is concentrated in a life intense,

Where not a beam, nor air, nor leaf is lost,
But hath a part of being, and a sense
Of that which is of all Creator and Defence.

2. EXPULSIVE WHISPERING.

Let the breath pass from the mouth with more force than in Effusive; so that a person could understand at about twice the distance of Effusive.

Examples.

Soldiers! you are now within a few steps of the enemy's outposts. Our scouts report them as slumbering in parties around their watchfires, and utterly unprepared for our approach. A swift and noiseless advance around that projecting rock, and we are upon them,—we capture them without the possibility of resistance.—One disorderly noise or motion may leave us at the mercy of their advanced guard. Let every man keep the strictest silence, under pain of instant death!

3. EXPLOSIVE WHISPERING.

Let the breath pass from the mouth in as abrupt and explosive a manner as possible.

Examples.

Hark! I hear the bugles of the enemy! They are on their march along the bank of the river. We must retreat instantly, or be cut off from our boats. I see the head of their column already rising over the height. Our only safety is in the screen of this hedge. Keep close to it; be silent; and stoop as you run. For the boats! Forward!

IV. QUALITY.

Quality has reference to the tone, or the kind of sound uttered.

The Qualities of Voice mostly used in reading or speaking, and which should receive the highest degree of culture are, the Pure Tone, the Orotund, the Aspirated, and the Guttural.

PURE TONE.

The Pure Tone is a clear, smooth, sonorous flow of

sound, adapted to express emotions of *joy*, *love*, and *tranquillity*.

Examples.

" JOY."

Shakspeare.

Come, let us to the castle.—
News, friends; our wars are done, the Turks are drown'd.
How does my old acquaintance of this isle?
Honey, you shall be well desired in Cyprus,
I have found great love amongst them. O my sweet,
I prattle out of fashion, and I dote
In mine own comforts.

" LOVE."

LINES WRITTEN IN A HIGHLAND GLEN.— *Wilson.*

Oh! that this lovely vale were mine!
Then, from glad youth to calm decline,
   My years would gently glide;
Hope would rejoice in endless dreams,
And Memory's oft-returning gleams
   By peace be sanctified!

"TRANQUILLITY."

SOLILOQUY OF DOUGLAS.—*Home.*

This is the place,—the centre of the grove;—
Here stands the oak, the monarch of the wood:
How sweet and solemn is this midnight scene!
The silver moon unclouded holds her way
Through skies where I could count each little star;
The fanning west wind scarcely stirs the leaves;
The river, rushing o'er its pebbled bed,
Imposes silence with a stilly sound.
In such a place as this, at such an hour,—
If ancestry may be in aught believed,—
Descending spirits have conversed with man,
And told the secrets of the world·unknown.

OROTUND. *

The Orotund is a full, deep, round, pure tone of voice, adapted to the declamatory style generally; and adapted

---

* The Orotund is, in reality, a fuller development of the Pure Tone.

especially to express, *sublime, impassioned* and *pathetic* emotions.

1. EFFUSIVE OROTUND.

Examples.

"SUBLIMITY."

MILTON'S INVOCATION OF LIGHT.

Hail! holy Light,—offspring of Heaven, first-born,
Or of the Eternal co-eternal beam
May I express thee unblamed? since God is light,
And never but in unapproached light,
Dwelt from eternity,—dwelt then in thee,
Bright effluence of bright Essence increate!
Or hear'st thou, rather, pure ethereal stream,
Whose fountain who shall tell?—Before the sun,
Before the heavens thou wert, and, at the voice
Of God, as with a mantle didst invest
The rising world of waters, dark and deep,
Won from the void and formless infinite.

"SUBLIMITY."

FROM THE BOOK OF PSALMS.

Bless the Lord, O my soul! O Lord, my God, Thou art very great. Thou art clothed with honor and majesty; who coverest thyself with light as with a garment; who stretchest out the heavens like a curtain: who layeth the beams of His chambers in the waters: who maketh the clouds His chariot; who walketh upon the wings of the wind; who laid the foundations of the earth, that it should not be removed forever.

2. EXPULSIVE OROTUND.

Examples.

"DECLAMATORY STYLE."

WEBSTER'S SPEECH OF JOHN ADAMS.

Sir, before God, I believe the hour is come. My judgment approves this measure; and my whole heart is in it. All that I have, and all that I am, and all that I hope, in this life, I am now ready here to stake upon it; and I leave off, as I began, that, live or die, survive or perish, I am for the declaration. It is my living sentiment; and, by the blessing of God, it shall be my dying sentiment:—independence *now*, and INDEPENDENCE FOREVER!

"IMPASSIONED."

FROM CAREY'S ODE ON ELOQUENCE.

Where rests the sword ?—where sleep the brave ?
Awake ! Cecropia's ally save
From the fury of the blast !
Burst the storm on Phocis' walls,—
Rise ! or Greece forever falls ;
Up ! or Freedom breathes her last !

3. EXPLOSIVE OROTUND.

Examples.

"IMPASSIONED."

ODE TO THE GREEKS.

Strike for the sires who left you free !
Strike for their sakes who bore you !
Strike for your homes and liberty,
And the Heaven you worship, o'er you !

"IMPASSIONED."

ANTONY, TO THE CONSPIRATORS.—*Shakspeare.*

Villains ! you did not threat, when your vile daggers
Hacked one another in the sides of Cæsar !
You showed your teeth like apes, and fawned like hounds,
And bowed like bondmen, kissing Cæsar's feet ;
Whilst damned Casca, like a cur, behind,
Struck Cæsar on the neck.—Oh ! flatterers !

ASPIRATED.

The Aspirated Tone is a forcible breathing or whispering utterance, and is used to express *fear, anger, terror,
revenge,* and *remorse.*

Examples.

"TERROR."

MACBETH, TO THE GHOST OF BANQUO.

Avaunt ! and quit my sight ! Let the earth hide thee !
Thy bones are marrowless, thy blood is cold :
Thou hast no speculation in those eyes
Which thou dost glare with !

Hence, horrible shadow!
Unreal mockery, hence!

"FEAR."

CALIBAN CONDUCTING STEPHANO AND TRINCULO TO THE CELL OF PROS-
PERO.—*Shakspeare.*

Pray you tread softly,—that the blind mole may not
Hear a footfall; we are now near his cell.
　　　　　Speak softly!
All's hushed as midnight yet.
　　　　　　　See'st thou here?
This is the mouth o' the cell: no noise! and enter.

GUTTURAL.

The Guttural is a deep, aspirated tone of voice, used to express *aversion, hatred, loathing,* and *contempt.*

Examples.

"AVERSION AND HATRED."

SHYLOCK, REGARDING ANTONIO.

How like a fawning publican he looks!
I hate him, for he is a Christian;
But more, for that, in low simplicity,
He lends out money gratis, and brings down
The rate of usuance with us here in Venice.
If I can catch him once upon the hip,
I will feed fat the ancient grudge I bear him!
He hates our sacred nation; and he rails,
Even there where merchants most do congregate,
On me, my bargains, and my well-won thrift,
Which he calls interest.—Cursed be my tribe,
If I forgive him!

"LOATHING AND CONTEMPT."

MASANIELLO, IN REPLY TO THE BASE SUGGESTIONS OF GENUINO.

I would that now
I could forget the monk who stands before me;
For he is like the accursed and crafty snake!
Hence! from my sight!—Thou Satan, get behind me,
Go from my sight!—I hate and I despise thee!

These were thy pious hopes; and I, forsooth,
Was in thy hands a pipe to play upon ;
And at thy music my poor soul to death
Should dance before thee !

V. ARTICULATION.

Articulation is the distinct utterance of all the oral elements in syllables and words, according to the most approved custom of pronouncing them. With faithful practice on the following examples, giving to each syllable and letter its proper sound, the student will find little difficulty in articulation.

Remember, that in good articulation, very much depends upon opening the mouth sufficiently, so that nothing can impede a round, full tone of voice.

A *daily practice*, upon the following examples, cannot be too strictly enjoined; because there is nothing that indicates Vocal Culture more plainly than good articulation.

Examples.

1. He beg*g*ed to be permit*t*ed to stay.

2. The foul*est* s*t*ain an*d* scan*dal* of our nature,
   Becomes i*ts* boas*t*. One *m*urder *m*akes a villain,
   *M*illions a hero.

3. Brigh*t* angels ! s*t*rike your loudes*t* s*t*rings,—
   Your sweet*est* voices raise.

, 4. I love my country's pine-cla*d h*ills,
   Her thousan*d* brigh*t* an*d g*ushing rills,
       Her sunshine an*d* her s*t*or*m*s ;
   He*r* rough an*d r*ugged *r*ocks that *r*ea*r*
   Their *h*oary *h*eads *h*igh in the air,
       In wil*d* fantastic for*m*s.

5. The c*r*icket kep*t* c*r*eeping ac*r*oss the crevices.

6. For *f*ear o*f* o*ff*ending the *f*rightful *f*ugitive, the *v*ile vagabond ventured to *v*ili*f*y the *v*enerable *v*eteran.

7. *Wh*ile *w*andering *wh*ere the *wh*irlpool *w*ends its *w*inding *w*ay,
   We *w*istfully *w*atched the *w*rathful *w*aters *w*ildly play.

8. The *st*ripling *str*anger *str*ayed *str*aight *t*oward the *str*uggling *str*eam.

9. The *sl*eepy *sl*uggard sits *sl*umbering silently.

10. All that's brigh*t* mus*t* fade,—
    The brightes*t st*ill the fleetes*t ;*
All tha*t's* *s*weet was made
    But to be los*t* when sweetes*t.*

11. He carves with classic chisel the Corinthian capital that crowns the column.

12. Now on his couch he *sh*runk and *sh*ivered.

13. Morn that now mee*t'st* the orie*nt* sun, now fly's*t.*

14. Yet say, should tyra*nts* learn a*t* las*t t*o feel,
    And the lou*d d*in of battle cease to bray ;
    Woul*d d*eath be foiled ? Would health, an*d str*ength, an*d* youth,
    Defy his power? *Has he* no a*rts* in *s*tore,
    No other shaf*ts* save those of war ? Alas !
    Even in the smile of peace—that smile which she*ds*
    A heavenly sun*sh*ine o'er the soul,—there ba*sks*
    That serp*ent*—LUXURY.

15. The Almighty sustai*ns* an*d* conduc*ts* the universe. It was He who separated the jarri*ng* elem*ents !* It was He who hu*ng* up the wo*rlds* in *empt*y space ! It is He who *preserves* them in their cir*cles,* an*d* imp*els* them in their course !

16. The bliss of man,—coul*d pr*ide that blessi*ng* find,—
    Is no*t t*o a*ct* or thin*k* bey*ond* manki*nd.*

17. All the orienta*l l*uster of the riche*st* ge*ms,* all the encha*nt*ing beauties of exterior shape, the exquisite of all forms, the loveliness of color, the harmony of soun*ds,* the heat an*d* brightne*ss* of the enlivening su*n,* the heroic virtue of the brave*st* mi*nds,* with the purity an*d* quickness of the highe*st* intelle*ct,* are all emanations from the Deity.

VI. MODULATION.*

MODULATION includes the consideration of Key, Variations, Force, and Rate.

---

* The terms and a part of the definitions in modulation are adopted from Mandeville.

KEY.

The KEY, otherwise called *pitch*, is the *predominating tone* of reading or speaking.

Accurately speaking, there are as many keys as there are half tones and even quarter tones of the voice; any one of which may be made at pleasure, the *predominating tone* of reading or speaking.

For convenience, and for practice, KEY is commonly divided into *low key*, *middle key*, and *high key*.

1. LOW KEY.

The Low Key should generally be used in expressing *deep solemnity, awe, amazement, horror, despair, melancholy,* and *deep grief.*

The exceedingly *low key* of these and similar states of feeling, is one of those universal facts which necessarily becomes a law of vocal expression, and consequently an indispensable rule of Elocution. Any passage strongly marked by the language of one of these emotions, becomes utterly inexpressive without its appropriate deep notes; and yet this fault is one of the most prevalent in reading, especially with the youth.

Examples.

"DEEP SOLEMNITY, AND AWE."

[Effusive and Expulsive orotund.]

CATO, IN SOLILOQUY.—*Addison.*

It must be so ;—Plato, thou reasonest well!
Else, whence this pleasing hope, this fond desire
This longing after immortality?
Or whence this secret dread, and inward horror,
Of falling into nought? Why shrinks the soul
Back on herself, and startles at destruction?
'T is the Divinity that stirs within us:
'T is Heaven itself that points out an hereafter,
And intimates Eternity to man.
Eternity!—thou pleasing,—dreadful thought!
Through what variety of untried being,
Through what new scenes and changes must we pass!
The wide, the unbounded prospect lies before me;
But shadows, clouds, and darkness, rest upon it.

"HORROR AND DESPAIR."
[Aspirated Quality.]

THE PESTILENCE.—*Porteous.*

At dead of night,
In sullen silence stalks forth PESTILENCE :
CONTAGION, close behind, taints all her steps
With poisonous dew : no smiting hand is seen,
No sound is heard ; but soon her secret path
Is marked with desolation : heaps on heaps
Promiscuous drop.   No friend, no refuge, near :
All, all is false and treacherous around,
All that they touch, or taste, or breathe, is DEATH !

" DEEP GRIEF."
[Effusive and Expulsive orotund.]

AFFLICTION AND DESOLATION.—*Young.*

In every varied posture, place, and hour,
How widowed every thought of every joy !
Thought, busy thought ! too busy for my peace !
Through the dark postern of time long elapsed,
Led softly, by the stillness of the night,
Led like a murderer, (and such it proves !)
Strays, (wretched rover !) o'er the pleasing past :
In quest of wretchedness perversely strays,
And finds all desert now.

2. MIDDLE KEY.

The Middle Key should generally be used in *common conversation*, in the delivery of a *literary* or *scientific essay,* a *doctrinal sermon*, a plain *practical oration* on any subject limited to purposes of mere utility, and demanding the action of reason and judgment.

Examples.

" LITERARY ESSAY."
[Declamatory style, Expulsive orotund.]

PURE LOVE.

Raleigh's cheerfulness, during his last days, was so great, and his fearlessness of death so marked, that the Dean of Westminster who attended

2

him, wondering at his deportment, reprehended the lightness of his manner. But Raleigh gave God thanks that he had never feared death; for it was but an opinion and an imagination; and, as for the manner of death, he had rather die so than in a burning fever; that some might have made shows outwardly; but he felt the joy within.

"EARNEST PRACTICAL ORATION."
[Declamatory style, Expulsive orotund.]
LOVE OF COUNTRY.—*Sidney Smith.*

Whence does this love of our country, this universal passion, proceed? Why does the eye ever dwell with fondness upon the scenes of infant life? Why do we breathe with greater joy the breath of our youth? Why are not other soils as grateful, and other heavens as gay? Why does the soul of man ever cling to that earth where it first knew pleasure and pain, and, under the rough discipline of the passions, was roused to the dignity of moral life? Is it only that our country contains our kindred and our friends? And is it nothing but a name for our social affections?

It cannot be this; the most friendless of human beings, has a country which he admires and extols, and which he would, in the same circumstances, prefer to all others under heaven. Tempt him with the fairest face of nature, place him by living waters under shadowy trees of Lebanon, open to his view all the gorgeous allurements of the sunniest climates, he will love the rocks and deserts of his childhood better than all these, and thou canst not bribe his soul to forget the land of his nativity.

3. HIGH KEY.

The High Key should generally be used in expressing *brisk, gay,* and *joyous* emotions; also the *extremes* of *pain, grief,* and *fear,* which from their preternaturally exciting power, cause the peculiar shrill, convulsive cries and shrieks which express these passions.

This key of voice, though seldom used in ordinary reading, ought to be *practiced thoroughly,* as it tends to give strength, scope, and command to the voice, and as it is frequently employed in public speaking. Almost every one can speak in a high key, while but few can do it without a shrill, unpleasant tone. It should not be forgotten, either, that it is not he who speaks the loudest who can be heard the furthest. A scientific observer remarks, "It is a curious fact in the history of sound, that the loudest noises always perish on the spot where they are produced, whereas musical notes will be heard at a great distance."

Examples.

"BRISK, JOYOUS STYLE."
[Expulsive Orotund.]
FROM THE HYMN OF THE STARS.—*Bryant.*

Away, away! through the wide, wide sky,—
The fair blue fields that before us lie,—
Each sun with the worlds that round him roll,
Each planet, poised on her turning pole,
With her isles of green, and her clouds of white,
And her waters that lie like fluid light!

For the source of glory uncovers his face,
And the brightness o'erflows unbounded space;
And we drink, as we go, the luminous tides
In our ruddy air and our blooming sides:
Lo! yonder the living splendors play!
Away! on our joyous path away!

Away, away!—In our blossoming bowers,
In the soft air wrapping these spheres of ours,
In the seas and fountains that shine with morn,
See, Love is brooding, and Life is born;
And breathing myriads are breaking from night,
To rejoice like us, in motion and light!

"GAY, BRISK."
[Pure Tone.]
SPRING.—*Bryant.*

Is this a time to be gloomy and sad,
　When our mother Nature laughs around;
When even the deep blue heavens look glad,
　And gladness breathes from the blossoming ground?

The clouds are at play, in the azure space,
　And their shadows at play on the bright green vale,
And here they stretch to the frolic chase,
　And there they roll on the easy gale.

And look at the broad-faced sun how he smiles
　On the dewy earth that smiles on his ray,
On the leaping waters and gay young isles,—
　Ay, look, and he'll smile thy gloom away.

TRANSITION IN KEY.

Examples.

"FROM HORROR TO TRANQUILLITY."

[From Very Low to Middle Key.]

STANZAS FROM A RUSSIAN POET.—*Bowring.*

Very Low.

How frightful the grave! how deserted and drear!
With the howls of the storm-wind, the creaks of the bier,
  And the white bones all clattering together!

Middle Key.

How peaceful the grave! its quiet how deep:
Its zephyrs breathe calmly; and soft is its sleep;
  And flowrets perfume it with ether.

"FROM RAPTURE TO GRIEF."

[From Very High to Low Key.]

Very High.

Ring joyous chords!—ring out again!
A swifter still and a wilder strain!
And bring fresh wreaths!—we will banish all
Save the free in heart from our festive hall.
On through the maze of the fleet dance, on!

Low Key.

But where are the young and the lovely?—gone!
Where are the brows with the red rose crowned,
And the floating forms with the bright zone bound?
And the waving locks and the flying feet,
That still should be where the mirthful meet?—
They are gone!—they are fled, they are parted all:
  Alas! the forsaken hall!

MONOTONE.

The Monotone, though perhaps not coming under the head of Key, will be far better understood if treated here, than elsewhere.

The Monotone is speaking without change of *key:* that

is, preserving a fulness of tone, without ascent or descent on the scale.

The Monotone when given in a low key, and without force, is much more audible than when the voice slides up and down.

Actors adopt this tone when repeating passages aside. It conveys the idea of being inaudible to those with them in the scene, by being in a lower tone; and by being in a Monotone becomes audible to the whole house.

Generally the Monotone requires a low tone of voice, with slow and prolonged utterance. It is the ONLY tone that can properly present the *supernatural* and *ghostly*.

This is the *best* tone, *by far*, to practice, in the cultivation of the voice.

Examples.

Milton.

1. High on a throne of royal state, which far
Outshone the wealth of Ormus or of Ind,
Or where the gorgeous East, with richest hand,
Showers on her kings barbaric pearl and gold,
Satan exalted sat!

2. How reverend is the face of this tall pile,
Whose ancient pillars rear their marble heads,
To bear aloft its arched and ponderous roof,
By its own weight made steadfast and immovable,
Looking tranquillity! It strikes an awe
And terror on my aching sight: the tombs
And monumental caves of death look cold,
And shoot a chillness to my trembling heart. .

Shakspeare.

3. I am thy father's spirit;
Doomed for a certain term to walk the night,
And, for the day confined to fast in fires,
Till the foul crimes, done in my days of nature,
Are burnt and purged away. But that I am forbid
To tell the secrets of my prison-house,
I could a tale unfold, whose lightest word
Would harrow up thy soul; freeze thy young blood;
Make thy two eyes, like stars, start from their spheres;

Thy knotted and combined locks to part,
And each.particular hair to stand on end,
Like quills upon the fretful porcupine:
But this eternal blazon must not be
To ears of flesh and blood:—List,—list,—O list!—
If thou didst ever thy dear father love,
Revenge his foul and most unnatural murder.

VARIATIONS.

By Vocal Variation, is meant the different movements of the voice, or *variations* from the key, in the delivery of a sentence. These are the Sweeps, the Bend, the Slides, and the Closes.

1. SWEEPS.

The most important are the Emphatic Sweeps.

The movement of the voice, which a development of the Emphatic Sweeps requires, is a sweep upward from the key to the word emphasized, and, coming down upon the word, with increased force, is carried below the key and again back to it. The upper movement is called the Upper Sweep: the lower movement, the Lower Sweep.

Thus :   Low'r Sweep ? Upp'r Sweep

Examples.

They were *gone* on your arrival?
You over*came* him in the struggle?
He rode to *Lon*don last week?

Accentual Sweeps take the same movement of the Emphatic, though very much diminished in extent, and are generally developed upon one syllable or word:—The Accentual Sweeps in this movement may be compared to the ripples upon a lake; while the Emphatic may be likened to the great waves of the sea.

The movement of the Accentual Sweeps may be observed, in the following sentence, if read without Emphasis. Thus :

Examples.

Night, sable goddess, from her ebon throne
In rayless majesty now stretches forth
Her leaden sceptre o'er a slumbering world.

2. BEND.

The Bend is a slight turn of the voice upward, at a pause of imperfect sense.

The use of the Bend in reading and speaking will be found of the greatest utility, as it gives life and animation to the subject: especially in opening an address use the Bend as much as possible, as it aids materially in gaining the good will and sympathy of the audience.

Examples.

Trained and instructed', strengthened by wise discipline', and guided by pure principle,' it ripens into an intelligence' but little lower than the angels.

Ladies,' and gentlemen,' our country at this hour,' not only needs patriotism in the field,' but also all the aid of noble hearts at home.

3. SLIDES.

The *Upward* Slide.   The *Downward* Slide.   The *Waving* Slide.   The *Double* Slide.

THE UPWARD SLIDE,

is a gradual rise of the voice upward through a series of tones, ceasing at the highest.   Thus: ————'

Examples.

Would you deny being useful to the present generation, because you have been wounded by the poisoned shaft of envy?

Are you a scholar, and shall the land of Muses ask your help in vain?

> Can the deep statesman, skilled in great design,
>   Protect but for a day precarious breath?
> Or the tuned follower of the sacred nine,
>   Soothe with his melody, insatiate death?

THE DOWNWARD SLIDE,

is the *reverse* of the Upward: carrying the voice downward through a series of tones, ceasing at the lowest.

Thus: ———— !

Examples.

Who is there so cold that did not weep when Mighty Cæsar fell?
Who but rather turns
To heaven's broad fire his unconstrained view,
Than to the glimmering of a waxen flame?

THE WAVING SLIDE,

has the precise movement of the Emphatic Sweeps.
Thus:

Examples.

They were *gone* on your arrival?
You joined the "Army of the Oriskany" on that occasion?
They visited Washington on Saturday?

THE DOUBLE SLIDE,

is used in the delivery of all questions where the disjunctive conjunction *or* is present: the *or* forming the point at which the one ends, and the other begins. The voice takes the movement of the Upward Slide to *or*, and the Downward Slide from it to the close.
Thus: ——— or! ———, ———; ———,

Examples.

Are the stars that gem the vault of the heavens above us, mere decorations of the night; or are they revolving suns and centres of planetary systems?

Was it a wailing bird of the gloom,
Which shrieked on the house of woe all night?
Or a shivering fiend that flew to a tomb?

4. CLOSES.

The Partial Close, } marked thus: (\ )
The Perfect Close, }   (.)
in the following examples.

The Partial Close is a fall of the voice at the end of one of the *parts* of a sentence to the key, or to a point near the key, preparatory to the Perfect Close.

The Perfect Close is a fall of the voice, at the end of a sentence, to a point generally below the key.

Examples of both in Connection.

Before closing this I wish to make one observation :\ I shall make it once for all.

History, as it has been written, is the genealogy of princes :\ the field book of conquerors.

FORCE.

Reading with greater or less Force, is simply reading with more or less volume of voice upon the same key. There are many reasons why we should be judicious in the use of Force. First, if too little Force be used, the rear portion of the audience will not hear distinctly. Secondly, if too much Force be used, the speaking will be too loud for those nearest the rostrum. Thirdly, the continued use of an unusual degree of Force, destroys the flexibility of the voice; and leaves no room for an increase of volume, when the nature of the sentence absolutely demands greater force.

STRESS, according to Dr. Rush, is but the rendering of *Force* perceptible or impressive, in *single sounds*.

There are, properly, three kinds: the Radical, the Median, and the Increasing.

1. The RADICAL is generally explosive, and falls on the first part of a sound.

Examples.

[Explosive Utterance, Orotund, High Key.]
Strike, for the sires who left your free !
Strike, for their sakes who bore you !
Strike for your homes and Liberty,
And the Heaven you worship o'er you !

[Explosive Utterance, Pure Tone, High Key.]
VOICE OF SPRING.—*Mrs. Hemans.*
Ye of the rose lip and the dew-bright eye
And the bounding footstep, to meet me fly !
2*

With the lyre and the wreath and the joyous lay,
  Come forth to the sunshine,—I may not stay.

[The same as before.]

SPRING.—*Bryant.*

There's a dance of leaves in that aspen bower,
  There's a titter of winds in that beechen tree,
There's a smile on the fruit, and a smile on the flower
  And a laugh from the brook that runs to the sea !

2. The MEDIAN is generally expulsive, and swells out towards the middle of a sound, and vanishes towards the close.

Examples.

[Effusive Utterance, Pure Tone, Middle Key.]

DEATH OF THE GOOD MAN.—*Bryant.*

Why weep ye, then, for him, who, having won
The bound of man's appointed years,—at last,
Life's blessings all enjoyed, life's labors done,
Serenely to his final rest has passed ;
While the soft memory of his virtues, yet,
Lingers like twilight hues, when the bright sun is set ?

His youth was innocent ; his riper age,
Marked with some act of goodness, every day ;
And, watched by eyes that loved him, calm and sage
Faded his late declining years away.
Cheerful he gave his being up, and went
To share the holy rest that waits a life well spent.

[Expulsive Utterance, Pure Tone, Middle Key.]
PLEASURES OF THE NATURALIST.—*Wood.*

Whether the naturalist be at home or abroad, in every different clime, and in every season of the year, universal nature is before him, and invites to a banquet richly replenished with whatever can invigorate his understanding, or gratify his mental taste.   The earth on which he treads, the air in which he moves, the sea along the margin of which he walks, all teem with objects that keep his attention perpetually awake, excite him to healthful activity, and charm him with an ever-varying succession of the beautiful, the wonderful, the useful, and the new.

3. The INCREASING, effusive at first, increases till the last moment of the sound, and ends with the explosive.

Examples.

[Aspirated Quality, Low Key.]

KING HENRY V. TO LORD SCROOP, ON THE DETECTION OF HIS TREASON.—
Shakspeare.

But oh!
What shall I say to thee, Lord Scroop, thou cruel
Ungrateful, savage, and inhuman creature!
Thou that didst bear the keys of all my counsels,
That knew'st the very bottom of my soul,
That almost might'st have coined me into gold,
Wouldst thou have practised on me for thy use?

[Aspirated and guttural Quality, Middle Key.]

QUEEN CONSTANCE, TO THE ARCHDUKE OF AUSTRIA.—*Shakspeare.*

Thou slave! thou wretch! thou coward!
Thou little valiant, great in villany!
Thou ever strong upon the stronger side!
Thou Fortune's champion, that dost never fight
But when her humorous ladyship is by
To teach thee safety!

RATE.

Rate must necessarily vary with the nature of the thought, and the emotion. It has been observed that the tendency of American orators is, to undue rapidity. The Rate should not be so *slow* that the Audience may anticipate what we are about to say; and (as good Articulation is one of the most necessary requisites of a good orator) it should not be so *fast*, that the Articulation is rendered indistinct. Generally *Slow* Rate should be practiced. Because in speaking thus, an orator has the air of self-possession,—can Articulate distinctly, and has, in reserve, the power to increase the Rate, where the nature of the sentence may absolutely demand it.

VII. DELIVERY.

All sentences are comprehended in three classes: the Declarative, the Interrogative, and the Exclamatory.

Declarative sentences state or declare something, of time past, present or future; affirmatively or negatively; as true or false; possible or impossible; &c.

Interrogative sentences are such as contain questions.

Exclamatory sentences are such as are employed to express emotion or passion.

DECLARATIVE.

Rule 1. Declarative sentences are delivered with the Bend at intermediate pauses, when life, cheerfulness, or joy is required, and the Partial Close, when sorrow, or great emphasis is required.

Examples.

1. He left his father's house' for the halls of the academy.

2. Fire of imagination,' strength of mind,' and firmness of soul,' are gifts of nature.

3. In man or woman,' but far most in man;'
   And most of all' in man that ministers
   And serves the altar,' in my soul I loathe'
   All affectation.'

4. I protest against the measure, as cruel,' oppressive,' tyrannous, and vindictive'.

INTERROGATIVE.

Interrogative sentences are either Definite, Indefinite, or Indirect.

DEFINITE.

The Definite are such as begin with verbs, and may be answered by *yes* or *no.*

Rule 2. Definite Interrogative Sentences are delivered with the Rising Slide ending only with the last word.

Examples.

1. Did not even-handed Justice, commend the poisoned chalice to their own lips?

    2. Is this a dagger which I see before me,
        The handle toward my hand?

3. Should not merchants be prompt in paying their debts?

4. Do you hear the rain, Mr. Caudle?

    5. Heard ye those loud contending waves,
        That shook Cecropia's pillared state?
    Saw ye the mighty from their graves,
        Look up, and tremble at their fate?

6. Does prodigal autumn to our age deny
    The plenty that once swelled beneath his sober eye?

7.   Will he quench the ray
    Infused by his own forming smile at first,
    And leave a work so far all blighted and accursed?

8. Will a man play tricks, will he indulge
    A silly, fond conceit of his fair form
    And just proportion, fashionable mien,
    And pretty face, in presence of his God?

9. Can we want obedience then
    To him, or possibly his love desert,
    Who formed us from the dust and placed us here,
    Full to the utmost measure of what bliss
    Human desires can seek or apprehend?

10. Canst thou with impious obloquy condemn
    The just decree of God, pronounced and sworn,
    That to his only Son, by right endued
    With regal sceptre, every soul in heaven
    Shall bend the knee, and in that honor due
    Confess him rightful king?

11. Will then the merciful One, who stamped our race
    With his own image, and who gave them sway
    O'er earth, and the glad dwellers on her face,
    Now that our flourishing nations far away
    Are spread, where'er the moist earth drinks the day,
    Forget the ancient care that taught and nursed
    His latest offspring?

EXCEPTIONS TO RULE 2.

There are, however, no Exceptions, save for the sake of *emphasis*.

Exception 1. When the same Definite question is repeated, the repetition should be delivered with the Downward Slide.

Examples.

1. Has he returned?   *Has he returned?*
2. Do you hear the rain?   Mr. Caudle.   *Do you hear the rain?*
3. Has the gentleman done?   *Has he completely done?*

Exception 2. A series of Definite Interrogatives should have the last member delivered with the Downward Slide.

Examples.

1. Do you know me, Sir?   Am I Dromio?
   Am I your man?   *Am I myself?*
2. *Shy.* Three thousand ducats: well.
   Bass. Ay, Sir, for three months.
   Shy. For three months; well.
   Bass. For the which, I told you, Antonio shall be bound.
   Shy. Antonio shall become bound; well.
   Bass. May you stead me? Will you pleasure me?
   Shall I know your answer?

INDEFINITE.

The Indefinite are such as begin with adverbs and relative pronouns, and cannot be answered by *yes* or *no*.

Rule 3. Indefinite Interrogative sentences are delivered with the Upper Emphatic sweep to the emphatic word, and the Downward Slide from it to the close.

Examples.

1. When may a man be said to be properly educated?
2. What advantages result from the possession of elegance, or delicacy of taste?
3. When was it that Rome attracted most strongly the admiration of

mankind, and impressed the deepest sentiment of fear on the hearts of her enemies?

4. What scourge for perjury
Can this dark monarchy afford false Clarence?

5. What constitutes a State?

6. What have I done, that thou darest wag thy tongue in noise against me?'

7. Whence is that knocking?

8. How is 't with me, when every noise appalls me?

EXCEPTION TO RULE 3.

Exception. An Indefinite repeated for the sake of *emphasis*, or to obtain a more *distinct answer*, is delivered with the Upward Slide.

Examples.

1. When will you go to Boston? Next week.
   When will you go to Boston? Next week.
2. *Falstaff.* A plague on all cowards, say I.
   Prince Henry. What's the matter?
   Fal. *What's the matter?* Here be four of us have taken a thousand pounds this morning.
   Prince H. Where is it, Jack? Where is it?
   Fal. *Where is it?* taken from us, it is.

INDIRECT.

The Indirect are interrogatives in a declarative form.

Rule 4. Indirect interrogative sentences are delivered with the Waving Slide: that is, the Upper Sweep to the emphatic word, and the Lower Sweep from it.   .

Examples.

1. You assisted at the Capitol this morning?
2. They visited Egypt before returning?
3. Surely you will return to-morrow?
4. I certainly must have seen you at Chicago?
5. Thou art not wont to join in the prattle of the common people at Rome?
6. Surely he will leave it in the care of his country?

EXCEPTION TO RULE 4.

Exception. In a series of Indirect interrogatives the last member should be delivered like a Declarative.

Examples.

1. You have an elegant show case at your window? Yes, sir. *And you seem highly pleased with it ?* Yes, sir.

2. You visited the Exposition at Paris? Yes, sir. You saw the Emperor of France? Yes, sir. And the Turkish train? Yes, sir. *On the whole, you must have seen very many wonders?* Yes, sir, many.

EXCLAMATORY.

Exclamatory sentences are Declarative, Interrogative, and Spontaneous.

All Exclamatory sentences are, in reality, either Declarative or Interrogative sentences, and are delivered with precisely the same movement of voice, but (for the sake of Exclamation) with a greater degree of emotion or passion expressed. Hence,

Rule 5. Exclamatory sentences are delivered like the Declarative and Interrogative sentences from which they are derived; except that they require in addition the peculiar effects of the emotions and passions.

Examples of Declarative.

1. I will paint the death-dew on his brow !
2. Shake off this downy sleep, death's counterfeit,
   And look on death itself !
3. She murmured as she died !
4. Think on thy chains !
5. Look on this wedge of gold !
6. The starless grave shall shine
   The portal of eternal day !

Examples of Interrogative.
DEFINITE.

1. Is that vile thing the cause of this !
2. Can it be possible !
3. Was it not a terrible night when we met on the beach !
4. Do you think they did the deed !

INDEFINITE.

1. Whence comes that noise !
2. Who ever thought
In such a homely piece of stuff, to see
    The mighty Senate's tool !
3. How his eyes glare !
4. Who did the murder !

INDIRECT.

1. You do not believe he joined in the riot ! '
2. Let them not die in that terrible manner !
3. He saved his family from the burning walls !
4. Thou wouldst not have me make a trial of my skill upon my child !

Examples of Spontaneous.

See there ! Behold ! Avaunt ! Hurra ! Hold ! Away ! Look !
Shame ! Lo ! Lush ! Hush !

They are called Spontaneous because they are generally uttered without deliberation.

While the preceding rules apply to simple sentences, there are *very few* compound sentences that are really exceptions to these rules; or, of which a thorough knowledge of them will not determine the delivery. Therefore, the student, *next in value* to a knowledge of the voice, should thoroughly acquaint himself with these rules.

VIII. PHONETIC LAUGHTER.

Laughter as an art, may be easily learned by the aid of Phonetics. It is one of the most interesting and healthy of all vocal exercises. There are in the English language thirty-two well defined varieties of laughter.

Eighteen are produced in connection with the Tonics *a, e, i, o, u;* nine with the Subtonics of *l, m, n, ng, r, th, v,* and *z;* and five with the Atonics of *f, h, s, th,* and *sh.*

In practicing the student should first utter a tonic, and

then prefixing the oral element of *h*, should produce in continued repetition the syllable; as, ā, hā, hā, hā, &c.; ă, hă, hă, &c.·

IX. GESTURE.

Gesture should be used only when it will aid in expressing language more forcibly; and, to be appropriate and impressive, it must always be natural; for, when Gesture appears studied and artificial, it obviously destroys the effect.

No speaker should be so prolific or eccentric in gesture, that his audience will notice any peculiarities of gesture, but will remember only, that all were graceful and appropriate. The learner will find the following rules of value.

1. The Gesture employed most frequently, is the movement used in handing a book or other article to a friend.

And what is the delivery of an oration, but simply the presentation of ideas to the audience?

POSITION OF THE HAND: The hand open: the first finger straight, the others slightly curved; and generally the palms of the hands open toward the audience, so that they may be seen by the audience.

2. The Argumentative, commonly called the "Henry Clay" gesture may, and should be used most frequently in debate, and argumentative declamation.

POSITION OF THE HAND : First finger straight, the others closed, or nearly so.

This gesture is very useful in earnest debate; as it was often remarked of Clay that the arguments seemed to drop from the end of his finger. These gestures, indeed, as they serve to bring the thoughts and arguments to a point, are of great value in any discourse.

3. The Fist, sometimes called the "Sledge-Hammer" gesture, should be used in the expression of the most earnest, powerful, *moving* sentiments where strong argu-

ments are to be brought out with telling effect. This gesture was a favorite one with Daniel Webster; and in those memorable debates with Hayne in the United States Senate, he is said to have riveted his arguments with the force of a giant, when at every appropriate place, he brought down his "Sledge-Hammer" gesture; as, in the expression, "Liberty *and* Union, now and for *ever*, *one* and *inseparable.*"

GESTURE, WHEN USED.

Save in debate and argumentative orations, gesture should seldom be used, except when referring to some object in nature.

1. When referring to the earth covered with snow, to withering famine, to desolation in whatever respect; or, when referring to death, or hell, always have the *palm* of the hand *downward;* and the arm raised but slightly from the body.

Examples.

The time
Of blossoms and green leaves is yet afar ;
And ere it comes, the encountering winds shall oft
Muster their wrath again, and rapid clouds
Shade heaven, and bounding on the frozen earth
Shall full their volleyed stores, rounded like hail
And white like snow, and the loud North again
Shall buffet the vexed forest in his rage.—BRYANT.

2. When referring to the earth robed in green, to the trees and flowers in bloom; to life, or to abundance, always have the *palm* of the hand *upward*, and often raised as high as the head.

Examples.

Now the bright morning star, day's harbinger,
Comes dancing from the east, and leads with her
The flowery May, who from her green lap throws
The yellow cowslip and the pale primrose.
Hail beauteous May, that dost inspire
Mirth and youth and warm desire!—MILTON.

In all cases, be careful to complete the gesture, where it is intended, at the instant of uttering the syllable or word; for, if it comes in before or lags behind the word, it will certainly detract from the effect.

X. RHETORICAL PAUSES.

Rhetorical Pauses are those which require a suspension of the voice in reading or speaking, although the construction of the sentence admits of no grammatical pause.

The Rhetorical pause occurs, either directly before, or directly after the utterance of an important thought; and is found as frequently where there is *not* as where there *is* a *grammatical* pause.

In the following examples Rhetorical pauses are denoted thus (‖); but in general, the student must be guided by the sense.

Examples.

1. And there lay the steed‖ with his nostril all wide,
   But through them there rolled‖ not the breath of his pride,
   And the foam of his gasping‖ lay white on the turf,
   And cold as the spray‖ of the rock-beaten surf.

2. The worst of slaves, is he ‖ whom passion ‖ rules.

3. Glory ‖ is like a circle ‖ in the water,
   Which never ceaseth ‖ to enlarge itself,
   Till, by broad spreading, it disperse ‖ to naught.

4. There is a land ‖ of every land the pride,
   Beloved by Heaven ‖ o'er all the world beside,
   Where brighter scenes ‖ dispense serener light,
   And milder moons ‖ imparadise the night;
   Oh, thou shalt find, ‖ howe'er thy footsteps roam,
   That land—thy country ‖ and that spot—thy home.

5. No self-plumed vanity ‖ was there,
   With fancy's consequence ‖ elate;
   Unknown to her ‖ the haughty air
   That means to speak ‖ superior state.

6. You may as well ‖ go stand upon the beach,
   And bid the main-flood ‖ bate his usual height;
   You may as well ‖ use question with the wolf,
   Why he hath made ‖ the ewe bleat for the lamb ;
   You may as well ‖ forbid the mountain pines
   To wag their high tops, ‖ and to make no noise,
   When they are fretted ‖ with the gusts of heaven ;
   You may as well ‖ do any thing that's hard,
   As seek to soften ❘ that, (than which, what's harder?)
   His Jewish heart.

7. Now the hungry ‖ lion roars,
   And the wolf ‖ behowls the moon ;
   While the heavy ‖ ploughman snores,
   With his weary ‖ task foredone.

8. Now the wasted ‖ brands do glow,
   While the screech-owl ‖ screeching-loud,
   Puts the wretch ‖ that lies in woe,
   In remembrance ‖ of his shroud.

9. She said ❘ and struck; ‖ deep entered ❘ in her side
   The piercing steel, ‖ with reeking purple dyed :
   Clogged ❘ in the wound, ‖ the cruel ❘ weapon stands,
   The spouting blood ‖ came streaming o'er her hands.
   Her sad attendants ‖ saw the deadly stroke,
   And with loud cries ‖ the sounding palace shook.

XI. EMPHASIS.

Emphasis is that change, or modulation of voice, that renders whatever the speaker desires to utter clear and expressive.

The various movements of the voice are given under Sweeps and Force, in Modulation. There can be no other *special* rules, except that the meaning of the selections to be rendered be *carefully* studied.

XII. PARENTHESIS.

The Parenthesis is generally delivered more rapidly, or in a more subdued tone than what precedes or follows it; and, if the Parenthesis follows a part of a sentence making imperfect sense, it terminates with the bend; otherwise with the Partial, or Perfect Close.

Examples.

1. Know then this truth, (enough for man to know,)
Virtue alone is happiness below.

2. I have seen charity (if charity it may be called) insult with an air of pity.

3. I am happy, said he (expressing himself with the warmest emotion), infinitely happy, in seeing you return.

4. Surely, in this age of invention, something may be struck out to obviate the necessity (if such necessity exist) of so tasking the human intellect.

5. Know ye not, brethren (for I speak to them that know the law), that the law hath dominion over a man as long as he liveth?

XIII. STYLE.

The student should never attempt to deliver any selection, until he first ascertains to what *style* it belongs.

If it be

1. ARGUMENTATIVE, he must deliver it as if debating; therefore earnest.

2. DESCRIPTIVE, he must deliver it as if actually describing some scene.

3. PERSUASIVE, he must use those looks, tones, and gestures appropriately used in persuasion.

XIV. THE PASSIONS.

The student should always have his mind so wrought up to the proper pitch in which the passion should be rendered, that he may, with ease, be able to deliver it correctly.

Great actors, before appearing in the character they are to personify, through force of will, work their minds up to the degree of passion required, and thus appear perfectly life-like.

Elocutionists, also, in exhibiting some vehement passion to a class, have brought their minds to such a pitch of phrensy, as to be several hours in overcoming its effects. Students should always, before attempting to express one of the passions, carefully examine in what Tone, Key, Force, and Rate it should be delivered: finding these, adapt the voice and expression to it, and then deliver it.

Examples.

1. "SCORN AND DEFIANCE."

[Explosive Orotund, Middle Key.]

FROM PARADISE LOST.—*Milton.*

Satan, [*to Death.*]   " Whence and what art thou, execrable shape!
That dar'st, though grim and terrible, advance
Thy miscreated front athwart my way
To yonder gates ?   Through them I mean to pass,—
That be assured,—without leave asked of thee :
Retire ! or taste thy folly ; and learn by proof,
Hell-born ! not to contend with spirits of heaven."

2. "WRATH AND THREATENING."

[Explosive Orotund, Low key.]

Death, [*in reply.*]   " Back to thy punishment,
False fugitive ! and to thy speed add wings ;
Lest with a whip of scorpions I pursue   ·
Thy lingering, or, with one stroke of this dart,
Strange horror seize thee, and pangs unfelt before ! "

3. "EXHORTING."

[Expulsive Orotund, High Key.]

But wherefore do you droop? why look you sad ?
Be great in act, as you have been in thought ;
Let not the world see fear, and sad distrust
Govern the motion of a kingly eye :
Be stirring as the time ; be fire with fire ;
Threaten the threatener, and outface the brow
Of bragging horror : so shall inferior eyes,
That borrow their behavior from the great,
Grow great by your example, and put on
The dauntless spirit of resolution.

4. "ANGER AND SCORN."

[Explosive Utterance, Aspirated Tone, Low Key.]

Thou slave! thou wretch! thou coward!
Thou little valiant, great in villainy!
Thou ever strong upon the stronger side!
Thou fortune's champion, thou dost never fight
But when her humorous ladyship is by
To teach thee safety! Thou art perjured too,
And sooth'st up greatness! What a fool art thou,
A ramping fool, to brag, and stamp, and sweat,
Upon my party! Thou cold-blooded slave,
Hast thou not spoke like thunder on my side?

5. "CAUTION."

[Effusive Utterance, Pure Tone, Low Key.]

Hush! lightly tread! still tranquilly she sleeps;—
I've watched, suspending e'en my breath, in fear
To break the heavenly spell. Move silently!

6. "PITY."

[Expulsive Orotund, Middle Key.]

Oh! sailor-boy, woe to thy dream of delight!
In darkness dissolves the gay frost-work of bliss—
Where now is the picture that Fancy touched bright,
Thy parents' fond pressure, and love's honeyed kiss?

Oh! sailor-boy! sailor-boy! never again
Shall home, love, or kindred, thy wishes repay;
Unblessed and unhonored, down deep in the main,
Full many a score fathom, thy frame shall decay.

No tomb shall e'er plead to remembrance for thee,
Or redeem form, or frame, from the merciless surge;
But the white foam of waves shall thy winding-sheet be,
And winds, in the midnight of winter, thy dirge.

7. "UNRELENTING OBSTINACY."

[Explosive Utterance, Aspirated, Low Key.]

I'll have my bond; I will not hear thee speak:
I'll have my bond; and therefore speak no more.
I'll not be made a soft and dull-eyed fool,
To shake the head, relent, and sigh, and yield

To Christian intercessors. Follow not;
I'll have no speaking! I will have my bond.

8. "GRIEF."

[Effusive and Expulsive, Orotund, High Key.]

My daughter, once the comfort of my age,
 Lured by a villain from her native home,
Is cast, abandon'd, on the world's wide stage,
 And doom'd in scanty poverty to roam.

My tender wife, sweet soother of my care!
 Struck with sad anguish at the stern decree,
Fell, lingering fell, a victim to despair;
 And left the world to wretchedness and me.

Pity the sorrows of a poor old man,
 Whose trembling limbs have borne him to your door,
Whose days are dwindled to the shortest span:
 Oh! give relief, and Heaven will bless your store.

9. "SELF REPROACH."

[Expulsive, Aspirated and Orotund, Middle Key.]

O what a rogue and peasant slave am I;
Is it not monstrous, that this player here,
But in a fiction, in a dream of passion,
Could force his soul so to his own counsel,
That, from her working, all his visage warmed,
Tears in his eyes, distraction in his aspect,
A broken voice, and his whole functions suiting,
With forms to his conceit; and all for nothing;
For Hec-u-ba! What's Hec-u-ba to him, or he to Hec-u-ba,
That he should weep for her?

10. "INTENSE FEAR."

[Expulsive, Aspirated, Low Key.]

Ah! mercy on my soul! What is that? My old friend's ghost?
They say none but wicked folks walk; I wish I were at the bottom of a
coal-pit. See! how long and pale his face has grown since his death; he
never was handsome; and death has improved him very much the wrong
way. Pray do not come near me! I wish'd you very well when you were
alive; but I could never abide a dead man, cheek by jowl with me.
Ah, ah, mercy on us! No nearer, pray; if it be only to take leave

3

of me that you are come back, I could have excused you the ceremony with all my heart; or if you—mercy on us! no nearer, pray, or, if you have wronged any body, as you always loved money a little, I give you the word of a frightened Christian; I will pray as long as you please for the deliverance or repose of your departed soul. My good, worthy, noble friend, do, pray disappear, as ever you would wish your old friend to come to his senses again.

· 11. "SUSPICION."

[Expulsive Orotund and Aspirated, Middle Key.]

Would he were fatter; but I fear him not:
Yet, if my name were liable to fear,
I do not know the man, I should avoid
So soon as this spare Cassius. He reads much;
He is a great observer, and he looks
Quite through the deeds of men.
    He loves no plays; he hears no music;
Seldom he smiles; and smiles in such a sort,
As if he mocked himself, and scorned his spirit,
That could be moved to smile at any thing.
Such men as he, be never at heart's ease,
While they behold a greater than themselves,
And therefore, are they very dangerous.

12. "REMORSE."

[Expulsive Orotund, Middle and Low Key.]

Oh! I have passed a miserable night,
So full of fearful dreams, of ugly sights,
That, as I am a Christian faithful man,
I would not spend another such a night,
Though 't were to buy a world of happy days,
So full of dismal terror was the time!
    My dream was lengthened after life:—
Oh! then began the tempest to my soul!—
    With that, methought, a legion of foul fiends
Environed me, and howled in mine ears
Such hideous cries, that, with the very noise,
I trembling waked, and, for a season after,
Could not believe but that I was in hell;
Such terrible impression made my dream!

13. "RESIGNATION."

[Effusive Orotund, Middle Key.]

O Thou, who dry'st the mourner's tear,
    How dark this world would be,
If, when deceived and wounded here,
    We could not fly to thee!

The friends who in our sunshine live,
    When winter comes, are flown;
And he who has but tears to give
    Must weep those tears alone.

But thou wilt heal that broken heart
    Which, like the plants that throw
Their fragrance from the wounded part,
    Breathes sweetness out of woe.

14. "SUBLIMITY."

[Expulsive Orotund, Middle Key.]

O thou vast Ocean!—ever-sounding sea!
Thou symbol of a dread immensity!
Thy voice is like the thunder, and thy sleep
Is as a giant's slumber, loud and deep.
I love to wander on thy pebbled beach,
Marking the sunlight at the evening hour,
And hearken to the thoughts thy waters teach—
"Eternity, eternity, and power."

15. "AWE."

[Expulsive Orotund, Low and Middle Key.]

A fearful hope—was all—the world contained:
Forests were set on fire; but, hour by hour,
They fell, and faded, and the crackling trunks
Extinguished with a crash, and all was black.
The brows of men, by the despairing light
Wore an unearthly aspect, as, by fits,
The flashes fell upon them. Some lay down,
And hid their eyes, and wept; and some did rest
Their chins upon their clenched hands, and smil'd;
And others hurried to and fro, and fed
Their funeral piles with fuel, and looked up,
With mad disquietude, on the dull sky,

The pall of a past world; and then again,
With curses, cast them down upon the dust,
And gnashed their teeth, and howled.

16. "SORROW."

[Expulsive Orotund, Middle and High Key.]

Seems, madam! nay, it is: I know not seems,
'T is not alone my inky cloak, good mother,
Nor customary suits of solemn black,
Nor windy suspiration of forced breath;
No, nor the fruitful river in the eye,
Nor the dejected 'havior of the visage,
Together with all forms, modes, shows of grief,
That can denote me truly: these, indeed, seem,
For they are actions that a man might play;
But I have that—within, which passeth show,
These—but the trappings and the suits of wo.

17. "FEAR."

[Expulsive Utterance, Aspirated, Low Key.]

Cicero.—Why are you breathless?—and why stare you so?
Casca.—Are you not moved, when all the sway of earth
Shakes, like a thing unfirm?   O Cicero!
I have seen tempests, when the scolding winds
Have riv'd the knotty oaks; and I have seen
The ambitious ocean swell, and rage, and foam,
To be exalted with the threatening clouds;
But never till to-night, never till now,
Did I go through tempests dropping fire.

18. "REVERENCE."

[Effusive Orotund, Low and Middle Key.]

O Lord, our Lord, how excellent is Thy name in all the earth! who hast set Thy glory above the heavens.   When I consider the heavens, the work of Thy fingers; the moon and the stars, which Thou hast ordained; what is man that Thou art mindful of him? and the son of man, that Thou visitest him?

For Thou hast made him a little lower than the angels, and hast crowned him with glory and honor.   Thou madest him to have dominion over the works of Thy hands: Thou hast put all things under his feet. O Lord, our Lord, how excellent is Thy name in all the earth!

19. "HORROR."

[Expulsive Utterance, Guttural, Low Key.]

Avaunt! and quit my sight! Let the earth hide thee!
Thy bones are marrowless, thy blood is cold:
Thou hast no speculation in those eyes
Which thou dost glare with! Hence, horrible shadow,
Unreal mockery, hence!

20. "JOY."

[Expulsive Utterance, Pure Tone, High Key.]

Come, let us to the castle.—
News, friends; our wars are done, the Turks are drown'd.
How does my old acquaintance of this isle?—
Honey, you shall be well desired in Cyprus,
I have found great love amongst them. O my sweet,
I prattle out of fashion, and I dote
In mine own comforts.—*Othello.*

21. "BITTER DENUNCIATION."

[Explosive Utterance, Guttural, Low Key.]

Thou den of Drunkards with the blood of princes!
Gehenna of the waters! thou sea Sodom!
Thus I devote thee to the infernal gods!
Thee, and thy serpent seed!—Slave, do thine office!
Strike as I struck the foe! Strike as I would
Have struck those tyrants! Strike deep as my curse!
Strike—and but once!

22. "HOPE."

[Expulsive Orotund, High Key.]

All's for the best! be sanguine and cheerful,
    Trouble and Sorrow are friends in disguise;
Nothing but Folly goes faithless and fearful,
    Courage forever is happy and wise:
All's for the best—if a man would but know it,
    Providence wishes us all to be blest;
This is no dream of the pundit or poet,
    Heaven is gracious, and—All's for the best!

All's for the best! set this on your standard,
    Soldier of sadness, or pilgrim of love,

Who to the shores of Despair may have wandered,
A way-wearied swallow, or heart-stricken dove ;
All's for the best !—be a man but confiding,
Providence tenderly governs the rest,
And the frail bark of his creature is guiding
Wisely and warily, all for the best.

23. "COMMAND."

[Expulsive Orotund, Middle Key.]

Still " Onward ! " was his stern exclaim ;
" Charge on the battery's jaws of flame !
Rush on the level gun !
·Each Hulan forward with his lance !
My steel-clad cuirassiers advance !
My guard, my chosen, charge for France—
France and Napoleon ! "

24. "MERCY."

[Effusive Orotund, Middle Key.]

The quality of mercy is not strain'd ;
It droppeth as the gentle rain from heaven
Upon the place beneath : it is twice bless'd ;
It blesseth him that gives, and him that takes :
'Tis mightiest—in the mightiest ; it becomes
The throned monarch—better than his crown;
His scepter shows the force of temporal power,
The attribute to awe—and majesty,
Wherein doth sit the dread and fear of kings ;
But mercy—is above this sceptered sway,
It is enthroned—in the hearts of kings,
It is an attribute——to God himself :
And earthly power—doth then show likest God's,
When mercy—seasons justice.

25. "REVENGE."

[Explosive Utterance, Aspirated and Guttural, Low Key.]

If it will feed nothing else, it will feed my revenge. He hath disgraced me, and hinder'd me of half a million ; laugh'd at my losses, mocked at my gains, scorn'd my nation, thwarted my barg-ins, cool'd my friends, heated mine enemies. And what's his reason ? I am a Jew ! Hath not a Jew eyes ? Hath not a Jew hands? organs, dimensions, senses, affections, passions ? Is he not fed with the same food ; hurt with the same weapons; subject to the same diseases; heal'd by the same means: warm'd and cool'd by the same summer and winter, as a Christian is?

If you stab us, do we not bleed? If you tickle us, do we not laugh? If you poison us, do we not die? And if you wrong us, shall we not revenge? If we are like you in the rest, we will resemble you in that. If a Jew wrong a Christian what is his humility? Revenge. If a Christian wrong a Jew, what should his sufferance be by Christian example? Why, Revenge. The villainy you teach me, I will execute; and it shall go hard, but I will better the instruction.

26. "ADORATION."

[Effusive Orotund, Middle Key.]

Thou art, O God! the life and light
Of all this wondrous world we see;
Its glow by day, its smile by night,
    Are but reflections caught from thee.
Where'er we turn, thy glories shine,
    And all things fair and bright are Thine!

When Day, with farewell beam, delays
    Among the opening clouds of even,
And we can almost think we gaze
    Through golden vistas into Heaven,
Those hues, that make the sun decline
    So soft, so radiant, Lord! are Thine.

27. "SURPRISE."

[Expulsive Orotund, High Key.]

Gone to be married; gone to swear a peace!
It is not so: thou hast misspoke, misheard!
Be well advised, tell o'er thy tale again:
It cannot be! thou dost but say 't is so;
What dost thou mean by shaking of thy head?
What means that hand—upon that breast of thine?
Why holds thine eye—that lamentable rheum?
Be these sad sighs—confirmers of thy words?
Then speak again; not all thy former tale,
But this one word—whether thy tale be true?

28. "ADMONITION."

[Expulsive Orotund, Middle Key.]

Give thy thoughts no tongue,
Nor any unproportioned thought his act.
Be thou familiar; but by no means vulgar.

The friends thou hast, and their adoption tried,
Grapple them to thy soul, with hooks of steel;
But do not dull thy palm—with entertainment
Of ev'ry new hatch'd, unfledg'd comrade. Beware
Of entrance into quarrel ! but, being in,
Bear it, that the opposer—may beware of thee.
Give every man thine ear, but few thy voice.
Take each man's censure, but reserve thy judgment.
Costly thy habit—as thy purse can buy,
But not expressed in fancy ; rich, not gaudy.
For the apparel—oft proclaims the man.
Neither a borrower, nor a lender be ;
For loan—oft loses both itself and friend,
And borrowing—dulls the edge of husbandry.
This above all—to thine own self be true,
And it must follow, as the night the day,
Thou canst not, then—be false to any man.

29. "REPROACH."

[Explosive Orotund and Aspirated, Low Key.]

Shame ! shame ! that in such a proud moment of life,
    Worth ages of history,—when, had you but hurl'd
One bolt at your bloody invader, that strife
    Between freemen and tyrants had spread through the world,—
That then,—O ! disgrace upon manhood !—e'en then
    You should falter,—should cling to your pitiful breath,—
Cower down into beasts, when you might have stood men,—
    And prefer a slave's life to a glorious death !

30. "ENVY AND HATRED."

[Explosive Utterance, Guttural, Low Key.]

How like a fawning publican he looks !
I hate him for he is a Christian;
But more for that, in low simplicity,
He lends out money gratis, and brings down
The rate of usance here with us in Venice.
If I can catch him once upon the hip,
I will feed fat the ancient grudge I bear him.
He hates our sacred nation ; and he rails,
Even there where merchants most do congregate,
On me, my bargains, and my well-won thrift,
Which he calls interest.   Cursed be my tribe,
If I forgive him.—*Merchant of Venice.*

XV. DIRECTIONS FOR STUDENTS.

1.—POSITION OF THE BODY.

The first, and certainly, one of the most important directions to students is, that he should stand erect, and firm, and in such a posture that the chest may be fully expanded, and easy play given to the organs of respiration and utterance.

2.—WEIGHT OF THE BODY.

The weight of the body should be thrown upon one foot, leaving the other free to be thrown backward or forwards; or the weight of the body changed to rest upon it, and thus continuing to change as often as fatigue, or the action in speaking may require.

When the weight is thus resting upon one foot, the feet should be nearly, but never quite at right angles to each other.

3.—POSITION OF THE HEAD.

The head should be held in an erect and natural position, as this, in delivery, chiefly contributes to the expression. For, when inclined to one side, it expresses languor; when drooped, humility; when turned upwards pride; and when stiff and rigid, it indicates a lack of ease and self-possession.

4.—THE EYES.

As the eyes are the light of the body, so, also, in delivery, they are the life of expression. They should occasionally glance toward the gesture, as that gives prominence, and attention to it; when we wish to refuse or condemn, the eyes should be turned from the object. Otherwise the eyes should be toward the audience, and assume an expression of earnestness.

5.—MOVING UPON THE STAGE.

Moving upon the stage, (while practicing,) even to excess, is advisable: because the grace of an orator is

3*

conspicuous in the case with which he moves and changes his position.

The student should, however, (except in cultivation,) be judicious in this practice; as too frequent movements upon the rostrum will indicate that he is disconcerted; always excepting, however, such orators as Gough.

6.—DRINKING WHILE SPEAKING.

The thirst, which is experienced by many speakers, is simply a lack of self-possession; and, as soon as the speaker is entirely at case, the thirst will disappear. But the more he drinks the more thirsty he will become, and the more difficult it will be for him to control his voice.

And the use of strong drink, for a stimulant while speaking, is one of the greatest mistakes an orator can make. For under the influence of stimulants the tendency is to speak with the utmost degree of force; and the result is hoarseness or a husky, squeaking tone. Students should never resort to stimulants of any kind, as they are injurious and unnatural.

7.—VOCAL EXERCISE.

"The management of the breath, in reading or speaking, requires great care so as not to be obliged to divide words from one another, which have so intimate a connection that they ought to be pronounced in the same breath, and without the least separation. Many sentences are marred and the force of the emphasis totally lost, by divisions being made in the wrong place."—*Sargent.*

"Reading aloud and recitation, are more useful and invigorating muscular exercises than is generally imagined; at least, when managed with due regard to the natural powers of the individual, so as to avoid effort and fatigue. Both require the varied activity of most of the muscles of the trunk to a degree of which few are conscious till their attention is turned to it."—*Combe:*

Exercising the vocal organs a few moments vigorously, about two hours before speaking in public, is an excellent practice to secure a good tone; but care should be taken that this practice be not prolonged so as to weary the organs, else they may not recover their natural elasticity before speaking.

8.—TOBACCO INJURIOUS TO THE VOICE.

"The use of tobacco, in any form, has a deleterious effect upon the speaking and breathing organs. It enfeebles the nervous system, and tends to make the voice dry, harsh, husky, and inflexible.

"Public speakers who are votaries of the weed, if they cannot give it up entirely, ought, by all means, to refrain from the use of it for several hours previous to speaking or engaging in any public vocal exercise. For this brief period of self-denial they will be rewarded by a clearness and fullness of tone, and a flexibility of voice which will surprise and delight them."—*Kidd.*

MODULATION.

Lloyd.

1. 'T is not enough the voice be sound and clear,
'T is modulation that must charm the ear.
That voice all modes of passion can express,
Which marks the proper words with proper stress:
But none emphatic can that speaker call,
Who lays an equal emphasis on all.
Some, o'er the tongue the labored measures roll,
Slow and deliberate as the parting toll;
Point every stop, mark every pause so strong,
Their words like stage processions stalk along.

2. All affectation but creates disgust;
And e'en in speaking, we may seem too just.
In vain for them the pleasing measure flows,
Whose recitation runs it all to prose;
Repeating what the poet sets not down,
The verb disjointing from its favorite noun,
While pause, and break, and repetition join
To make a discord in each tuneful line.

3. Some placid natures fill the allotted scene
With lifeless drawls, insipid and serene;
While others thunder every couplet o'er,
And almost crack your ears with rant and roar.
More nature oft, and finer strokes are shown
In the low whisper, than tempestuous tone;
And Hamlet's hollow voice and fixed amaze,
More powerful terror to the mind conveys,
Than he, who, swollen with impetuous rage,
Bullies the bulky phantom of the stage.

4. He who, in earnest, studies o'er his part,
Will find true nature cling about his heart.
The modes of grief are not included all
In the white handkerchief and mournful drawl !
A single look more marks the internal woe,
Than all the windings of the lengthened Oh !
Up to the face the quick sensation flies,
And darts its meaning from the speaking eyes :
Love, transport, madness, anger, scorn, despair,
And all the passions, all the soul is there.

Every student should carefully analyze that epitome of instruction, " HAMLET'S INSTRUCTION TO THE PLAYERS." He will be delighted to notice that the " Great Artist " has presented in a single page a concise summary of invaluable suggestions.

HAMLET'S INSTRUCTION TO THE PLAYERS.

Speak the speech, I pray you,' as I *pronounced* it to you :' trippingly on the tongue;' but if you *mouth* it, as *many* of our players do,' I had as lief the town-*crier* spake my lines. Nor do not saw the air too much with your hand *thus*, but use all *gently;* ' for in the very torrent, tempest, and, (as I may say,) *whirlwind* of your passion,' you must acquire and beget a *temperance*, that may give it *smoothness*.' O, it offends me to the *soul*, to hear a robustious periwig-pated fellow tear a passion to tatters, to very *rags*, to split the ears of the groundlings;' who, for the *most* part, are capable of nothing but inexplicable dumb shows and noise. Pray you, *avoid* it. Be not too *tame* neither,' but let your own discretion be your *tutor*. Suit the action to the *word;* ' the word to the *action:* ' with this special *observance:* ' that you o'*erstep* not the modesty of *nature;* ' for any thing so over-*done* is from the purpose of *playing;* ' whose end, both at the first and now, was, and is, to hold, as 'twere, the mirror up to *nature;* to show virtue her own *feature;* ' scorn her own *image;* ' and the very age and *body* of the time,' his form and *pressure*. Now this, overdone or come tardy off,' though it make the unskilful *laugh*, cannot but make the judicious *grieve;* ' the censure of which *one*, must, in your allowance, o'erweigh a whole theatre of *others*. O, there be players, that I have seen play, and heard others praise, and that *highly*, (not to speak it *profanely*,) that, neither having the accent of *Christians*, nor the gait of Christian, pagan, or *man*, have so strutted and bellowed, that I have thought some of nature's *journeymen* had made men, and not made them *well:* ' they imitated humanity so *abominably*.

Selections.

I.—RICHTER'S DREAM.

1. INTO the great vestibule of heaven, God called up a man from dreams, saying, " Come thou hither, and see the glory of my house." And, to the servants that stood around His throne, He said, " Take him, and undress him from his robes of flesh : cleanse his vision, and put a new breath into his nostrils ; only touch not with any change his human heart—the heart that weeps and trembles."

2. It was done ; and, with a mighty angel for his guide, the man stood ready for his infinite voyage ; and from the terraces of heaven, without sound or farewell, at once they wheeled away into endless space. Sometimes, with solemn flight of angel wings, they fled through Gaarahs of darkness—through wildernesses of death, that divided the world of life : sometimes they swept over frontiers that were quickening under the prophetic motions from God.

3. Then, from a distance that is counted only in heaven, light dawned for a time through a sleepy film ; by unutterable pace the light swept to them ; they by unutterable pace to the light. In a moment, the rushing of planets was upon them : in a moment, the blazing of suns was around them.

4. Then came eternities of twilight, that revealed, but were not revealed. On the right hand and on the left, towered mighty constellations, that by self-repetition and

answers from afar, that by counter-positions, built up triumphal gates, whose architraves—whose archways—horizontal, upright—rested, rose—at attitudes by spans—that
seemed ghostly from infinitude. Without measure were
the architraves, past number were the archways, beyond
memory the gates.

5. Within were stairs that scaled the eternities below :
above was below—below was above, to the man stripped
of gravitating body : depth was swallowed up in height
insurmountable : height was swallowed up in depth unfathomable. Suddenly, as thus they rode from infinite to
infinite : suddenly, as thus they tilted over abysmal worlds,
a mighty cry arose,· that systems more mysterious, that
worlds more billowy, other heights and other depths, were
coming—were nearing—were at hand.

6. Then the man sighed, and stopped, and shuddered,
and wept. His overladen heart uttered itself in tears ;
and he said, "Angel, I will go no farther; for the spirit of
man acheth with this infinity. Insufferable is the glory of
God. Let me lie down in the grave, and hide me from the
persecutions of the Infinite ; for end, I see, there is none."

7. And from all the listening stars that shone around,
issued a choral cry, "The man speaks truly : end there is
none that ever yet we heard of." "End ! is there none ? "
the angel solemnly demanded : "Is there indeed no end!
and is this the sorrow that kills you ? " But no voice
answered that he might answer himself. Then the angel
threw up his glorious hands toward the heaven of heavens,
saying, "End, is there none to the universe of God ? Lo!
also there is no beginning."

———◆———

II.—DEATH-BED OF BENEDICT ARNOLD.

GEORGE LEPPARD.

1. FIFTY years ago, in a rude garret, near the loneliest
suburbs of the city of London, lay a dying man. He
was but half dressed ; though his legs were concealed in

long military boots. An aged minister stood beside the rough couch. The form was that of a strong man grown old through care more than age. There was a face that you might look upon but once, and yet wear it in your memory forever.

2. Let us bend over the bed, and look upon that face. A bold forehead seamed by one deep wrinkle visible between the brows—long locks of dark hair, sprinkled with gray; lips firmly set, yet quivering, as though they had a life separate from the life of the man; and then, two large eyes—vivid, burning, unnatural in their steady glare. Ay, there was something terrible in that face—something so full of unnaturable loneliness—unspeakable despair, that the aged minister started back in horror. But look! those strong arms are clutching at the vacant air: the death-sweat stands in drops on that bold brow—the man is dying. Throb—throb—throb—beats the death-watch in the shattered wall. " Would you die in the faith of the Christian ? " faltered the preacher, as he knelt there on the damp floor.

3. The white lips of the death-stricken man trembled, but made no sound. Then, with the strong agony of death upon him, he rose into a sitting posture. For the first time he spoke. " Christian ! " he echoed in that deep tone which thrilled the preacher to the heart : " Will that faith give me back my honor ? Come with me, old man, come with me, far over the waters. Ha! we are there! This is my native town. Yonder is the church in which I knelt in childhood : yonder the green on which I sported when a boy. But another flag waves yonder, in place of the flag that waved when I was a child.

4. " And listen, old man, were I to pass along the streets, as I passed when but a child, the very babes in their cradles would raise their tiny hands, and curse me! The graves in yonder churchyard would shrink from my footsteps ; and yonder flag would rain a baptism of blood upon my head ! "

5. That was an awful death-bed. The minister had watched "the last night" with a hundred convicts in their cells, but had never beheld a scene so terrible as this. Suddenly the dying man arose : he tottered along the floor. With those white fingers, whose nails were blue with the death-chill, he threw open a valise. He drew from thence a faded coat of blue, faced with silver, and the wreck of a battle-flag.

6. "Look ye, priest! this faded coat is spotted with my blood!" he cried, as old memories seemed stirring at his heart. "This coat I wore, when I first heard the news of Lexington : this coat I wore, when I planted the banner of the stars on Ticonderoga! that bullet-hole was pierced in the fight of Quebec ; and now, I am a—let me whisper it in your ear!" He hissed that single burning word into the minister's ear.: "Now help me, priest! help me to put on this coat of blue ; for you see"—and a ghastly smile came over his face—"there is no one here to wipe the cold drops from my brow : no wife : no child. I must meet Death alone ; but I will meet him, as I have met him in battle, without a fear!"

7. And, while he stood arraying his limbs in that worm-eaten coat of blue and silver, the good minister spoke to him of faith in Jesus. Yes, of that great faith, which pierces the clouds of human guilt, and rolls them back from the face of God. "Faith!" echoed that strange man, who stood there, erect, with the death-chill on his brow, "Faith! Can it give me back my honor? Look ye, priest! there, over the waves, sits George Washington, telling to his comrades the pleasant story of the eight years' war : there, in his royal balls, sits George of England, bewailing, in his idiotic voice, the loss of his colonies! And here am I!—I, who was the first to raise the flag of freedom, the first to strike a blow against that king—here am I, dying! oh, dying like a dog!"

8. The awe-stricken preacher started back from the look of the dying man, while throb—throb—throb—beats

the death-watch, in the shattered wall. "Hush! silence along the lines there!" he muttered, in that wild, absent tone, as though speaking to the dead; "silence along the lines! not a word—not a word, on peril of your lives! Hark you, Montgomery! we will meet in the centre of the town:—we will meet there in victory, or die!—Hist! silence, my men—not a whisper, as we move up those steep rocks! Now on, my boys—now on! Men of the wilderness, we will gain the town! Now up with the banner of the stars—up with the flag of freedom, though the night is dark, and the snow falls! Now! now, one more blow, and Quebec is ours!"

9. And look! his eye grows glassy. With that word on his lips, he stands there—ah! what a hideous picture of despair: erect, livid, ghastly: there for a moment, and then he falls!—he is dead! Ah, look at that proud form, thrown cold and stiff upon the damp floor. In that glassy eye there lingers, even yet, a horrible energy—a sublimity of despair. Who is this strange man lying there alone, in this rude garret: this man, who, in all his crimes, still treasured up in that blue uniform, that faded flag? Who is this being of horrible remorse—this man, whose memories seem to link something with heaven, and more with hell?

10. Let us look at that parchment and flag. The aged minister unrolls that faded flag; it is a blue banner gleaming with thirteen stars. He unrolls that parchment: it is a colonel's commission in the Continental army addressed to BENEDICT ARNOLD! And there, in that rude hut, while·the death-watch throbbed like a heart in the shattered wall: there, unknown, unwept, in all the bitterness of desolation, lay the corse of the patriot and the traitor.

11. Oh that our own true Washington had been there, to sever that good right arm from the corse; and, while the dishonored body rotted into dust, to bring home that noble arm, and embalm it among the holiest memories of the past. For that right arm struck many a gallant blow

for freedom : yonder at Ticonderoga, at Quebec, Champlain, and Saratoga—that arm, yonder, beneath the snow white mountains, in the deep silence of the river of the dead, first raised into light the Banner of the Stars.

III.—WHAT THE SEA SAID TO ME.

1. By the sandy sea-shore strolling,
   List'ning to the surges rolling,
   And their never ceasing bowling,
   　　　　'Mong the rocks.

   Surely, 'tis no idle notion,
   That the sparkling, seething ocean,
   With its rhythmic, breathing motion,
   　　　　With me talks.

2. " Ocean, with thy locks so hoary,
   Thou must have a wondrous story,
   Tale of ancient love or glory,
   　　　　Laid in store."

   Softly said the sea as sighing,
   With a lover's voice replying,
   Made by wavelets ever dying
   　　　　On the shore.

3. " Sad and lonely once I wandered
   Round a shoreless world and pondered,
   Wondering wherefore power was squandered,
   　　　　Making me.

   Now, since heaven has kindly fated
   I like Adam should be mated,
   Why I wandering, wondering waited,
   　　　　Now I see.

4. I've a sweetheart, I'm a lover,
   In my arms I clasp her ever,
   Nothing ever shall us sever,
   　　　　Sea and land.

   Now I know what heavenly bliss is,
   While I feel such love as this is,

Brimming o'er in ceaseless kisses,
On the strand.

5. Robe of green on forest bowers,
Covering prairies decked with flowers,
Woven in my loom of showers,
I present.

Fruits of spring and summer's growing,
Autumn's garners overflowing,
These are gifts of my bestowing,
Yearly sent.

6. Clouds that round the mountains hover,
Snow-caps that their bald heads cover,
Fountains cool I give that ever
Bubbling flow.

Fairest gifts of earthly blessing,
Ever fondest love confessing,
Yet that love not half expressing,
I bestow."

IV.—RIGHT TRIUMPHANT.

SHAKSPEARE.

1. Know'st thou not,
That when the searching eye of heaven is hid
Behind the globe, and lights the lower world,
Then thieves and robbers range abroad unseen,
In murders, and in outrage, bloody here ;
But when, from under this terrestrial ball,
He fires the proud tops of the eastern pines,
And darts his light through every guilty hole,
Then murders, treasons, and detested sins,
The cloak of night being pluck'd from off their backs
Stand bare and naked, trembling at themselves?

2. So when this thief, this traitor, Bolingbroke,—
Who all this while hath revell'd in the night,
Whilst we were wandering with the antipodes,—
Shall see us rising in our throne the east,
His treasons will sit blushing in his face
Not able to endure the sight of day,
But, self-affrighted, trembling at his sin.

3. Not all the water in the rough rude sea
Can wash the balm from an anointed king :
The breath of worldly men cannot depose
The deputy elected by the Lord :
For every man that Bolingbroke hath press'd,
To lift shrewd steel against our golden crown,
God for his Richard hath in heavenly pay
A glorious angel : then, if angels fight,
Weak men must fall ; *for heaven still guards the right.*

V.—SEEING THE SUN AT MIDNIGHT.

1. In July, 1865, Hon. J. H. Campbell, United States Minister to Norway, with a party of American gentlemen, went far enough north to see the sun at midnight. It was in 69 degrees north latitude, and they ascended a cliff 1,000 feet high above the Arctic sea.

2. The scene is thus described : " It was late, but still sunlight. The Arctic ocean stretched away in silent vastness at our feet ; the sound of its waves scarcely reached our airy lookout ; away in the north the huge old sun swung low along the horizon like a slow beat of the pendulum in the tall clock in our grandfather's parlor corner. We all stood silent looking at our watches. When both hands came together at 12, midnight, the full, round orb hung triumphantly above the wave : a bridge of gold running due north spangled the waters between us and him.

3. There he shone in silent majesty which knew no setting. We involuntarily took off our hats—no word was spoken. Combine, if you can, the most brilliant sunset and sunrise you ever saw, and its beauties will pale before the gorgeous coloring which now lit up the ocean, heaven and mountain. In half an hour the sun had swung up perceptibly on its beat, the colors changed to those of morning, a fresh breeze rippled over the florid sea, one songster after another piped up in the grove behind us— we had slid into another day."

VI.—THE BLUE AND THE GRAY.

[The women of Columbus, Mississippi, animated by noble sentiments, have shown themselves impartial in their offerings made to the memory of the dead. They strewed flowers alike on the graves of the Confederate and of the National soldiers.]

1. By the flow of the island river,
    Whence the fleets of iron have fled,
   Where the blades of the grave-grass quiver,
    Asleep on the ranks of the dead :—
      Under the sod and the dew,
       Waiting the judgment day ;
      Under the one, the Blue,
       Under the other, the Gray.

2. These in the robings of glory,
    Those in the gloom of defeat,
   All with the battle blood gory,
    In the dusk of eternity meet :—
      Under the sod and the dew,
       Waiting the judgment day ;
      Under the laurel, the Blue,
       Under the willow, the Gray.

3. From the silence of sorrowful hours
    The desolate mourners go,
   Lovingly laden with flowers
    Alike for the friend and the foe :—
      Under the sod and the dew,
       Waiting the judgment day ;—
      Under the roses, the Blue,
       Under the lilies, the Gray.

4. So with an equal splendor,
    The morning sun-rays fall,
   With a touch impartially tender,
    On the blossoms blooming for all :
      Under the sod and the dew,   ·
       Waiting the judgment day ;—
      Broidered with gold, the Blue ;
       Mellowed with gold, the Gray.

5. So, when the Summer calleth,
    On forest and field of grain,

With an equal murmur falleth
The cooling drip of the rain :
Under the sod and the dew,
Waiting the judgment day ;
Wet with the rain, the Blue,
Wet with the rain, the Gray.

6. Sadly, but not upbraiding,
The generous deed was done ;
In the storm of the years that are fading,
No braver battle was won :
Under the sod and the dew,
Waiting the judgment day ;
Under the blossoms, the Blue,
Under the garlands, the Gray.

7. No more shall the war-cry sever,
Or the winding rivers be red ;
They banish our anger forever
When they laurel the graves of our dead !
Under the sod and the dew,
Waiting the judgment day ;
Love and tears for the Blue,
Tears and love for the Gray.

-----◆-----

VII.—TOUSSAINT L'OUVERTURE.

WENDELL PHILLIPS.

[Toussaint L'Ouverture, who has been pronounced one of the greatest statesmen and generals of the nineteenth century, saved his master and family by hurrying them on board a vessel at the insurrection of the negroes of Hayti. He then joined the negro army, and soon found himself at their head. Napoleon sent a fleet with French veterans, with orders to bring him to France at all hazards. But all the skill of the French soldiers could not subdue the negro army ; and they finally made a treaty, placing Toussaint L'Ouverture governor of the island. The negroes no sooner disbanded their army, than a squad of soldiers seized Toussaint by night, and taking him on board a vessel, hurried him to France. There he was placed in a dungeon, and finally starved to death.]

1. If I stood here to-night to tell the story of Napoleon, I should take it from the lips of Frenchmen, who find no language rich enough to paint the great general of the century. If I were to tell you the story of Washington, I should take it from your hearts—you who think no

marble white enough, in which to carve the name of the Father of his Country.

2. But I am to tell you the story of a negro, Toussaint L'Ouverture, who has left hardly one written line. I am to glean it from the reluctant testimony of his enemies, men who despised him because he was a negro and a slave, hated him because he had beaten them in battle. You remember that Macauly says, comparing Cromwell with Napoleon, that Cromwell showed greater military genius on this account, he never saw an army till he was forty: Napoleon from a boy was educated in the best military schools of Europe.

3. Cromwell manufactured his army. Napoleon at nineteen was placed at the head of the best troops Europe ever saw. They both conquered, but, says Macauly, with such disadvantages, the Englishman showed the greater genius. Whether you allow the result or not, you will at least allow that that is a fair mode of measurement.

4. Now apply it to Toussaint. Cromwell never saw an army till he was forty: this man never saw a soldier till he was fifty. Cromwell manufactured his army—out of what? Englishmen—the best blood of Europe. With it he conquered what? Englishmen—their equals.

5. This man manufactured his army out of what? Out of what you call the despicable race of negroes, debased, demoralized, by two hundred years of slavery. Yet out of this mixed, and as you say despicable mass, he forged a thunderbolt and hurled it—at what? At the proudest blood in Europe—the Spaniard, and sent him home: at the most warlike blood in Europe—the Frenchman, and put him under his feet: at the pluckiest blood in Europe—the English, and they skulked home to Jamaica. Now if Cromwell was a general, at least, this man was a soldier. It is not by quantity, but by quality we measure genius.

6. Cromwell was only a soldier: his fame stops there. Not one line, in the statute book of Britain, can be traced to him. The state he founded went down with him to his

grave. But this man no sooner found himself at the helm of state, than the ship steadied, with an upright keel, and began to evince a statesmanship as marvellous as his military genius.

7. It was 1798, a time when religious intolerance poisoned every page of England's statute book: when every state in the Union, save Rhode Island, was but another name for bigotry. This man remember was a negro, you say that is a superstitious blood. He was uneducated, you say that makes a man narrow minded. He was a Catholic; many say that is but another name for intolerance. Yet, Negro, Catholic, Slave, he took his place beside Roger Williams and said to his committee, " Make it the first line of my constitution, that I know no difference between religious beliefs."

8. Now blue-eyed Saxon, proud of your race, go back with me sixty years; select what statesman you please: let him be either American or Englishman, let him have a brain the result of six generations of culture, let him have the richest culture of university routine, crown his temples with the silver locks of seventy years, and show me the man of Saxon lineage, for whom his most sanguine admirers will wreathe a laurel, rich as embittered foes, have placed on the brow of this negro.

9. I would call him Napoleon; but Napoleon made his way to empire over broken oaths, and through a sea of blood. This man never broke his word, and his last words uttered to his son in France were these, " My boy, you will some day go back to St. Domingo, forget that France murdered your father." I would call him Cromwell, but Cromwell was only a soldier, and the state he founded did go down with him to the grave. I would call him Washington, but the great Virginian held slaves.

10. You think me a fanatic to-night, for you read history not with your eyes but with your prejudices. But fifty years hence when impartial history gets written, some Plutarch of later days will put Phocian for the

Greek, Brutus for the Roman, Hampden for England, Fayette for France, choose Washington as the bright consummate flower of our earlier civilization; then, dipping his pencil in sunlight, will write in the clear blue above them all, the name of the soldier, the statesman, and the martyr, Toussaint L'Ouverture.

———◆———

VIII.—THE DRUNKARD'S DAUGHTER.

[We cannot find words to express our emotions when we first read the following touching verses. They stir the soul to its very depths, and we defy a man of feeling to read them with a tearless eye. A young lady, whose life had been made wretched by the drunkenness of her father, is the author; and none but one who has "walked woe's depths," could write such a powerful piece. She wrote and sent it to a friend, who had told her that she was a "monomaniac," in bitter hatred of the "deadly cup."—*St. Louis Press.*]

1. Go, feel what I have felt,
   Go, bear what I have borne;
   Sink 'neath the blow a father dealt,
   And the cold proud world's scorn;
   Thus struggle on from year to year,
   Thy sole relief the tear.

2. Go, weep as I have wept,
   O'er a loved father's fall,
   See every cherished promise swept,
   Youth's sweetness turned to gall;
   Hope's faded flowers strewn all the way,
   That led me up to woman's day.

3. Go, kneel as I have knelt,
   Implore, beseech and pray,
   Strive the besotted heart to melt,
   The downward course to stay:
   Be cast, with bitter tears, aside,
   Thy prayers burlesqued, thy tears defied.

4. Go, stand where I have stood,
   And see the strong man bow,
   With gnashing teeth, lips bathed in blood,
   And cold the livid brow;
   Go, catch his wandering glance, and see
   There mirror'd, his soul's misery.

4

5. Go, hear what I have heard,
    The sobs of sad despair,
  As memory's feeling fount hath stirr'd
    And its revealing there
  Have told him what he might have been
  Had he the drunkard's fate foreseen.

6. Go, to my mother's side,
    And her crushed spirit cheer,
  Thine own deep anguish hide,
    Wipe from her cheek the tear :
  Mark her dimm'd eye, her furrow'd brow,
  The gray that streaks her dark hair now,
  Her toil-worn frame, her trembling limb,
  And trace the ruin back to him
  Whose plighted faith in early youth
  Promised eternal love and truth :

7. But who, foresworn, hath yielded up
  This promise to the deadly cup,
  And led down from love and light,
  From all that made her pathway bright,
  And chained her there, 'mid want and strife,
  That lowly thing, a Drunkard's Wife,
  And stamp'd on childhood's brow so mild,
  That withering blight, a Drunkard's Child.

8. Go, hear, and see, and feel, and know
    All that my soul hath felt and known :
  Then look upon the wine cup's glow,
    See if its brightness can atone.
  Think if its flavor you will try,
  If all proclaimed—" 'Tis drink and die ! "

9. Tell me I hate the bowl !
    Hate is a feeble word—
  I loathe, abhor—my very soul
    With strong disgust is stirr'd
  Whene'er I see, or hear, or tell
  Of that dark beverage of hell !

IX.—VIRGIL'S HADES.   *Literal Translation.*
                                                    WILEY.
1. At length th' accursed gates are open'd, grating on their horrid
  Sounding hinges.   " Yonder seest thou what figure guards the

Passage ? and what the gate ?   A dreadful Hydra there, with fifty
Black and gaping mouths, more terrible, by far, than any
Fury, holds her seat within.   Then Tartarus itself, in
Course toward the Shades, sinks down as far as twice the distance,
Measured by the eye, *from earth to heaven.*

2.   " Here the ancient
Progeny of Earth, th' Titanian youth, by thunderbolts hurled
Down, lie welt'ring in the abyss.   Here too, I saw the sons of
Alœus, gigantic forms, who sought to rend the heavens,
Hurling from his lofty throne immortal Jove.   And here I
Saw Salmoneus in torture suffering, for having
Dared to imitate the light'nings and the bolts of Jove.
Drawn by horses, in his chariot, proud, and brandishing a torch, he
Rode through Greece triumphant and the midst of Elis ; and the
Honor of th' Immortals boasting claimed : foolish mortal !
Who, with brazen car and tramp o' his horn-hoofed steeds, the rushing
Storms and dreadful roaring thunder sought to imitate.
But th' almighty Sire hurled an awful bolt, (not harmless
Firebrands he, nor torches' smoky light,) and cast him headlong
To the Shades, amid a roaring whirlwind.

3.   "Tityus too, you
Might have seen, the foster-child of all-producing Earth :
Whose awful body reaches over nine unbroken acres ;
And a vulture, monstrous bird, with hooked beak, is ever
Feasting on his entrails ; nor is any respite given,
But the fibres ever springing up afresh creates new
Food for punishment.   Why need I mention Sirithous the
Lapithæ, and Ixion above whom threat'ning hangs a
Black and flinty rock, that ev'ry moment swinging round seems
Falling?   Golden standards unto lofty couches glisten ;
And in view are banquets furnished out with regal splendor :
Near them, thund'ring with her voice and brandishing her torch on
High, the eldest of the Furies sits and guards the banquets.

4. "Here, too, are those who with their brothers lived at enmity : had
Treated ill a parent ; or had wrought deceit against a
Client ; or the miserly, who brooded o'er acquired
Wealth alone, nor sought division with their kindred ; these by
Far most numerous ; and those who for adultery were
Slain ; and who in impious wars had joined, and hesitated
Not to violate their plighted faith to lawful masters :
There in prison 'wait their punishment.   Nor kind, nor shape, nor
In what state the punishment, they seek to be informed.

5. "Others heave up rolling stones, and hang fast bound to wheels. There
Sits, and shall forever sit, unhappy Theseus. And
Phlegyas, wretchedest, admonishes ; and with a solemn
Voice proclaims throughout the Shades, ' Warn'd seek righteousness,
and
Not contemn the gods.' Another sold for gold his country :
Raising into rule a domineering tyrant : made and
Unmade laws for gold. And one attempted marriage rites
Unlawful with his daughter. All have dared some heinous crime and
'Complished what they dared. Had I a hundred tongues, a hundred
Mouths, and voice of sounding iron, I could not comprehend the
Species of their crimes, nor numerate their punishments."

X.—THE BEAUTIFUL LAND.

1. There's a beautiful land by the spoiler untrod,
   Unclouded by sorrow or care ;
   It is lighted alone by the presence of God,
   Whose throne and whose temple are there ;
   Its crystalline streams with a murmurous flow,
   Meander through valleys of green,
   And its mountains of jasper are bright in the glow
   Of a splendor no mortal hath seen.

2. And throngs of glad singers with jubilant breath
   Make the air with their melodies rife ;
   And one known on earth as the angel of death,
   Shines here as an angel of life !
   And infinite tenderness beams from his eyes,
   On his brow is a heavenly calm,
   And his voice as it thrills thro' the depths of the skies
   Is as sweet as the seraphim's psalm.

3. Through the musical groves of this beautiful land
   Walk the souls which were faithful in this,
   And their foreheads by the breath of the zephyrs are fanned
   That evermore murmur of bliss ;
   They taste the rich fruitage that hangs from the trees
   And breathe the sweet odor of flowers
   More fragrant than ever were kissed by the breeze
   In Araby's loveliest bowers.

4. Old prophets, whose words were a spirit of flame
   Blazing out o'er the darkness of time,

And martyrs, whose courage no torture could tame,
  Nor turn from their purpose sublime ;
And saints and confessors, a numberless throng,
  Who were loyal to truth and to right,
And left as they walked thro' the darkness of wrong
  Their foot-prints encircled with light..

5. And the dear little children who went to their rest
  Ere their lives had been sullied by sin,
While the angel of morning still tarried a guest,
  Their spirit's pure temple within—
All are there, all are there—in the beautiful land,
  The land by the spoiler untrod,
And their foreheads by the breath of the breezes are fanned
  That blow from the gardens of God.

6. My soul hath looked in thro' the gateway of dreams
  On the city all paved with pure gold,
And heard the sweet flow of its murmurous streams,
  As through the green valleys they rolled :
And though it still waits on this desolate strand
  A pilgrim and stranger on earth,
Yet it knew, in that glimpse of the beautiful land,
  That it gazed on the home of its birth.

XI.—PROSE SELECTIONS.

1.—GROWING OLD.

1. How stealthily the years creep upon us, one by one, until some day we are startled to find ourselves grown old ! It is curious to see what different estimates people put upon old age at different periods of their own lives. To the youth in his teens, the man of middle age appears quite antiquated, but when he himself arrives at forty years, he can scarce believe he is no longer young, and is astonished to see so many who were but infants the other day now jostling him as full grown men in the race of life. Said one gentleman to another once in our hearing, " What has become of all the old men ? When you and I were boys there were many old gentlemen about, but they

seem to be all gone?" "Ah," said his friend with a smile, "ask these youngsters where the old men are. They'll tell you—and you will find yourself among them!"

2.—MEMORY.

1. MEMORIES of some kind we all have—it is the one thing which makes the man himself. If it be true that every particle of our bodies is changed once in seven years, memory is the surest guardian of personal identity. Cicero, after long thinking about it concluded that it was the strongest proof that the soul was immaterial and immoral. Destroy it, and the chief value of life would be taken away. What would an existence be worth that had not, could never have, any yesterday—to which came no tender whispers from the morning land of youth, no words whose very echo thrills steady-going old age with indefinable bliss? To forget is indeed to be annihilated.

3.—FACTS WORTH KNOWING.

1. IT is not what people eat, but what they digest, that makes them strong. It is not what they gain, but what they save, that makes them rich. It is not what they read, but what they remember, that makes them learned. It is not what they profess, but what they practice, that makes them good.

4.—A NOBLEMAN AND HIS JESTER.

1. THERE was a certain lord who kept a jester in his house, (as many great men did in olden days of their pleasure,) to whom the lord gave a staff, and charged him to keep it till he should meet with one who was a greater fool than himself, and if he should meet with such a one, to deliver it over to him.

Not many years after, his lord fell sick, and, indeed was sick unto death. The jester came to see him, and was told by his sick lord that he must now shortly leave him.

" And whither wilt thou go ? " said the jester.

" Into another world," said the lord.

" And when wilt thou come again ? within a month ? "

" No."

" Within a year ? "

" No."

" When, then ? "

" Never."

" Never! and what provision hast thou made for thy entertainment whither thou goest ? "

" None at all."

' " No! " said the jester. " None at all ? Here, take thy staff, then. Art thou going away forever ? Hast thou made no preparation for a journey from which thou shalt never return ? Take my staff then, for I will not be guilty of such folly as this."

5.—GREATNESS.

1. ONLY moral greatness is truly sublime. The gladiator may discipline his sinews, and almost compete in strength even with his maddened adversary. And there are modern as well as ancient names, which awaken pity, if not contempt, for their owners, on account of the fearful perversion of their splendid talents. But when we read or hear of HOWARD, the illustrious philanthropist, the soul—debased as it may be—bends with instinctive homage, and feels as if a ray from his beatified spirit illumed and purified its purposes.

2. While NAPOLEON, like the fabled genii, traversed the affrighted earth, marked his footsteps with human blood, our own WASHINGTON rose like another luminary upon the dark and troubled scene of American politics, and with no marvelous intellectual ability,—but in the tranquil might of moral majesty,—he pursued the narrow path of duty, and blenched neither to the power of enemies, nor to the influence of affection. He had no noonday brightness,—no declining splendor. His whole course

was light and glory; and he left a heavenly and perennial brilliancy on the national horizon.

6.—LIFE.

1. LIFE bears us on, like the current of a mighty river. Our boat, at first, glides down the narrow channel, through the playful murmurings of the little brook, and the windings of its happy border. The trees shed their blossoms over our young heads; the flowers on the brink seem to offer themselves to our hands; we are happy in hope, and we grasp eagerly at the beauties around us; but the stream hurries us on, and still our hands are empty.

2. Our course in youth and manhood is along a wider and deeper flood, and amid objects more striking and magnificent. We are animated by the moving picture of enjoyment and industry, which passes before us: we are excited by some short-lived success, or depressed and made miserable by some equally short-lived disappointment. But our energy and our dependence are both in vain. The stream bears us on, and our joys and our griefs are alike left behind us; we may be shipwrecked, but we cannot anchor; our voyage may be hastened, but it cannot be delayed; whether rough or smooth, the river hastens toward its home, till the roaring of the ocean is in our ears, and the tossing of the waves is beneath our heel, and the land lessens from our eyes, and the floods are lifted up around us, and we take our last leave of the earth, and its inhabitants; and of our further voyage there is no witness but the Infinite and Eternal.

7.—VULGAR WORDS.

1. THERE is as much connection between the words and the thoughts, as there is between the thoughts and the words; the latter are not only the expression of the former, but they have power to react upon the soul and leave the stain of corruption there.

2. A young man who allows himself to use profane

and vulgar words, has not only shown that there is a foul spot on his mind, but by the utterance of that word he extends that spot and inflames it, till by indulgence it will soon pollute and ruin the whole soul.

3. Be careful of your words, as well as of your thoughts. If you can control the tongue, that no improper words be pronounced by it, you will soon be able to control the mind and save it from corruption. You extinguish the fire by smothering it, or prevent bad thoughts bursting out in language. Never utter a word, anywhere, which you would be ashamed to speak in the presence of the most religious man. Try this practice a little, and you will soon have command of yourself.

XII.—CATILINE TO HIS ARMY, NEAR FÆSULÆ.

BEN JONSON.

1.   I NEVER yet knew, Soldiers, that in fight
     Words added virtue unto valiant men ;
     Or that a General's oration made
     An army full or stand : but how much prowess,
     Habitual or natural, each man's breast
     Was owner of, so much in act it showed.
     Whom neither glory nor danger can excite,
     'Tis vain to attempt with speech.

2.   Two armies wait us, Soldiers ; one from Rome
     The other from the provinces of Gaul.
     The sword must now direct and cut our passage.
     I only, therefore, wish you, when you strike,
     To have your valors and your souls about you ;
     And think you carry in your laboring hands
     The things you seek,—glory and liberty !
     For by your swords the Fates must be instructed !
     If we can give the blow, all will be safe ;
     We shall not want provision, nor supplies ;
     The colonies and free towns will lie open ;
     Where, if we yield to fear, expect no place,
     Nor friend, to shelter those whom their own fortune
     And ill-used arms have left without protection.

4*

3.   You might have lived in servitude or exile,
     Or safe at Rome, depending on the great,
     But that you thought those things unfit for men ;
     And, in that thought, my friends, you then were valiant ;
     For no man ever yet changed peace for war
     But he that meant to conquer.   Hold that purpose.
     Meet the opposing army in that spirit.
     There's more necessity you should be such,
     In fighting for yourselves, than they for others.
     He's base who trusts his feet, whose hands are armed.

4.   Methinks I see Death and the Furies waiting
     What we will do, and all the Heaven at leisure
     For the great spectacle.   Draw, then, your swords,
     And, should our destiny begrudge our virtue
     The honor of the day, let us take care
     To sell ourselves at such a price as may
     Undo the world to buy us !

XIII.—SPARTACUS TO THE GLADIATORS AT CAPUA.

E. KELLOGG.

1. IT had been a day of triumph in Capŭa. Lentŭlus, returning with victorious eagles, had amused the populace with the sports of the amphitheatre to an extent hitherto unknown even in that luxurious city. The shouts of revelry had died away; the roar of the lion had ceased; the last loiterer had retired from the banquet; and the lights in the palace of the victor were extinguished.

2. The moon, piercing the tissue of fleecy clouds, silvered the dew-drops on the corslet of the Roman sentinel, and tipped the dark waters of the Vulturnus with a wavy, tremulous light. No sound was heard, save the last sob of some retiring wave, telling its story to the smooth pebbles of the beach ; and then all was still as the breast when the spirit has departed. In the deep recesses of the amphitheatre, a band of gladiators were assembled ; their muscles still knotted with the agony of conflict, the foam upon their lips, the scowl of battle yet lingering on their

brows; when Spartăcus, starting forth from amid the throng, thus addressed them :

3. " Ye call me chief; and ye do well to call *him* chief who, for twelve long years, has met upon the arēna every shape of man or beast the broad empire of Rome could furnish, and who never yet lowered his arm. If there be one among you who can say, that ever, in public fight or private brawl, my actions did belie my tongue, let him stand forth, and say it. If there be three in all your company dare face me on the bloody sands, let them come on. And yet I was not always thus,—a hired butcher, a savage chief of still more savage men !

4. " My ancestors came from old Sparta, and settled among the vine-clad rocks and citron groves of Syrasella. My early life ran quiet as the brooks by which I sported; and when, at noon, I gathered the sheep beneath the shade, and played upon the shepherd's flute, there was a friend, the son of a neighbor, to join me in the pastime. We led our flocks to the same pasture, and partook together our rustic meal.

5. " One evening, after the sheep were folded, and we were all seated beneath the myrtle which shaded our cottage, my grandsire, an old man, was telling of Marăthon, and Leuctra; and how, in ancient times, a little band of Spartans, in a defile of the mountains, had withstood a whole army. I did not then know what war was; but my cheeks burned, I knew not why, and I clasped the knees of that venerable man, until my mother, parting the hair from off my forehead, kissed my throbbing temples, and bade me go to rest, and think no more of those old tales and savage wars. That very night, the Romans landed on our coast. I saw the breast that had nourished me trampled by the hoof of the war-horse; the bleeding body of my father flung amidst the blazing rafters of our dwelling !

6. " To-day I killed a man in the arēna; and, when I broke his helmet-clasps, behold ! he was my friend. He

knew me, smiled faintly, gasped, and died;—the same
sweet smile upon his lips that I had marked, when, in
adventurous boyhood, we scaled the lofty cliff to pluck the
first ripe grapes, and bear them home in childish triumph.
I told the prætor that the dead man had been my friend,
generous and brave; and I begged that I might bear away
the body, to burn it on a funeral pile, and mourn over its
ashes. Ay! upon my knees, amid the dust and blood of
the arēna, I begged that poor boon, while all the assembled maids and matrons, and the holy virgins they call
Vestals, and the rabble, shouted in derision, deeming it
rare sport, forsooth, to see Rome's fiercest gladiator turn
pale and tremble at sight of that piece of bleeding clay!
And the prætor drew back as I were pollution, and sternly
said,—' Let the carrion rot; there are no noble men but
Romans!' And so, fellow-*gladiators*, must you, and so
must I, die like dogs.

7. " O, Rome! Rome! thou hast been a tender nurse to
me. Ay! thou hast given, to that poor, gentle, timid
shepherd-lad, who never knew a harsher tone than a flute-
note, muscles of iron and a heart of flint; taught him to
drive the sword through plaited mail and links of rugged
brass, and warm it in the marrow of his foe;—to gaze into
the glaring eye-balls of the fierce Numidian lion, even as a
boy upon a laughing girl! And he shall pay thee back,
until the yellow Tiber is red as frothing wine, and in its
deepest ooze thy life-blood lies curdled!

8. " Ye stand here now like giants, as ye are! The
strength of brass is in your toughened sinews; but to-
morrow some Roman Adōnis, breathing sweet perfume
from his curly locks, shall with his lily fingers pat your red
brawn, and bet his sestérces upon your blood. Hark!
hear ye yon lion roaring in his den? 'Tis three days since
he tasted flesh; but to-morrow he shall break his fast
upon yours,—and a dainty meal for him ye will be!

9. " If ye are *beasts*, then stand here like fat oxen, waiting for the butcher's knife! If ye are *men*,—follow me!

Strike down yon guard, gain the mountain passes, and there do bloody work, as did your sires at Old Thermopylæ! Is Sparta dead? Is the old Grecian spirit frozen in your veins, that you do crouch and cower like a belabored hound beneath his master's lash. O, comrades! warriors! Thracians!—if we must fight, let us fight for *ourselves*. If we must slaughter, let us slaughter our *oppressors!* If we must die, let it be under the clear sky, by the bright waters, in noble, honorable battle!"

XIV.—WOLSEY'S FALL.

SHAKSPEARE.

1.   FAREWELL, a long farewell, to all my greatness!
This is the state of man; to-day he puts forth
The tender leaves of hope, to-morrow blossoms,
And bears his blushing honors thick upon him;
The third day comes a frost—a killing frost;
And when he thinks, good easy man! full surely
His greatness is a ripening—nips the root,
And then he falls, as I do.

2.   I have ventured,
Like little wanton boys, that swim on bladders,
These many summers in a sea of glory,
But far beyond my depth: my high-blown pride
At length broke under me, and now has left me,
Weary and old with service, to the mercy
Of a rude stream that must forever hide me.

3.   Vain pomp and glory of this world, I hate ye!
I feel my heart new opened; oh! how wretched
Is that poor man that hangs on princes' favors!
There is, betwixt that smile he would aspire to,
That sweet aspect of princes and his ruin,
More pangs and fears than wars or women have;
And when he falls, he falls like Lucifer,
Never to hope again.

XV.—THE RUM MANIAC.

ALLISON.

1.   "Say, Doctor, may I not have rum,
To quench this burning thirst within?
Here on this cursed bed I lie,
And cannot get one drop of gin.
I ask not health, nor even life—
Life! what a curse it's been to me!
I'd rather sink in deepest hell,
Than drink again its misery.

2.   "But, Doctor, may I not have rum?
One drop alone is all I crave:
Grant this small boon—I ask no more—
Then I'll defy—yes, e'en the grave;
Then, without fear, I'll fold my arms,
And bid the monster strike his dart,
To haste me from this world of woe,
And claim his own—this ruined heart.

3.   "A thousand curses on his head
Who gave me first the poisoned bowl,
Who taught me first this bane to drink—
Drink—death and ruin to my soul.
My soul! oh cruel, horrid thought!
Full well I know thy certain fate;
With what instinctive horror shrinks
The spirit from that awful state!

4.   "Lost—lost—I know forever lost!
To me no ray of hope can come:
My fate is sealed; my doom is——
But give me rum; I will have rum.
But, Doctor, don't you see him there?
In that dark corner low he sits;
See! how he sports his fiery tongue,
And at me burning brimstone spits!

5.   "Say, don't you see this demon fierce?
Does no one hear? will no one come?
Oh save me—save me—I will give—
But rum! I must have—will have rum!
Ah! now he's gone; once more I'm free;
He—the boasting knave and liar—
He said that he would take me off
Down to —— But there! my bed's on fire!

6.   " Fire ! water ! help ! come, haste—I'll die ;
Come, take me from this burning bed :
The smoke—I'm choking—cannot cry ;
There now—it's catching at my head !
But see ! again that demon's come ;
Look ! there he peeps through yonder crack ;
Mark how his burning eyeballs flash !
How fierce he grins ! what brought him back ?

7.   There stands his burning coach of fire ;
He smiles and beckons me to come—
What are those words he's written there ?
' In hell, we never want for rum ! ' "
One loud, one piercing shriek was heard ;
One yell rang out upon the air ;
One sound, and one alone, came forth—
The victim's cry of wild despair.

8.   " Why longer wait ? I'm ripe for hell ;
A spirit's sent to bear me down :
There, in the regions of the lost,
I sure will wear a fiery crown.
Damned, I know, without a hope !—
One moment more, and then I'll come !—
And there I'll quench my awful thirst
With boiling, burning, fiery rum ! "

XVI.—WHAT MAKES A HERO ?
HENRY TAYLOR.

1. WHAT makes a hero ?—not success, not fame,
Inebriate merchants, and the loud acclaim
Of glutted Avarice,—caps tossed up in air,
Or pen of journalist with flourish fair ;
Bell pealed, stars, ribbons, and a titular name—
These, though his rightful tribute, he can spare ;
His rightful tribute, not his end or aim,
Or true reward ; for never yet did these
Refresh the soul, or set the heart at ease.
What makes a hero ?—An heroic mind,
Expressed in action, in endurance proved.

2. And if there be preëminence of right
Derived through pain well suffered, to the height

Of rank heroic, 'tis to bear unmoved,
Not toil, not risk, not rage of sea or wind,
Not the brute fury of barbarians blind,
    But worse—ingratitude and poisonous darts,
    Launched by the country he has served and loved ;
This, with a free, unclouded spirit pure,
This, in the strength of silence to endure,
    A dignity to noble deeds imparts,
    Beyond the gauds and trappings of renown ;
    This is the hero's complement and crown ;
This missed, one struggle had been wanting still,—
One glorious triumph of the heroic will,
    One self-approval in his heart of hearts.

XVII.—THE TRUE KING.   *Translated from Seneca.*

LEIGH HUNT.

1. 'TIS not wealth that makes a King,
    Nor the purple coloring ;
    Nor a brow that's bound with gold,
    Nor gate on mighty hinges rolled.
    The King is he, who, void of fear,
    Looks abroad with bosom clear ;
    Who can tread ambition down,
    Nor be swayed by smile or frown ;

2. Nor for all the treasure cares,
    That mine conceals, or harvest wears,
    Or that golden sands deliver,   .
    Bosomed in a glassy river.
    What shall move his placid might ?
    Not the headlong thunder-light,
    Nor all the shapes of slaughter's trade,
    With onward lance, or fiery blade.

3. Safe, with wisdom for his crown
    He looks on all things calmly down ;
    He welcomes Fate, when Fate is near
    Nor taints his dying breath with fear.
    No—to fear not earthly thing,
    This it is that makes the King ;
    And all of us, whoe'er we be
    May carve us out that royalty.

XVIII.—BRUTUS ON THE DEATH OF LUCRETIA.

PAYNE.

1. Thus, thus, my friends! fast as our breaking hearts
    Permitted utterance, we have told our story:
    And now, to say one word of the imposture—
    The mask necessity has made me wear.
    When the ferocious malice of your king—
    King! do I call him?—when the monster, Tarquin,
    Slew, as most of you may well remember,
    My father, Marcus, and my elder brother,
    Envying at once their virtues and their wealth,
    How could I hope a shelter from his power,
    But in the false face I have worn so long?

2. Would you know why I summoned you together?
    Ask ye what brings me here?   Behold this dagger,
    Clotted with gore!   Behold that frozen corse!
    See where the lost Lucretia sleeps in death!
    She was the mark and model of the time,
    The mold in which each female face was formed,
    The very shrine and sacristy of virtue!

3. The worthiest of the worthy! not the nymph
    Who met old Numa in his hallowed walks,
    And whispered in his ear her strains divine,
    Can I conceive beyond her!—the young choir
    Of vestal virgins bent to her!—Such a mind,
    Might have abashed the boldest libertine,
    And turned desire to reverential love
    And holiest affection!

4. Oh my countrymen!
    You all can witness when that she went forth
    It was a holiday in Rome: old age
    Forgot its crutch; labor its task! all ran;
    And mothers, turning to their daughters, cried
    "There, there's Lucretia!"—Now look ye where she lies,
    That beauteous flower, that innocent sweet rose,
    Torn up by ruthless violence—gone! gone!

5. Say—would you seek instructions! would you seek
    What ye should do?—Ask ye yon conscious walls
    Which saw his poisoned brother, saw the crime
    Committed there, and they will cry, Revenge!—

Ask yonder senate-house, whose stones are purple
With human blood, and it will cry, Revenge !
Go to the tomb where lie his murdered wife,
And the poor queen who loved him as her son,
Their unappeased ghosts will shriek, Revenge !
The temples of the gods, the all-viewing heaven,—
The gods themselves—will justify the cry,
And swell the general sound—Revenge ! Revenge !

XIX.—RICHARD II. ON THE VANITY OF POWER.

SHAKSPEARE.

1.   OF comfort no man speak :
Let's talk of graves, of worms, and epitaphs ;
Make dust our paper, and with rainy eyes
Write sorrow on the bosom of the earth.
Let's choose executors and talk of wills :
And yet not so—for what can we bequeath,
Save our depos-ed bodies to the ground ?
Our lands, our lives, and all are Bolingbroke's,
And nothing can we call our own, but death,
And that small model of our barren earth,
Which serves as paste and cover to our bones.

2.   For heaven's sake let us sit upon the ground,
And tell sad stories of the death of kings—
How some have been deposed, some slain in war ;
Some haunted by the ghosts they have deposed ;
Some poisoned by their wives, some sleeping killed ;
All murdered—for within the hollow crown,
That rounds the mortal temples of a king,
Keeps death his court, and there the antic sits,
Scoffing his state, and grinning at his pomp ;
Allowing him a breath, a little scene
To monarchize, be feared and killed with looks ;
Infusing him with self and vain conceit—
As if this flesh which walls about our life,
Were brass impregnable : and humored thus,
Comes at the last and with a little pin
Bores through his castle wall, and—farewell, king !

XX.—THE PASSING OF THE RUBICON.

KNOWLES.

1. A GENTLEMAN, Mr. President, speaking of Cæsar's
benevolent disposition, and of the reluctance with which
he had entered into the civil war, observes, "How long
did he pause upon the brink of the Rubicon?" How
came he to the brink of that river! How dared he cross
it! Shall private men respect the boundaries of private
property, and shall a man pay no respect to the boundaries
of his country's rights? How dared he cross that river!
Oh, but he paused upon the brink! He should have perished upon the brink ere he had crossed it! Why did he
pause? Why does a man's heart palpitate when he is on
the point of committing an unlawful deed? Why does
the very murderer, his victim sleeping before him, and his
glaring eye taking the measure of the blow, strike wide
of the mortal part? Because of conscience! 'Twas that
made Cæsar pause upon the brink of the Rubicon. Compassion! What compassion? The compassion of an
assassin, that feels a momentary shudder as his weapon
begins to cut!

2. Cæsar paused upon the brink of the Rubicon!
What was the Rubicon? The boundary of Cæsar's province. From what did it separate his province? From his
country. Was that country a desert? No; it was cultivated and fertile, rich and populous! Its sons were men
of genius, spirit, and generosity! Its daughters were
lovely, susceptible, and chaste! Friendship was its inhabitant! Love was its inhabitant! Domestic affection
was its inhabitant! Liberty was its inhabitant! All
bounded by the stream of the Rubicon! What was
Cæsar, that stood upon the bank of that stream? A
traitor, bringing war and pestilence into the heart of that
country. No wonder that he paused—no wonder if, his
imagination wrought upon by his conscience, he had beheld blood instead of water, and heard groans instead of
murmurs! No wonder, if some gorgon horror had turned

him into stone upon the spot! But, no!—he cried, "The die is cast!" He plunged!—he crossed!—and Rome was free no more!

XXI.—THE UNION.

WEBSTER.

1. I PROFESS, sir, in my career hitherto, to have kept steadily in view the prosperity and honor of the whole country, and the preservation of our federal union. It is to that union, we owe our safety at home, and our consideration and dignity abroad. It is to that union, that we are chiefly indebted for whatever makes us most proud of our country. That union we reached only by the discipline of our virtues, in the severe school of adversity. It had its origin in the necessities of disordered finance, prostrate commerce, and ruined credit. Under its benign influences, these great interests immediately awoke as from the dead, and sprang forth with newness of life. Every year of its duration has teemed with fresh proof of its utility and its blessings; and, although our territory has stretched out wider and wider, and our population spread further and further, they have not outrun its protection or its benefits. It has been to us all a copious fountain of national, social, and personal happiness.

2. I have not allowed myself, sir, to look beyond the union, to see what might lie hidden in the dark recess behind. I have not coolly weighed the chances of preserving liberty, when the bonds that unite us together shall be broken asunder. I have not accustomed myself to hang over the precipice of disunion, to see whether, with my short sight, I can fathom the abyss below; nor could I regard him as a safe counsellor in the affairs of the government, whose thoughts should be mainly bent on considering, not how the union might best be preserved, but how tolerable might be the condition of the people, when it shall be broken up and destroyed.

3. While the union lasts, we have high, exciting, gratifying prospects spread out before us, for us and our children. Beyond that, I seek not to penetrate the veil. God grant, that in my day, at least, that curtain may not rise. God grant, that on my vision never may be opened what lies behind. When my eyes shall be turned to behold, for the last time, the sun in heaven, may I not see him shining on the broken and dishonored fragments of a once glorious union; on states dissevered, discordant, belligerent; our land rent with civil feuds, or drenched, it may be, in fraternal blood!

4. Let my last feeble and lingering glance rather behold the gorgeous ensign of the republic, now known and honored throughout the earth, still full high advanced, its arms and trophies streaming in their original lustre, not a stripe erased or polluted, not a single star obscured, bearing, for its motto, no such miserable interrogatory as, *What is all this worth?* nor those other words of delusion and folly, *Liberty first, and union afterward;* but everywhere, spread all over, in characters of living light, blazing on all its ample folds, as they float over the sea, and over the land, and on every wind, and under the whole heavens, that other sentiment, dear to every true American heart—*Liberty* AND *Union, now and forever; one and inseparable!*

XXII.—EXTRACT FROM THE LAST SPEECH OF ROBERT EMMET.

1. I HAVE been charged with that importance in the efforts to emancipate my country, as to be considered the key-stone of the combination of Irishmen, or, as your lordship expressed it, "The life and blood of the conspiracy." You do me honor over-much: you have given to the subaltern all the credit of a superior. There are men engaged in this conspiracy, who are not only superior to me, but even to your own conceptions of yourself, my lord; men,

before the splendor of whose genius and virtues I should bow with respectful deference, and who would think themselves dishonored to be called your friend—who would not disgrace themselves by shaking your blood-stained hand.

2. What, my lord, shall you tell me, on the passage to that scaffold, which that tyranny, of which you are only the intermediary executioner, has erected for my murder, that I am accountable for all the blood that has been, and will be shed, in this struggle of the oppressed against the oppressor? Shall you tell me this, and must I be so very a slave as not to repel it? I do not fear to approach the omnipotent Judge, to answer for the conduct of my whole life; and am I to be appalled and falsified by a mere remnant of mortality here? by you too, who, if it were possible to collect all the innocent blood that you have shed in your unhallowed ministry, in one great reservoir, your lordship might swim in it.

3. Let no man dare, when I am dead, to charge me with dishonor! let no man attaint my memory, by believing that I could have engaged in any cause but that of my country's liberty and independence; or, that I could have become the pliant minion of power, in the oppression, or the miseries, of my countrymen. The proclamation of the provisional government speaks forth our views; no inference can be tortured from it, to countenance barbarity, or debasement at home, or subjection, humiliation, or treachery from abroad. I would not have submitted to a foreign invader, for the same reason that I would resist the foreign and domestic oppressor; in the dignity of freedom, I would have fought upon the threshold of my country, and its enemy should enter only by passing over my lifeless corpse. Am I, who have lived but for my country, and who have subjected myself to the dangers of the jealous and watchful oppressor, and the bondage of the grave, only to give my countrymen their rights, and my country her independence, and am I to be loaded with calumny, and not suffered to resent or repel it? No, God forbid!

4. If the spirits of the illustrious dead participate in the concerns and cares of those who are dear to them in this transitory life, O, ever dear and venerated shade of my departed father, look down with scrutiny upon the conduct of your suffering son; and see if I have even for a moment deviated from those principles of morality and patriotism, which it was your care to instill into my youthful mind; and for which I am now to offer up my life. My lords, you are impatient for the sacrifice. The blood which you seek, is not congealed by the artificial terrors which surround your victim; it circulates warmly and unruffled, through the channels which God created for noble purposes, but which you are bent to destroy, for purposes so grievous, that they cry to heaven.

5. Be yet patient! I have but a few words more to say. I am going to my cold and silent grave: my lamp of life is nearly extinguished; my race is run: the grave opens to receive me, and I sink into its bosom! I have but one request to ask at my departure from this world,— it is the charity of its silence! Let no man write my epitaph: for, as no man, who knows my motives, dare now vindicate them, let not prejudice or ignorance asperse them. Let them, and me, repose in obscurity and peace, and my tomb remain uninscribed, until other times, and other men, can do justice to my character: when my country takes her place among the nations of the earth, then, and not till then, let my epitaph be written. I have done.

XXIII.—TELL ON HIS NATIVE HILLS.

KNOWLES.

1.   Oh, with what pride I used
    To walk these hills, and look up to my God,
    And bless him that the land was free. 'T was free—
    From end to end, from cliff to lake 't was free!
    Free as our torrents are that leap our rocks,
    And plow our valleys, without asking leave!

Or as our peaks, that wear their caps of snow
In very presence of the regal sun !

2.   How happy was it then !   I loved
Its very storms.   Yes, I have sat
In my boat at night, when, midway o'er the lake,
The stars went out, and down the mountain gorge
The wind came roaring.   I have sat and eyed
The thunder breaking from his cloud, and smiled
To see him shake his lightnings o'er my head,
And think I had no master save his own !

3.   On yonder jutting cliff—o'ertaken there
By the mountain blast, I've laid me flat along,
And while gust followed gust more furiously,
As if to sweep me o'er the horrid brink,
And I have thought of other lands, whose storms
Are summer-flaws to those of mine, and just
Have wished me there—the thought that mine was free
Has checked that wish, and I have raised my head,
And cried in thraldom to that furious wind,
Blow on !—this is the land of liberty !

XXIV.—ONE YEAR AGO.

1. What stars have faded from our sky !
What hopes unfolded but to die !
What dreams so fondly pondered o'er,
Forever lost the hues they wore ?
How like a death-knell, sad and slow,
Tolls through the soul, " one year ago ! "

2. Where is the face we loved to greet,
The form that graced the fireside seat,
The gentle smile, the winning way,
That blessed our life-path day by day ?
Where fled those accents soft and low
That thrilled our hearts " one year ago ! "

3. Ah, vacant is the fireside chair,
The smile that won, no longer there ;
From door and hall, from porch and lawn,
The echo of the voice is gone,
And we who linger, only know
How much we lost, " one year ago ! "

4. Beside her grave the marble white
Keeps silent guard by day and night.
Serene she sleeps, nor heeds the tread
Of footsteps o'er her lowly bed :
Her pulseless breast no more may know
The pangs of life, " one year ago ! "

5. " But why repine ? " A few more years,
A few more broken sighs and tears,
And we, enlisted with the dead,
Shall follow where her steps have fled,
To that far world rejoicing go
To which she passed " one year ago ! "

XXV.—MACBETH TO THE DAGGER.

SHAKSPEARE.

1. Is this a dagger which I see before me,
The handle toward my hand ?   Come, let me clutch thee—
I have thee not ; and yet I see thee still.
Art thou not, fatal vision, sensible
To feeling, as to sight ? or art thou but
A dagger of the mind ? a false creation
Proceeding from the heat-oppressed brain ?
I see thee yet, in form as palpable
As this which now I draw.

2.   Thou marshal'st me the way that I was going ;
And such an instrument I was to use.
Mine eyes are made the fools o' the other senses,
Or else worth all the rest. I see thee still ;
And on thy blade and dudgeon, gouts of blood,
Which was not so before.   There's no such thing !—
It is the bloody business, which informs
Thus to mine eyes.

3.   Now o'er the one-half world,
Nature seems dead, and wicked dreams abuse
The curtained sleep : now witchcraft celebrates
Pale Hecate's offerings ; and withered Murder,
—Alarumed by his sentinel, the wolf,
Whose howl 's his watch—thus with his stealthy pace,
Toward his design moves like a ghost.

5

4.　Thou sure and firm-set earth,
Hear not my steps, which way they walk, for fear
Thy very stones prate of my whereabout ;
And take the present horror from the time,
Which now suits with it.　Whiles I threat, he lives—
Words to the heat of deeds too cold breath gives ;
I go, and it is done ; the bell invites me.
Hear it not, Duncan ; for it is a knell
That summons thee to heaven, or to hell.

XXVI.—THE INDIAN HUNTER.

ELIZA COOK.

1. Oh ! why does the white man follow my path,
Like the hound on the tiger's track ?
Does the flush on my dark cheek waken his wrath,—
Does he covet the bow at my back ?

2. He has rivers and seas where the billows and breeze
Bear riches for him alone ;
And the sons of the wood never plunge in the flood,
Which the white man calls his own.

3. Then why should he come to the streams where none
But the red man dares to swim ?
Why, why should he wrong the hunter,—one
Who never did harm to him ?

4. The Father above thought fit to give
The white man corn and wine ;
There are golden fields where he may live,
But the forest shades are mine.

5. The Eagle hath its place of rest ;
The wild horse, where to dwell ;
And the spirit that gave the bird its nest,
Made me a home as well.

6. Then back ! go back from the red man's track ;
For the hunter's eyes grow dim,
To find that the white man wrongs the one
Who never did harm to him.

XXVII.—PRENTICE'S BEST POEM.

[The following is the poem read by George D. Prentice of the Louisville Journal at the unvailing of the Clay statue—pronounced the best effort of his life by his admirers :]

1. HAIL ! true and glorious semblance, hail !
   Of him, the noblest of our race,
We seem, at lifting of thy vail,
   To see again his living face !
To hear the stirring words once more,
   That like the storm-god's cadence pealed
With mightier power from shore to shore
   Than thunders of the battle-field.

2. Lo ! that calm, high, majestic look,
   That blinds our gaze as by a spell,
It is the same that erst-while shook
   The traitors on whose souls it fell !
Oh that he were again in life !
   To wave, as once, his wand of power,
And scatter far the storms of strife
   That o'er our country darkly lower.

3. Again, again, and yet again
   He rolled back passion's roaring tide,
When the fierce souls of hostile men
   Each other's wildest wrath defied :
Alas ! alas ! dark storms at length
   Sweep o'er our half-wrecked ship of state,
And there seem none with will and strength
   To save her from her awful fate !

4. But thou, majestic image, thou
   Wilt in thy lofty place abide,
And many a manly head will bow
   While gazing on a nation's pride ;
And while his hallowed ashes lie
   Afar beneath old Ashland's sod,
One gaze at thee should sanctify
   Our hearts to country and to God.

5. We look on thee, we look on thee,
   Proud statue, glorious and sublime,
And years as if by magic flee,
   And leave us in his grand old time !

Oh, he was born to bless our race
As ages after ages roll,
We see the image of his face—
Earth has no image of his soul !

6. Proud statue ! if the nation's life,
For which he toiled through all his years,
Must vanish in our wicked strife
And leave but groans, and blood, and tears ;
If all to anarchy be given,
And ruin all our land assail,
He'll turn away his eyes to heaven,
And o'er thee we will cast thy vail.

XXVIII.—THE UNSEEN BATTLE-FIELD.

1. There is an unseen battle-field
In every human breast,
Where two opposing forces meet,
But where they seldom rest.

2. That field is vailed from mortal sight,
'Tis only seen by One
Who knows alone where victory lies,
When each day's fight is done.

3. One army clusters strong and fierce,
Their chief of demon form ;
His brow is like the thunder-cloud,
His voice the bursting storm,

4. His captains, Pride, and Lust, and Hate,
Whose troops watch night and day,
Swift to detect the weakest point,
And thirsting for the fray.

5. Contending with this mighty force
Is but a little band ;
Yet there, with an unquailing front,
Those warriors firmly stand !

6. Their leader is a God-like form,
Of countenance serene ;
And glowing on his naked breast
A simple cross is seen.

7. His captains, FAITH, and HOPE, and LOVE,
   Point to that wondrous sign ;
   And, gazing on it, all receive
   Strength from a Source divine.

8. They feel it speak a glorious truth,
   A truth as great as sure,
   That to be victors they must learn
   To love, confide, endure.

9. That faith sublime in wildest strife
   Imparts a holy calm ;
   For every deadly blow a shield,
   For every wound a balm.

10. And when they win that battle-field,
   Past toil is quite forgot ;
   The plain where carnage once had reigned,
   Becomes a hallowed spot :

11. A spot where flowers of joy and peace
   Spring from the fertile sod,
   And breathe the perfume of their praise
   On every breeze—to God.

XXIX.—WHAT CONSTITUTES A STATE.

SIR WILLIAM JONES.

1.   WHAT constitutes a state ?
Not high-raised battlements, or labored mound,
   Thick wall, or moated gate :
Not cities proud with spires and turrets crowned,
   Not bays and broad-armed ports,
Where, laughing at the storm, rich navies ride ;
   Not starred and spangled courts,
Where low-born baseness wafts perfume to pride.

2.   ·No ; *men*, high-minded *men*,
With power as far above dull brutes indued,
   In forest, brake, or den,
As beasts excel cold rocks and brambles rude :
   Men who their duties know,
But know their rights ; and knowing, dare maintain,
   Prevent the long-aimed blow,
And crush the tyrant while they rend the chain :
   These constitute a state ;

3. And sovereign law, that state's collected will,
      O'er thrones and globes elate,
   Sits empress, crowning good, repressing ill :
      Smit by her sacred frown,
   The fiend Discretion, like a vapor, sinks,
      And e'en the all-dazzling crown
   Hides his faint rays, and at her bidding shrinks.

———◆———

XXX.—POETICAL SELECTIONS.

1.—Eloquence of Silence.
Miss Mary A. Wheaton.

1. At midnight's hour, when o'er the sleeping world
   The white wings of the angels are unfurled,
   And the wild surging tides of life that rushed
   So restlessly through human hearts lie hushed ;
   When all the air is fragrant with the balm
   Of blossoms breathing sweet and holy calm,
   O'er the tired spirit, then there steal away
   Voices to us we never hear by day,
   Faint echoes from the world unseen that roll
   Through the dim, silent chambers of the soul.

2.—True Refinement.
Holland's Kathrina.

1. One thing I learned : that she who thus had joined
   This cluster of disciples was not born
   And reared among their number ; that was plain.
   I saw it in her bearing and her dress ;
   In that unconsciousness of self that comes
   Of gentle breeding, and society
   Of gentle men and women ; in the ease
   With which she bore the awkward deference
   Of those that spoke with her adown the aisle ;
   In distant and admiring gaze of men,
   And the cold scrutiny of village girls
   Who passed for belles.

3.—Forgive and Forget.
Charles Swain.

1. Forgive and forget ! why, the world would be lonely,
   The garden a wilderness left to deform,

If the flowers but remembered the chilling blast only,
  And the fields gave no verdure for fear of the storm.
Oh, still in thy loveliness emblem the flower,
  Give the fragrance of feeling to sweeten life's way;
And prolong not again the brief cloud of an hour,
  With tears that but darken the rest of the day!

2. Forgive and forget! there's no breast so unfeeling,
    But some gentle thoughts of affection there live;
  And the best of us all require something concealing,
    Some heart that with smiles can forget and forgive.
  Then away with the clouds from those beautiful eyes,
    That brow was no home for such frowns to have met;
  O, how could our spirits e'er hope for the skies,   -
    If Heaven refused—TO FORGIVE AND FORGET?

4.—THE FLIGHT OF A SINGLE SOUL.

1. As the light leaf, whose fall to ruin bears
  Some trembling insect's little world of cares,
  Descends in silence,—while around waves on
  The mighty forest, reckless what is gone!
  Such is man's doom,—and ere an hour be flown;
  Start not, then, trifler!—such may be thine own!

5.—GENIUS UNEMPLOYED.

HOLLAND.

1. OF all the dull, dead weights man ever bore,
  Sure, none can wear the soul with discontent
  Like consciousness of power unused.   To feel
  That one has gift to move the multitude,—
  To act upon the life of human kind
  By force of will, or fire of eloquence,
  Or voice of lofty art, and yet, to feel
  No stir of mighty motive in the soul
  To action or endeavor; to behold
  The fairest prizes of this fleeting life
  Borne off by patient men who, day by day,
  By bravest toil and struggle, reach the heights
  Of great achievement, toiling, struggling thus
  With a strong joy, and with a fine contempt
  For soft and selfish passion; to see this,
  Yet cling to such a passion, like a slave
  Who hugs his chains in sluggish impotence,

Refusing freedom lest he lose the crust
The chain of bondage warrants him—ah ! this
Is misery indeed !

6.—THE ANGEL OF SLEEP.

1. HE drops his plumy, snow-soft wings,
    He waves his balmy hand,
And wide the gate of silence swings
    That guards the shadowy land.
Forgot is Time, the sentinel
    That stands outside the door ;
The gloomy train of cares as well
    That clogged our steps before ;
Oh river of oblivion !
    Thy draughts are sweet and deep,
For memory slumbers on her throne,
    Rocked by the angel, Sleep.

2. There is a face whose loveliness
    Is marred by hues of care ;
But sleep hath swept it with his kiss,
    And made it smooth and fair.
There is a worn and weary brain,
    That rests until the morn :
There is a heart which beats with pain,
    That feels no more forlorn.
Oh, Death's fair brother, how divine
    Must be that slumber deep,
More sweet, more calm, more free than thine,
    When His beloved sleep.

7.—WHERE GOD APPEARS.

1. MEN dream of God as far
    Beyond the highest star.
      His throne they place
      In some far space,
        Where one
        Vast, central sun,
In awful power, and light, and grandeur rolls,
And all the movements of all worlds controls.

    2. Not there
      Does He appear ;

We need not cleave the air
To find Him near.
   His Spirit dwells
   In smallest cells.
  Within the breast,
  We test
His love and might.
  In Solar-Plexus deep,
  Our souls their vigils keep :
   And there,
   In hour of prayer,
Heaven dawns upon the sight.
In that effulgent light
The living God is near,
And to the pure in heart doth evermore appear.

8.—LIFE OF MAN.

BEAUMONT.

1. LIKE to the falling of a star,
Or as the flights of eagles are,
Or like the fresh spring's gaudy hue,
Or silver drops of morning dew,
Or like a wind that chafes the flood,
Or bubbles which on water stood :
E'en such is man, whose borrowed light
Is straight called in and paid to-night :
The wind blows out, the bubble dies ;
The spring entombed in autumn lies ;
The dew's dried up, the star is shot,
The flight is past, and man forgot.

9.—THE PILOT.

THOMAS HAYNES BAYLY.

1. O, PILOT ! 'tis a fearful night,—there's danger on the deep ;
I'll come and pace the deck with thee,—I do not dare to sleep.
Go down ! the sailor cried, go down ; this is no place for thee :
Fear not ; but trust in Providence, wherever thou mayst be.

2. Ah ! pilot, dangers often met we all are apt to slight,
And thou hast known these raging waves but to subdue their might.
It is not apathy, he cried, that gives this strength to me :
Fear not ; but trust in Providence, wherever thou mayst be.

3. On such a night the sea engulfed my father's lifeless form ;
My only brother's boat went down in just so wild a storm ;
5*

And such, perhaps, may be my fate ; but still I say to thee,
Fear not ; but trust in Providence, wherever thou mayst be.

10.—IMMORTALITY.

R. H. DANA.

1. "MAN, thou shalt never die ! " Celestial voices
Hymn it unto our souls : according harps,
By angel fingers touched, when the mild stars
Of morning sang together, sound forth still
The song of our great immortality !
Thick-clustering orbs on this our fair domain,
The tall, dark mountains, and the deep-toned seas,
Join in this solemn, universal song.
O listen, ye our spirits ! drink it in
From all the air ! 'Tis in the gentle moonlight ;
'Tis floating mid day's setting glories ; night,
Wrapped in her sable robe, with silent step,
Comes to our bed, and breathes it in our ears.
Night and the dawn, bright day and thoughtful eve,
All time, all bounds, the limitless expanse,
As one vast mystic instrument, are touched
By an unseen, living hand, and conscious chords
Quiver with joy in this great jubilee :
The dying hear it ; and, as sounds of earth
Grow dull and distant, wake their passing souls
To mingle in this heavenly harmony.

11.—ABOU BEN ADHEM.

LEIGH HUNT.

1. ABOU BEN ADHEM (may his tribe increase !)
Awoke one night from a deep dream of peace,
And saw within the moonlight of his room,
Making it rich, and like a lily in bloom,
An angel writing in a book of gold.
Exceeding peace had made Ben Adhem bold,
And, to the presence in the room, he said,
" What writest thou ? " The vision raised its head,
And, with a look made of all sweet accord,
Answered, " The names of those who love the Lord ! "
" And is mine one ? " asked Abou.—" Nay, not so,"
Replied the angel. Abou spake more low,
But cheerly still ; and said—" I pray thee, then,
Write me as one that loves his fellow-men."

The angel wrote and vanished. The next night
It came again, with a great wakening light,
And showed the names whom love of God had blest;
And lo! Ben Adhem's name led all the rest!

12.—ATHEISM REPROVED.

From the ITALIAN.

1. " THERE is no God," the fool in secret said,—
 " There is no God that rules or earth or sky ! "
Tear off the band that folds the wretch's head,
 That God may burst upon his faithless eye !
Is there no God ?—the stars, in myriads spread,
 If he look up, the blasphemy deny ;
While his own features, in the mirror read,
 Reflect the image of Divinity.

2. Is there no God ?—the stream that silv'ry flows,
 The air he breathes, the ground he treads, the trees,
The flowers, the grass, the sands, each wind that blows,
 All speak of God ; through one voice agrees,
And eloquent His dread existence shows ;—
 Blind to thyself, ah, see Him, fool, in these !

XXXI.—STORY OF LOGAN, A MINGO CHIEF.

1. In the spring of the year 1774, a robbery and murder were committed on an inhabitant of the frontiers of Virginia by two Indians of the Shawanese tribe. The neighboring whites, according to their custom, undertook to punish this outrage in a summary way. Colonel Cresap, a man infamous for the many murders he had committed on those much injured people, collected a party, and proceeded down the Kanhaway in quest of vengeance. Unfortunately, a canoe of women and children, with one man only, was seen coming from the opposite shore unarmed, and unsuspecting any hostile attack from the whites. Cresap and his party concealed themselves on the bank of the river ; and the moment the canoe reached the shore, singled out their objects, and at one fire killed every person in it.

2. This happened to be the family of Logan, who had long been distinguished as the friend of the whites. This unworthy return provoked his vengeance. He accordingly signalized himself in the war which ensued. In the autumn of the same year, a decisive battle was fought at the mouth of the Great Kanhaway, between the collected forces of the Shawanese, Mingoes, and Delawares, and a detachment of the Virginia militia. The Indians were defeated and sued for peace. Logan, however, disdained to be seen among the suppliants; but, lest the sincerity of a treaty should be disturbed, from which so distinguished a chief absented himself, he sent by a messenger, the following speech, to be delivered to Lord Dunmore.

3. "I appeal to any white man to say, if ever he entered Logan's cabin hungry, and he gave him no meat; if ever he came cold and naked, and he clothed him not. During the last long and bloody war, Logan remained idle in his cabin, an advocate for peace. Such was my love for the whites, that my countrymen pointed as they passed by, and said, *Logan is the friend of white men.* I had even thought to have lived with you, had it not been for the injuries of one man,—Colonel Cresap, the last spring in cold blood, and unprovoked, murdered all the relations of Logan, not even sparing my women and children.

4. "There runs not a drop of my blood in the veins of any living creature. This called on me for revenge. I have sought it; I have killed many; I have fully glutted my vengeance. For my country, I rejoice at the beams of peace; but do not harbor a thought that mine is the joy of fear. Logan never felt fear. He will not turn on his heel to save his life. Who is there to mourn for Logan? Not one."

XXXII.—SPEECH OF A SCYTHIAN EMBASSADOR TO ALEX-
ANDER.

1. WHEN the Scythian embassadors waited on Alex-

ander the Great, they gazed on him a long time without speaking a word, being very probably surprized, as they formed a judgment of men from their air and stature, to find that his did not answer the high idea they entertained of him from his fame. At last, the oldest of the embassadors addressed him thus: "Had the gods given thee a body proportioned to thy ambition, the whole universe would have been too little for thee. With one hand thou wouldst touch the East and with the other the West; and, not satisfied with this, thou wouldst follow the sun, and know where he hides himself.

2. "But what have we to do with thee? We never set foot in thy country. May not those who inhabit woods be allowed to live without knowing who thou art, and whence thou comest? We will neither command over, nor submit to any man. And that thou mayest be sensible what kind of people the Scythians are, know that we received from Heaven, as a rich present, a yoke of oxen, a ploughshare, a dart, a javelin and a cup. These we make use of, both with our friends and against our enemies.

3. "To our friends we give corn, which we procure by the labor of our oxen; with them we offer wine to the gods in our cup; and with regard to our enemies, we combat at a distance with our arrows, and near at hand with our javelins. But thou, who boasted thy coming to extirpate robbers, art thyself the greatest robber upon earth. Thou hast plundered all nations thou overcamest; thou hast possessed thyself of Lybia, invaded Syria, Persia and Bactriana; thou art forming a design to march as far as India, and now thou comest hither to seize upon our herds of cattle.

4. "The great possessions thou hast, only make thee covet the more eagerly what thou hast not. If thou art a god, thou oughtest to do good to mortals, and not deprive them of their possessions. If thou art a mere man, reflect always on what thou art. They whom thou shalt not molest will be thy true friends: the strongest friendships

being contracted between equals ; and they are esteemed
equals, who have not tried their strength against each
other. But do not suppose that those whom thou con-
querest can love thee."

———————♦———————

XXXIII.—SINGULAR ADVENTURE OF GENERAL PUTNAM.

1. WHEN General Putnam first moved to Pomfret, in
Connecticut, in the year 1739, the country was new and
much infested with wolves. Great havoc was made
among the sheep by a she-wolf which, with her annual
whelps, had for several years continued in that vicinity.
The young ones were commonly destroyed by the vigilance
of the hunters ; but the old one was too sagacious to be
ensnared by them. This wolf, at length, became such an
intolerable nuisance, that Mr. Putnam entered into a combination with five of his neighbors to hunt alternately until
they could destroy her. Two by rotation, were to be constantly in pursuit. It was known, that, having lost the
toes from one foot, by a steel-trap, she made one track
shorter than the other.

2. By this vestige the pursuers recognized, in a light
snow, the route of this pernicious animal. Having followed her to Connecticut river, and found she had turned
back in a direct course towards Pomfret, they immediately returned, and by ten o'clock the next morning the blood-
hounds had driven her into a den, about three miles distant
from the house of Mr. Putnam. The people soon collected
with dogs, guns, straw, fire and sulphur to attack the common enemy. With this apparatus several unsuccessful efforts
were made to force her from the den. The hounds came
back badly wounded, and refused to return. The smoke
of blazing straw had no effect. Nor did the fumes of burnt
brimstone, with which the cavern was filled, compel her to
quit the retirement.

3. Wearied with such fruitless attempts (which had

brought the time to ten o'clock at night), Mr. Putnam tried once more to make his dog enter, but in vain; he proposed to his negro man to go down into the cavern and shoot the wolf. The negro declined the hazardous service. Then it was that their master, angry at the disappointment, and declaring that he was ashamed at having a coward in his family, resolved himself to destroy the ferocious beast, lest she should escape through some unknown fissure of the rock. His neighbors strongly remonstrated against the perilous enterprise ; but he knowing that wild animals were intimidated by fire, and having provided several strips of birch bark, the only combustible material which he could obtain, which would afford light in this deep and darksome cave, prepared for his descent.

4. Having accordingly divested himself of his coat and waistcoat, and having a long rope fastened round his legs, by which he might be pulled back, at a concerted signal, he entered, head foremost, with a blazing torch in his hand. Having groped his passage till he came to a horizontal part of the den, the most terrifying darkness appeared in front of the dim circle of light afforded by his torch. It was silent as the house of death. None but monsters of the desert had ever before explored this solitary mansion of horror. He cautiously proceeding onward came to an ascent which he slowly mounted on his hands and knees, until he discovered the glaring eye-balls of the wolf, which was sitting at the extremity of the cavern. Startled at the sight of fire, she gnashed her teeth and gave a sullen growl.

5. As soon as he had made the necessary discovery, he kicked the rope as a signal for pulling him out. The people at the mouth of the den, who had listened with painful anxiety, hearing the growling of the wolf, and supposing their friend to be in the most imminent danger, drew him forth with such celerity that he was stripped of his clothes, and severely bruised. After he had adjusted his clothes, and loaded his gun with nine buck shot, holding a torch in

one hand and the musket in the other, he descended a second time. When he drew nearer than before, the wolf assuming a still more fierce and terrible appearance, howling, rolling her eyes, snapping her teeth, and dropping her head between her legs, was evidently, in the attitude and on the point of springing at him.

6. At this critical instant, he levelled and fired at her head. Stunned with the shock, and suffocated with the smoke, he immediately found himself drawn out of the cave. But having refreshed himself and permitted the smoke to dissipate, he went down the third time. Once more he came within sight of the wolf, which appearing very passive, he applied the torch to her nose ; and perceiving her dead, he took hold of her ears, and then kicking the rope (still tied round his legs) the people above with no small exultation dragged them both out together.

----&----

XXXIV.—THE AGED PRISONER RELEASED FROM THE BASTILE.

1. Nowhere else on earth, perhaps, has human misery, by human means been rendered so lasting, so complete or remediless as in that despotic prison, the Bastile. This the following case may suffice to evince : the particulars of which are translated from that elegant and energetic writer, Mr. Mercier. The heinous offence which merited an imprisonment surpassing torture, and rendering death a blessing, was no more than some unguarded expressions, implying disrespect towards the late Gallic monarch, Louis XV.

2. Upon the accession of Louis XVI. to the throne, the ministers then in office, moved by humanity, began their administration with an act of clemency and justice. They inspected the registers of the Bastile, and set many prisoners at liberty. Among those, there was an old man who had groaned in confinement for forty-seven years,

between four thick and cold stone walls. Hardened by adversity, which strengthens both the mind and constitution, when they are not overpowered by it, he had resisted the horrors of his long imprisonment, with an invincible and manly spirit.

3. His locks, white, thin, and scattered, had almost acquired the rigidity of iron; whilst his body, environed for so long a time by a coffin of stone, had borrowed from it a firm and compact habit. The narrow door of his tomb, turning upon its grating hinges, opened not as usual by halves, and an unknown voice announced his liberty, and bade him depart. Believing this to be a dream, he hesitated; but at length rose up and walked forth with trembling steps, amazed at the space he traversed. The stairs of the prison, the halls, the court seemed to him vast, immense, and almost without bounds.

4. He stopped from time to time, and gazed around like a bewildered traveller. His vision was with difficulty reconciled to the clear light of day. He contemplated the heavens as a new object. His eyes remained fixed, and he could not even weep. Stupefied with his newly acquired power of changing his position, his limbs, like his tongue, refused, in spite of his efforts, to perform their office. At length he got through the formidable gates. When he felt the motion of the carriage which was prepared to transport him to his former habitation, he screamed out and uttered some inarticulate sounds; and as he could not bear this new movement, he was obliged to descend. Supported by a benevolent arm, he sought out the street where he had formerly resided: he found it, but no trace of his house remained: one of the public edifices occupied the spot where it stood.

5. He now saw nothing which brought to his recollection, either that particular quarter, the city itself, or the objects with which he was formerly acquainted. The houses of his nearest neighbors, which were fresh in his

5*

memory, had assumed a new appearance. In vain were his looks directed to all the objects around him : he could discover nothing of which he had the smallest remembrance. Terrified, he stopped and fetched a deep sigh. To him what did it import, that the city was peopled with living creatures? None of them were alive to him : he was unknown to all the world, and he knew nobody ; and while he wept he regretted his dungeon.

6. At the name of the Bastile, which he often pronounced and even claimed as an asylum, and the sight of his clothes which marked his former age, the crowd gathered around him : curiosity blended with pity excited their attention. The most aged asked him many questions, but had no remembrance of the circumstances which he recapitulated. At length accident brought to his way an ancient domestic, now a superannuated porter, who, confined to his lodge for fifteen years, had barely sufficient strength to open the gate. Even *he* did not know the master he had served ; but informed him that grief and misfortune had brought his wife to the grave thirty years before ; that his children were gone abroad to distant climes, and that of all his relations and friends, none now remained.

7. This recital was made with the indifference which people discover for events long passed and almost forgotten. The miserable man groaned, and groaned alone. The crowd around, offering only unknown features to his view, made him feel the excesses of his calamities, even more than he would have done in the dreadful solitude which he had left. Overcome with sorrow, he presented himself before the minister, to whose humanity he owed that liberty which was now a burden to him. Bowing down, he said, " Restore me again to that prison from which you have taken me. I cannot survive the loss of my nearest relations ; of my friends ; and in one word, of a whole generation. Is it possible in the same moment to be informed of this universal destruction, and not wish for death ?

8. " This general mortality, which to others comes slowly and by degrees, has to me been instantaneous, the operation of a moment. While secluded from society, I lived with myself only; but here I can neither live with myself, nor with this new race, to whom my anguish and despair appear only as a dream." The minister was melted; he caused the old domestic to attend this unfortunate person, as only *he* could talk to him of his family. This discourse was the single consolation which he received; for he shunned intercourse with the new race, born since he had been exiled from the world; and he passed his time in the midst of Paris in the same solitude as he had done while confined in a dungeon for almost half a century. But the chagrin and mortification of meeting no person who could say to him, "We were formerly known to each other," soon put an end to his life.

XXXV.—THE POWER OF HABIT.

J. B. GOUGH.

1. I REMEMBER once riding from Buffalo to the Niagara Falls. I said to a gentleman, "What river is that, sir?"

"That," he said, "is Niagara river."

"Well, it is a beautiful stream," said I; "bright and fair and glassy; how far off are the rapids?"

"Only a mile or two," was the reply.

"Is it possible that only a mile from us we shall find the water in the turbulence which it must show near to the Falls?"

"You will find it so, sir." And so I found it; and the first sight of Niagara I shall never forget. Now, launch your bark on that Niagara river; it is bright, smooth, beautiful and glassy. There is a ripple at the bow; the silver wake you leave behind adds to your enjoyment.

2. Down the stream you glide, oars, sails and helm in proper trim, and you set out on your pleasure excursion. Suddenly some one cries out from the bank, " Young men, ahoy!"

"What is it?"

"The rapids are below you."

"Ha! hah! we have heard of the rapids, but we are not such fools as to get there. If we go too fast, then we shall up with the helm and steer to the shore; we will set the mast in the socket, hoist the sail, and speed to the land. Then on, boys; don't be alarmed—there is no danger."

"Young men, ahoy there!"

"What is it?"

"The rapids are below you!"

3. "Ha! hah! we will laugh and quaff; all things delight us. What care we for the future! No man ever saw it. Sufficient for the day is the evil thereof. We will enjoy life while we may; will catch pleasure as it flies. This is enjoyment; time enough to steer out of danger when we are sailing swiftly with the current."

"Young men, ahoy!"

"What is it?"

"Beware! Beware! The rapids are below you!"

Now you see the water foaming all around. See how fast you pass that point! Up with the helm! Now turn! Pull hard! quick! quick! quick! pull for your lives! pull till the blood starts from thy nostrils, and the veins stand like whip-cords upon thy brow! Set the mast in the socket! hoist the sail!—ah! ah! it is too late! "Shrieking, cursing, howling, blaspheming, over they go."

Thousands go over the rapids every year, through the power of habit, crying all the while, "When I find out that it is injuring me I will give it up!"

XXXVI.—SENDING RELIEF TO IRELAND, 1847.

S. S. Prentiss.

1. WE have assembled, not to respond to shouts of triumph from the West,* but to answer the cry of want

---

* Referring to the victories in Mexico, the news of which had been recently received.

and suffering which comes from the East. The Old World stretches out her arms to the New. The starving parent supplicates the young and vigorous child for bread. There lies, upon the other side of the wide Atlantic, a beautiful island, famous in story and in song. Its area is not so great as that of the State of Louisiana, while its population is almost half that of the Union. It has given to the world more than its share of genius and of greatness. It has been prolific in statesmen, warriors, and poets. Its brave and generous sons have fought successfully all battles but their own.

2. In wit and humor it has no equal, while its harp, like its history, moves to tears, by its sweet but melancholy pathos. Into this fair region God has seen fit to send the most terrible of all those fearful ministers who fulfil his inscrutable decrees. The earth has failed to give her increase; the common mother has forgotten her offspring, and her breast no longer affords them their accustomed nourishment. Famine, gaunt and ghastly famine, has seized a nation in its strangling grasp; and unhappy Ireland, in the sad woes of the present, forgets, for a moment, the gloomy history of the past.

3. O, it is terrible, in this beautiful world, which the good God has given us, and in which there is plenty for us all, that men should die of starvation! You, who see, each day, poured into the lap of your city food sufficient to assuage the hunger of a nation, can form but an imperfect idea of the horrors of famine. In battle, in the fulness of his pride and strength, little recks the soldier whether the hissing bullet sings his sudden requiem, or the cords of life are severed by the sharp steel. But he who dies of hunger wrestles alone, day after day, with his grim and unrelenting enemy.

4. The blood recedes, the flesh deserts, the muscles relax, and the sinews grow powerless. At last, the mind, which, at first, had bravely nerved itself for the contest, gives way, under the mysterious influences which govern

its union with the body. Then he begins to doubt the existence of an overruling Providence; he hates his fellow-men, and glares upon them with the longings of a cannibal, and, it may be, dies blaspheming!

5. Who will hesitate to give his mite to avert such awful results? Surely not the citizens of New Orleans, ever famed for deeds of benevolence and charity. Freely have your hearts and purses opened, heretofore, to the call of suffering humanity. Nobly did you respond to oppressed Greece and to struggling Poland. Within Erin's borders is an enemy more cruel than the Turk, more tyrannical than the Russian. Bread is the only weapon that can conquer him. Let us, then, load ships with this glorious munition, and, in the name of our common humanity, wage war against this despot Famine. Let us, in God's name, " cast our bread upon the waters," and if we are selfish enough to desire it back again, we may recollect the promise, that it shall return to us after many days.

----------◆----------

XXXVII.—IRISH ALIENS AND ENGLISH VICTORIES.
SHEIL.

1. I SHOULD be surprised, indeed, if, while you are doing us wrong, you did not profess your solicitude to do us justice. From the day on which Strongbow set his foot upon the shore of Ireland, Englishmen were never wanting in protestations of their deep anxiety to do us justice: even Strafford, the deserter of the People's cause,—the renegade Wentworth, who gave evidence in Ireland of the spirit of instinctive tyranny which predominated in his character: even Strafford, while he trampled upon our rights, and trod upon the heart of the country, protested his solicitude to do justice to Ireland.

2. What marvel is it, then, that Gentlemen opposite should deal in such vehement protestations? There is, however, one man, of great abilities,—not a member of

this House, but whose talents and whose boldness have placed him in the topmost place in his party,—who, disdaining all imposture, and thinking it the best course to appeal directly to the religious and national antipathies of the people of this country, abandoning all reserve, and flinging off the slender veil by which his political associates affect to cover, although they cannot hide, their motives, distinctly and audaciously tells the Irish People that they are not entitled to the same privileges as Englishmen; and pronounces them, in any particular which could enter his minute enumeration of the circumstances by which fellow-citizenship is created, in race, identity and religion, to be aliens: to be aliens in race, to be aliens in country, to be aliens in religion! Aliens! good heavens! was Arthur, Duke of Wellington, in the House of Lords,— and did he not start up and exclaim, "HOLD! I HAVE SEEN THE ALIENS DO THEIR DUTY!"

3. The Duke of Wellington is not a man of an excitable temperament. His mind is of a cast too martial to be easily moved; but, notwithstanding his habitual inflexibility, I cannot help thinking that, when he heard his Roman Catholic countrymen (for we are his countrymen) designated by a phrase as offensive as the abundant vocabulary of his eloquent confederate could supply,—I cannot help thinking that he ought to have recollected the many fields of fight in which we have been contributors to his renown.

4. "The battles, sieges, fortunes that he has passed," ought to have come back upon him. He ought to have remembered that, from the earliest achievement in which he displayed that military genius which has placed him foremost in the annals of modern warfare, down to that last and surpassing combat which has made his name imperishable,—from Assaye to Waterloo, the Irish soldiers, with whom your armies are filled, were the inseparable auxiliaries to the glory with which his unparalleled successes have been crowned. Whose were the arms that

drove your bayonets at Vimiéra through the phalanxes
that never reeled in the shock of war before ?

5. What desperate valor climbed the steeps and filled
the moats at Badajos ? * All his victories should have
rushed and crowded back upon his memory,—Vimiéra,
Badajos, Salamanca, Albuéra, Toulouse, and, last of all,
the *Greatest*. Tell me,—for you were there,—I appeal to
the gallant soldier before me (Sir Henry Hardinge), from
whose opinions I differ, but who bears, I know, a generous
heart in an intrepid breast: tell me,—for you must needs
remember,—on that day when the destinies of mankind
were trembling in the balance, while death fell in showers,
when the artillery of France was levelled with a precision
of the most deadly science,—when her legions, incited by
the voice and inspired by the example of their mighty leader, rushed again and again to the onset,—tell me if, for an
instant, when to hesitate for an instant was to be lost, the
" aliens " blenched ?

6. And when, at length, the moment for the last and
decided movement had arrived, and the valor which had
so long been wisely checked was, at last, let loose : when,
with words familiar, but immortal, the great captain commanded the great assault: tell me if Catholic Ireland
with less heroic valor than the natives of this your own
glorious country precipitated herself upon the foe ?   The
blood of England, Scotland, and of Ireland, flowed in the
same stream, and drenched the same field.   When the
chill morning dawned, their dead lay cold and stark together: in the same deep pit their bodies were deposited:
the green corn of spring is now breaking from their com-
mingled dust : the dew falls from Heaven upon their union
in the grave.   Partakers in every peril, in the glory shall
we not be permitted to participate ; and shall we be told,
as a requital, that we are estranged from the noble country for whose salvation our life-blood was poured out ?

---

* Pronounced *Ba-dah-yhôs*.

XXXVIII.—PROSE SELECTIONS.

1.—REMARKABLE PATIENCE.

1. THE most extraordinary instance of patience on record, in modern times, is that of an Illinois judge, who listened silently for two days while a couple of wordy attorneys contended about the construction of an act of the Legislature, and then ended the controversy by quietly remarking : " Gentlemen, the law is repealed."

2.—CURIOSITY.

1. A TRAVELLER going from Erie to Pittsburg, fell in with a Yankee, each being mounted on a horse. The first was rather inclined to taciturnity, and bore with great patience the questions with which the New Englander bored him from time to time. Finally, upon the Yankee noticing that he had lost an arm and inquiring the reason, he replied, "I will tell you, my friend, if you will promise on your honor to ask no more questions." The promise was made. " Well," said the stranger, " it was bit off." The Yankee rode on in silence for several miles, but in an agony of curiosity. At last, in a transport of despair he exclaimed, " I vow to gracious, I would give a shilling to know what bit it off."

3.—COLONEL RICE.

1. COLONEL RICE spent the winter in Lexington, Kentucky. A friend of his went out to visit him. "Some Sunday," says the Colonel, "I want you to hearken to our church bells here. There's four of 'em. Each of 'em sounds out its own denominational call.

" There's the Episcopal. That is a heavy, deep-toned, sonorous bell. Now you see if that don't ring out—'Postolic succession ! 'Postolic succession !

" Then the old Presbyterian : that's most as deep-sounding, and that says—Eternal damnation ! Eternal damnation ! Eternal damnation !

6

"The Baptist is quicker—a sharp, snappy bell, and that says rapid—Come up and be dipped! Come up and be dipped! Come up and be dipped! Come up and be dipped!

"But the Methodist: that's a crowner; it talks right out—Room—for—all! Room—for—all! Room—for—all!

4.—A QUAKER WOMAN'S SERMON.

1. "My dear friends there are three things I very much wonder at. The first is, that children should throw stones, clubs, and brickbats up into fruit trees to knock down fruit; if they would let it alone it would fall itself. The second is, that men should be so foolish, and so wicked, as to go to war and kill each other; if let alone they would die themselves. And the third and last thing that I wonder at, is that young men should be so unwise as to go after the young women; if they would stay at home the young women would come after them."

5.—THE SUNKEN LAKE.

1. THE *Sentinel*, published at Jacksonville, Oregon, says: "Several of our citizens returned last week from a visit to the great Sunken Lake, situated in Cascade mountains, about 75 miles north-east from Jacksonville. This lake rivals the famous valley of Sinbad, the sailor. It is thought to average 2,000 feet down to the water all around. The walls are almost perpendicular, running down into the water, and leaving no beach. The depth of the water is unknown, and its surface is smooth and unruffled, and it lies so far below the surface of the mountain that the air currents do not affect it. Its length is estimated at 12 miles, and its breadth at 10.

2. No living man ever has, and probably never will be able to reach the water's edge. It lies silent, still and mysterious in the bosom of the ' everlasting hills ' like a huge well, scooped out by the hands of the giant genii of the mountain in unknown ages gone by, and around it the

primeval forest watch and ward are keeping. The visiting party fired a rifle several times into the water at an angle of 42 degrees, and were able to denote several seconds of time from the report of the gun until the ball struck the water. Such seems incredible, but is vouched for by some of our most trustworthy citizens. The lake is certainly a most remarkable curiosity."

6.—WANTED A RECEIPT.

1. Jo SOCABSIN, a Penobscot Indian, was sued for the sum of $5 by a white man, before Squire Johnson. On the day of the trial, Jo made his appearance and tendered the requisite amount for debt and costs, and demanded a receipt in full.

" Why, Jo, it is unnecessary," said the Squire.

" Oh, yes, me want 'um receipt sartin."

" I tell you, Jo, a receipt will do you no good."

" Sartin, Squire Johnson, I want 'um."

" What do you want it for, Jo?"

" Oh, spose me die and go to Heaven: then spose they say—' Well, Jo Socabsin, you owe any man now?' Then me say, ' No.' ' Very well, did you payum Ben Johnson?' ' Oh yes, me payum.' ' Well, then, spose you show 'um receipt!' Then me have to run all over hell, to huntum up Squire Johnson."

XXXIX.—THE UNION.

MRS. SARAH T. BOLTON.

1. DISSOLVE the Union! Let the blush of shame
  Hide, with its crimson glow, the brazen cheek
Of him who dares avow the traitorous aim.
  'Tis not the true, the wise, the good, who speak
  Words of such fearful import: 'tis the weak,
Drunk with fanaticism's poisoned wine,
  Who, reckless of the future, blindly seek
To hold their saturnalia at the shrine
That noble souls have held, and still must hold, divine.

2. Dissolve the Union ! madmen, would you rend
    The glorious motto from our country's crest ?
Would ye despoil the stars and stripes that send
Home, food, protection, to the world's oppressed ?
Have ye no reverence for the high bequest,
That' our immortal sires bestowed ere while ?
Has sin effaced the image God impressed
On your humanity, that you could smile,
To see the lurid flames of freedom's funeral pile ?

3. Dissolve the Union !   In the day and hour
    Ye rend the blood-cemented ties in twain,
The fearful cloud of civil war shall lower
    On every old blue hill and sunny plain,
    From torrid Mexico to frigid Maine !
Dissolve the Union !   No, ye cannot part,
    With idle words, the blessed ties that bind,
In one the interests of the mighty heart,
    That treasure up the hopes of all mankind.
Awhile, perhaps, the blind may lead the blind,
From beaten paths to quagmires, ere they find
The ray that shone so beautiful and bright,
Was but a phantom lure to deeper, darker night.

4. Dissolve the Union !   Never !   Ye may sow
    The seeds of vile dissension through the land,
May madly aim a parricidal blow,
    And show your disregard of all its grand
    Eternal interests ; but a noble 'band
Of patriots, tried, and true, will still remain,
    With heart to heart, and sinewy hand to hand,
To guard from foul dishonor's cankering stain,
The jewels God has shrined in freedom's holy fane.

5. Dissolve the Union !—perish first the page
    That gave to human sight the hideous scrawl :
Let not the freemen of a future age
    Read these detested words : they would recall
    Shame, madness, imbecility, and all
That mars the noontide glory of our time.
    True to the undivided, stand or fall,
To waver now is little less than crime,
To battle for the right is glorious, is sublime.

XL.—THE FIREMAN.

F. S. HILL.

1. HARK! that alarm-bell, 'mid the wintry storm!
Hear the loud shout! the rattling engines swarm.
Hear that distracted mother's cry to save
Her darling infant from a threatened grave!
That babe who lies in sleep's light pinions bound,
And dreams of heaven, while hell is raging round!
Forth springs the Fireman—stay! nor tempt thy fate!—
He hears not—heeds not—nay, it is too late!
See how the timbers crash beneath his feet!
O, which way now is left for his retreat?
The roaring flames already bar his way,
Like ravenous demons raging for their prey!
He laughs at danger,—pauses not for rest,
Till the sweet charge is folded to his breast.

2. Now, quick, brave youth, retrace your path,—but, lo!
A fiery gulf yawns fearfully below!
One desperate leap!—lost! lost!—the flames arise,
And paint their triumph on the o'erarching skies!
Not lost! again his tottering form appears!
The applauding shouts of rapturous friends he hears!
The big drops from his manly forehead roll,
And deep emotions thrill his generous soul.

3. But struggling nature now reluctant yields;
Down drops the arm the infant's face that shields,
To bear the precious burthen all too weak;
When, hark!—the mother's agonizing shriek!
Once more he's roused,—his eye no longer swims,
And tenfold strength reanimates his limbs;
He nerves his faltering frame for one last bound,—
"Your child!" he cries, and sinks upon the ground!

4. And his reward you ask;—reward he spurns;
For him the father's generous bosom burns,—
For him on high the widow's prayer shall go,—
For him the orphan's pearly tear-drop flow.
His boon,—the richest e'er to mortals given,—
Approving conscience, and the smile of Heaven!

From GRIFFITH's *Elocution.*

XLI.—LAY OF THE MADMAN.

1. MANY a year hath passed away,
   Many a dark and dismal year,
   'Since last I roamed in the light of day,
   Or mingled my own with another's tear ;
   Woe to the daughters and sons of men—
   Woe to them all when I roam again !

2. Here have I watched, in this dungeon cell,
   Longer than Memory's tongue can tell ;
   Here have I shrieked, in my wild despair,
   When the damned fiends, from their prison came,
   Sported and gamboled, and mocked me here
   · With their eyes of fire, and their tongues of flame,
   Shouting forever and aye my name !
   And I strove in vain to burst my chain,
   And longed to be free as the winds again,
   That I might spring in the wizard ring,
   And scatter them back to their hellish den !
   Woe to the daughters and sons of men—
   Woe to them all, when I roam again !

3. How long have I been in this dungeon here,
   · Little I know, and nothing I care ;
   What to me is the day, or night,
   Summer's heat, or autumn sere,
   Spring-tide flowers, or winter's blight,
   ·Pleasure's smile, or sorrow's tear ?
   Time ! what care I for thy flight,
   Joy ! I spurn thee with disdain ;
   Nothing love I but this clanking chain ;
   Once I broke from its iron hold,
   Nothing I said, but silent, and bold,
   Like the shepherd that watches his gentle fold,
   Like the tiger that crouches in mountain lair,
   Hours upon hours so watched I here ;
   Till one of the fiends that had come to bring
   Herbs from the valley and drink from the spring,
   Stalked through my dungeon entrance in !
   Ha ! how he shrieked to see me free—
   Ho ! how he trembled, and knelt to me,
   He, who had mocked me many a day,
   And barred me out from its cheerful ray—

Gods! how I shouted to see him pray!
I wreathed my hands in the demon's hair,
And choked his breath in its muttered prayer,
And danced I then, in wild delight,
To see the trembling wretch's fright!

4. Gods! how I crushed his hated bones!
'Gainst the jagged wall and the dungeon stones;
And plunged my arm adown his throat,
    And dragged to life his beating heart,
And held it up that I might gloat,
    To see its quivering fibres start!
Ho! how I drank of the purple flood,
Quaffed, and quaffed again, of blood,
Till my brain grew dark, and I knew no more,
Till I found myself on this dungeon floor,
Fettered and held by this iron chain;
    Ho! when I break its links again,
    Ha! when I break its links again,
Woe to the daughters and sons of men!

XLII.—THE MOUNTAINS OF LIFE.

J. G. CLARK.

1. THERE'S a land far away, 'mid the stars, we are told,
    Where they know not the sorrows of time:
Where the pure waters wander through valleys of gold,
    And life is a treasure sublime;
'Tis the land of our God, 'tis the home of the soul,
Where the ages of splendor eternally roll,
Where the way-weary traveller reaches his goal,
    On the evergreen Mountains of Life.

2. Our gaze cannot soar to that beautiful land,
    But our visions have told of its bliss,
And our souls by the gale of its gardens are fanned,
    When we faint in the desert of this;
And we sometimes have longed for its holy repose,
When our spirits were torn with temptations and woes,
And we've drank from the tide of the river that flows
    From the evergreen Mountains of Life.

3. O, the stars never tread the blue heavens at night,
    But we think where the ransomed have trod;

And the day never smiles from his palace of light,
  But we feel the bright smile of our God.
We are travelling homeward through changes and gloom,
To a kingdom where pleasures unceasingly bloom,
And our guide is the glory that shines through the tomb,
  From the evergreen Mountains of Life.

————————◆————————

XLIII.—SCOTT AND THE VETERAN.

BAYARD TAYLOR.

1. AN old and crippled veteran to the War Department came.
  He sought the Chief who led him, on many a field of fame:
  The Chief who shouted, " Forward ! " where'er his banner rose,
  And bore his stars in triumph behind the flying foes.
  " Have you forgotten, General," the battered soldier cried,
  " The days of eighteen hundred twelve, when I was at your side ?
  Have you forgotten Johnson, that fought at Lundy's Lane ?
  'Tis true, I'm old, and pensioned, but I want to fight again."
  " Have I forgotten ? " said the Chief, " my brave old soldier, No !
  And here's the hand I gave you then, and let it tell you so ;
  But you have done your share, my friend ; you're crippled, old, and
    gray,
  And we have need of younger arms and fresher blood to-day."

2. " But, General ! " cried the veteran, a flush upon his brow,
  " The very men who fought with us, they say, are traitors now ;
  They've torn the flag of Lundy's Lane, our old red, white, and blue,
  And while a drop of blood is left, I'll show that drop is true.
  I'm not so weak but I can strike, and I've a good old gun
  To get the range of traitors' hearts, and pick them one by one.
  Your Minie rifles, and such arms, it a'n't worth while to try ;
  I couldn't get the hang o' them, but I'll keep my powder dry ! "
  " God bless you, comrade ! " said the Chief—" God bless your loyal heart !
  But younger men are in the field, and claim to have their part.

3. They'll plant our sacred banner in each rebellious town,
  And woe, henceforth, to any hand that dares to pull it down ! "
  " But, General,"—still persisting—the weeping veteran cried
  " I am young enough to follow, so long as *you're* my guide .
  And some, you know, must bite the dust, and that, at least, can I ;
  So, give the young ones place to fight, but me a place to die :
  If they should fire on Pickens, let the Colonel in command
  Put me upon the rampart, with the flag-staff in my hand ;

No odds how hot the cannon smoke, or how the shells may fly,
I'll hold the Stars and Stripes aloft, and hold them till I die !

4. I'm ready, General, so you let a post to me be given,
Where Washington can see me, as he looks from highest Heaven,
And says to Putnam, at his side, or, may be, General Wayne,
' There stands old Billy Johnson, who fought at Lundy's Lane ! '
And when the fight is hottest, before the traitors fly,
When shell and ball are screeching, and bursting in the sky,
If any shot should hit me, and lay me on my face,
My soul would go to Washington's, and not to Arnold's place ! "

---◆---

XLIV.—DRUNKARDS NOT ALL BRUTES.

JOHN B. GOUGH.

1. I SAID when I began, that I was a trophy of this movement; and therefore the principal part of my work has been (not ignoring other parts) in behalf of those who have suffered as I have suffered. You know there is a great deal said about the reckless victims of this foe being " brutes." No, they are not brutes. I have labored for about eighteen years among them and I never have found a brute. I have had men swear at me : I have had a man dance around me as if possessed of a devil, and spit his foam in my face ; but he is not a brute.

2. I think it is Charles Dickens who says : " Away up a great many pair of stairs, in a very remote corner, easily passed by, there is a door, and on that door is written ' woman.' " And so in the heart of the vile outcast, away up a great many pair of stairs, in a very remote corner, easily passed by, there is a door, on which is written " man." Here is our business to find that door. It may take a time ; but begin and knock. Don't get tired ; but remember God's long suffering for us and keep knocking a long time if need be. Don't get weary if there is no answer ; remember Him whose locks were wet with dew.

3. Knock on—just try it—*you* try it ; and just so sure as you do, just so sure, by-and-by, will the quivering lip and starting tear tell you have knocked at the heart of a

6*

man, and not of a brute. It is because these poor wretches *are* men, and not brutes that we have hopes of them. They said " he is a brute—let him alone." I took him home with me and kept the " brute " fourteen days and nights, through his delirium ; and he nearly frightened Mary out of her wits, once chasing her about the house with a boot in his hand. But she recovered her wits, and he recovered his.

4. He said to me, " You wouldn't think I had a wife and child ? " " Well, I shouldn't." " I have, and—God bless her little heart—my little Mary is as pretty a little thing as ever stepped," said the " brute." I asked, " where do they live ? " " They live two miles away from here." " When did you see them last ? " " About two years ago." Then he told me his story. I said, " you must go back to your home again."

5. " I mus'nt go back—I won't—my wife is better without me than with me ! I will not go back any more ; I have knocked her, and kicked her, and abused her ; do you suppose I will go back again ? " I went to the house with him ; I knocked at the door and his wife opened it. " Is this Mrs. Richardson ? " " Yes, sir." " Well, that is Mr. Richardson. And Mr. Richardson, that is Mrs. Richardson. Now come into the house." They went in. The wife sat on one side of the room and the " brute " on the other. I waited to see who would speak first; and it was the woman. But before she spoke she fidgetted a good deal.

6. She pulled her apron till she got hold of the hem, and then she pulled it down again. Then she folded it up closely, and jerked it out through her fingers an inch at a time, and then she spread it all down again ; and then she looked all about the room and said, " Well, William ? " And the " brute " said, " Well, Mary ? " He had a large handkerchief round his neck, and she said, " You had better take the handkerchief off, William ; you'll need it when you go out." He began to fumble about it.

7. The knot was large enough ; he could have untied

it if he liked; but he said, "Will you untie it, Mary?" and she worked away at it; but *her* fingers were clumsy, and she couldn't get it off; their eyes met, and the love-light was not all quenched; she opened her arms gently and he fell into them. If you had seen those white arms clasped about his neck, and he sobbing on her breast, and the child looking in wonder first at one and then at the other, you would have said "It is not a brute; it is a man, with a great, big, warm heart in his breast."

XLV.—AN APPEAL TO THE PATRIOTISM OF SOUTH CAROLINA.

ANDREW JACKSON.

1. FELLOW CITIZENS of my native State! let me not only admonish you, as the first magistrate of our common country, not to incur the penalty of its laws, but use the influence that a father would over his children whom he saw rushing to certain ruin. In that paternal language, with that paternal feeling, let me tell you, my countrymen, that you are deluded by men who either are deceived themselves or wish to deceive you. Mark under what pretenses you have been led on to the brink of insurrection and treason, on which you stand.

2. You were told that this opposition might be peaceably,—might be constitutionally made,—that you might enjoy all the advantages of the Union, and bear none of its burdens. Eloquent appeals to your passions, to your State pride, to your native courage, to your sense of real injury, were used to prepare you for the period when the mask which concealed the hideous features of DISUNION, should be taken off. It fell, and you were made to look with complacency on objects which not long since you would have regarded with horror.

3. Look back at the acts which have brought you to this state: look forward to the consequences, to which it must inevitably lead. Something more is necessary. Contemplate the condition of that country, of which you still

form an important part! Consider its government, uniting
in one bond of common interest and general protection, so
many different States: giving to all their inhabitants the
proud title of AMERICAN CITIZENS: protecting their commerce: securing their literature and their arts: facili-
tating their intercommunication: defending their frontiers; and making their name respected in the remotest
parts of the earth!

4. Consider the extent of its territory, its increasing
and happy population, its advance in arts which render life
agreeable, and the sciences which elevate the mind! See
education spreading the lights of religion, humanity, and
general information, into every cottage in this wide extent
of our territories and states! Behold it as the asylum
where the wretched and the oppressed find refuge and
support! Look on this picture of happiness and honor,
and say, "WE, TOO, ARE CITIZENS OF AMERICA; Carolina
is one of these proud States; her arms have defended,—
her best blood has cemented this happy Union!" And
then add, if you can, without horror and remorse, "This
happy Union we will dissolve: this picture of peace and
prosperity we will deface: this free intercourse we will
interrupt: these fertile fields we will deluge with blood:
the protection of that glorious flag we renounce: the very
name of AMERICANS we discard."

5. And for what, mistaken men! for what do you
throw away these inestimable blessings; for what would
you exchange your share in the advantages and honor of
the Union? For the *dream* of a separate independence,
a DREAM interrupted by bloody conflicts with your neighbors, and a vile dependence on foreign power? If your
leaders could succeed in establishing a separation, what
would be your situation? Are you united at home: are
you free from the apprehensions of civil discord, with all
its fearful consequences? Do our neighboring republics,
every day suffering some new revolution, or contending
with some new insurrection,—do they excite your envy?

6. But the dictates of a high duty oblige me solemnly to announce that you cannot succeed. The laws of the United States must be executed, I have no discretionary power on the subject: my duty is emphatically pronounced in the constitution. Those who told you that you might peaceably prevent their execution, deceived you: they could not have been deceived themselves. They know that a forcible opposition could alone prevent the execution of the laws, and they know that such opposition must be repelled. Their object is disunion; but be not deceived by names; *disunion*, by armed force, is TREASON.

7. Are you really ready to incur its guilt? If you are, on the heads of the instigators of the act, be the dreadful consequences: on their heads be the dishonor, but on yours may fall the punishment: on your unhappy state will inevitably fall all the evils of the conflict you force upon the government of your country. It cannot accede to the mad project of disunion, of which you would be the first victims: its first magistrate cannot, if he would, avoid the performance of his duty: the consequence must be fearful for you, distressing to your fellow-citizens here, and to the friends of good government throughout the world.

8. Its enemies have beheld our prosperity with a vexation they could not conceal,—it was a standing refutation of their slavish doctrines, and they will point to our discord with the triumph of malignant joy. It is yet in your power to disappoint them. There is yet time to show that the descendants of the Pinckneys, the Sumters, the Rutledges, and of the thousand other names which adorn the pages of your Revolutionary history, will not abandon that Union, to support which so many of them fought, and bled, and died.

9. I adjure you, as you honor their memories,—as you love the cause of freedom, to which they dedicated their lives,—as you prize the peace of your country, the lives of its best citizens, and your own fair fame, to retrace your steps. Snatch from the archives of your state the

disorganizing edict of its convention : bid its members to reassemble and promulgate the decided expressions of your will to remain in the path which alone can conduct you to safety, prosperity, and honor: tell them that, compared to disunion, all other evils are light, because that brings with it an accumulation of all: declare that you will never take the field unless the star-spangled banner of your country shall float over you : that you will not be stigmatized when dead, and dishonored and scorned while you live, as the authors of the first attack on the constitution of your country!

10. Its destroyers you cannot be. You may disturb its peace : you may interrupt the course of its prosperity : you may cloud its reputation for stability,—but its tranquillity will be restored, its prosperity will return, and the stain upon its national character will be transferred and remain an eternal blot on the memory of those who caused the disorder.

11. May the great Ruler of nations grant, that the signal blessings, with which He has favored ours, may not, by the madness of party or personal ambition, be disregarded and lost ; and may His wise providence bring those who have produced this crisis, to see the folly, before they feel the misery, of civil strife ; and inspire a returning veneration for that Union which, if we may dare to penetrate His designs, He has chosen as the only means of attaining the high destinies, to which we may reasonably aspire.

---◆---

XLVI.—ADVICE TO A YOUNG LAWYER.

JUDGE STORY.

1. WHENE'ER you speak, remember every cause
Stands not on eloquence, but stands on laws :
Pregnant in matter, in expression brief,
Let every sentence stand in bold relief ;
On trifling points nor time nor talents waste,
A sad offence to learning and to taste ;

AND ORATORY.

135

Nor deal with pompous phrase, nor e'er suppose
Poetic flights belong to reasoning prose.

2. Loose declamation may deceive the crowd,
And seem more striking as it grows more loud ;
But sober sense rejects it with disdain,
As nought but empty noise, and weak as vain.
The froth of words, the schoolboy's vain parade
Of books and cases—all his stock in trade—
The pert conceits, the cunning tricks and play
Of low attorneys, strung in long array,
The unseemly jest, the petulant reply,
That chatters on, and cares not how, or why,
Strictly avoid—unworthy themes to scan,
They sink the speaker and disgrace the man,
Like the false lights, by flying shadows cast,
Scarce seen when present and forgot when past.

3. Begin with dignity ; expound with grace
Each ground of reasoning in its time and place ;
Let order reign throughout—each topic touch,
Nor urge its power too little, nor too much ;
Give each strong thought its most attractive view,
In diction clear and yet severely true,
And as the arguments in splendor grow,
Let each reflect its light on all below ;
When to the close arrived, make no delays
By petty flourishes, or verbal plays,
But sum the whole in one deep solemn strain,
Like a strong current hastening to the main.

XLVII.—OUR DUTIES TO THE REPUBLIC.
JUDGE STORY.

1. THE Old World has already revealed to us, in its
unsealed books, the beginning and end of all its own
marvellous struggles in the cause of liberty.   Greece,
lovely Greece,

"The land of scholars and the nurse of arms,"

where Sister Republics, in fair procession, chanted the
praises of liberty and the Gods,—where and what is she ?
For two thousand years the oppressor has ground her to

the earth. Her arts are no more. The last sad relics of her temples are but the barracks of a ruthless soldiery. The fragments of her columns and her palaces are in the dust, yet beautiful in ruins. She fell not when the mighty were upon her. Her sons were united at Thermopylæ and Marathon; and the tide of her triumph rolled back upon the Hellespont. She was conquered by her own factions. She fell by the hands of her own People.

2. The man of Macedonia did not the work of destruction. It was already done, by her own corruptions, banishments, and dissensions. Rome, republican Rome, whose eagles glanced in the rising and setting sun,—where and what is she? The eternal city yet remains, proud even in her desolation, noble in her decline, venerable in the majesty of religion, and calm as in the composure of death. The malaria has but travelled in the paths worn by her destroyers. More than eighteen centuries have mourned over the loss of her empire. A mortal disease was upon her vitals before Cæsar had crossed the Rubicon; and Brutus did not restore her health by the deep probings of the Senate-chamber. The Goths, and Vandals, and Huns, the swarms of the North, completed only what was already begun at home. Romans betrayed Rome. The Legions were bought and sold; but the People offered the tribute money.

3. We stand the latest, and, if we fail, probably the last experiment of self-government by the People. We have begun it under circumstances of the most auspicious nature. We are in the vigor of youth. Our growth has never been checked by the oppressions of tyranny. Our constitutions have never been enfeebled by the vices or luxuries of the Old World. Such as we are, we have been from the beginning,—simple, hardy, intelligent, accustomed to self-government, and to self-respect. The Atlantic rolls between us and any formidable foe. Within our own territory, stretching through many degrees of latitude and longitude, we have the choice of many prod-

ucts, and many means of independence. The Government is mild. The Press is free. Religion is free. Knowledge reaches, or may reach, every home. What fairer prospect of success could be presented? What means more adequate to accomplish the sublime end? What more is necessary than for the People to preserve what they have themselves created?

4. Already has the age caught the spirit of our institutions. It has already ascended the Andes, and snuffed the breezes of both oceans. It has infused itself into the life-blood of Europe, and warmed the sunny plains of France and the lowlands of Holland. It has touched the philosophy of Germany and the North; and, moving onward to the South, has opened to Greece the lessons of her better days. Can it be that America, under such circumstances, can betray herself? Can it be that she is to be added to the catalogue of Republics, the inscription upon whose ruins is: THEY WERE, BUT THEY ARE NOT? Forbid it, my countrymen! Forbid it, Heaven!

XLVIII.—LOVE OF COUNTRY AND HOME.
JAMES MONTGOMERY.

1. THERE is a land, of every land the pride,
Beloved by Heaven o'er all the world beside;
Where brighter suns dispense serener light,
And milder moons emparadise the night;—
There is a spot of earth supremely blest,
A dearer, sweeter spot than all the rest,
Where man, creation's tyrant, casts aside
His sword and sceptre, pageantry and pride,
While in his softened looks benignly blend
The sire, the son, the husband, brother, friend;—
" Where shall that *land*, that *spot of earth*, be found? "
Art thou a man?—a patriot?—look around!
O, thou shalt find, howe'er thy footsteps roam,
That land thy country, and that spot thy home!

2. On Greenland's rocks, o'er rude Kamschatka's plains,
In pale Siberia's desolate domains;

When the wild hunter takes his lonely way,
Tracks through tempestuous snows his savage prey,
Or, wrestling with the might of raging seas,
Where round the Pole the eternal billows freeze,
Plucks from their jaws the stricken whale, in vain
Plunging down headlong through the whirling main ;
His wastes of snow are lovelier in his eye
Than all the flowery vales beneath the sky,
And dearer far than Cæsar's palace-dome,
His cavern-shelter, and his cottage-home.

3. O'er China's garden-fields and peopled floods,
In California's pathless world of woods ;
Round Andes' heights, where Winter, from his throne
Looks down in scorn upon the Summer zone ;
By the gay borders of Bermuda's isles,
Where Spring with everlasting verdure smiles ;
On pure Madeira's vine-robed hills of health ;
In Java's swamps of pestilence and wealth ;
Where Babel stood, where wolves and jackals drink
'Midst weeping willows, on Euphrates' brink ;

4. On Carmel's crest ; by Jordan's reverend stream,
Where Canaan's glories vanished like a dream ;
Where Greece, a spectre, haunts her heroes' graves,
And Rome's vast ruins darken Tiber's waves ;
Where broken-hearted Switzerland bewails
Her subject mountains and dishonored vales ;
Where Albion's rocks exult amidst the sea,
Around the beauteous isle of Liberty ;—
Man, through all ages of revolving time,
Unchanging man, in every varying clime,
Deems his own land of every land the pride,
Beloved by Heaven o'er all the world beside ;
His home the spot of earth supremely blest,
A dearer, sweeter spot than all the rest !

XLIX.—THE ISLE OF LONG AGO.

B. F. TAYLOR.

1. O, A WONDERFUL stream is the river Time,
    As it runs through the realm of tears,
With a faultless rhythm and a musical rhyme,
And a boundless sweep and a surge sublime,
    As it blends with the Ocean of Years.

2. How the winters are drifting, like flakes of snow,
     · And the summers, like buds between ;
And the year in the sheaf—so they come and they go,
On the river's breast, with its ebb and flow,
     As it glides in the shadow and sheen.

3. There 's a magical isle up the river of Time,
     · Where the softest of airs are playing;
There 's a cloudless sky and a tropical clime,
And a song as sweet as a vesper chime,
     And the Junes with the roses are staying.

4. And the name of that Isle is the Long Ago,
     And we bury our treasures there;
There are brows of beauty and bosoms of snow— .
There are heaps of dust—but we loved them so !—
     There are trinkets and tresses of hair ;

5. There are fragments of song that nobody sings,
     And a part of an infant's prayer ;
There 's a lute unswept, and a harp without strings
There are broken vows and pieces of rings,
     And the garments that she used to wear.

6. There are hands that are waved, when the fairy shore
     By the mirage is lifted in air ;
And we some times hear, through the turbulent roar,
Sweet voices we heard in the days gone before,
     When the wind down the river is fair.

7. O, remembered for aye, be the blessed Isle,
     All the day of our life till night—
When the evening comes with its beautiful smile,
And our eyes are closing to slumber awhile,
     May that " Greenwood " of Soul be in sight!

————◆————

L.—TIME'S MIDNIGHT VOICE.

EDWARD YOUNG.

1. CREATION sleeps. 'T is as the general pulse
Of life stood still, and Nature made a pause,
An awful pause! prophetic of her end.
    The bell strikes one. We take no note of time,
But from its loss. To give it, then, a tongue,
Is wise in man. As if an angel spoke,

I feel the solemn sound.   If heard aright,
It is the knell of my departed hours.
Where are they ?   With the years beyond the flood !
It is the signal that demands despatch:

2. How much is to be done !   My hopes and fears
Start up alarmed, and o'er life's narrow verge
Look down—on what ? a fathomless abyss !
A dread eternity !   How surely mine !
And can eternity belong to me,
Poor pensioner on the bounties of an hour ?
    How poor, how rich, how abject, how august,
How complicate, how wonderful, is man !
How passing wonder He who made him such !
Who centred in our make such strange extremes
From different natures marvellously mixed,
Connection exquisite of distant worlds !

3. Distinguished link in being's endless chain !
Midway from nothing to the Deity !
A beam ethereal, sullied, and absorpt !
Though sullied, and dishonored, still divine
Dim miniature of greatness absolute !
An heir of glory ! a frail child of dust !
Helpless immortal ! insect infinite !
A worm ! a god !—I tremble at myself,
And in myself am lost !   At home a stranger,
Thought wanders up and down, surprised, aghast,
And wondering at her own: how Reason reels !

4. O what a miracle to man is man,
Triumphantly distressed !   What joy, what dread
Alternately transported, and alarmed !
What can preserve my life, or what destroy ?
An angel's arm can't snatch me from the grave ;
Legions of angels can't confine me there !
Even silent night proclaims my soul immortal !

LI.—THE COMMON LOT.

JAMES MONTGOMERY.

1. ONCE, in the flight of ages past,
    There lived a man ; and Who was He ?

Mortal! howe'er thy lot be cast,
  That Man resembled Thee.
Unknown the region of his birth,
  The land in which he died unknown:
His name has perished from the earth;
  This truth survives alone:—

2. That joy and grief, and hope and fear,
    Alternate triumphed in his breast;
  His bliss and woe,—a smile, a tear!—
    Oblivion hides the rest.
  The bounding pulse, the languid limb,
    The changing spirit's rise and fall;
  We know that these were felt by him,
    For these are felt by all.

3. He suffered,— but his pangs are o'er;
    Enjoyed, — but his delights are fled;
  Had friends, — his friends are now no more
    And foes, — his foes are dead.
  He loved, — but whom he loved the grave
    Hath lost in its unconscious womb:
  O, she was fair!— but naught could save
    Her beauty from the tomb.

4. He saw whatever thou hast seen;
    Encountered all that troubles thee:
  He was — whatever thou hast been;
    He is — what thou shalt be.
  The rolling seasons, day and night,
    Sun, moon and stars, the earth and main,
  Erewhile his portion, life and light,
    To him exist in vain.

5. The clouds and sunbeams, o'er his eye
    That once their shades and glory threw,
  Have left in yonder silent sky
    No vestige where they flew:
  The annals of the human race,
    Their ruins, since the world began,
  Of *him* afford no other trace
    Than this, — THERE LIVED A MAN!

LII.—THE ATLANTIC TELEGRAPH.

[Successfully laid between Europe and America July 27, 1866.]

GEO. LANSING TAYLOR.

1. GLORY to God above!
   The Lord of life and love!
Who makes his curtains clouds and waters dark;
   Who spreads his chambers on the deep,
   While all its armies silence keep,
Whose hand of old, world-rescuing, steered the ark;
   Who led Troy's bands exiled,
   And Genoa's god-like child,
   And Mayflower, grandly wild,
And now has guided safe a grander bark
   Who, from her iron loins
   Has spun the thread that joins
Two yearning worlds made one with lightning spark.

2. Praise God! praise God! praise God!
   The sea obeyed his rod,
What time his saints marched down its deeps of yore;
   And now for Commerce, Science, Peace,
   Redemption, Freedom, Love's increase,
   He bids great ocean's barriers cease.
While flames celestial flash from shore to shore!
And nations pause 'mid battles' deadliest roar,
Till Earth's one heart swells upward and brims o'er
   With thanks! thanks! thanks and praise!
   To him who lives always!
   Who reigns through endless days!
      While halleluias sweet
      Roll up as incense meet,
And all Earth's crowns are cast before his feet!

3. "And there was no more sea,"
   Spake in rapt vision he
Who "a new heaven and a new earth" beheld,
   And lo! we see the day
   That ends its weltering sway,
And weds the nations, long asunder held!
   Ten years of toil, of failure, fear,
   Thousands to scorn and few to cheer,
   What are they now to ears that hear,
   To eyes that see their triumph near!

When lightning flames the ends of earth shall weld,
And wrong and right, by lightning beams dispelled,
    Shall lift from all man's race,
    And God the Father's face
Shall smile o'er all the world millennial grace!

    4. FRANKLIN! and MORSE! and FIELD!
    Great shades of centuries yield!
Make way for these in your sublimest throng!
Heroes of blood, great in immortal wrong,
Stoop your helmed heads and blush! O seers of song,
    Of blood and strife no longer sing;
    In heavenlier transport smite the string,
    Soar, soar on purer, rapter wing,
    Till all the throbbing azure ring
        The song that erst began :
        " Good will and peace toward man,"
        Redeemed and bought with blood,
        One mighty brotherhood!
And every bond that brings heart nearer heart,
Shall bring man nearer God, and bear a part
    In that great work benign,
The work of love, that makes all worlds divine!

LIII.—THE GLADIATOR.

1. STILLNESS reigned in the vast amphitheater, and from the countless thousands that thronged the spacious inclosure, not a breath was heard. Every tongue was mute with suspense, and every eye strained with anxiety toward the gloomy portal, where the gladiator was momentarily expected to enter. At length the trumpet sounded, and they led him forth into the broad arena. There was no mark of fear upon his manly countenance, as with majestic step and fearless eye he entered. He stood there, like another Apollo, firm and unbending as the rigid oak. His fine proportioned form was matchless, and his turgid muscles spoke his giant strength.

2. "I am here," he cried, as his proud lip curled in scorn, " to glut the savage eyes of Rome's proud populace.

Aye, like a dog you throw me to a beast; and what is my offense? Why, forsooth, I am a *Christian.* But know, ye can not fright my soul, for it is based upon a foundation stronger than the adamantine rock. Know ye, whose hearts are harder than the flinty stone, my heart quakes not with fear; and here I aver, I would not change conditions with the blood-stained Nero, crowned though he be, not for the wealth of Rome. Blow ye your trumpet—I am ready."

3. The trumpet sounded, and a long, low growl was heard to proceed from the cage of a half-famished Numidian Lion, situated at the farthest end of the arena. The growl deepened into a roar of tremendous volume, which shook the enormous edifice to its very center. At that moment, the door was thrown open, and the huge monster of the forest sprung from his den, with one mighty bound to the opposite side of the arena. His eyes blazed with the brilliancy of fire, as he slowly drew his length along the sand, and prepared to make a spring upon his formidable antagonist. The gladiator's eye quailed not: his lip paled not; but he stood immovable as a statue, waiting the approach of his wary foe.

4. At length, the lion crouched himself into an attitude for springing, and with the quickness of lightning, leaped full at the throat of the gladiator. But he was prepared for him, and bounding lightly on one side, his falchion flashed for a moment over his head, and in the next it was deeply dyed in the purple blood of the monster. A roar of redoubled fury again resounded through the spacious amphitheater, as the enraged animal, mad with anguish from the wound he had just received, wheeled hastily round, and sprung a second time at the Nazarene.

5. Again was the falchion of the cool and intrepid gladiator, deeply planted in the breast of his terrible adversary; but so sudden had been the second attack, that it was impossible to avoid the full impetus of his bound, and he staggered and fell upon his knee. The monster's paw

was upon his shoulder, and he felt his hot fiery breath upon his cheek, as it rushed through his wide distended nostrils. The Nazarene drew a short dagger from his girdle, and endeavored to regain his feet. But his foe, aware of his design, precipitating himself upon him, threw him with violence to the ground.

6. The excitement of the populace was now wrought up to a high pitch, and they waited the result with breathless suspense. A low growl of satisfaction now announced the noble animal's triumph, as he sprang fiercely upon his prostrate enemy. But it was of short duration; the dagger of the gladiator pierced his vitals, and together they rolled over and over, across the broad arena. Again the dagger drank deep of the monster's blood, and again a roar of anguish reverberated through the stately edifice.

7. The Nazarene, now watching his opportunity, sprung with the velocity of thought from the terrific embrace of his enfeebled antagonist, and regaining his falchion which had fallen to the ground in the struggle, he buried it deep in the heart of the infuriated beast. The noble king of the forest, faint from the loss of blood, concentrated all his remaining strength in one mighty bound; but it was too late; the last blow had been driven home to the center of life, and his huge form fell with a mighty crash upon the arena, amid the thundering acclamations of the populace.

LIV.—HENRY V. AT HARFLEUR.
SHAKSPEARE.

1. Once more unto the breach, dear friends, once more;
Or close the wall up with our English dead.
In peace there's nothing so becomes a man
As modest stillness and humility;
But when the blast of war blows in our ears,
Then imitate the action of the tiger;
Stiffen the sinews, summon up the blood,
Disguise fair nature with hard-favored rage;
Then lend the eye a terrible aspect;

7

Let it pry through the portage of the head
Like the brass cannon ; let the brow o'erwhelm it,
As fearfully as doth a gall-ed rock
O'erhang and jutty his confounded base,
Swilled with the wild and wasteful ocean.

2. Now set the teeth, and stretch the nostril wide,
Hold hard the breath, and bend up every spirit
To his full hight. Now on, you noblest English,
Whose blood is fetched from fathers of war-proof ;
Fathers, that like so many Alexanders,
Have in these parts from morn till even fought,
And sheathed their swords for lack of argument :
Be copy now to men of grosser blood,
And teach them how to war !

3. And you, good yeomen,
Whose limbs are made in England, show us here
The mettle of your pasture ; let us swear
That you are worth your breeding, which I doubt not ;
For there is none of you so mean and base
That hath not noble luster in your eye ;
I see you stand like grayhounds in the slips,
Straining upon the start : the game 's a-foot ;
Follow your spirit ; and, upon this charge,
Cry, Heaven for Harry, England, and St. George !

--------◆--------

LV.—SEVEN AGES OF MAN.

SHAKSPEARE.

1. ALL the world 's a stage,
And all the men and women merely players :
They have their exits and their entrances,
And one man in his time plays many parts,
His acts being seven ages. At first, the infant,
Mewling and puking in the nurse's arms.
Then, the whining school-boy, with his satchel,
And shining morning face, creeping like snail
Unwillingly to school. And then, the lover,
Sighing like a furnace, with a woeful ballad
Made to his mistress' eyebrow. Then, a soldier,
Full of strange oaths, and bearded like a pard,
Jealous in honor, sudden and quick in quarrel,
Seeking the bubble reputation
Even in the cannon's mouth.

2. And then, the justice,
   In fair round belly, with good capon lined,
   With eyes severe, and beard of formal cut,
   Full of wise saws and modern instances :
   And so he plays his part.   The sixth age shifts
   Into the lean and slippered pantaloon,
   With spectacles on nose, and pouch on side ;
   His youthful hose, well saved, a world too wide
   For his shrunk shank, and his big manly voice,
   Turning again toward childish treble, pipes
   And whistles in his sound.   Last scene of all,
   That ends this strange, eventful history,
   Is second childishness, and mere oblivion ;
   Sans teeth, sans eyes, sans taste, sans every thing.

---◆---

LVI.—PARRHASIUS.

N. P. WILLIS.

1. PARRHASIUS stood, gazing forgetfully
   Upon his canvas.   There Prometheus lay,
   Chained to the cold rocks of Mount Caucasus,
   The vulture at his vitals, and the links
   Of the lame Lemnian festering in his flesh ;
   And, as the painter's mind felt through the dim,
   Rapt mystery, and plucked the shadows forth
   With his far-reaching fancy, and with form
   And color clad them, his fine, earnest eye
   Flashed with a passionate fire, and the quick curl
   Of his thin nostril, and his quivering lip,
   Were like the winged god's breathing from his flight.

2.   " Bring me the captive now !
   My hand feels skillful, and the shadows lift
   From my waked spirit airily and swift ;
       And I could paint the bow
   Upon the bended heavens ; around me play
   Colors of such divinity to-day.

3.   " Ha ! bind him on his back !
   Look ! as Prometheus in my picture here !
   Quick ! or he faints ! stand with the cordial near !
       Now, bend him to the rack !
   Press down the poisoned links into his flesh !
   And tear agape that healing wound afresh !

4.　　"So! let him writhe! How long
Will he live thus? Quick, my good pencil, now!
What a fine agony works upon his brow!
Ha! gray-haired, and so strong!
How fearfully he stifles that short moan!
Gods! if I could but paint a dying groan!

5.　　"'Pity' thee? So I do;
I pity the dumb victim at the altar;
But does the robed priest for his pity falter?
I'd rack thee, though I knew
A thousand lives were perishing in thine;
What were ten thousand to a fame like mine?

6.　　"Ah! there's a deathless name!
A spirit that the smothering vault shall spurn,
And, like a steadfast planet, mount and burn;
And though its crown of flame
Consumed my brain to ashes as it won me;
By all the fiery stars! I'd pluck it on me!

7.　　"Ay, though it bid me rifle
My heart's last fount for its insatiate thirst;
Though every life-strung nerve be maddened first;
Though it should bid me stifle
The yearning in my throat for my sweet child,
And taunt its mother till my brain went wild!

8.　　"All! I would do it all,
Sooner than die, like a dull worm, to rot;
Thrust foully in the earth to be forgot.
Oh heavens! but I appall
Your heart, old man! forgive—ha! on your lives
Let him not faint! rack him till he revives!

9.　　"Vain—vain—give o'er. His eye
Glazes apace. He does not feel you now.
Stand back! I'll paint the death dew on his brow!
Gods! if he do not die
But for one moment—one—till I eclipse
Conception with the scorn of those calm lips!

10.　　"Shivering! Hark! he mutters
Brokenly now; that was a difficult breath;
Another? Wilt thou never come, oh, Death?
Look! how his temple flutters!

Is his heart still ?   Aha ! lift up his head !
He shudders—gasps—Jove help him—so, he's dead ! "

11. How like a mountain devil in the heart
Rules this unreined ambition !   Let it once
But play the monarch, and its haughty brow
Glows with a beauty that bewilders thought
And unthrones peace forever.   Putting on
The very pomp of Lucifer, it turns
The heart to ashes, and with not a spring
Left in the desert for the spirit's lip,
We look upon our splendor, and forget
The thirst of which we perish !

LVIL—THE SEMINOLE'S DEFIANCE.

G. W. PATTEN.

1. BLAZE, with your serried columns !   I will not bend the knee ;
The shackle ne'er again shall bind the arm which now is free !
I've mailed it with the thunder, when the tempest muttered low ;
And where it falls, ye well may dread the lightning of its blow.
I've scared you in the city : I've scalped you on the plain :
Go, count your chosen where they fell beneath my leaden rain !
I scorn your proffered treaty : the pale-face I defy :
Revenge is stamped upon my spear, and " blood " my battle-cry !

2. Some strike for hope of booty ; some to defend their all :—
I battle for the joy I have to see the white man fall.
I love, among the wounded, to hear his dying moan,
And catch, while chanting at his side, the music of his groan.
Ye've trailed me through the forest : ye've tracked me o'er the stream ;
And struggling through the everglade your bristling bayonets gleam.
But I stand as should the warrior, with his rifle and his spear :
The scalp of vengeance still is red, and warns you—" Come not here ! "

3. Think ye to find my homestead ?—I gave it to the fire.
My tawny household do ye seek ?—I am a childless sire.
But, should ye crave life's nourishment, enough I have, and good :
I live on hate—'tis all my bread ; yet light is not my food.
I loathe you with my bosom !   I scorn you with mine eye !
And I'll taunt you with my latest breath, and fight you till I die !
I ne'er will ask for quarter, and I ne'er will be your slave ;
But I'll swim the sea of slaughter till I sink beneath the wave !

LVIII.—UNIVERSAL SUFFRAGE, May 20, 1850.

VICTOR HUGO.

1. UNIVERSAL suffrage!—what is it but the overthrow of violence and brute force—the end of the material and the beginning of the moral fact? What was the Revolution of February intended to establish in France, if not this? And now it is proposed to abolish this sacred right! And what is its abolition, but the reïntroduction of the right of insurrection? Ye Ministers and men of State, who govern, wherefore do you venture on this mad attempt? I will tell you. It is because the People have deemed worthy of their votes men whom you judge worthy of your insults! It is because the People have presumed to compare your promises with your acts; because they do not find your Administration altogether sublime; because they have dared peaceably to instruct you through the ballot-box!

2. Therefore it is, that your anger is roused, and that, under the pretence that Society is in peril, you seek to chastise the People,—to take them in hand! And so, like that maniac of whom History tells, you beat the ocean with rods! And so you launch at us your poor little laws, furious but feeble! And so you defy the spirit of the age, defy the good sense of the public, defy the Democracy, and tear your unfortunate finger-nails against the granite of universal suffrage!

Go on, Gentlemen! Proceed! Disfranchise, if you will, three millions of voters, four millions, nay, eight millions out of nine! Get rid of all these! It will not matter. What you cannot get rid of is your own fatal incapacity and ignorance; your own antipathy for the mind, which was named John Huss, and which did not die on the funeral-pile of Constance; which was named Luther, and shook orthodoxy to its centre; which was named Voltaire, and shook faith; which was named Mirabeau, and shook royalty.

3. It is the human mind, which, since history began,

has transformed societies and governments according to a law progressively acceptable to the reason,—which has been theocracy, aristocracy, monarchy, and which is to-day democracy. It is the human mind, which has been Babylon, Tyre, Jerusalem, Athens, and which to-day is Paris; which has been, turn by turn, and sometimes all at once, error, illusion, schism, protestation, truth; it is the human mind, which is the great pastor of the generations, and which, in short, has always marched towards the Just, the Beautiful, and the True, enlightening multitudes, elevating life, raising more and more the head of the People towards the Right, and the head of the individual towards God!

4. And now I address myself to the alarm party,—not in this Chamber, but wherever they may be, throughout Europe,—and I say to them: "Consider well what you would do; reflect on the task that you have undertaken; and measure it well before you commence. Suppose you should succeed: when you have destroyed the Press, there will remain something more to destroy,—Paris! When you have destroyed Paris, there will remain France. When you have destroyed France, there will remain the human mind." I repeat it, let this great European alarm party measure the immensity of the task which, in their heroism, they would attempt. Though they annihilate the Press to the last journal, Paris to the last pavement, France to the last hamlet, they will have done nothing. There will remain yet for them to destroy something always paramount, above the generations, and, as it were, between man and his Maker;—something that has written all the books, invented all the arts, discovered all the worlds, founded all the civilizations;—something which will always grasp, under the form of Revolutions, what is not yielded under the form of progress;—something which is itself unseizable as the light, and unapproachable as the sun,—and which calls itself the human mind!

LIX.—DEATH'S FINAL CONQUEST.

JAMES SHIRLEY.

1. THE glories of our blood and state
   Are shadows, not substantial things;
   There is no armor against Fate;
   Death lays his icy hand on Kings!
        Sceptre, Crown,
        Must tumble down,
   And in the dust be equal made
   With the poor crooked scythe and spade.

2. Some men with swords may reap the field,
   And plant fresh laurels where they kill;
   But their strong nerves at last must yield,—
   They tame but one another still.
        Early or late,
        They stoop to Fate,
   And must give up their conquering breath,
   When they, pale captives, creep to Death.

3. The garlands wither on your brow!—
   Then boast no more your mighty deeds:
   Upon Death's purple altar now
   See where the victor-victim bleeds!
        All heads must come
        To the cold tomb:
   Only the actions of the just
   Smell sweet, and blossom in the dust.

LX.—GENERAL GRANT TO THE ARMY.—1865.

U. S. GRANT.

1. SOLDIERS of the Armies of the United States! By
your patriotic devotion to your country in the hour of
danger and alarm, your magnificent fighting, bravery, and
endurance, you have maintained the supremacy of the
Union and the Constitution, overthrown all armed opposition to the enforcement of the laws, and of the proclama-
tions forever abolishing Slavery—the cause and pretext
of the Rebellion—and opened the way to the rightful
authorities, to restore order and inaugurate peace on a

permanent and enduring basis on every foot of American soil. Your marches, sieges, and battles, in distance, duration, resolution, and brilliancy of results, dim the luster of the world's past military achievements, and will be the patriot's precedent in defence of Liberty and the right in all time to come. In obedience to your country's call, you left your homes and families and volunteered in its defence.

2. Victory has crowned your valor and secured the purpose of your patriotic hearts; and with the gratitude of your countrymen and the highest honors a great and free nation can accord, you will soon be permitted to return to your homes and families, conscious of having discharged the highest duty of American citizens. To achieve these glorious triumphs, and to secure to yourselves, your countrymen, and posterity the blessings of free institutions, tens of thousands of your gallant comrades have fallen and sealed the priceless legacy with their lives. The graves of these a grateful nation bedews with tears, honors their memories, and will ever cherish and support their stricken families.

LXI.—HOTSPUR'S DESCRIPTION OF A FOP.

SHAKSPEARE.

1. My liege, I did deny no prisoners.
But I remember, when the fight was done,
When I was dry with rage, and extreme toil,
Breathless, and faint, leaning upon my sword,
Came there a certain lord, neat, trimly dressed,
Fresh as a bridegroom; and his chin, new reaped,
Showed like stubble-land at harvest home.

2. He was perfumed like a milliner;
And, twixt his finger and his thumb, he held
A pouncet-box, which, ever and anon,
He gave his nose. And still he smiled, and talked,
And as the soldiers bore dead bodies by,
He called them untaught knaves, unmannerly,

7*

To bring a slovenly, unhandsome corse
Betwixt the wind and his nobility.

3. With many holiday and lady terms,
He questioned me ; among the rest, demanded
My prisoners, in her majesty's behalf ;
I then, all smarting with my wounds, being galled
To be so pestered with a popinjay,
Out of my grief and my impatience,
Answered negligently—I know not what—
He should, or should not ; for he made me mad,
To see him shine so brisk, and smell so sweet,
And talk so like a waiting gentlewoman,
Of guns, and drums, and wounds—heaven save the mark—
And telling me the sovereign'st thing on earth,
Was spermaceti—for an inward bruise :

4. And that it was great pity—so it was—
That villanous saltpeter should be digged
Out of the bowels of the harmless earth,
Which many a good, tall fellow had destroyed
So cowardly ; and, but for these vile guns,
He would himself have been a soldier.

5. This bald, unjointed chat of his, my lord,
I answered indirectly, as I said ;
And I beseech you, let not his report
Come current, for an accusation,
Betwixt my love, and your high majesty.

———————◆———————

LXII.—THE GAMBLER'S WIFE.

COATES.

1. Dark is the night ! how dark—no light—no fire !
Cold, on the hearth, the last faint sparks expire !
Shivering she watches by the cradle side,
For him who pledged her love—last year a bride !

2. " Hark ! 'tis his footstep ! No—'tis past : 'tis gone :
Tick !—Tick !—How wearily the time crawls on !
Why should he leave me thus ? He once was kind !
And I believed 'twould last—how mad !—how blind !

3. " Rest thee, my babe !—rest on !—'tis hunger's cry !
Sleep !—for there is no food ! the fount is dry !

Famine and cold their wearying work have done,
My heart must break !—and thou !" The clock strikes one.

4. " Hush ! 'tis the dice-box ! Yes, he's there, he's there,
For this ! for this he leaves me to despair !
Leaves love ! leaves truth ! his wife ! his child ! for what ?
The wanton's smile—the villain—and the sot !

5. " Yet I'll not curse him ! No ! 'tis all in vain !
'Tis long to wait, but sure he'll come again !
And I could starve and bless him, but for you,
My child !—his child !—O fiend !" The clock strikes two.

6. " Hark ! how the sign-board creaks ! The blast howls by !
Moan ! moan ! A dirge swells through the cloudy sky !
Ha ! 'tis his knock ! he comes !—he comes once more !
'Tis but the lattice flaps ! Thy hope is o'er.

7. " Can he desert me thus ? He knows I stay
Night after night in loneliness to pray
For his return—and yet he sees no tear !
No ! no ! it cannot be. He will be here.

8. " Nestle more closely, dear one, to my heart !
Thou'rt cold ! thou'rt freezing ! But we will not part.
Husband !—I die !—Father !—It is not he !
Oh God ! protect my child !" The clock strikes three.

9. They're gone ! they're gone ! the glimmering spark hath fled.
The wife and child are numbered with the dead !
On the cold hearth, out-stretched in solemn rest,
The child lies frozen on its mother's breast !
The gambler came at last—but all was o'er—
Dead silence reigned around—The clock struck four !

———◆———

LXIII.—CASSIUS AGAINST CÆSAR.

SHAKSPEARE.

1. Honor is the subject of my story,
I cannot tell what you, and other men,
Think of this life ; but for my single self,
I had as lief not be, as live to be
In awe of such a thing as I, myself.
I was born as free as Cæsar ; so were you ;
We have both fed as well ; and we can both
Endure the winter's cold as well as he.

2. For, once upon a raw and gusty day,
   The troubled Tiber chafing with its shores,
   Cæsar says to me—" Darest thou, Cassius, now
   Leap in with me, into this angry flood,
   And swim to yonder point ? "—Upon the word,
   Accoutred as I was, I plungëd in,
   And bade him follow ; so, indeed he did.
   The torrent roared, and we did buffet it ;
   With lusty sinews, throwing it aside,
   And stemming it, with hearts of controversy.
   But ere we could arrive the point proposed,
   Cæsar cried—" Help me, Cassius, or I sink."

3. I, as Æneas, our great ancestor,
   Did from the flames of Troy, upon his shoulder
   The old Anchises bear, so, from the waves of Tiber
   Did I the tired Cæsar ; and this man
   Is now become a god ; and Cassius is
   A wretched creature, and must bend his body,
   If Cæsar carelessly but nod to him.

4. He had a fever when he was in Spain,
   And when the fit was on him, I did mark
   How he did shake : 'tis true, this god did shake ;
   His coward lips did from their color fly ;
   And that same eye, whose bend doth awe the world,
   Did lose its luster ; I did hear him groan,
   Aye, and that tongue of his, that bade the Romans
   Mark him, and write his speeches in their books,
   " Alas ! " it cried—" Give me some drink, Titinius."

5. Ye gods ! it doth amaze me,
   A man of such a feeble temper should
   So get the start of the majestic world,
   And bear the palm alone.
   Why, man, he doth bestride the narrow world,
   Like a Colossus, and we, petty men,
   Walk under his huge legs, and peep about,
   To find ourselves dishonorable graves.

6. Men, at some time, are masters of their fates :
   The fault, dear Brutus, is not in our stars,
   But in ourselves, that we are underlings.
   Brutus and Cæsar ! What should be in that Cæsar ?
   Why should that name be sounded more than yours ?

Write them together : yours is as fair a name ;
Sound them : it doth become the mouth as well ;
Weigh them : it is as heavy : conjure with 'em :
Brutus will start a spirit as soon as Cæsar.

7. Now, in the name of all the gods at once,
Upon what meats doth this our Cæsar feed,
That he hath grown so great? Age, thou art ashamed ;
Rome, thou hast lost the breed of noble bloods.
When went there by an age, since the great flood,
But it was famed with more than with one man ?
When could they say, till now, that talked of Rome,
That her wide walls encompassed but one man ?
Oh ! you and I have heard our fathers say,
There was a Brutus once, that would have brooked
The infernal devil, to keep his state in Rome,
As easily as a king.

———◆———

LXIV.—RIENZI'S ADDRESS TO THE ROMANS.

MISS MITFORD.

1. I COME not here to talk. You know too well
The story of our thralldom. We are slaves !
The bright sun rises to his course and lights
A race of slaves ! He sets, and his last beams
Fall on a slave ; not such as, swept along
By the full tide of power, the conqueror led
To crimson glory and undying fame :
But base, ignoble slaves ; slaves to a horde
Of petty tyrants, feudal despots, lords,
Rich in some dozen paltry villages ;
Strong in some hundred spearmen ; only great
In that strange spell—a name.

2. Each hour, dark fraud,
Or open rapine, or protected murder,
Cry out against them. But this very day
An honest man, my neighbor—there he stands—
Was struck—struck like a dog, by one who wore
The badge of Ursini ; because, forsooth,
He tossed not high his ready cap in air,
Nor lifted up his voice in servile shouts,
At sight of that great ruffian ! Be we men,

And suffer such dishonor ? men, and wash not
The stain away in blood ?   Such shames are common :
I have known deeper wrongs ; I, that speak to ye.
I had a brother once—a gracious boy,
Full of gentleness, of calmest hope,
Of sweet and quiet joy : there was the look
Of heaven upon his face, which limners give
To the beloved disciple.

3.   How I loved
That gracious boy !   Younger by fifteen years,
Brother at once, and son !   He left my side,
A summer bloom on his fair check, a smile
Parting his innocent lips.   In one short hour,
That pretty, harmless boy was slain !   I saw
The corse, the mangled corse, and then I cried
For vengeance !   Rouse, ye Romans !   rouse, ye slaves !
Have ye brave sons ?   Look in the next fierce brawl
To see them die.   Have ye fair daughters ?   Look
To see them live, torn from your arms, distained,
Dishonored ; and if ye dare call for justice,
Be answered by the lash !

4.   Yet this is Rome,
That sat on her seven hills, and, from her throne
Of beauty, ruled the world !   Yet we are Romans !
Why, in that elder day, to be a Roman,
Was greater than a king ! and once again—
Hear me, ye walls, that echoed to the tread
Of either Brutus !   once again, I swear,
The eternal city shall be free.

---- ◆ ----

LXV.—THE SAILOR-BOY'S DREAM.

DIMOND.

1. In slumbers of midnight the sailor-boy lay ;
      His hammock swung loose at the sport of the wind ;
    But watch-worn and weary, his cares flew away,
      And visions of happiness danced o'er his mind.

2. He dreamed of his home, of his dear native bowers,
      And pleasures that waited on life's merry morn ;
    While memory stood sidewise, half-covered with flowers,
      And restored every rose, but secreted its thorn.

3. Then fancy her magical pinions spread wide,
   And bade the young dreamer in ecstasy rise—
Now far, far behind him the green waters glide,
   And the cot of his forefathers blesses his eyes.

4. The jessamine clambers in flower o'er the thatch,
   And the swallow sings sweet from her nest in the wall :
All trembling with transport, he raises the latch,
   And the voices of loved ones reply to his call.

5. A father bends o'er him with looks of delight,
   His cheek is impearled with a mother's warm tear,
And the lips of the boy in a love-kiss unite
   With the lips of the maid whom his bosom holds dear.

6. The heart of the sleeper beats high in his breast,
   Joy quickens his pulse—all his hardships seem o'er,
And a murmur of happiness steals through his rest—
   "Oh God thou hast blest me—I ask for no more."

7. Ah ! what is that flame, which now bursts on his eye ?
   Ah ! what is that sound which now 'larums his ear ?
'Tis the lightning's red glare, painting hell on the sky !
   'Tis the crash of the thunder, the groan of the sphere !

8. He springs from his hammock—he flies to the deck :
   Amazement confronts him with images dire—
Wild winds and mad waves drive the vessel a wreck—
   The masts fly in splinters—the shrouds are on fire !

9. Like mountains the billows tremendously swell—
   In vain the lost wretch calls on Mercy to save :
Unseen hands of spirits are ringing his knell,
   And the death-angel flaps his broad wing o'er the wave !

10. Oh ! sailor-boy, woe to thy dream of delight !
    In darkness dissolves the gay frost-work of bliss—
Where now is the picture that fancy touched bright,
    Thy parent's fond pressure, and love's honeyed kiss ?

11. Oh ! sailor-boy ! sailor-boy ! never again
    Shall home, love, or kindred, thy wishes repay :
Unblessed and unhonored, down deep in the main,
    Full many a score fathom, thy frame shall decay.

12. No tomb shall e'er plead to remembrance for thee,
    Or redeem form or frame from the merciless surge :
But the white foam of waves shall thy winding-sheet be,
    And winds, in the midnight of winter, thy dirge.

13. On beds of green sea-flowers thy limbs shall be laid ;
    Around thy white bones the red coral shall grow ;
    Of thy fair yellow locks threads of amber be made,
    And every part suit to thy mansion below.

14. Days, months, years, and ages, shall circle away,
    And still the vast waters above thee shall roll :
    Earth loses thy pattern forever and aye—
    Oh ! sailor-boy ! sailor-boy ! peace to thy soul.

———◆———

LXVI.—BERNARDO DEL CARPIO.

MRS. HEMANS.

1. THE warrior bowed his crested head, and tamed his heart of fire,
   And sued the haughty king to free his long-imprisoned sire :
   " I bring thee here my fortress-keys, I bring my captive train,
   I pledge thee faith, my liege, my lord !—O ! break my father's chain ! "

2. " Rise, rise ! even now thy father comes, a ransomed man, this day !
   Mount thy good horse ; and thou and I will meet him on his way."
   Then lightly rose that loyal son, and bounded on his steed,
   And urged, as if with lance in rest, the charger's foamy speed.

3. And lo ! from far, as on they pressed, there came a glittering band,
   With one that 'midst them stately rode, as a leader in the land :
   " Now haste, Bernardo, haste ! for there, in very truth, is he,
   The father whom thy faithful heart hath yearned so long to see."

4. His dark eye flashed, his proud breast heaved, his cheek's hue came
       and went :
   He reached that gray-haired chieftain's side, and there, dismounting,
       bent ;
   A lowly knee to earth he bent, his father's hand he took—
   What was there in its touch that all his fiery spirit shook ?

5. That hand was cold—a frozen thing—it dropped from his like lead ! ·
   He looked up to the face above—the face was of the dead !
   A plume waved o'er the noble brow—the brow was fixed and white ;
   He met, at last, his father's eyes—but in them was no sight !

6. Up from the ground he sprang and gazed ; but who could paint that
       gaze ?
   They hushed their very hearts, that saw its horror and amaze—
   They might have chained him, as before that stony form he stood ;
   For the power was stricken from his arm, and from his lip the blood.

7. "Father!" at length he murmured low, and wept like childhood then:
   Talk not of grief till thou hast seen the tears of warlike men!
   He thought on all his glorious hopes, and all his young renown—
   He flung his falchion from his side, and in the dust sat down.

8. Then covering with his steel-gloved hands his darkly mournful brow,
   "No more, there is no more," he said, "to lift the sword for, now:
   My king is false—my hope betrayed! My father—O! the worth,
   The glory, and the loveliness, are passed away from earth!

9. "I thought to stand where banners waved, my sire, beside thee, yet!
   I would that there our kindred blood on Spain's free soil had met!
   Thou wouldst have known my spirit, then—for thee my fields were won;
   And thou hast perished in thy chains, as though thou hadst no son!"

10. Then, starting from the ground once more, he seized the monarch's rein,
    Amid the pale and wildered looks of all the courtier train;
    And, with a fierce, o'ermastering grasp, the rearing war-horse led,
    And sternly set them face to face—the king before the dead:

11. "Came I not forth, upon thy pledge, my father's hand to kiss?
    Be still, and gaze thou on, false king! and tell me what is this?
    The voice, the glance, the heart I sought—give answer, where are they?
    If thou wouldst clear thy perjured soul, send life through this cold
         clay!

12. "Into these glassy eyes put light—be still! keep down thine ire!
    Bid these white lips a blessing speak—this earth is not my sire:
    Give me back him for whom I strove, for whom my blood was shed?
    Thou canst not?—and a king!—his dust be mountains on thy head!"

13. He loosed the steed—his slack hand fell—upon the silent face
    He cast one long, deep, troubled look, then turned from that sad place:
    His hope was crushed, his after fate untold in martial strain—
    His banner led the spears no more, amid the hills of Spain.

LXVII.—ORATION AGAINST VERRES.

CICERO.

1. I ASK now, Verres, what have you to advance against this charge? Will you pretend to deny it? Will you pretend that any thing false, that even any thing exaggerated is alleged against you? Had any prince, or any state, committed the same outrage against the privileges of Roman citizens, should we not think we had suffi-

cient reason for declaring immediate war against them ? What punishment, then, ought to be inflicted on a tyrannical and wicked pretor, who dared, at no greater distance than Sicily, within sight of the Italian coast, to put to the infamous death of crucifixion that unfortunate and innocent citizen, Publius Gavius Cosanus, only for his having asserted his privilege of citizenship, and declared his intention of appealing to the justice of his country against a cruel oppressor, who had unjustly confined him in prison at Syracuse, whence he had just made his escape ? The unhappy man, arrested as he was going to embark for his native country, is brought before the wicked pretor. With eyes darting fury, and a countenance distorted with cruelty, he orders the helpless victim of his rage to be stripped, and rods to be brought : accusing him, but without the least shadow of evidence, or even of suspicion, of having come to Sicily as a spy.

2. It was in vain that the unhappy man cried out, " I am a Roman citizen, I have served under Lucius Pretius, who is now at Panormus, and will attest my innocence." The bloodthirsty pretor, deaf to all he could urge in his own defence, ordered the infamous punishment to be inflicted. Thus, fathers, was an innocent Roman citizen publicly mangled with scourging ; while the only words he uttered amid his cruel sufferings were, " I am a Roman citizen ! " With these he hoped to defend himself from violence and infamy. But of so little service was this privilege to him, that while he was asserting his citizenship, the order was given for his execution—for his execution upon the cross !

3. O liberty ! O sound once delightful to every Roman ear ! O sacred privilege of Roman citizenship ! once sacred, now trampled upon ! But what then—is it come to this ? Shall an inferior magistrate, a governor, who holds his power of the Roman people, in a Roman province, within sight of Italy, bind, scourge, torture with fire and red-hot plates of iron, and at last put to the infamous

death of the cross, a Roman citizen? Shall neither the cries of innocence expiring in agony, nor the tears of pitying spectators, nor the majesty of the Roman commonwealth, nor the fear of the justice of his country, restrain the licentious and wanton cruelty of a monster, who, in confidence of his riches, strikes at the root of liberty and sets mankind at defiance?

LXVIII.—FROM THE FIRST ORATION AGAINST CATILINE.
CICERO.

1. How far wilt thou, O Catiline, abuse our patience? How long shall thy madness outbrave our justice? To what extremities art thou resolved to push thy unbridled insolence of guilt? Canst thou behold the nocturnal arms that watch the palatium : the guards of the city : the consternation of the citizens; all the wise and worthy clustering into consultation; this impregnable situation of the seat of the senate, and the reproachful looks of the fathers of Rome? Canst thou, I say, behold all this, and yet remain undaunted and unabashed? Art thou sensible that thy measures are detected?

2. Art thou sensible that this senate, now thoroughly informed, comprehends the full extent of thy guilt? Point me out the senator ignorant of thy practices, during the last and the preceding night; of the place where you met, the company you summoned, and the crime you concerted. The senate is conscious, the consul is witness to this : yet mean and degenerate—the traitor lives! Lives! did I say? He mixes with the senate : he shares in our counsels : with a steady eye he surveys us : he anticipates his guilt: he enjoys his murderous thoughts, and coolly marks us out for bloodshed. Yet we, boldly passive in our country's cause, think we act like Romans if we can escape his frantic rage.

3. Long since, O Catiline! ought the consul to have doomed thy life a forfeit to thy country; and to have

directed upon thy own head the mischief thou hast long been meditating for ours. Could the noble Scipio, when sovereign pontiff, as a private Roman kill Tiberius Gracchus for a slight encroachment upon the rights of this country; and shall we, her consuls, with persevering patience endure Catiline, whose ambition is to desolate a devoted world with fire and sword?

4. There was—there was a time, when such was the spirit of Rome, that the resentment of her magnanimous sons more sternly crushed the Roman traitor, than the most inveterate enemy. Strong and weighty, O Catiline! is the decree of the senate we can now produce against you; neither wisdom is wanting in this state, nor authority in this assembly; but we, the consuls, we are defective in our duty.

LXIX.—DEGENERACY OF ATHENS.

DEMOSTHENES.

1. SUCH, O men of Athens! were your ancestors: so glorious in the eye of the world; so bountiful and munificent to their country; so sparing, so modest, so self-denying, to themselves. What resemblance can we find, in the present generation, to these great men? At the time when your ancient competitors have left you a clear stage, when the Lacedemonians are disabled, the Thebans employed in troubles of their own, when no other state whatever is in a condition to rival or molest you—in short, when you are at full liberty, when you have the opportunity and the power to become once more the sole arbiters of Greece—you permit, patiently, whole provinces to be wrested from you: you lavish the public money in scandalous and obscure uses: you suffer your allies to perish in time of peace, whom you preserved in time of war; and, to sum up all, you yourselves, by your mercenary court, and servile resignation to the will and pleasure of designing, insidious leaders, abet, encourage, and

strengthen, the most dangerous and formidable of your enemies. Yes, Athenians, I repeat it, you yourselves are the contrivers of your own ruin.

2. Lives there a man who has confidence enough to deny it? Let him arise and assign, if he can, any other cause of the success and prosperity of Philip. "But," you reply, "what Athens may have lost in reputation abroad she has gained in splendor at home. Was there ever a greater appearance of prosperity and plenty? Is not the city enlarged? Are not the streets better paved, houses repaired and beautified?" Away with such trifles! Shall I be paid with counters? An old square new vamped up! a fountain! an aqueduct! Are these acquisitions to boast of? Cast your eyes upon the magistrate under whose ministry you boast these precious improvements. Behold the despicable creature, raised all at once from dirt to opulence, from the lowest obscurity to the highest honors. Have not some of these upstarts built private houses and seats vying with the most sumptuous of our public palaces? And how have their fortunes and their power increased, but as the commonwealth has been ruined and impoverished?

LXX.—TELL ME, YE WINGED WINDS.

CHARLES MACKAY.

1. TELL me, ye winged winds,
   That round my pathway roar,
   Do you not know some spot
   Where mortals weep no more?
   Some lone and pleasant dell,
   Some valley in the west,
   Where, free from toil and pain,
   The weary soul may rest?
The loud wind softened to a whisper low,
And sighed for pity as it whispered—"No!"

2. Tell me, thou mighty deep,
   Whose billows round me play,

Know'st thou some favored spot,
Some island far away,
Where weary man may find
The bliss for which he sighs,
Where sorrow never lives
And friendship never dies?
The loud waves rolling in perpetual flow,
Stopped for a while, and sighed to answer—" No ! "

3. And thou, serenest moon,
That with such holy face
Dost look upon the earth,
Asleep in night's embrace,
Tell me, in all thy round,
Hast thou not seen some spot,
Where miserable man
Might find a happier lot?
Behind a cloud the moon withdrew in woe,
And a voice sweet, but sad, responded—" No ! "

4. Tell me, my secret soul,
O ! tell me, Hope and Faith,
Is there no resting-place
From sorrow, sin, and death?
Is there no happy spot,
Where mortals may be blest,
Where grief may find a balm,
And weariness a rest?
Faith, Hope, and Love—best boons to mortals given—
Waved their bright wings, and whispered—" Yes ! in heaven ! "

LXXI.—SPEECH OF PATRICK HENRY.

PATRICK HENRY.

1. I HAVE but one lamp by which my feet are guided ;
and that is the lamp of experience. I know of no way
of judging of the future but by the past. And, judging
by the past, I wish to know what there has been, in the
conduct of the British ministry, for the last ten years, to
justify those hopes with which gentlemen have been
pleased to solace themselves, and the house? Is it that
insidious smile with which our petition has been lately

received ? Trust it not, sir ; it will prove a snare to your feet. Suffer not yourselves to be betrayed with a kiss. Ask yourselves how this gracious reception of our petition comports with those warlike preparations which cover our waters, and darken our land. Are fleets and armies necessary to a work of love and reconciliation ? Have we shown ourselves so unwilling to be reconciled, that force must be called in to win back our love ?

2. Let us not deceive ourselves, sir. These are the implements of war and subjugation—the last arguments to which kings resort. I ask gentlemen, sir, what means this martial array, if its purpose be not to force us to submission ? Can gentlemen assign any other possible motive for it ? Has Great Britain any enemy in this quarter of the world, to call for all this accumulation of navies and armies ? No, sir, she has none. They are meant for us : they can be meant for no other. They are sent over to bind and rivet upon us those chains which the British ministry have been so long forging. And what have we to oppose to them ? Shall we try argument ? Sir, we have been trying that for the last ten years. Have we any thing new to offer upon the subject ? Nothing.

3. We have held the subject up in every light of which it is capable ; but it has been all in vain. Shall we resort to entreaty and humble supplication ? What terms shall we find which have not been already exhausted ? Let us not, I beseech you, sir, deceive ourselves longer. Sir, we have done every thing that could be done to avert the storm which is now coming on. We have petitioned : we have remonstrated : we have supplicated : we have prostrated ourselves before the throne, and have implored its interposition to arrest the tyrannical hands of the ministry and parliament. Our petitions have been slighted : our remonstrances have produced additional violence and insult : our supplications have been disregarded, and we have been spurned with contempt from the foot of the throne.

4. In vain, after these things, may we indulge the fond hope of peace and reconciliation. There is no longer any room for hope. If we wish to be free; if we mean to preserve inviolate those inestimable privileges, for which we have been so long contending; if we mean not basely to abandon the noble struggle, in which we have been so long engaged, and which we have pledged ourselves never to abandon, until the glorious object of our contest shall be obtained, we must fight! I repeat it, sir, we must fight!

5. An appeal to arms, and to the God of hosts, is all that is left us. They tell us, sir, that we are weak, unable to cope with so formidable an adversary. But when shall we be stronger? Will it be the next week or the next year? Will it be when we are totally disarmed, and when a British guard shall be stationed in every house? Shall we gather strength by irresolution and inaction? Shall we acquire the means of effectual resistance by lying supinely on our backs, and hugging the delusive phantom of hope, until our enemies shall have bound us hand and foot?

6. Sir, we are not weak if we make a proper use of those means which the God of nature hath placed in our power. Three millions of people, armed in the holy cause of liberty, and in such a country as that which we possess, are invincible by any force which our enemy can send against us. Besides, sir, we shall not fight our battles alone. There is a just God who presides over the destinies of nations, and who will raise up friends to fight our battles for us. The battle, sir, is not to the strong alone, it is to the vigilant, the active, the brave. Besides, sir, we have no election. If we were base enough to desire it, it is now too late to retire from the contest. There is no retreat but in submission and slavery. Our chains are forged. Their clanking may be heard on the plains of Boston! The war is inevitable, and let it come! I repeat it, sir, let it come!

7. It is in vain, sir, to extenuate the matter. Gentlemen

may cry peace, peace, but there is no peace. The war is actually begun! The next gale that sweeps from the North will bring to our ears the clash of resounding arms! Our brethren are already in the field! Why stand we here idle! What is it that gentlemen wish? what would they have? Is life so dear, or peace so sweet, as to be purchased at the price of chains and slavery? Forbid it, Almighty God! I know not what course others may take, but as for me, give me liberty, or give me death!

———————◆———————

LXXII.—CATILINE'S LAST HARANGUE TO HIS ARMY.

CROLY.

1. BRAVE comrades! all is ruined! I disdain
   To hide the truth from you. The die is thrown!
   And now, let each that wishes for long life
   Put up his sword, and kneel for peace to Rome.
   Ye are all free to go.—What! no man stirs!
   Not one!—a soldier's spirit in you all?
   Give me your hands! (This moisture in *my* eyes
   Is womanish—'twill pass.) My noble hearts!
   Well have you chosen to die! For, in my mind,
   The grave is better than o'erburthened life;—
   Better the quick release of glorious wounds,
   Than the eternal taunts of galling tongues;—
   Better the spear-head quivering in the heart,
   Than daily struggle against Fortune's *curse;*—

2. Better, in manhood's muscle and high blood,
   To leap the gulf, than totter to its edge
   In poverty, dull pain, and base decay.
   Once more, I say,—are ye resolved?
   Then, each man to his tent, and take the arms
   That he would love to die in,—for, *this hour*,
   We storm the Consul's camp.—A last farewell!
   When next we meet, we 'll have no time to look,
   How parting clouds a soldier's countenance:
   Few as we are, we 'll rouse them with a peal
   That shall shake Rome!
   Now to your cohorts' heads,—the word's—*Revenge*.

8

LXXIII.—THE AMERICAN FLAG.

J. R. DRAKE.

1. WHEN Freedom, from her mountain height,
    Unfurled her standard to the air,
  She tore the azure robe of night,
    And set the stars of glory there.
  She mingled with its gorgeous dyes
  The milky baldric of the skies,
  And striped its pure celestial white,
  With streakings of the morning light;
  Then, from his mansion in the sun,
  She called her eagle bearer down,
  And gave into his mighty hand
  The symbol of her chosen land.

2. Majestic monarch of the cloud,
    Who rear'st aloft thy regal form,
  To hear the tempest trumpings loud
    And see the lightning lances driven,
  When strive the warriors of the storm,
    And rolls the thunder-drum of Heaven,—
  Child of the Sun! to thee 'tis given
    To guard the banner of the free:
  To hover in the sulphur smoke:
  To ward away the battle-stroke;
  And bid its blendings shine afar,
  Like rainbows on the cloud of war,
    The harbingers of victory!

3. Flag of the brave! thy folds shall fly,
  The sign of hope and triumph high.
  When speaks the signal trumpet tone,
  And the long line comes gleaming on,—
  Ere yet the life-blood, warm and wet,
  Has dimmed the glistening bayonet,—
  Each soldier's eye shall brightly turn
  To where thy sky-born glories burn;
  And, as his springing steps advance,
  Catch war and vengeance from the glance.
  And, when the cannon-mouthings loud
  Heave in wild wreaths the battle shroud,
  And gory sabres rise and fall
  Like shoots of flame on midnight's pall,

Then shall thy meteor glances glow,
  And cowering foes shall fall beneath
Each gallant arm that strikes below
  That lovely messenger of death.

4. Flag of the seas! on ocean's wave
  Thy stars shall glitter o'er the brave.
When Death, careering on the gale,
Sweeps darkly round the bellied sail,
And frighted waves rush wildly back,
Before the broadside's reeling rack,
Each dying wanderer of the sea
Shall look at once to Heaven and thee;
And smile to see thy splendors fly,
In triumph, o'er his closing eye.

5. Flag of the free heart's hope and home!
  By angel hands to Valor given!
Thy stars have lit the welkin dome,
  And all thy hues were born in Heaven.
Forever float that standard sheet!
  Where breathes the foe but falls before us,
With Freedom's soil beneath our feet,
  And Freedom's banner streaming o'er us?

LXXIV.—BURIAL OF SIR JOHN MOORE, 1809.

Rev. CHARLES WOLFE.

1. Not a drum was heard, not a funeral note,
  As his corse to the rampart we hurried;
Not a soldier discharged his farewell shot
  O'er the grave where our hero we buried.
We buried him darkly, at dead of night,
  The sods with our bayonets turning;
By the struggling moonbeams' misty light,
  And the lantern dimly burning.

2. No useless coffin enclosed his breast,
  Nor in sheet, nor in shroud, we wound him;
But he lay, like a warrior taking his rest,
  With his martial cloak around him.
Few and short were the prayers we said,
  And we spoke not a word of sorrow;
But we steadfastly gazed on the face of the dead,
  And we bitterly thought of the morrow.

3. We thought, as we hollowed his narrow bed,
   And smoothed down his lonely pillow,
That the foe and the stranger would tread o'er his head,
   And we far away on the billow!
Lightly they 'll talk of the spirit that 's gone,
   And o'er his cold ashes upbraid him;
But little he 'll reck, if they let him sleep on,
   In the grave where a Briton has laid him!

4. But half of our heavy task was done,
   When the clock struck the hour for retiring,
And we heard by th' distant and random gun,
   That the foe was sullenly firing.
Slowly and sadly we laid him down,
   From the field of his fame, fresh and gory!
We carved not a line, we raised not a stone,
   But we left him—alone with his glory!

LXXV.—THE BATTLE OF HOHENLINDEN, 1800.

THOMAS CAMPBELL.

1. On Linden when the sun was low,
   All bloodless lay the untrodden snow,
   And dark as winter was the flow
       Of Iser, rolling rapidly.

2. But Linden saw another sight,
   When the drum beat at dead of night,
   Commanding fires of death to light
       The darkness of her scenery.

3. By torch and trumpet fast arrayed,
   Each warrior drew his battle-blade,
   And furious every charger neighed,
       To join the dreadful revelry.

4. Then shook the hills with thunder riven,
   Then rushed the steeds to battle driven,
   And louder than the bolts of Heaven
       Far flashed the red artillery.

5. And redder yet those fires shall glow
   On Linden's hills of blood-stained snow,
   And darker yet shall be the flow
       Of Iser rolling rapidly.

6. 'T is morn; but scarce yon lurid sun
    Can pierce the war-clouds, rolling dun,
    While furious Frank and fiery Hun
        Shout in their sulphurous canopy.

7. The combat deepens. On, ye brave
    Who rush to glory, or the grave!
    Wave, Munich, all thy banners wave!
        And charge with all thy chivalry!

8. Ah! few shall part where many meet,
    The snow shall be their winding-sheet.
    And every turf beneath their feet
        Shall be a soldier's sepulchre.

LXXVI.—POETICAL SELECTIONS.

1.—NOVEMBER.

W. C. BRYANT.

1. YET one smile more, departing, distant sun!
    One mellow smile through the soft vapory air,
    Ere, o'er the frozen earth, the loud winds run,
    Or snows are sifted o'er the meadows bare.
    One smile on the brown hills and naked trees,
        And the dark rocks whose summer wreaths are cast,
    And the blue gentian flower, that in the breeze
        Nods lonely, of her beauteous race the last.
    Yet a few sunny days, in which the bee
        Shall murmur by the hedge that skirts the way,
    The cricket chirp upon the russet lea,
        And man delight to linger in thy ray.
    Yet one rich smile, and we will try to bear
    The piercing winter frost, and winds, and darkened air.

2.—THE CONSTITUTION.

W. C. BRYANT.

1. GREAT were the thoughts, and strong the minds
        Of those who framed in high debate,
    The immortal league of love, that binds
        Our fair broad Empire, State with State.
    And deep the gladness of the hour,
        When as the auspicious task was done,
    In solemn trust, the sword of power,
        Was given to glory's spotless son.

2. The noble race is gone—the suns
    Of sixty years have risen and set;
But the bright links, those chosen ones,
    So strongly forged, are brighter yet.
Wide as our own free race increase—
    Wide shall extend the elastic chain,
And bind in everlasting peace,
    State after State,—a mighty train.

3.—The Avenger of Slander.

From Victor Hugo.

                "Sire, at your hands
I had the right to claim all meet respect
That majesty to majesty accords:
You are the king!—I am—a father!
The eminence of years o'ertops a throne.
Upon your brows and mine, as well,
There rests a crown!—a crown
To which no eye of insult dare be raised.
The golden *fleur-de-lis* your diadem,
And mine, the silvery locks of age.
King, when the sacrilegious hand
On yours is laid, from you the quick,
Terrible redress!
But when dishonor smites the coronet
That Time has hallowed on a father's head,
God is the avenger!"

4.—The Press.

Adaptation from Ebenezer Elliot.

1. God said—"Let there be light!"
    Grim darkness felt His might,
        And fled away:
Then startled seas and mountains cold
Shone forth, all bright in blue and gold,
        And cried—"'T is day! 't is day!"

2. "Hail, holy light!" exclaimed
    The thunderous cloud that flamed
        O'er daisies white;
And lo! the rose, in crimson dressed,
Leaned sweetly on the lily's breast,
        And, blushing, murmured—"Light."

3. Then was the skylark born;
   Then rose the embattled corn;
     Then floods of praise
Flowed o'er the sunny hills of noon;
And then, in stillest night, the moon
     Poured forth her pensive rays.

4. Lo, Heaven's bright bow is glad!
   Lo, trees and flowers, all clad
     In glory, bloom!
And shall the immortal sons of God
Be senseless as the trodden clod,
     And darker than the tomb?

5. No, by the *mind* of man!
   By the swart artisan!
     We will aspire!
Our souls have holy light within,
And every form of grief and sin
     Shall see and feel its fire.

6. By all we hope of Heaven,
   The shroud of souls is riven!
     Mind, mind alone
Is light, and hope, and life, and power!
Earth's deepest night, from this blessed hour,—
     The night of mind,—is gone!

7. "The Press!" all lands shall sing:
   The Press, the Press we bring,
     All lands to bless.
O, pallid Want! O, Labor stark!
Behold! we bring the second ark!
     The Press, the Press, the Press!

5.—THOUGHTS OF A SCHOOLMATE—ONCE LOVED.

1. I THOUGHT of thee when the spring sent forth
     Fresh grass and sweet wild flowers,
   And the green leaves gave their shelter out
     To form the young year's bowers.
   And my thoughts of thee resembled then
     The breath of the fragrant breeze,
   That wafted o'er meadows cool and green,
     And soft through the new-clad trees.

2. I thought of thee in the summer time,
   When the sun sent forth its heat,
   To ripen the orchard's rosy fruit,
   And the golden ears of wheat.
   And my thought of thee was like the glow
   Of the warmth that parched the land :
   It beamed as the eastern sunshine beams
   On desert plains of sand.

3. I thought of thee when the autumn wind
   Swept wildly o'er hill and vale,
   And russet leaves were carried away
   On the breath of the drifting gale.
   And my thought of thee grew wilder then,
   As wild as the moaning blast,
   That seemed to tell with every sob
   Of dead hopes rushing past.

4. And now I think in the dim nights lone,
   When the stars shed out no glow,
   And o'er rock and hill, and deep dark sea,
   The winter fog hangs low.
   And sad, oh, sad! is my thought of thee,
   As I ponder o'er and o'er,
   On the many seasons lost in the shade
   Of a past that returns no more!

6.—THE LOVE OF COUNTRY.

SIR WALTER SCOTT.

1. BREATHES there a man with soul so dead,
   Who never to himself hath said,
   "This is my own, my native land"?
   Whose heart hath ne'er within him burned,
   As home his footsteps he hath turned,
   From wandering on a foreign strand?
   If such there breathe, go, mark him well
   For him no minstrel raptures swell!
   High though his titles, proud his name,
   Boundless his wealth as wish can claim:
   Despite those titles, power, and pelf,
   The wretch, concentred all in self
   Living, shall forfeit fair renown,
   And, doubly dying, shall go down
   To the vile dust, from whence he sprung,
   Unwept, unhonored, and unsung.

7.—ENVY.

1. EVERY thing contains within itself
   The seeds and sources of its own corruption:
   The cankering rust corrodes the brightest steel:
   The moth frets out your garment, and the worm
   Eats its slow way into the solid oak;
   But envy, of all evil things the worst,
   The same to-day, to-morrow, and forever,
   Saps and consumes the heart in which it works.

LXXVII.—SOLILOQUY OF THE DYING ALCHEMIST.

N. P. WILLIS.

1. THE night wind with a desolate moan swept by;
   And the old shutters of the turret swung,
   Creaking upon their hinges; and the moon,
   As the torn edges of the clouds flew past,
   Struggled aslant the stained and broken panes
   So dimly, that the watchful eye of death
   Scarcely was conscious when it went and came.

2.   The silent room,
   From its dim corners, mockingly gave back
   His rattling breath; the humming in the fire
   Had the distinctness of a knell; and when
   Duly the antique horologe beat one,
   He drew a phial from beneath his head,
   And drank. And instantly his lips compressed,
   And, with a shudder in his skeleton frame,
   He rose with supernatural strength, and sat
   --Upright, and communed with himself:—

3.   "I did not think to die
   Till I had finished what I had to do:
   I thought to pierce th' eternal secret through
        With this my mortal eye:
   I felt,—O God! it seemeth even now
   This can not be the death-dew on my brow!

4.   "And yet it is,—I feel,
   Of this dull sickness at my heart, afraid;   .
   And in my eyes the death-sparks flash and fade;
        And something seems to steal
   Over my bosom like a frozen hand,—
   Binding its pulses with an icy band.
   8*

5.   "And this is death ! But why
Feel I this wild recoil ?   It can not be
Th' immortal spirit shuddereth to be free !
      Would it not leap to fly·
Like a chain'd eaglet at its parent's call ?
I fear,—I fear,—that this poor life is all !

6.   "Yet thus to pass away !—
To live but for a hope that mocks at last,—
To agonize, to strive, to watch, to fast,
      To waste the light of day,
Night's better beauty, feeling, fancy, thought,
All that we have and are,—for this,—for naught !

7.   "Grant me another year,
God of my spirit !—but a day,—to win
Something to satisfy this thirst within !
      I would *know* something here !
Break for me but one seal that is unbroken !
Speak for me but one word that is unspoken !

8.   "Vain,—vain!—my brain is turning
With a swift dizziness, and my heart grows sick,
And these hot temple-throbs come fast and thick,
      And I am freezing,—burning,—
Dying! O God! if I might only live !
My phial————Ha! it.thrills me,—I revive.

9.   "Aye,—were not man to die
He were too mighty for this narrow sphere !
Had he but time to brood on knowledge here,—
      Could he but train his eye,—
Might he but wait the mystic word and hour,—
Only his Maker would transcend his power !

10.   "Earth has no mineral strange,—
Th' illimitable air no hidden wings,—
Water no quality in covert springs,
      And fire no power to change,—
Seasons no mystery, and stars no spell,
Which the unwasting soul might not compel.

11.   "Oh, but for time to track
The upper stars into the pathless sky :
To see th' invisible spirits, eye to eye :
      To hurl the lightning back :
To tread unhurt the sea's dim-lighted halls :
To chase Day's chariot to the horizon-walls ;

12.   " And more, much more,—for now
The life-sealed fountains of my nature move,—
To nurse and purify this human love,—
    To clear the godlike brow
Of weakness and mistrust, and bow it down
Worthy and beautiful, to the much-loved one,—

13.   " This were indeed to feel
The soul-thirst slaken at the living stream,—
To live,—O God! that life is but a dream!
    And death———Aha! I reel,—
Dim,—dim,—I faint,—darkness comes o'er my eye,—
Cover me! save me!——God of Heaven! I die!"

14. 'Twas morning, and the old man lay alone.
No friend has closed his eyelids, and his lips,
Open and ashy pale, th' expression wore
Of his death-struggle. His long silvery hair
Lay on his hollow temples thin and wild,
His frame was wasted, and his features wan
And haggard as with want, and in his palm
His nails were driven deep, as if the throe
Of the last agony had wrung him sore.

LXXVIII.—THE BELLS.

EDGAR A. POE.

1. HEAR the sledges with the bells, silver bells—
What a world of merriment their melody foretells!
How they tinkle, tinkle, tinkle, in the icy air of night!
While the stars that oversprinkle all the heavens, seem to twinkle
    With a crystalline delight—
Keeping time, time, time, in a sort of Runic rhyme,
To the tintinnabulation that so musically wells
From the bells, bells, bells, bells, bells, bells, bells—
From the jingling and the tinkling of the bells.

2. Hear the mellow wedding-bells, golden bells,
What a world of happiness their harmony foretells!
Through the balmy air of night how they ring out their delight!
From the molten-golden notes, all in tune,
    What a liquid ditty floats
To the turtle-dove that listens, while she gloats on the moon!
    O, from out the sounding cells,
What a gush of euphony voluminously wells!

How it swells, how it dwells
On the Future! how it tells of the rapture that impels
To the swinging and the ringing of the bells, bells, bells—
Of the bells, bells, bells, bells, bells, bells, bells—
To the rhyming and the chiming of the bells.

3. Hear the loud alarum-bells, brazen bells!
What a tale of terror, now, their turbulency tells!
In the startled ear of night how they scream out their affright!
Too much horrified to speak, they can only shriek, shriek,
    Out of tune,
In the clamorous appealing to the mercy of the fire,
In a mad expostulation with the deaf and frantic fire
Leaping higher, higher, higher, with a desperate desire,
And a resolute endeavor, now—now to sit or never,
    By the side of the pale-faced moon.
O, the bells, bells, bells, what a tale their terror tells of Despair!
How they clang, and clash, and roar! what a horror they outpour
On the bosom of the palpitating air!
    Yet the ear it fully knows,
    By the twanging and the clanging, how the danger ebbs and flows;
    Yet the ear distinctly tells,
In the jangling, and the wrangling, how the danger sinks and swells,
By the sinking or the swelling in the anger of the bells, of the bells,
Of the bells, bells, bells, bells, bells, bells, bells—
In the clamor and the clangor of the bells!

4. Hear the tolling of the bells, iron bells!
What a world of solemn thought their monody compels!
In the silence of the night, how we shiver with affright
    At the melancholy menace of their tone!
For every sound that floats from the rust within their throats
    Is a groan.
And the people—ah, the people—they that dwell up in the steeple
    All alone,
And who tolling, tolling, tolling, in that muffled monotone,
Feel a glory in so rolling on the human heart a stone—
They are neither man nor woman—they are neither brute nor human,
    They are ghouls:
And their king it is who tolls; and he rolls, rolls, rolls, rolls,
A pæan from the bells! and his merry bosom swells
With the pæan of the bells! and he dances and he yells:
Keeping time, time, time, in a sort of Runic rhyme,
    To the pæan of the bells, of the bells:

Keeping time, time, time, in a sort of Runic rhyme,
To the throbbing of the bells, of the bells, bells, bells—
    To the sobbing of the bells:
Keeping time, time, time, as he knells, knells, knells,
In a happy Runic rhyme, to the rolling of the bells—
Of the bells, bells, bells, to the tolling of the bells,
Of the bells, bells, bells, bells, bells, bells, bells—
To the moaning and the groaning of the bells.

LXXIX.—THE OLD CONTINENTALS.

GUY HUMPHREY McMASTER.

1. In their ragged regimentals
      Stood the old Continentals,
          Yielding not,
      When the Grenadiers were lunging,
      And like hail fell the plunging
          Cannon-shot:
          When the files
          Of the isles,
From the smoky night encampment, bore the banner of the rampant
          Unicorn,
And grummer, grummer, grummer rolled the roll of the drummer,
          Through the morn!

2. Then with eyes to the front all,
      And with guns horizontal,
          Stood our sires;
      And the balls whistled deadly,
      And in streams flashing redly
          Blazed the fires;
          As the roar
          On the shore,
Swept the strong battle-breakers o'er the green-sodded acres
          Of the plain;
And louder, louder, louder, cracked the black gunpowder,
          Cracking amain!

3. Now like smiths at their forges
      Worked the red St. George's
          Cannoniers;
      And the "villainous saltpetre"
      Rang a fierce, discordant metre
          Round their ears;

As the swift
Storm-drift,
With hot sweeping anger, came the horse-guards' clangor
On our flanks.
Then higher, higher, higher, burned the old-fashioned fire
Through the ranks!

4. Then the old-fashioned Colonel
Galloped through the white infernal
Powder-cloud ;
And his broad sword was swinging,
And his brazen throat was ringing
Trumpet loud.
Then the blue
Bullets flew,
And the trooper-jackets redden at the touch of the leaden
Rifle-breath.
And rounder, rounder, rounder, roared the iron six-pounder,
Hurling death !

LXXX.—ONCE I WAS PURE.

1. O! THE snow, the beautiful snow,
Filling the sky and the earth below:
Over the housetops, over the street,
Over the heads of the people you meet,
Dancing,
Flirting,
Skimming along,
Beautiful snow ! It can do nothing wrong,
Flying to kiss a fair lady's cheek,
Clinging to lips in a frolicsome freak,
Beautiful snow from the heaven above
Pure as an angel, as gentle as love !

2. O! the snow, the beautiful snow,
How the flakes gather and laugh as they go !
Whirling about in its maddening fun,
It plays in its glee with every one,
Chasing,
Laughing,
Hurrying by,
It lights up the face and it sparkles the eye !

And even the dogs, with a bark and a bound,
Snap at the crystals that eddy around:
The town is alive, and its heart in a glow,
To welcome the coming of beautiful snow.

3. How the wild crowd goes swaying along,
Hailing each other with humor and song !
How the gay sledges, like meteors, flash by,
Bright for the moment, then lost to the eye ;
    Ringing,
        Swinging,
            Dashing they go,
Over the crest of the beautiful snow ;
Snow so pure when it falls from the sky,
To be trampled in mud by the crowd rushing by,
To be trampled and tracked by the thousands of feet,
Till it blends with the filth in the horrible street.

4. Once I was pure as the snow—but I fell !
Fell like the snow-flakes from heaven to hell :
Fell to be trampled as filth in the street :
Fell to be scoffed, to be spit on and beat :
    Pleading,
        Cursing,
            Dreading to die,
Selling my soul to whoever would buy,
Dealing in shame for a morsel of bread,
Hating the living and fearing the dead :
Merciful God ! have I fallen so low ?
And yet I was once like the beautiful snow.

5. Once I was fair as the beautiful snow,
With an eye like its crystal, a heart like its glow :
Once I was loved for my innocent grace—
Flattered and sought for the charms of my face :
    Father,
        Mother,
            Sisters all,
God, and myself, I have lost by my fall.
The veriest wretch that goes shivering by,
Will take a wide sweep lest I wander too nigh ;
For all that is on or above me, I know,
There is nothing as pure as the beautiful snow.

6. How strange it should be that this beautiful snow
Should fall on a sinner with nowhere to go !

How strange it should be, when the night comes again,
If the snow and the ice struck my desperate brain,
  Fainting,
   Freezing,
    Dying alone,
Too wicked for prayer, too weak for my moan
To be heard in the crazy town,
Gone mad in the joy of the snow coming down,
To lie and to die in my terrible woe,
With a bed and a shroud of the beautiful snow.

———◆———

LXXXI.—PRESIDENT LINCOLN'S SPEECH AT THE GETTYS-BURG CEMETERY.

1. FOURSCORE and seven years ago our fathers brought forth upon this continent a new nation, conceived in liberty, and dedicated to the proposition that all men are created equal. Now we are engaged in a great civil war, testing whether that nation, or any nation so conceived and so dedicated, can long endure. We are met on a great battle-field of that war. We have come to dedicate a portion of that field as a final resting-place for those who gave their lives that that nation might live.

2. It is altogether fitting and proper that we should do this. But in a larger sense we cannot dedicate, we cannot consecrate, we cannot hallow this ground. The brave men, living and dead, who struggled here, have consecrated it far above our power to add or detract. The world will little note, nor long remember what we say here, but it can never forget what they did here. It is for us, the living, rather to be dedicated here to the unfinished work which those who fought here have thus far so nobly advanced.

3. It is rather for us to be here dedicated to the great task remaining before us, that from these honored dead we take increased devotion to that cause for which they gave the last full measures of devotion: that we here highly resolve that these dead shall not have died in vain: that this nation, under God, shall have a new birth of freedom,

and that Government *of* the people, *by* the people, and *for* the people, shall not perish from the earth.

LXXXII.—CHARACTER OF BLANNERHASSETT.
WIRT.

In 1807, Aaron Burr and others, among whom was Blannerhassett, were tried on an indictment for treason against the government of the United States. They were accused of a design to take possession of New Orleans, and to erect the country watered by the Mississippi and its branches, into an independent government. They were acquitted for want of evidence, though it was generally believed that Burr was guilty. The beautiful island, upon which Blannerhassett resided, is situated in the Ohio river, about 270 miles above Cincinnati. His former residence is now in ruins, but the island is still an object of curiosity to the traveller.

1. Let us put the case between Burr and Blannerhassett. Let us compare the two men, and settle the question of precedence between them. Who, then, is Blannerhassett? A native of Ireland, a man of letters, who fled from the storms of his own country, to find quiet in ours. Possessing himself of a beautiful island in the Ohio, he rears upon it a palace, and decorates it with every romantic embellishment of fancy. A shrubbery, that Shenstone might have envied, blooms around him. Music, that might have charmed Calypso and her nymphs, is his. An extensive library spreads its treasures before him. A philosophical apparatus offers to him all the secrets and mysteries of nature. Peace, tranquillity, and innocence shed their mingled delights around him.

2. The evidence would convince you, that this is but a faint picture of the real life. In the midst of all this peace, this innocent simplicity, and this tranquillity, this feast of the mind, this pure banquet of the heart, the destroyer comes : he comes to change this paradise into a hell. A stranger presents himself. Introduced to their civilities, by the high rank which he had lately held in his country, he soon finds his way to their hearts by the dignity and elegance of his demeanor, the light and beauty of his conversation, and the seductive and fascinating power of his address.

3. The conquest was not difficult. Innocence is ever simple and credulous. Conscious of no design itself, it suspects none in others. It wears no guard before its breast. Every door, and portal, and avenue of the heart is thrown open, and all who choose it, may enter. Such was the state of Eden, when the serpent entered its bowers. The prisoner, in a more engaging form, winding himself into the open and unpracticed heart of the unfortunate Blannerhassett, found but little difficulty in changing the native character of that heart, and the objects of its affection. By degrees, he infuses into it the fire of his own courage : a daring and desperate thirst for glory : an ardor panting for great enterprises, for all the storm, and bustle, and hurricane of life.

4. In a short time, the whole man is changed, and every object of his former life is relinquished. No more he enjoys the tranquil scene : it has become flat and insipid to his taste. His books are abandoned. His retort and crucible are thrown aside. His shrubbery blooms and breathes its fragrance upon the air in vain : he likes it not. His ear no longer drinks the rich melody of music : it longs for the trumpet's clangor and the cannon's roar. Even the prattle of his babes, once so sweet, no longer affects him ; and the angel smile of his wife, which hitherto touched his bosom with ecstacy so unspeakable, is now unseen and unfelt.

5. Greater objects have taken possession of his soul. His imagination has been dazzled by visions of diadems, of stars, and garters, and titles of nobility. He has been taught to burn, with restless emulation, at the names of great heroes and conquerors. His enchanted island is destined soon to relapse into a wilderness ; and, in a few months, the beautiful and tender partner of his bosom, whom he lately " permitted not- the winds of summer to visit too roughly," we find shivering, at midnight, on the winter banks of the Ohio, and mingling her tears with the torrents, that froze as they fell.

6. Yet this unfortunate man, thus deluded from his in-

terest and his happiness, thus seduced from the paths of innocence and peace, thus confounded in the toils that were deliberately spread for him, and overwhelmed by the mastering spirit and genius of another—this man, thus ruined and undone, and made to play a subordinate part in this grand drama of guilt and treason, this man is to be called the principal offender, while he, by whom he was thus plunged in misery, is comparatively innocent, a mere accessory!

7. Is this reason? Is it law? Is it humanity? Neither the human heart nor the human understanding, will bear a perversion so monstrous and absurd! so shocking to the soul! so revolting to reason! Let Aaron Burr, then, not shrink from the high destination which he has courted; and having already ruined Blannerhassett, in fortune, character, and happiness, forever, let him not attempt to finish the tragedy, by thrusting that ill-fated man between himself and punishment.

LXXXIII.—ON THE TRIAL OF A MURDERER.

DANIEL WEBSTER.

1. An aged man, without an enemy in the world, in his own house, and in his own bed, is made the victim of butcherly murder for mere pay. Truly, here is a new lesson for painters and poets. Whoever shall hereafter draw the portrait of murder, if he will show it, as it has been exhibited in an example, where such example was least to have been looked for, in the very bosom of our New England society, let him not give it the grim visage of Moloch, the brow knitted by revenge, the face black with settled hate, and the blood-shot eye emitting livid fires of malice: let him draw, rather, a decorous, smooth-faced, bloodless demon: a picture in repose, rather than in action; not so much an example of human nature in its depravity and in its paroxysms of crime, as an infernal nature, a fiend in the ordinary display and development of his character.

2. The deed was executed with a degree of self-possession and steadiness, equal to the wickedness with which it
was planned. The circumstances now clearly in evidence,
spread out the whole scene before us. Deep sleep had
fallen on the destined victim, and on all beneath his roof.
A healthful old man, to whom sleep was sweet; the first
sound slumbers of the night held him in their soft but
strong embrace. The assassin enters through the window,
already prepared, into an unoccupied apartment. With
noiseless foot he paces the lonely hall, half lighted by the
moon : he winds up the ascent of the stairs, and reaches
the door of the chamber. Of this, he moves the lock, by
soft and continued pressure, till it turns on its hinges ; and
he enters, and beholds his victim before him. The room
was uncommonly open to the admission of light. The face
of the innocent sleeper was turned from the murderer, and
the beams of the moon, resting on the gray locks of his
aged temple, showed him where to strike. The fatal blow
is given ! and the victim passes without a struggle or a
motion, from the repose of sleep to the repose of death !

3. It is the assassin's purpose to make sure work ; and
he yet plies the dagger, though it was obvious that life had
been destroyed by the blow of the bludgeon. He even
raises the aged arm, that he may not fail in his aim at the
heart ; and replaces it again over the wounds of the pon-
iard ! To finish the picture, he explores the wrist for the
pulse ! He feels it, and ascertains that it beats no longer !
It is accomplished. The deed is done. He retreats, re-
traces his steps to the window, passes out through it as he
came in, and escapes. He has done the murder : no eye
has seen him, no ear has heard him. The secret is his own,
and it is safe !

4. Ah ! gentlemen, that was a dreadful mistake. Such
a secret can be safe nowhere. The whole creation of God
has neither nook nor corner, where the guilty can bestow
it, and say it is safe. Not to speak of that eye which
glances through all disguises, and beholds every thing as in

the splendor of noon : such secrets of guilt are never safe from detection, even by men. True, it is, generally speaking, that "murder will out." True it is, that Providence hath so ordained, and doth so govern things, that those who break the great law of heaven, by shedding men's blood, seldom succeed in avoiding discovery. Especially, in a case exciting so much attention as this, discovery must come, and will come, sooner or later. A thousand eyes turn at once to explore every man, every thing, every circumstance connected with the time and place : a thousand ears catch every whisper : a thousand excited minds intensely dwell on the scene,—shedding all their light, and ready to kindle, at the slightest circumstance, into a blaze of discovery.

5. Meantime, the guilty soul cannot keep its own secret. It is false to itself, or rather, it feels an irresistible impulse to be true to itself. It labors under its guilty possession, and knows not what to do with it. The human heart was not made for the residence of such an inhabitant. It finds itself preyed on by a torment, which it does not acknowledge to God nor man. A vulture is devouring it, and it can ask no sympathy nor assistance, either from heaven or earth. The secret which the murderer possesses, soon comes to possess him ; and like the evil spirits of which we read, it overcomes him, and leads him whithersoever it will. He feels it beating at his heart, rising to his throat, and demanding disclosure. He thinks the whole world sees it in his face, reads it in his eyes, and almost hears its workings in the very silence of his thoughts. It has become his master. It betrays his discretion, it breaks down his courage, it conquers his prudence. When suspicions from without begin to embarrass him, and the net of circumstances to entangle him, the fatal secret struggles with still greater violence to burst forth. It *must* be confessed, it *will* be confessed : there is no refuge from confession but suicide, and suicide is confession.

LXXXIV.—CHARGE OF THE LIGHT BRIGADE.

ALFRED TENNYSON.

1. Half a league, half a league,
    Half a league onward,
   All in the valley of death
       Rode the six hundred.
   " Forward, the Light Brigade :
   Charge for the guns ! " he said.
   Into the valley of death,
       Rode the six hundred.

2. " Forward, the Light Brigade ! "
   Was there a man dismayed ?
   Not though the soldiers knew
       Some one had blundered :
   Theirs not to make reply,
   Theirs not to reason why,
   Theirs but to do and die :
   Into the valley of death
       Rode the six hundred.

3. Cannon to right of them,
   Cannon to left of them,
   Cannon in front of them
       Volleyed and thundered :
   Stormed at with shot and shell,
   Boldly they rode and well :
   Into the jaws of death,
   Into the mouth of hell,
       Rode the six hundred.

4. Flashed all their sabers bare,
   Flashed as they turned in air,
   Sab'ring the gunners there,
   Charging an army, while
       All the world wondered :
   Plunged in the battery smoke,
   Right through the line they broke :
   Cossack and Russian
   Reeled from the saber-stroke,
       Shattered and sundered.
   Then they rode back, but not,
       Not the six hundred.

5. Cannon to right of them,
Cannon to left of them,
Cannon behind them,
  Volleyed and thundered :
Stormed at with shot and shell,
While horse and hero fell,
They that had fought so well,
Came through the jaws of death,
Back from the mouth of hell,
  All that was left of them,
    Left of six hundred.

6. When can their glory fade ?
O, the wild charge they made !
  All the world wondered.
Honor the charge they made !
Honor the Light Brigade,
  Noble six hundred !

LXXXV.—" EXCELSIOR ! "

LONGFELLOW.

1. The shades of night were falling fast,
As through an Alpine village passed
A youth, who bore, 'mid snow and ice,
A banner with the strange device,
    " Excelsior ! "

2. His brow was sad : his eye, beneath,
Flashed like a falchion from its sheath :
And like a silver clarion rung
The accents of that unknown tongue,
    " Excelsior ! "

3. In happy homes he saw the light
Of household fires gleam warm and bright :
Above, the spectral glaciers shone ;
And from his lips escaped a groan,
    " Excelsior ! "

4. " Try not the pass ! " the old man said,
" Dark lowers the tempest overhead :
The roaring torrent 's deep and wide ! "
And loud that clarion voice replied,
    " Excelsior ! "

5. "Oh! stay," the maiden said, "and rest
Thy weary head upon this breast! "—
A tear stood in his bright blue eye;
But still he answered, with a sigh,
        " Excelsior ! "

6. " Beware the pine-tree's withered branch !
Beware the awful avalanche ! "
This was the peasant's last good-night ;—
A voice replied, far up the hight,
        " Excelsior ! "

7. At break of day, as heavenward
The pious monks of Saint Bernard
Uttered the oft-repeated prayer,
A voice cried through the startled air,
        " Excelsior ! "

8. A traveller, by the faithful hound,
Half-buried in the snow was found,
Still grasping in his hand of ice
That banner with the strange device,
        " Excelsior ! "

9. There, in the twilight cold and gray,
Lifeless, but beautiful, he lay ;
And from the sky, serene and far,
A voice fell, like a falling star—
        " Excelsior ! "

LXXXVI.—SOLILOQUY OF KING RICHARD III.

SHAKSPEARE.

1. GIVE me another horse—bind up my wounds—
Have mercy, Jesu—soft: I did but dream !
O, coward conscience, how dost thou afflict me !
The lights burn blue. It is now dead midnight.
What do I fear? Myself? There's none else by.
Richard loves Richard : that is, I am I.
Is there a murderer here? No : yes ; I am.
Then fly. What! From myself? Great reason, why?
Lest I revenge. What? Myself on myself?
I love myself? Wherefore? For any good
That I myself have done unto myself?
O, no : alas ! I rather hate myself,
For hateful deeds committed by myself.

2. I am a villain : yet I lie : I am not.
Fool, of thyself speak well—fool, do not flatter—
My conscience hath a thousand several tongues ;
And every tongue brings in a several tale ;
And every tale condemns me for a villain.
Perjury, perjury, in the highest degree,—
Murder, stern murder, in the direst degree,
Throng to the bar, crying all, Guilty ! guilty !
I shall despair. There is no creature loves me,
And, if I die, no soul will pity me ;
Nay ; wherefore should they ; since that I myself
Find in myself no pity to myself?—
Methought the souls of all that I had murdered
Came to my tent, and every one did threat
To-morrow's vengeance on the head of Richard.

LXXXVII.—MOONLIGHT AND MUSIC.

SHAKSPEARE.

1. How sweet the moonlight sleeps upon this bank !
Here will we sit, and let the sounds of music
Creep in our ears : soft stillness, and the night,
Become the touches of sweet harmony.
Sit, Jessica : Look, how the floor of heaven
Is thick inlaid with patines of bright gold :
There's not the smallest orb, which thou beholdest,
But in his motion like an angel sings,
Still quiring to the young-eyed cherubim :
But, while this muddy vesture of decay
Doth grossly close it in, we cannot hear it—
Come, ho ! and wake Diana with a hymn ;
With sweetest touches pierce your mistress' ear,
And draw her home with music.

2. Do thou but note a wild and wanton herd,
Or race of youthful and unhandled colts,
Fetching mad bounds, bellowing, and neighing loud,
Which is the hot condition of their blood ;
If they but hear perchance a trumpet sound,
Or any air of music touch their ears,
You shall perceive them make a mutual stand,
Their savage eyes turned to a modest gaze,
9

By the sweet power of music. Therefore, the poet
Did feign that Orpheus drew trees, stones, and floods:
Since nought so stockish hard, and full of rage,
But music for the time doth change his nature.
The man that hath no music in himself,
Nor is not moved with concord of sweet sounds,
Is fit for treasons, stratagems, and spoils:
The motions of his spirit are dull as night,
And his affections dark as Erebus:
Let no such man be trusted.

LXXXVIII.—THE ISLES OF GREECE.

BYRON.

1. THE isles of Greece! the isles of Greece!
    Where burning Sappho loved and sung:
    Where grew the arts of war and peace:
      Where Delos rose, and Phœbus sprung!
    Eternal summer gilds them yet;
    But all, except their sun, is set.

2. The mountains look on Marathon—
      And Marathon looks on the sea;
    And musing there an hour alone,
      I dreamed that Greece might still be free;
    For, standing on the Persian's grave,
    I could not deem myself a slave.

3. 'Tis something, in the dearth of fame,
      Though linked among a fettered race,
    To feel at least a patriot's shame,
      Even as I sing, suffuse my face;
    For what is left the poet here?
    For Greeks a blush—for Greece a tear.

4. Must we but weep o'er days more blessed?
      Must we but blush?—Our fathers bled—
    Earth! render back from out thy breast
      A remnant of our Spartan dead!
    Of the three hundred grant but three,
    To make a new Thermopylæ.

5. What! silent still? and silent all?
      Ah! no;—the voices of the dead
    Sound like a distant torrent's fall,
      And answer, "Let one living head,

But one arise,—we come, we come !"
'Tis but the living who are dumb.

6. In vain—in vain : strike other chords :
   Fill high the cup with Samian wine !
Leave battles to the Turkish hordes,
   And shed the blood of Scio's vine !—
Hark ! rising to the ignoble call,
How answers each bold bacchanal !

7. The tyrant of the Chersonese
   Was freedom's best and bravest friend :
That tyrant was Miltiades !
   O that the present hour would lend
Another despot of the kind !
Such chains as his were sure to bind.

8. Trust not for freedom to the Franks—
   They have a king who buys and sells.
In native swords and native ranks
   The only hope of courage dwells ;
But Turkish force and Latin fraud
Would break your shield, however broad.

9. Place me on Sunium's marble steep,
   Where nothing, save the waves and I,
May hear our mutual murmurs sweep ;
   There, swan-like, let me sing and die :
A land of slaves shall ne'er be mine—
Dash down yon cup of Samian wine !

LXXXIX.—WHAT IS TIME?

MARSDEN.

1. I ASKED an aged man, a man of cares,
   Wrinkled, and curved, and white with hoary hairs :
"Time is the warp of life," he said, " oh tell
The young, the fair, the gay, to weave it *well*."

2. I asked the ancient, venerable dead,
   Sages who wrote, and warriors who bled :
From the cold grave a hollow murmur flowed,
" Time sowed the seed we reap in this abode ! "

3. I asked the dying sinner, ere the tide
   Of life had left his veins : " Time ! " he replied :
" I've lost it ! Ah, the treasure ! " and he died.

4. I asked a spirit lost; but oh, the shriek
  That pierced my soul! I shudder while I speak!
  It cried, " A particle! a speck! a mite
  Of endless years, duration infinite!"

5. I asked my Bible; and, methinks, it said,
  " Time is the *present hour :* the past is fled :
  Live! live to-day! to-morrow never yet
  On any human being rose or set."

6. I asked old Father Time himself, at last;
  But in a moment, he flew swiftly past,
  His chariot was a cloud, the viewless wind
  His noiseless steeds, which left no trace behind.

7. I asked the mighty Angel who shall stand
  One foot on sea, and one on solid land :
  " I now declare, the mystery is o'er :
  Time *was*," he cried, " but Time shall be no more!"

XC.—DEATH AND THE DRUNKARD.

1. His form was fair, his cheek was health :
  His word a bond, his purse was wealth;
  With wheat his field was covered o'er,
  Plenty sat smiling at his door.
  His wife, the fount of ceaseless joy :
  Now laughed his daughter, played his boy :
  His library, though large, was read
  Till half its contents decked his head.
  At morn, 'twas health, wealth, pure delight,
  'Twas health, wealth, peace, and bliss at night.
  I wished not to disturb his bliss :
  'Tis gone! but all the fault is his.

2. The social glass I saw him seize,
  The more with festive wit to please,
  Daily increase his love of cheer :
  Ah, little thought he *I* was near!
  Gradual indulgence on him stole,
  Frequent became the midnight bowl.
  I, in that bowl, the *headache* placed,
  Which, with the juice, his lips embraced.
  Shame next I mingled with the draught :
  Indignantly he drank, and laughed.

3. In the bowl's bottom, *bankruptcy*
I placed : he drank with tears and glee.
Remorse did I into it pour :
He only sought the bowl the more.
I mingled, next, *joint torturing pain :*
Little the more did he refrain.
The *dropsy* in the cup I mixed ;
Still to his mouth the cup was fixed.
My emissaries thus in vain
I sent, the mad wretch to restrain.

4. On the bowl's bottom, then, *myself*
I threw : the most abhorrent elf
Of all that mortals hate or dread ;
And thus in horrid whispers said,
"Successless ministers I've sent,
Thy hastening ruin to prevent :
Their lessons naught : then here am I :
Think not my threatenings to defy.
Swallow this, this thy last will be,
For with it, thou must swallow me."

5. Haggard his eyes, upright his hair,
Remorse his lips, his cheeks despair :
With shaking hands the bowl he clasp'd,
My meatless limbs his carcass grasp'd
And bore it to the church-yard, where
Thousands, ere I would call, repair.

6. Death speaks : ah, reader, dost thou hear ?
Hast thou no lurking cause to fear ?
Has not o'er *thee* the sparkling bowl,
Constant, commanding, sly control ?
Betimes reflect, betimes beware,
Though ruddy, healthful now, and fair :
Before slow reason lose the sway,
Reform : postpone another day,
You soon may mix with common clay.

XCI.—HAMLET'S SOLILOQUY.

SHAKSPEARE.

1. To be or not to be—that is the question !
Whether 'tis nobler in the mind to suffer

The stings and arrows of outrageous fortune,
Or to take arms against a sea of troubles,
And, by opposing, end them : To die—to sleep—
No more !—and, by a sleep, to say we end
The heart-ache, and the thousand natural shocks
That flesh is heir to—'tis a consummation
Devoutly to be wished.

2. To die—to sleep :
   To sleep ?—perchance to dream—aye, there's the rub !
   For, in that sleep of death, what dreams may come,
   When we have shuffled off this mortal coil,
   Must give us pause !   There's the respect,
   That makes calamity of so long life :
   For who would bear the whips and scorns of time,
   The oppressor's wrong, the proud man's contumely,
   The pangs of despised love, the law's delay,
   The insolence of office, and the spurns
   That patient merit of the unworthy takes—
   When he himself might his quietus make
   With a bare bodkin ?

3. Who would fardels bear,
   To groan and sweat under a weary life,
   But that the dread of something after death—
   That undiscovered country, from whose bourne
   No traveller returns—puzzles the will,
   And makes us rather bear those ills we have,
   Than fly to others that we know not of !

4. Thus, conscience does make cowards of us all :
   And thus, the native hue of resolution
   Is sicklied o'er with the pale cast of thought ;
   And enterprises of great pith and moment,
   With this regard, their currents turn awry,
   And lose the name of action.

XCII.—THE MANIAC.

LEWIS.

1. STAY, jailer, stay, and hear my woe !
   She is not mad that kneels to thee ;
   For what I'm now, too well I know,
   And what I was, and what should be.

I'll rave no more in proud despair :
  My language shall be mild, though sad :
But yet I firmly, truly swear,
  I am not mad, I am not mad.

2. My tyrant husband forged the tale
    Which chains me in this dismal cell :
  My fate unknown my friends bewail—
    Oh ! jailer, haste that fate to tell :
  Oh ! haste my father's heart to cheer :
    His heart at once 'twill grieve and glad
  To know, though kept a captive here,
    I am not mad, I am not mad.

3. He smiles in scorn, and turns the key :
    He quits the grate : I knelt in vain :
  His glimmering lamp, still, still I see—
    'Tis gone ! and all is gloom again.
  Cold, bitter cold !—No warmth ! no light !—
    Life, all thy comforts once I had ;
  Yet here I'm chained, this freezing night,
    Although not mad : no, no, not mad.

4. 'Tis sure some dream, some vision vain :
    What ! I—the child of rank and wealth—
  Am I the wretch who clanks this chain,
    Bereft of freedom, friends, and health ?
  Ah ! while I dwell on blessings fled,
    Which never more my heart must glad,
  How aches my heart, how burns my head,
    But 'tis not mad : no, 'tis not mad.

5. Hast thou, my child, forgot, ere this,
    A mother's face, a mother's tongue ?
  She'll ne'er forget your parting kiss,
    Nor round her neck how fast you clung ;
  Nor how with her you sued to stay ;
    Nor how that suit your sire forbade ;
  Nor how—I'll drive such thoughts away ;
    They'll make me mad, they'll make me mad.

6. His rosy lips, how sweet they smiled !
    His mild blue eyes, how bright they shone !
  None ever bore a lovelier child ;
    And art thou now forever gone ?

And must I never see thee more,
My pretty, pretty, pretty lad ?
I will be free ! unbar the door !
I am not mad : I am not mad.

7. Oh ! hark ! what mean those yells and cries ?
His chain some furious madman breaks :
He comes—I see his glaring eyes :
Now, now, my dungeon-grate he shakes.
Help ! help !—he's gone !—oh ! fearful woe,
Such screams to hear, such sights to see !
My brain, my brain—I know, I know,
I am not mad, but soon shall be.

8. Yes, soon ; for, lo you !—while I speak—
Mark how yon demon's eyeballs glare !
He sees me : now, with dreadful shriek,
He whirls a serpent high in air.
Horror !—the reptile strikes his tooth
Deep in my heart, so crushed and sad :
Ay, laugh, ye fiends : I feel the truth :
Your task is done—I'm mad ! I'm mad !

XCIII.—DARKNESS.

BYRON.

1. I HAD a dream, which was not all a dream.
The bright sun was extinguished, and the stars
Did wander, darkling, in the eternal space,
Rayless and pathless, and the icy earth
Swung blind and blackening in the moonless air.
Morn came and went—and came, and brought no day,
And men forgot their passions, in the dread
Of this their desolation ; and all hearts
Were chilled into a selfish prayer for light.
And they did live by watch-fires ; and the thrones,
The palaces of crowned kings, the huts,
The habitations of all things which dwell,
Were burnt for beacons : cities were consumed,
And men were gathered round their blazing homes,
To look once more into each other's face.
Happy were those who dwelt within the eye
Of the volcanoes and their mountain torch.

2. A fearful hope was all the world contained :
   Forests were set on fire ; but, hour by hour,
   They fell and faded ; and the crackling trunks
   Extinguished with a crash—and all was black.
   The brows of men, by their despairing light,
   Wore an unearthly aspect, as, by fits,
   The flashes fell upon them.   Some lay down,
   And hid their eyes, and wept ; and some did rest
   Their chins upon their clenched hands, and smiled ;
   And others hurried to and fro, and fed
   Their funeral piles with fuel, and looked up,
   With mad disquietude, on the dull sky,
   The pall of a past world ; and then again
   With curses, cast them down upon the dust,
   And gnashed their teeth, and howled.   The wild birds shrieked,
   And, terrified, did flutter on the ground,   .
   And flap their useless wings : the wildest brutes
   Came tame, and tremulous ; and vipers crawled
   And twined themselves among the multitude,
   Hissing, but stingless—they were slain for food.

3. And War, which for a moment was no more,
   Did glut himself again :—a meal was bought
   With blood, and each sat sullenly apart,
   Gorging himself in gloom : no love was left :
   All earth was but one thought—and that was death,
   Immediate and inglorious, and the pang
   Of famine fed upon all entrails.   Men
   Died ; and their bones were tombless as their flesh
   The meager by the meager were devoured.
   Even dogs assailed their masters,—all save one,
   And he was faithful to a corse, and kept
   The birds, and beasts, and famished men at bay,
   Till hunger clung them, or the drooping dead
   Lured their lank jaws : himself sought out no food,
   But, with a piteous, and perpetual moan,
   And a quick, desolate cry, licking the hand
   Which answered not with a caress—he died.

4. The crowd was famished by degrees.   But two
   Of an enormous city did survive,
   And they were enemies.   They met beside
   The dying embers of an altar-place,
   Where had been heaped a mass of holy things
   For an unholy usage.   They raked up,
   9*

And, shivering, scraped with their cold, skeleton hands,
The feeble ashes; and their feeble breath
Blew for a little life, and made a flame,
Which was a mockery. Then they lifted
Their eyes as it grew lighter, and beheld
Each other's aspects—saw, and shrieked, and died;
Even of their mutual hideousness they died,
Unknowing who he was, upon whose brow
Famine had written Fiend.

5.   The world was void:
The populous and the powerful was a lump,
Seasonless, herbless, treeless, manless, lifeless:
A lump of death, a chaos of hard clay.
The rivers, lakes, and ocean, all stood still,
And nothing stirred within their silent depths.
Ships, sailorless, lay rotting on the sea,
And their masts fell down piecemeal: as they dropped
They slept on the abyss, without a surge,—
The waves were dead: the tides were in their grave:
The moon, their mistress, had expired before:
The winds were withered in the stagnant air,
And the clouds perished: Darkness had no need
Of aid from them—she was the universe.

XCIV.—THE AMBITIOUS YOUTH.

E. Burritt.

The incident described in this selection occurred, some years since, at the Natural Bridge, in Virginia. This bridge is an immense mass of rock, thrown by the hand of nature over a considerable stream of water, thus forming a natural passage over the stream.

1. THERE are three or four lads standing in the channel below the natural bridge, looking up with awe to that vast arch of unhewn rocks, which the Almighty bridged over these everlasting abutments, "when the morning stars sang together." The little piece of sky spanning those measureless piers, is full of stars, although it is mid-day. It is almost five hundred feet from where they stand, up those perpendicular bulwarks of limestone to the key-rock of that vast arch, which appears to them only the size of a man's hand. The silence of death is rendered more im-

pressive by the little stream that falls from rock to rock
down the channel. .The sun is darkened, and the boys
have unconsciously uncovered their heads, as if standing
in the presence-chamber of the Majesty of the whole earth.

2. At last, this feeling begins to wear away : they begin to look around them. They see the names of hundreds
cut in the limestone abutments. A new feeling comes over
their young hearts, and their knives are in their hands, in
an instant. " What man has done, man can do," is their
watchword, as they draw themselves up and carve their
names a foot above those of a hundred full-grown men who
had been there before them. They are all satisfied with
this feat of physical exertion except one, whose example
illustrates perfectly the forgotten truth, that there is no
royal road to intellectual eminence. This ambitious youth
sees a name just above his reach, a name that will be green
in the memory of the world, when those of Alexander,
Cesar, and Bonaparte shall rot in oblivion. It was the
name of WASHINGTON. Before he marched with Braddock
to that fatal field, he had been there and left his name a
foot above all his predecessors.

3. It was a glorious thought of the boy, to write his
name, side by side with that of the great father of his
country. He grasps his knife with a firmer hand; and,
clinging to a little jutting crag, he cuts again into the limestone, about a foot above where he stands : he then reaches
up and cuts another place for his hands. It is a dangerous
adventure ; but as he puts his feet and hands into those
notches, and draws himself up carefully to his full length,
he finds himself a foot above every name chronicled in
that mighty wall. While his companions are regarding
him with concern and admiration, he cuts his name in rude
capitals, large and deep, into that flinty album. His knife
is still in his hand, and strength in his sinews, and a new-
created aspiration in his heart. Again he cuts another
niche, and again he carves his name in large capitals.

4. This is not enough. Heedless of the entreaties of

his companions, he cuts and climbs again. The graduations of his ascending scale grow wider apart. He measures his length at every gain he cuts. The voices of his friends wax weaker and weaker, till their words are finally lost on his ear. He now, for the first time, casts a look beneath him. Had that glance lasted a moment, that moment would have been his last. He clings with a convulsive shudder to his little niche in the rock. An awful abyss awaits his almost certain fall. He is faint with severe exertion, and trembling from the sudden view of the dreadful destruction to which he is exposed. His knife is worn half-way to the haft. He can hear the voices, but not the words, of his terror-stricken companions below. What a moment! What a meager chance to escape destruction! There was no retracing his steps. It is impossible to put his hands into the same niche with his feet, and retain his slender hold a moment.

5. His companions instantly perceive this new and fearful dilemma, and await his fall with emotions that " freeze their young blood." He is too high, too faint, to ask for his father and mother, his brothers and sisters, to come and witness or avert his destruction. But one of his companions anticipates his desire. Swift as the wind, he bounds down the channel, and the situation of the fated boy is told upon his father's hearth-stone.

6. Minutes of almost eternal length roll on ; and there are hundreds standing in that rocky channel, and hundreds on the bridge above, all holding their breath, and awaiting the fearful catastrophe. The poor boy hears the hum of new and numerous voices both above and below. He can just distinguish the tones of his father, who is shouting with all the energy of despair, " *William! William! don't look down! Your mother, and Henry, and Harriet, are all here praying for you! Don't look down! Keep your eye toward the top!*" The boy did not look *down*. His eye is fixed like a flint toward Heaven, and his young heart on him who reigns there.

7. He grasps again his knife. He cuts another niche, and another foot is added to the hundreds that remove him from the reach of human help from below. How carefully he uses his wasting blade! How anxiously he selects the softest places in that vast pier! How he avoids every flinty grain! How he economizes his physical powers, resting a moment at each gain he cuts. How every motion is watched from below. There stand his father, mother, brother, and sister, on the very spot, where, if he falls, he will not fall alone.

8. The sun is now half way down the west. The lad has made fifty additional niches in that mighty wall, and now finds himself directly under the middle of that vast arch of rocks, earth, and trees. He must cut his way in a new direction, to get from under this overhanging mountain. The inspiration of hope is dying in his bosom: its vital heat is fed by the increased shouts of hundreds perched upon cliffs and trees, and others, who stand with ropes in their hands on the bridge above, or with ladders below. Fifty gains more must be cut, before the longest rope can reach him. His wasting blade strikes again into the limestone. The boy is emerging painfully, foot by foot, from under that lofty arch.

9. Spliced ropes are ready in the hands of those who are leaning over the outer edge of the bridge. Two minutes more and all will be over. The blade is worn to the last half inch. The boy's head reels: his eyes are starting from their sockets. His last hope is dying in his heart: his life must hang upon the next gain he cuts. That niche is his last. At the last faint gash he makes, his knife, his faithful knife, falls from his nerveless hand, and ringing along the precipice, falls at his mother's feet. An involuntary groan of despair runs like a death-knell through the channel below, and all is still as the grave.

10. At the hight of nearly three hundred feet, the devoted boy lifts his hopeless heart and closing eyes to commend his soul to God. 'Tis but a moment—there!—one

foot swings off!—he is reeling—trembling—toppling over into eternity! Hark! a shout falls on his ear from above! The man who is lying with half his length over the bridge, has caught a glimpse of the boy's head and shoulders. Quick as thought, the noosed rope is within reach of the sinking youth. No one breathes. With a faint convulsive effort, the swooning boy drops his arms into the noose. Darkness comes over him, and with the words, God! and mother! whispered on his lips just loud enough to be heard in heaven, the tightening rope lifts him out of his last shallow niche. Not a lip moves while he is dangling over that fearful abyss: but when a sturdy Virginian reaches down and draws up the lad, and holds him up in his arms before the tearful, breathless multitude, such shouting, such leaping and weeping for joy, never greeted the ear of human being so recovered from the yawning gulf of eternity.

XCV.—SOLILOQUY OF A DRUNKARD'S WIFE.

1. TIME was, when much he loved me;
When we walked out, at close of day, t' inhale
The vernal breeze. Ah, well do I remember,
How, then, with careful hand, he drew my mantle
Round me, fearful lest the evening dews
Should mar my fragile health. Yes, then his eye
Looked kindly on me when my heart was sad.
How tenderly he wiped my tears away,
While from his lips the words of gentle soothing
In softest accents fell!

2. How blest my evenings too, when wintery blasts
Were howling round our peaceful dwelling!
Oh, it was sweet, the daily task performed,
By the sweet hearth and cheerful fire, to sit
With him I loved: to view with glistening eye,
And all a parent's fondness, the budding graces
Of our little ones.

3. Then ye had a father,
My lovely babes, my more than helpless orphans.

Your mother more than widowed grief has known:
Yes, sharper pangs than those who mourn the dead,
Seized on my breaking heart, when first I knew
My lover, husband—oh, my earthly all—
Was dead to virtue; when I saw the man
My soul too fondly loved, transformed to brute.
Oh, it was then I tasted gall and wormwood!

4. Then the world looked dreary: fearful clouds
Quick gathered round me: dark forebodings came:
The grave, before, was terror; now it smiled:
I longed to lay me down in peaceful rest,
There to forget my sorrows. But I lived,
And, oh, my God! what years of woe have followed!
I feel my heart is broken. He who vowed
To cherish me—before God's altar vowed—
Has done the deed. And shall I then upbraid him—
The husband of my youthful days—the man
To whom I gave my virgin heart away?
Patient I'll bear it all.

5. Peace, peace, my heart!
'Tis almost o'er. A few more stormy blasts,
And then this shattered, broken frame will fall,
And sweetly slumber where
The wicked cease from troubling,
And the weary are at rest.

* * *

XCVI.—BINGEN ON THE RHINE.

MRS. NORTON.

1. A soldier of the Legion lay dying in Algiers,
There was lack of woman's nursing, there was dearth of woman's tears;
But a comrade stood beside him, while his life-blood ebbed away,
And bent, with pitying glances, to hear what he might say.
The dying soldier faltered, as he took that comrade's hand,
And he said, "I never more shall see my own, my native land:
Take a message, and a token, to some distant friends of mine,
For I was born at Bingen—at Bingen on the Rhine.

2. "Tell my brothers and companions, when they meet and crowd around
To hear my mournful story in the pleasant vineyard ground,
That we fought the battle bravely, and when the day was done,
Full many a corse lay ghastly pale, beneath the setting sun.

And midst the dead and dying, were some grown old in wars,
The death-wound on their gallant breasts, the last of many scars:
But some were young—and suddenly beheld life's morn decline;
And one had come from Bingen—fair Bingen on the Rhine!

3. " Tell my mother that her other sons shall comfort her old age,
And I was aye a truant bird, that thought his home a cage:
For my father was a soldier, and even as a child
My heart leaped forth to hear him tell of struggles fierce and wild;
And when he died, and left us to divide his scanty hoard,
I let them take whate'er they would, but kept my father's sword,
And with boyish love I hung it where the bright light used to shine,
On the cottage-wall at Bingen—calm Bingen on the Rhine!

4. " Tell my sister not to weep for me, and sob with drooping head,
When the troops are marching home again, with glad and gallant tread;
But to look upon them proudly, with a calm and steadfast eye,
For her brother was a soldier too, and not afraid to die.
And if a comrade seek her love, I ask her in my name
To listen to him kindly, without regret or shame;
And to hang the old sword in its place (my father's sword and mine),
For the honor of old Bingen—dear Bingen on the Rhine!

5. " There's another—not a sister: in the happy days gone by,
You'd have known her by the merriment that sparkled in her eye:
Too innocent for coquetry,—too fond for idle scorning,—
Oh! friend, I fear the lightest heart makes sometimes heaviest mourning:
Tell her the last night of my life (for ere the moon be risen
My body will be out of pain—my soul be out of prison),
I dreamed I stood with *her*, and saw the yellow sunlight shine
On the vine-clad hills of Bingen—fair Bingen on the Rhine!

6. " I saw the blue Rhine sweeping along—I heard, or seemed to hear
The German songs we used to sing, in chorus sweet and clear;
And down the pleasant river, and up the slanting hill,
The echoing chorus sounded, through the evening calm and still;
And her glad blue eyes were on me as we passed with friendly talk
Down many a path beloved of yore, and well-remembered walk,
And her little hand lay lightly, confidingly in mine:
But we'll meet no more at Bingen—loved Bingen on the Rhine!"

7. His voice grew faint and hoarser,—his grasp was childish weak,—
His eyes put on a dying look,—he sighed and ceased to speak:
His comrade bent to lift him, but the spark of life had fled,—
The soldier of the Legion, in a foreign land—was dead!

And the soft moon rose up slowly, and calmly she looked down
On the red sand of the battle-field, with bloody corpses strown:
Yea, calmly on that dreadful scene her pale light seemed to shine,
As it shone on distant Bingen—fair Bingen on the Rhine!

XCVII.—NEW ENGLAND AND THE UNION.

S. S. PRENTISS.

1. GLORIOUS New England! thou art still true to thy ancient fame, and worthy of thy ancestral honors. On thy pleasant valleys rest, like sweet dews of morning, the gentle recollections of our early life; around thy hills and mountains cling, like gathering mists, the mighty memories of the Revolution; and far away in the horizon of thy past gleam, like thy own bright northern lights, the awful virtues of our pilgrim sires! But while we devote this day to the remembrance of our native land, we forget not that in which our happy lot is cast.

2. We exult in the reflection, that though we count by thousands the miles which separate us from our birthplace, still our country is the same. We are no exiles meeting upon the banks of a foreign river, to swell its waters with our homesick tears. Here floats the same banner which rustled above our boyish heads, except that its mighty folds are wider, and its glittering stars increased in number.

3. The sons of New England are found in every State of the broad republic! In the East, the South, and the unbounded West, their blood mingles freely with every kindred current. We have but changed our chamber in the paternal mansion; in all its rooms we are at home, and all who inhabit it are our brothers. To us the Union has but one domestic hearth; its household gods are all the same. Upon us, then, peculiarly devolves the duty of feeding the fires upon that kindly hearth; of guarding with pious care those sacred household gods.

4. We cannot do with less than the whole Union; to us it admits of no division. In the veins of our children

flows northern and southern blood: how shall it be separated?—who shall put asunder the best affections of the heart, the noblest instincts of our nature? We love the land of our adoption; so do we that of our birth. Let us ever be true to both; and always exert ourselves in maintaining the unity of our country, the integrity of the republic. Accursed, then, be the hand put forth to loosen the golden cord of union! thrice accursed the traitorous lips which shall propose its severance!

XCVIII.—A PSALM OF LIFE.

H. W. LONGFELLOW.

1. TELL me not in mournful numbers,
  Life is but an empty dream!
 For the soul is dead that slumbers,
  And things are not what they seem.

2. Life is real! Life is earnest!
  And the grave is not its goal:
 Dust thou art, to dust returnest,
  Was not written of the soul.

3. Not enjoyment, and not sorrow,
  Is our destined end and way,
 But to act, that each to-morrow
  Find us further than to-day.

4. Art is long, and time is fleeting,
  And our hearts, though stout and brave,
 Still, like muffled drums, are beating
  Funeral marches to the grave.

5. In the world's broad field of battle,
  In the bivouac of life,
 Be not like dumb, driven cattle!
  Be a hero in the strife!

6. Trust not Future, howe'er pleasant!
  Let the dead Past bury its dead!
 Act!—act in the living Present!
  Heart within, and God o'er head.

7. Lives of great men all remind us
　　We can make our lives sublime,
　　And, departing, leave behind us
　　　Footprints on the sands of time:

8. Footprints, that perhaps another,
　　Sailing o'er life's solemn main,
　　A forlorn and shipwreck'd brother,
　　　Seeing, shall take heart again.

9. Let us, then, be up and doing,
　　With a heart for any fate:
　　Still achieving, still pursuing,
　　　Learn to labor and to wait.

XCIX.—AFFECTATION IN THE PULPIT.

WILLIAM COWPER.

1. IN man or woman,—but far most in man,
And most of all in man that ministers　.
And serves the altar,—in my soul I loathe
All affectation.　'T is my perfect scorn:
Object of my implacable disgust.
What!—will a man play tricks,—will he indulge
A silly, fond conceit of his fair form,
And just proportion, fashionable mien,
And pretty face,—in presence of his God?
Or will he seek to dazzle me with tropes,
As with the diamond on his lily hand,
And play his brilliant parts before my eyes,
When I am hungry for the bread of life?
He mocks his Maker, prostitutes and shames
His noble office, and, instead of truth,
Displaying his own beauty, starves his flock!
Therefore, avaunt all attitude, and stare,
And start theatric, practised at the glass!
I seek divine simplicity in him
Who handles things divine; and all besides,
Though learned with labor, and though much admired
By curious eyes and judgments ill-informed,
To me is odious as the nasal twang
Heard at conventicle, where worthy men,
Misled by custom strain celestial themes
Through the pressed nostril, spectacle-bestrid.

2.   I venerate the man whose heart is warm,
Whose hands are pure, whose doctrine and whose life,
Coïncident, exhibit lucid proof
That he is honest in the sacred cause.
To such I render more than mere respect,
Whose actions say that they respect themselves.
But loose in morals, and in manners vain,
In conversation frivolous, in dress
Extreme, at once rapacious and profuse:
Frequent in park with lady at his side,   ˝
Ambling and prattling scandal as he goes;
But rare at home, and never at his books,
Or with his pen, save when he scrawls a card:
Constant at routs, familiar with a round
Of ladyships—a stranger to the poor:
Ambitious of preferment for its gold;
And well prepared, by ignorance and sloth,
By infidelity and love of world,
To make God's work a sinecure—a slave
To his own pleasures and his patron's pride;—
From such apostles, O, ye mitred heads,
Preserve the Church! and lay not careless hands
On skulls that cannot teach, and will not learn!

C.—LEAP FOR LIFE.

GEO. P. MORRIS.

1.   OLD Ironsides at anchor lay
In the harbor of Mahon:
A dead calm rested on the bay,
And the winds to sleep had gone:
When little Jack, the captain's son,
With gallant hardihood,
Climbed shroud and spar, and then upon
The main truck rose and stood.

2.   A shudder ran through every vein,
All hands were turned on high:
There stood the boy with dizzy brain,
Between the sea and sky.
No hold had he above, below,
Alone he stood in air:
At that far height none dared to go:
No aid could reach him there.

3. We gazed, but not a man could speak,
　　With horror all aghast:
　In groups, with pallid brow and cheek,
　　We watched the quivering mast.
　The atmosphere grew thick and hot,
　　And of a lurid hue,
　As riveted unto the spot
　　Stood officers and crew.

4. The father came on deck,—he gasped,
　　"Oh God! thy will be done!"
　Then suddenly a rifle grasped,
　　And aimed it at his son;—
　"Jump! far out, boy, into the wave,
　　Jump, or I fire!" he said:
　"This chance alone your life can save,
　　Jump! jump!"　The boy obeyed.

5. He sunk, he rose, he lived, he moved,
　　He for the ship struck out—
　On board we hailed the lad beloved,
　　With many a manly shout:
　His father drew, with silent joy,
　　Those wet arms round his neck,
　And folded to his heart the boy,
　　Then fainted on the deck.

CI.—"CLEON AND I."

CHARLES MACKAY

1. CLEON hath a million acres,—ne'er a one have I:
　Cleon dwelleth in a palace,—in a cottage, I:
　Cleon hath a dozen fortunes,—not a penny, I;
　But the poorer of the twain is Cleon, and not I.

2. Cleon, true, possesseth acres,—but the landscape, I:
　Half the charms to *me* it yieldeth money cannot buy:
　Cleon harbors sloth and dulness,—freshening vigor, I:
　He in velvet, I in fustian,—richer man am I.

3. Cleon is a slave to grandeur,—free as thought am I:
　Cleon fees a score of doctors,—need of none have I.
　Wealth-surrounded, care-environed, Cleon fears to die:
　Death may come,—he'll find me ready,—happier man am I.

4. Cleon sees no charms in Nature,—in a daisy, I :
Cleon hears no anthems ringing in the sea and sky.
Nature sings to me forever,—earnest listener I :
State for state, with all attendants, who would change? Not I.

———◆———

CII.—THE PROBLEM FOR THE UNITED STATES.

REV. HENRY A. BOARDMAN.

1. THIS Union cannot expire as the snow melts from the rock, or a star disappears from the firmament. When it falls, the crash will be heard in all lands. Wherever the winds of Heaven go, that will go, bearing sorrow and dismay to millions of stricken hearts ; for the subversion of this Government will render the cause of Constitutional Liberty hopeless throughout the world. What Nation can govern itself, if this Nation cannot ? What encouragement will any People have to establish liberal institutions for themselves, if ours fail ? Providence has laid upon us the responsibility and the honor of solving that problem in which all coming generations of men have a profound interest,—whether the true ends of Government can be secured by a popular representative system.

2. In the munificence of his goodness, He put us in possession of our heritage, by a series of interpositions scarcely less signal than those which conducted the Hebrews to Canaan ; and He has, up to this period, withheld from us no immunities or resources which might facilitate an auspicious result. Never before was a People so advantageously situated for working out this great problem in favor of human liberty ; and it is important for us to understand that the world so regards it.

3. If, in the frenzy of our base sectional jealousies, we dig the grave of the Union, and thus decide this question in the negative, no tongue may attempt to depict the disappointment and despair which will go along with the announcement, as it spreads through distant lands. It will be America, after fifty years' experience, giving in her

adhesion to the doctrine that man was not made for self-government. It will be Freedom herself proclaiming that Freedom is a chimera : Liberty ringing her own knell, all over the globe.

4. And, when the citizens or *subjects* of the Governments which are to succeed this Union shall visit Europe, and see, in some land now struggling to cast off its fetters, the lacerated and lifeless form of Liberty laid prostrate under the iron heel of Despotism, let them remember that the blow which destroyed her was inflicted by their own country.

> "So the struck Eagle, stretched upon the plain,
> No more through rolling clouds to soar again,
> Viewed his own feather on the fatal dart,
> And winged the shaft that quivered in his heart.
> Keen were his pangs, but keener far to feel
> He nursed the pinion which impelled the steel ;
> While the same plumage that had warmed his nest
> Drank the last life-drop of his bleeding breast."

CIII.—THE AMERICAN EXPERIMENT OF SELF-GOVERNMENT.

EDWARD EVERETT.

1. WE are summoned to new energy and zeal by the high nature of the experiment we are appointed in Providence to make, and the grandeur of the theatre on which it is to be performed. At a moment of deep and general agitation in the Old World, it pleased Heaven to open this last refuge of humanity. The attempt has begun and is going on, far from foreign corruption, on the broadest scale, and under the most benignant prospects ; and it certainly rests with us to solve the great problem in human society, —to settle, and that forever, the momentous question,— whether mankind can be trusted with a purely popular system of Government ?

2. One might almost think, without extravagance, that the departed wise and good, of all places and times, are looking down from their happy seats to witness what shall

now be done by us—that they who lavished their treasures
and their blood of old,—who spake and wrote, who labored,
fought and perished, in the one great cause of Freedom
and Truth,—are now hanging, from their orbs on high,
over the last solemn experiment of humanity.

3. As I have wandered over the spots once the scene
of their labors, and mused among the prostrate columns of
their senate-houses and forums, I have seemed almost to
hear a voice from the tombs of departed ages, from the
sepulchres of the Nations which died before the sight.
They exhort us, they adjure us, to be faithful to our trust.
They implore us, by the long trials of struggling humanity:
by the blessed memory of the departed : by the dear faith
which has been plighted by pure hands to the holy cause
of truth and man : by the awful secrets of the prison-house,
where the sons of freedom have been immured: by the
noble heads which have been brought to the block : by the
wrecks of time, by the eloquent ruins of Nations,—they
conjure us not to quench the light which is rising on the
world.   Greece cries to us by the convulsed lips of her
poisoned, dying Demosthenes; and Rome pleads with us
in the mute persuasion of her mangled Tully.

CIV.—THE SHIP OF STATE.

Rev. Wm. P. Lunt.

1. Break up the Union of these States, because there
are acknowledged evils in our system?   Is it so easy a
matter, then, to make everything in the actual world con-
form exactly to the ideal pattern we have conceived, in
our minds, of absolute right ?   Suppose the fatal blow were
struck, and the bonds which fasten together these States
were severed, would the evils and mischiefs that would be
experienced by those who are actually members of this
vast Republican Community be all that would ensue ?
Certainly not.   We are connected with the several Nations

and Races of the world as no other People has ever been connected.

2. We have opened our doors, and invited emigration to our soil from all lands. Our invitation has been accepted. Thousands have come at our bidding. Thousands more are on the way. Other thousands still are standing a-tiptoe on the shores of the Old World, eager to find a passage to the land where bread may be had for labor, and where man is treated as man. In our political family almost all Nations are represented. The several varieties of the race are here subjected to a social fusion, out of which Providence designs to form a "new man."

3. We are in this way teaching the world a great lesson, —namely, that men of different languages, habits, manners and creeds, can live together, and vote together, and, if not pray and worship together, yet in near vicinity, and do all in peace, and be, for certain purposes at least, one People. And is not this lesson of some value to the world, especially if we can teach it not by theory merely, but through a successful example? Has not this lesson, thus conveyed, some connection with the world's progress towards that far-off period to which the human mind looks for the fulfilment of its vision of a perfect social state? It may safely be asserted that this Union could not be dissolved without disarranging and convulsing every part of the globe.

4. Not in the indulgence of a vain confidence did our fathers build the Ship of State, and launch it upon the waters. We will exclaim, in the noble words of one of our poets:

"Thou, too, sail on, O Ship of State!
Sail on, O Union, strong and great!
Humanity with all its fears,
With all the hopes of future years,
Is hanging breathless on thy fate!
We know what Master laid thy keel,
What Workmen wrought thy ribs of steel,
Who made each mast, and sail, and rope,

10

What anvils rang, what hammers beat,
In what a forge and what a heat
Were shaped the anchors of thy hope !
Fear not each sudden sound and shock,—
'T is of the wave and not the rock :
'T is but the flapping of the sail,
And not a rent made by the gale!
In spite of rock and tempest roar,
In spite of false lights on the shore,
Sail on, nor fear to breast the sea!
Our hearts, our hopes, are all with thee.
Our hearts, our hopes, our prayers, our tears,
Our faith triumphant o'er our fears,
Are all with thee,—are all with thee ! "

CV.—IN THE MINES.

1. Leave the sluice and " tom " untended,
    Shadows darken on the river :
In the cañon day is ended,
    Far above the red rays quiver :
Lay aside the bar and spade,
    Let the pick-axe cease from drifting,
See how much the claim has paid
    Where the gold dust has been sifting.

2. Tell no tales of wizard charm
    In the myths of ages olden,
When the sorcerer's potent arm
    Turned all earthly things to golden :
Pick and spade are magic rods
    In the brawny hands of miners :
Mightier than the ancient gods,
    Laboring men are true diviners.

3. Gather round the blazing fire
    In the deepening darkness gleaming,
While the red tongues leaping, higher,
    Seem like banners upward streaming :
Stretched around the fiery coals,
    Lulled into luxurious dreaming,
Half-a-dozen hungry souls
    Watch the iron kettle steaming.

4. Break the bread with ready hand,
    Labor crowns it with a blessing—
Now the hungry crowd looks bland,
    Each a smoking piece possessing :
Pass the ham along this way,
    Quick, before the whole is taken :
Hang philosophy, we say,
    If we only save our bacon !

5. Spread the blankets on the ground,
    We must toil again to-morrow,
Labor brings us slumber sound
    No luxurious couch can borrow :
Watch the stars drift up the sky,
    Bending softly down above us,
Till in dreams our spirits fly
    Homeward to the friends who love us.

6. As the needle, frail and shivering,
    On the ocean wastes afar,
Veering, changing, trembling, quivering,
    Settles on the polar star ;
So, in souls of those who roam,
    Love's magnetic fires are burning,
To the loved ones left at home
    Throbbing hearts are ever turning.

CVI.—THE FAMILY MEETING.

CHARLES SPRAGUE.

1.   We are all here !
      Father, mother,
      Sister, brother,
All who hold each other dear :
Each chair is filled—we're *all at home ;*
To-night let no cold stranger come :
It is not often thus around
Our old familiar hearth we're found :
Bless, then, the meeting and the spot,
For once be every care forgot :
Let gentle Peace assert her power,
And kind Affection rule the hour ;
      We're all—all here.

2.   We're *not* all here!
Some are away—the dead ones dear,
Who thronged with us this ancient hearth,
And gave the hour to guiltless mirth.
Fate, with a stern, relentless hand,
Looked in and thinned our little band:
Some like a night-flash passed away,
And some sank, lingeiing, day by day:
The quiet graveyard—some lie there—
And cruel Ocean has his share—
                We're *not* all here.

3.   We *are* all here!
Even they—the dead—though dead, so dear:
Fond Memory, to her duty true,
Brings back their faded forms to view.
How lifelike, through the mist of years,
Each well-remembered face appears!
We see them as in times long past;
From each to each kind looks are cast:
We hear their words, their smiles behold:
They're round us as they were of old—
                We *are* all here.

4   We are all here!
                Father, mother,
                Sister, brother,
You that I love with love so dear.
This may not long of us be said;
Soon must we join the gathered dead;
And by the hearth we now sit round,
Some other circle will be found.
Oh! then, that wisdom may we know
Which yields a life of peace below;
So, in the world to follow this,
May each repeat, in words of bliss,
                " We're all—all *here!* "

CVII.—CHARACTER OF TRUE ELOQUENCE.

DANIEL WEBSTER.

1. WHEN public bodies are to be addressed on momentous occasions, when great interests are at stake, and strong
passions excited, nothing is valuable in speech, further than

it is connected with high intellectual and moral endowments. Clearness, force, and earnestness, are the qualities which produce conviction. True eloquence, indeed, does not consist in speech. It cannot be brought from far. Labor and learning may toil for it, but they will toil in vain. Words and phrases may be marshaled in every way, but they cannot compass it. It must exist in the man, in the subject, and in the occasion.

2. Affected passion, intense expression, the pomp of declamation, all may aspire after it: they cannot reach it. It comes, if it come at all, like the outbreaking of a fountain from the earth, or the bursting forth of volcanic fires, with spontaneous, original, native force.

3. The graces taught in the schools, the costly ornaments and studied contrivances of speech, shock and disgust men, when their own lives, and the fate of their wives, their children, and their country, hang on the decision of the hour. Then, words have lost their power, rhetoric is vain, and all elaborate oratory contemptible. Even genius itself then feels rebuked and subdued, as in the presence of higher qualities. Then, patriotism is eloquent: then, self-devotion is eloquent.

4. The clear conception, outrunning the deductions of logic, the high purpose, the firm resolve, the dauntless spirit, speaking on the tongue, beaming from the eye, informing every feature, and urging the whole man onward, right onward, to his object—this, this is eloquence; or, rather, it is something greater and higher than all eloquence,—it is action, noble, sublime, godlike action.

CVIII.—ELEGY IN A COUNTRY CHURCH-YARD.

GRAY.

1. THE curfew tolls the knell of parting day!
   The lowing herd winds slowly o'er the lea:
   The plowman homeward plods his weary way,
   And leaves the world to darkness, and to me.

2. Now fades the glimm'ring landscape on the sight,
   And all the air a solemn stillness holds,
   Save where the beetle wheels his droning flight,
   And drowsy tinklings lull the distant folds:

3. Save, that from yonder ivy-mantled tower,
   The moping owl does to the moon complain
   Of such as, wand'ring near her secret bower,
   Molest her ancient, solitary reign.

4. Beneath those rugged elms, that yew-tree's shade,
   Where heaves the turf in many a mold'ring heap,
   Each in his narrow cell forever laid,
   The rude forefathers of the hamlet sleep.

5. The breezy call of incense-breathing morn,
   The swallow, twitt'ring from the straw-built shed,
   The cock's shrill clarion, or the echoing horn,
   No more shall rouse them from their lowly bed.

6. For them no more the blazing hearth shall burn,
   Or busy housewife ply her evening care;
   Nor children run to lisp their sire's return,
   Or climb his knees the envied kiss to share.

7. Oft did the harvest to their sickle yield:
   Their furrow oft the stubborn glebe has broke:
   How jocund did they drive their team afield!
   How bow'd the woods beneath their sturdy stroke!

8. Let not ambition mock their useful toil,
   Their homely joys, and destiny obscure;
   Nor grandeur hear, with a disdainful smile,
   The short and simple annals of the poor.

9. The boast of heraldry, the pomp of power,
   And all that beauty, all that wealth e'er gave,
   Await, alike, the inevitable hour:
   The paths of glory lead but to the grave.

10. Nor you, ye proud, impute to these the fault,
    If mem'ry o'er their tomb no trophies raise,
    Where, through the long-drawn aisle and fretted vault,
    The pealing anthem swells the note of praise.

11. Can storied urn or animated bust,
    Back to its mansion call the fleeting breath?
    Can honor's voice provoke the silent dust,
    Or flattery soothe the dull, cold ear of death?

12. Perhaps, in this-neglected spot, is laid
    Some heart once pregnant with celestial fire:
Hands that the rod of empire might have swayed,
    Or waked to ecstasy the living lyre.

13. But knowledge to their eyes her ample page,
    Rich with the spoils of time, did ne'er unroll:
Chill penury repressed their noble rage,
    And froze the genial current of the soul.

14. Full many a gem of purest ray serene,
    The dark, unfathom'd caves of ocean bear:
Full many a flower is born to blush unseen,
    And waste its sweetness on the desert air.

15. Some village Hampden, that, with dauntless breast,
    The little tyrant of his field withstood:
Some mute, inglorious Milton here may rest:
    Some Cromwell, guiltless of his country's blood.

16. The applause of list'ning senates to command,
    The threats of pain and ruin to despise,
To scatter plenty o'er a smiling land,
    And read their hist'ry in a nation's eyes,

17. Their lot forbade; nor, circumscribed alone
    Their glowing virtues, but their crimes confined:
Forbade to wade through slaughter to a throne,
    And shut the gates of mercy on mankind:

18. The struggling pangs of conscious truth to hide:
    To quench the blushes of ingenuous shame;
Or heap the shrine of luxury and pride,
    With incense kindled at the muse's flame.

19. Far from the madding crowd's ignoble strife,
    Their sober wishes never learn'd to stray:
Along the cool, sequestered vale of life,
    They kept the noiseless tenor of their way.

20. Yet e'en these bones, from insult to protect,
    Some frail memorial still, erected nigh,
With uncouth rhymes and shapeless sculpture deck'd,
    Implores the passing tribute of a sigh.

21. Their names, their years, spell'd by the unletter'd muse,
    The place of fame and elegy supply;
And many a holy text around she strews,
    Teaching the rustic moralist to die.

22. For who, to dumb forgetfulness a prey,
    This pleasing, anxious being e'er resign'd:
  Left the warm precincts of the cheerful day,
    Nor cast one longing, ling'ring look behind?

23. On some fond breast the parting soul relics:
    Some pious drops the closing eye requires:
  E'en from the tomb the voice of nature cries,
    E'en in our ashes live their wonted fires.

24. For thee, who, mindful of the unhonor'd dead,
    Dost in these lines their artless tale relate,
  If, chance, by lonely contemplation led,
    Some kindred spirit shall inquire thy fate,

25. Haply some hoary-headed swain may say,
    " Oft have we seen him at the peep of dawn,
  Brushing, with hasty step, the dews away,
    To meet the sun upon the upland lawn.

26. There, at the foot of yonder nodding beech,
    That wreathes its old, fantastic roots so high,
  His listless length, at noontide would he stretch,
    And pore upon the brook that bubbles by.

27. Hard by yon wood, now smiling as in scorn,
    Mutt'ring his wayward fancies, he would rove:
  Now, drooping, woeful, wan, like one forlorn,
    Or crazed with care, or cross'd in hopeless love.

28. One morn, I miss'd him on the accustom'd hill,
    Along the heath, and near his fav'rite tree:
  Another came; nor yet beside the rill,
    Nor up the lawn, nor at the woods was he.

29. The next, with dirges due, in sad array,
    Slow through the church-yard path, we saw him borne.
  Approach, and read (for *thou canst* read) the lay,
    'Graved on the stone beneath yon aged thorn."

THE EPITAPH.

30. Here rests his head upon the lap of earth,
    A youth to Fortune, and to Fame, unknown:
  Fair Science frown'd not on his humble birth
    And Melancholy mark'd him for her own.

31. Large was his bounty, and his soul, sincere:
    Heaven did a recompense as largely send:
  He gave to Mis'ry all he had,—a tear:
    He gain'd from Heav'n—'t was all he wish'd—a friend.

32. No further seek his merits to disclose,
    Or draw his frailties from their dread abode :
    (There they alike in trembling hope repose,)
    The bosom of his Father, and his God.

CIX.—AN EVENING ADVENTURE.

1. Not long since a gentleman was travelling in one of the counties of Virginia, and about the close of the day stopped at a public house to obtain refreshment and spend the night. He had been there but a short time, before an old man alighted from his gig, with the apparent intention of becoming his fellow guest at the same house. As the old man drove up, he observed that both the shafts of his gig were broken, and that they were held together by withes, formed from the bark of a hickory sapling. Our traveller observed further, that he was plainly clad, that his knee-buckles were loosened, and that something like negligence pervaded his dress. Conceiving him to be one of the honest yeomanry of our land, the courtesies of strangers passed between them, and they entered the tavern. It was about the same time, that an addition of three or four young gentlemen was made to their number: most, if not all of them, of the legal profession.

2. As soon as they became conveniently accommodated, the conversation was turned, by one of the latter, upon the eloquent harangue which had that day been displayed at the bar. It was replied by the other, that he had witnessed, the same day, a degree of eloquence, no doubt equal, but it was from the pulpit. Something like a sarcastic rejoinder was made as to the eloquence of the pulpit, and a warm and able altercation ensued, in which the merits of the Christian religion became the subject of discussion. From six o'clock until eleven, the young champions wielded the sword of argument, adducing with ingenuity and ability every thing that could be said pro and con.

10*

3. During this protracted period, the old gentleman listened with the meekness and modesty of a child, as if he was adding new information to the stores of his own mind; or perhaps he was observing with a philosophic eye, the faculties of the youthful mind, and how new energies are evolved by repeated action; or perhaps, with patriotic emotion, he was reflecting upon the future destinies of his country, and on the rising generation, upon whom those future destinies must devolve; or, most probably, with a sentiment of moral and religious feeling, he was collecting an argument which no art would be "able to elude, and no force to resist." Our traveller remained a spectator, and took no part in what was said.

4. At last, one of the young men, remarking that it was impossible to combat with long and established prejudices, wheeled around, and with some familiarity, exclaimed, "Well, my old gentleman, what think *you* of these things?" If, said the traveller, a streak of vivid lightning had at that moment crossed the room, their amazement could not have been greater than it was from what followed. The most eloquent and unanswerable appeal that he had ever heard or read was made for nearly an hour, by the old gentleman. So perfect was his recollection, that every argument urged against the Christian religion, was met in the order in which it was advanced. Hume's sophistry on the subject of miracles, was, if possible, more perfectly answered, than it had already been done by Campbell. And in the whole lecture there was so much simplicity and energy, pathos and sublimity, that not another word was uttered.

5. An attempt to describe it, said the traveller, would be an attempt to paint the sunbeams. It was now a matter of curiosity and inquiry, who the old gentleman was. The traveller concluded that it was the preacher from whom the pulpit eloquence was heard; but no,—it was JOHN MARSHALL, the CHIEF JUSTICE OF THE UNITED STATES.

CX.—THREE DAYS IN THE LIFE OF COLUMBUS.

DELAVIGNE.

1. On the deck stood Columbus : the ocean's expanse,
   Untried and unlimited, swept by his glance.
   "Back to Spain ! " cry his men : " Put the vessel about !
   We venture no further through danger and doubt."—
   "Three days, and I give you a world ! " he replied :
   "Bear up, my brave comrades ;—three days shall decide."
   He sails,—but no token of land is in sight :
   He sails,—but the day shows no more than the night :
   On, onward he sails, while in vain o'er the lee
   The lead is plunged down through a fathomless sea.

2. The pilot, in silence, leans mournfully o'er
   The rudder which creaks mid the billowy roar :
   He hears the hoarse moan of the spray-driving blast,
   And its funeral wail through the shrouds of the mast.
   The stars of far Europe have sunk from the skies,
   And the great Southern Cross meets his terrified eyes ;
   But, at length, the slow dawn, softly streaking the night,
   Illumes the blue vault with its faint crimson light.
   " Columbus ! 'tis day, and the darkness is o'er."—
   " Day ! and what dost thou see ? "—" Sky and ocean.   No more ! "

3. The second day's past, and Columbus is sleeping,
   While Mutiny near him its vigil is keeping :
   " Shall he perish ? "—" Ay ! death ! " is the barbarous cry ;
   " He must triumph to-morrow, or, perjured, must die ! "
   Ungrateful and blind !—shall the world-linking sea,
   He traced for the Future, his sepulchre be ?
   Shall that sea, on the morrow, with pitiless waves,
   Fling his corse on that shore which his patient eye craves ?
   The corse of an humble adventurer, then :
   One day later,—Columbus, the first among men !

4. But, hush ! he is dreaming !—A veil on the main,
   At the distant horizon, is parted in twain,
   And now, on his dreaming eye,—rapturous sight !—
   Fresh bursts the New World from the darkness of night !
   O, vision of glory ! how dazzling it seems !
   How glistens the verdure ! how sparkle the streams !
   How blue the far mountains ! how glad the green isles ;
   And the earth and the ocean, how dimpled with smiles :
   " Joy ! joy ! " cries Columbus, " this region is mine ! "—
   Ah ! not e'en its name, wondrous dreamer, is thine !

5. But, lo ! his dream changes ;—a vision less bright
Comes to darken and banish that scene of delight.
The gold-seeking Spaniards, a merciless band,
Assail the meek natives, and ravage the land.
He sees the fair palace, the temple on fire,
And the peaceful Cazique, 'mid their ashes expire :
He sees, too,—O, saddest ! O, mournfullest sight !—
The crucifix gleam in the thick of the fight.
More terrible far than the merciless steel
Is the upifted cross in the red hand of Zeal !

6. Again the dream changes. Columbus looks forth,
And a bright constellation beholds in the North.
'Tis the herald of empire ! A People appear,
Impatient of wrong, and unconscious of fear !
They level the forest : they ransack the seas :
Each zone finds their canvas unfurled to the breeze.
"Hold !" Tyranny cries ; but their resolute breath
Sends back the reply, "INDEPENDENCE OR DEATH !"
The ploughshare they turn to a weapon of might,
And, defying all odds, they go forth to the fight.

7. They have conquered ! The People, with grateful acclaim
Look to Washington's guidance from Washington's fame ;—
Behold Cincinnatus and Cato combined
In his patriot heart and republican mind.
O, type of true manhood ! What sceptre or crown
But fades in the light of thy simple renown ?
And lo ! by the side of the Hero, a Sage,
In Freedom's behalf, sets his mark on the age :
Whom Science adoringly hails, while he wrings
The lightning from Heaven, the sceptre from kings !

8. At length, o'er Columbus slow consciousness breaks,—
"Land ! land !" cry the sailors ; "land ! land !"—he awakes—
He runs,—yes ! behold it !—it blesseth his sight :
The land ! O, dear spectacle ! transport ! delight !
O, generous sobs, which he cannot restrain !
What will Ferdinand say ? and the Future ? and Spain ?
He will lay this fair land at the foot of the Throne :
His King will repay all the ills he has known :
In exchange for a world what are honors and gains ?
Or a crown ? But how *is* he rewarded ?—with chains !

CXI.—DESTRUCTION OF THE PHILISTINES.

MILTON.

1. Occasions drew me early to the city;
And, as the gates I entered with sunrise,
The morning trumpets festival proclaimed
Through each high street: little I had despatched,
When all abroad was rumored that this day
Samson should be brought forth, to show the People
Proof of his mighty strength in feats and games.
I sorrowed at his captive state, but minded
Not to be absent at that spectacle.

2. The building was a spacious theatre
Half round, on two main pillars vaulted high,
With seats where all the lords, and each degree
Of sort, might sit, in order to behold:
The other side was open, where the throng
On banks and scaffolds under sky might stand:
I among these aloof obscurely stood.
The feast and noon grew high, and sacrifice
Had filled their hearts with mirth, high cheer, and wine,
When to their sports they turned. Immediately
Was Samson as a public servant brought,
In their state livery clad: before him pipes,
And timbrels,—on each side went armed guards,
Both horse and foot,—before him and behind,
Archers, and slingers, cataphracts and spears.

3. At sight of him, the People with a shout
Rifted the air, clamoring their god with praise,
Who had made their dreadful enemy their thrall.
He, patient, but undaunted, where they led him,
Came to the place; and what was set before him,
Which without help of eye might be essayed,
To heave, pull, draw or break, he still performed
All with incredible, stupendous force:
None daring to appear antagonist.
At length, for intermission sake, they led him
Between the pillars: he his guide requested
(For so from such as nearer stood we heard),
As over-tired, to let him lean a while
With both his arms on those two massy pillars
That to the arched roof gave main support.

4. He, unsuspicious, led him: which when Samson
Felt in his arms, with head a while inclined,

And eyes fast fixed he stood, as one who prayed,
Or some great matter in his mind revolved :
At last with head erect, thus cried aloud :—
" Hitherto, Lords, what your commands imposed
I have performed, as reason was, obeying,
Not without wonder or delight beheld :
Now of my own accord such other trial
I mean to show you of my strength, yet greater,
As with amaze shall strike all who behold."

5. This uttered, straining all his nerves, he bowed :
As with the force of winds and waters pent,
When mountains tremble, those two massy pillars
With horrible convulsion to and fro
He tugged, he shook, till down they came, and drew
The whole roof after them, with burst of thunder
Upon the heads of all who sat beneath,
Lords, ladies, captains, counsellors, or priests,
Their choice nobility and flower, not only
Of this, but each Philistian city round,
Met from all parts to solemnize this feast.
Samson, with these inmixed, inevitably
Pulled down the same destruction on himself :
The vulgar only 'scaped, who stood without.

CXII.—SATAN'S ENCOUNTER WITH DEATH.

MILTON.

1. BLACK it stood as night,
Fierce as ten furies, terrible as hell,
And shook a dreadful dart : what seemed his head
The likeness of a kingly crown had on.
Satan was now at hand ; and from his seat
The monster moving onward came as fast,
With horrid strides : hell trembled as he strode.
The undaunted fiend what this might be admired,
Admired, not feared : God and His Son except,
Created thing naught valued he, nor shunned.
And with disdainful look thus first began :—

2. " Whence, and what art thou, execrable shape !
That darest, though grim and terrible, advance
Thy miscreated front athwart my way

To yonder gates ?   Through them I mean to pass,
That be assured, without leave asked of thee :
Retire, or taste thy folly; and learn by proof,
Hell-born ! not to contend with spirits of Heaven ! "
  To whom the goblin, full of wrath, replied :—

3. " Art thou that traitor angel, art thou he,
Who first broke peace in Heaven, and faith, till then
Unbroken, and in proud rebellious arms
Drew after him the third part of Heaven's sons
Conjured against the Highest; for which both thou
And they, outcast from God, are here condemned
To waste eternal days in woe and pain ?
And reckon'st thou thyself with spirits of Heaven,
Hell-doomed ! and breathest defiance here and scorn,
Where I reign king, and, to enrage thee more
Thy king and lord !   Back to thy punishment,
False fugitive ! and to thy speed add wings :
Lest with a whip of scorpions I pursue
Thy lingering, or with one stroke of this dart ·
Strange horror seize thee, and pangs unfelt before."

4. So spake the grisly terror; and in shape,
So speaking, and so threatening, grew ten-fold
More dreadful and deform : on the other side,
Incensed with indignation, Satan stood
Unterrified, and like a comet burned,
That fires the length of Ophiuchus huge
In the Arctic sky, and from his horrid hair
Shakes pestilence and war.   Each at the head
Levelled his deadly aim : their fatal hands
No second stroke intend ; and such a frown
Each cast at the other, as when two black clouds,
With Heaven's artillery fraught, come rattling on
Over the Caspian ; then stand front to front
Hovering a space, till winds the signal blow
To join their dark encounter in mid air :

5. So frowned the mighty combatants, that hell
Grew darker at their frown : so matched they stood ;
For never but once more was either like
To meet so great a foe ; and now great deeds
Had been achieved, whereof all hell had rung,
Had not the snaky sorceress that sat
Fast by hell-gate, and kept the fatal key,
Risen, and with hideous cry rushed between.

CXIII.—BELSHAZZAR'S FEAST.

T. S. Hughes.

1. Joy holds her court in great Belshazzar's hall,
Where his proud lords attend their monarch's call.
The rarest dainties of the teeming East
Provoke the revel and adorn the feast.
And now the monarch rises :—" Pour," he cries
" To the great gods, the Assyrian deities !
Pour forth libations of the rosy wine
To Nebo, Bel, and all the powers divine !
Those golden vessels crown, which erewhile stood
Fast by the oracle of Judah's God,
Till that accursed race—"

2.   But why, O king !
Why dost thou start, with livid cheek ?—why fling
The untasted goblet from thy trembling hand ?
Why shake thy joints, thy feet forget to stand ?
Why roams thine eye, which seems in wild amaze
To shun some object, yet returns to gaze,—
Then shrinks again appalled, as if the tomb
Had sent a spirit from its inmost gloom ?

3. Awful the horror, when Belshazzar raised
His arm, and pointed where the vision blazed !
For see ! enrobed in flame, a mystic shade,
As of a hand, a red right-hand, displayed !
And, slowly moving o'er the wall, appear
Letters of fate, and characters of fear.
In deathlike silence grouped, the revellers all
Fix their glazed eyeballs on the illumined wall.
See ! now the vision brightens,—now 'tis gone,
Like meteor flash, like Heaven's own lightning flown !
But, though the hand hath vanished, what it writ
Is uneffaced. Who will interpret it ?
In vain the sages try their utmost skill :
The mystic letters are unconstrued still.

4. " Quick, bring the Prophet !—let his tongue proclaim
The mystery of that visionary flame."
The holy Prophet came, and stood upright,
With brow serene, before Belshazzar's sight.
The monarch pointed trembling to the wall :
" Behold the portents that our heart appal !

Interpret them, O Prophet! thou shalt know
What gifts Assyria's monarch can bestow."

5. Unutterably awful was the eye
Which met the monarch's; and the stern reply
Fell heavy on his soul: " Thy gifts withhold,
Nor tempt the Spirit of the Law, with gold.
Belshazzar, hear what these dread words reveal!
That lot on which the Eternal sets his seal.
Thy kingdom numbered, and thy glory flown,
The Mede and Persian revel on thy throne.
Weighed in the balance, thou hast kicked the beam:
See to yon Western sun the lances gleam,
Which, ere his Orient rays adorn the sky,
Thy blood shall sully with a crimson dye."
In the dire carnage of that night's dread hour,
Crushed mid the ruins of his crumbling power,
Belshazzar fell beneath an unknown blow—
His kingdom wasted, and his pride laid low!

CXIV.—THE NEW-YEAR'S NIGHT OF AN UNHAPPY MAN.
RICHTER.

1. On new-year's night, an old man stood at his window, and looked, with a glance of fearful despair, up to the immovable, unfading heaven, and down upon the still, pure, white earth, on which no one was now so joyless and sleepless as he. His grave stood near him: it was covered only with the snows of age, not with the verdure of youth; and he brought with him out of a whole, rich life, nothing but errors, sins, and diseases; a wasted body; a desolate soul; a heart full of poison; and an old age full of repentance. The happy days of his early youth passed before him, like a procession of specters, and brought back to him that lovely morning, when his father first placed him on the cross-way of life, where the right hand led by the sunny paths of virtue, into a large and quiet land, full of light and harvests; and the left plunged by the subterranean walks of vice, into a black cave, full of distilling poison, of hissing snakes, and of dark, sultry vapors.

2. Alas, the snakes were hanging upon his breast, and the drops of poison on his tongue; and he now, at length, felt all the horror of his situation. Distracted, with unspeakable grief, and with face up-turned to heaven, he cried, "My father! give me back my youth! O, place me once again upon life's cross-way, that I may choose aright." But his father and his youth were long since gone. He saw phantom-lights dancing upon the marshes, and disappearing at the church-yard; and he said, "These are my foolish days!" He saw a star shoot from heaven, and glittering in its fall, vanish upon the earth. "Behold an emblem of my career," said his bleeding heart, and the serpent tooth of repentance digged deeper into his wounds.

3. His excited imagination showed him specters flying upon the roof, and a skull, which had been left in the charnel-house, gradually assumed his own features. In the midst of this confusion of objects, the music of the new-year flowed down from the steeple, like distant church-melodies. His heart began to melt. He looked around the horizon, and over the wide earth, and thought of the friends of his youth, who now, better and happier than he, were the wise of the earth, prosperous men, and the fathers of happy children; and he said, "Like you, I also might slumber, with tearless eyes, through the long nights, had I chosen aright in the outset of my career. Ah, my father! had I hearkened to thy instructions, I too might have been happy."

4. In this feverish remembrance of his youthful days, the skull bearing his features, seemed slowly to rise from the door of the charnel-house. At length, by that superstition, which, in the new-year's night, sees the shadow of the future, it became a living youth. He could look no longer: he covered his eyes: a thousand burning tears streamed down, and fell upon the snow. In accents scarcely audible, he sighed disconsolately: "Oh, days of my youth, return, return!" And they *did* return. It had only been a horrible dream. But, although he was still a youth, his *errors* had been a *reality*. And he thanked God, that he,

still young, was able to pause in the degrading course of vice, and return to the sunny path which leads to the land of harvests.

5. Return with him, young reader, if thou art walking in the same downward path, lest his *dream* become *thy reality.* For if thou turnest not now, in the spring-time of thy days, vainly, in after years, when the shadows of age are darkening around thee, shalt thou call, " Return, oh beautiful days of youth ! " Those beautiful days, gone, gone forever, and hidden in the shadows of the misty past, shall close their ears against thy miserable cries, or answer thee in hollow accents, " *Alas ! we return no more.*"

CXV.—THE CLOSING YEAR.

G. D. Prentice.

1. 'Tis midnight's holy hour, and silence now
  Is brooding, like a gentle spirit, o'er
  The still and pulseless world. Hark ! on the winds,
  The bell's deep tones are swelling ;—'tis the knell
  Of the departed year. No funeral train
  Is sweeping past ; yet, on the stream and wood,
  With melancholy light, the moonbeams rest
  Like a pale, spotless shroud : the air is stirred,
  As by a mourner's sigh ; and, on yon cloud,
  That floats so still and placidly through heaven,
  The spirits of the Seasons seem to stand,
  Young Spring, bright Summer, Autumn's solemn form,
  And Winter, with his aged locks,—and breathe
  In mournful cadences, that come abroad
  Like the far wind-harp's wild, touching wail,
  A melancholy dirge o'er the dead year,
  Gone from the earth forever.

2.   'Tis a time
  For memory and for tears. Within the deep,
  Still chambers of the heart, a specter dim,
  Whose tones are like the wizard voice of Time,
  Heard from the tomb of ages, points its cold
  And solemn finger to the beautiful
  And holy visions, that have passed away,
  And left no shadow of their loveliness

On the dead waste of life. The specter lifts
The coffin-lid of Hope, and Joy, and Love,
And bending mournfully above the pale,
Sweet forms that slumber there, scatters dead flowers
O'er what has passed to nothingness.

3.   The year
Has gone, and with it, many a glorious throng
Of happy dreams. Its mark is on each brow,
Its shadow, in each heart. In its swift course,
It waved its scepter o'er the beautiful ;
And they are not. It laid its pallid hand
Upon the strong man ; and the haughty form
Is fallen, and the flushing eye is dim.
It trod the hall of revelry, where thronged
The bright and joyous ; and the tearful wail
Of stricken ones is heard, where erst the song
And reckless shout resounded. It passed o'er
The battle-plain, where sword, and spear, and shield,
Flashed in the light of mid-day ; and the strength
Of serried hosts is shivered, and the grass,
Green from the soil of carnage, waves above   .
The crushed and moldering skeleton. It came,
And faded like a wreath of mist at eve ;
Yet, ere it melted in the viewless air,
It heralded its millions to their home,
In the dim land of dreams.

4.   Remorseless Time !
Fierce spirit of the glass and scythe ! What power
Can stay him in his silent course, or melt
His iron-heart to pity ! On, still on,
He presses, and forever. The proud bird,—
The condor of the Andes, that can soar
Through heaven's unfathomable depths, or brave
The fury of the northern hurricane,
And bathe his plumage in the thunder's home,—
Furls his broad wing at night-fall, and sinks down
To rest upon his mountain crag ; but Time
Knows not the weight of sleep or weariness,
And Night's deep darkness has no chain to bind
His rushing pinion.

5.   Revolutions sweep ,
O'er earth, like troubled visions o'er the breast

Of dreaming sorrow : cities rise and sink
Like bubbles on the water : fiery isles
Spring blazing from the ocean, and go back
To their mysterious caverns : mountains rear
To heaven their bold and blackened cliffs, and bow
Their tall heads to the plain ; and empires rise,
Gathering the strength of hoary centuries,
And rush down, like the Alpine avalanche,
Startling the nations ; and the very stars,
Yon bright and glorious blazonry of God,
Glitter awhile in their eternal depths,
And, like the Pleiad, loveliest of their train,
Shoot from their glorious spheres, and pass away
To darkle in the trackless void ; yet Time,
Time, the tomb-builder, holds his fierce career,
Dark, stern, all pitiless, and pauses not
Amid the mighty wrecks that strew his path,
To sit and muse, like other conquerors,
Upon the fearful ruin he hath wrought.

CXVI.—A REPUBLIC OF PRAIRIE-DOGS.

W. IRVING.

1. ON returning from our excursion, I learned that a burrow, or village, as it is termed, of prairie-dogs had been discovered upon the level summit of a hill, about a mile from the camp. Having heard much of the habits and peculiarities of these little animals, I determined to pay a visit to the community. The prairie-dog is, in fact, one of the curiosities of the Far West, about which travelers delight to tell marvelous tales, endowing him, at times, with something of the political and social habits of a rational being, and giving him systems of civil government and domestic economy, almost equal to what they used to bestow upon the beaver.

2. The prairie-dog is an animal of the cony kind, about the size of a rabbit. He is of a very sprightly, mercurial nature : quick, sensitive, and somewhat petulant. He is very gregarious, living in large communities, sometimes of

several acres in extent, where innumerable little heaps of earth, show the entrances to the subterranean cells of the inhabitants, and the well-beaten tracks, like lanes and streets, show their mobility and restlessness. According to the accounts given of them, they would seem to be continually full of sport, business, and public affairs: whisking about hither and thither, as if on gossiping visits to each other's houses, or congregating in the cool of the evening, or after a shower, and gamboling together in the open air.

3. Sometimes, especially when the moon shines, they pass half the night in revelry, barking or yelping with short, quick, yet weak tones, like those of very young puppies. While in the hight of their playfulness and clamor, however, should there be the least alarm, they all vanish into their cells in an instant, and the village remains blank and silent. In case they are hard pressed by their pursuers, without any hope of escape, they will assume a pugnacious air, and a most whimsical look of impotent wrath and defiance. Such are a few of the particulars that I could gather about the habits of this little inhabitant of the prairies, who, with his pigmy republic, appears to be a subject of much whimsical speculation and burlesque remarks, among the hunters of the Far West.

4. It was toward evening that I set out, with a companion, to visit the village in question. Unluckily, it had been invaded in the course of the day by some of the rangers, who had shot two or three of its inhabitants, and thrown the whole sensitive community into confusion. As we approached, we could perceive numbers of the inhabitants seated at the entrance of their cells, while sentinels seem to have been posted on the out-skirts, to keep a look out. At sight of us, the picket-guards scampered in and gave the alarm; whereupon, every inhabitant gave a short yelp or bark, and dived in his hole, his heels twinkling in the air, as if he had thrown a somerset.

5. We traversed the whole village, or republic, which covered an area of about thirty acres; but not a whisker

of an inhabitant was to be seen. We probed their cells as far as the ramrods of our rifles would reach, but in vain. Moving quietly to a little distance, we lay down upon the ground, and watched for a long time, silent and motionless. By and by, a cautious old burgher would slowly put forth the end of his nose, but instantly draw it in again. Another, at a greater distance, would emerge entirely; but, catching a glance of us, would throw a somerset and plunge back again into his hole. At length, some who resided on the opposite side of the village, taking courage from the continued stillness, would steal forth, and hurry off to a distant hole, the residence, possibly, of some family connection or gossiping friend, about whose safety they were solicitous, or with whom they wished to compare notes about the late occurrences. Others, still more bold, assembled in little knots in the streets and public places, as if to discuss the recent outrages offered to the commonwealth, and the atrocious murders of their fellow burghers.

6. We rose from the ground, and moved forward to take a nearer view of these public proceedings, when, yelp! yelp! yelp!—there was a shrill alarm passed from mouth to mouth: the meeting suddenly dispersed: feet twinkled in the air in every direction, and, in an instant, all had vanished into the earth.

7. The dusk of the evening put an end to our observations, but the train of whimsical comparisons produced in my brain, by the moral attributes which I had heard given to these little, politic animals, still continued after my return to camp; and, late in the night, as I lay awake, after all the camp was asleep, and heard, in the stillness of the hour, a faint clamor of shrill voices from the distant village, I could not help picturing to myself the inhabitants gathered together in noisy assembly and windy debate, to devise plans for the public safety, and to vindicate the invaded rights and insulted dignity of the republic.

CXVII.—THANATOPSIS.

BRYANT.

[*Thanatopsis* is composed of the Greek words, *thanatos* meaning *death*, and *opsis*, a *view*. Together, therefore, they signify *a view of death* or "Reflections on Death."]

1.   To him, who, in the love of nature, holds
      Communion with her visible forms, she speaks
      A various language ; for his gayer hours
      She has a voice of gladness, and a smile
      And eloquence of beauty, and she glides
      Into his dark musings, with a mild
      And gentle sympathy, that steals away
      Their sharpness, ere he is aware.

2.   When thoughts
      Of the last bitter hour, come like a blight
      Over thy spirit, and sad images
      Of the stern agony, and shroud, and pall,
      And breathless darkness, and the narrow house,
      Make thee to shudder and grow sick at heart ;
      Go forth into the open sky, and list
      To nature's teaching, while from all around,
      Comes a still voice :—

3.   " Yet a few days, and thee,
      The all-beholding sun shall see no more
      In all his course ; nor yet, in the cold ground,
      Where thy pale form was laid with many tears,
      Nor in the embrace of ocean, shall exist
      Thy image. Earth, that nourished thee, shall claim
      Thy growth, to be resolved to earth again ;
      And, lost each human trace, surrendering up
      Thine individual being, shalt thou go
      To mix forever with the elements,
      To be a brother to th' insensible rock
      And to the sluggish clod, which the rude swain
      Turns with his share and treads upon.

4.   The oak
      Shall send his roots abroad, and pierce thy mold.
      Yet not to thy eternal resting place
      Shalt thou retire alone, nor could'st thou wish
      Couch more magnificent. Thou shalt lie down
      With patriarchs of the infant world, with kings,

The powerful of the earth, the wise, the good,
Fair forms, and hoary seers of ages past,
All in one mighty sepulcher.

5.   The hills,
Rock-ribbed, and ancient as the sun : the vales,
Stretching in pensive quietness between :
The venerable woods : rivers that move
In majesty, and the complaining brooks
That make the meadows green ; and, poured round all,
Old ocean's gray and melancholy waste,
Are but the solemn decorations all
Of the great tomb of man. The golden sun,
The planets, all the infinite host of heaven,
Are shining on the sad abodes of death,
Through the still lapse of ages.

6.   All that tread
The globe, are but a handful, to the tribes
That slumber in its bosom. Take the wings
Of morning, and the Barcan desert pierce,
Or lose thyself in the continuous woods
Where rolls the Oregon, and hears no sound
Save its own dashings—yet—the dead are there ;
And millions in those solitudes, since first
The flight of years began, have laid them down
In their last sleep : the dead reign there alone.

7. So shalt *thou* rest ; and what if thou shalt fall
Unnoticed by the living ; and no friend
Take note of thy departure ?   All that breathe
Will share thy destiny. The gay will laugh
When thou are gone ; the solemn brood of care
Plod on ; and each one, as before, will chase
His favorite phantom ; yet all these shall leave
Their mirth and their enjoyments, and shall come
And make their bed with thee. As the long train
Of ages glide away, the sons of men,
The youth in life's green spring, and he who goes
In the full strength of years, matron and maid,
The bowed with age, the infant in the smiles
And beauty of its innocent age cut off,—
Shall, one by one, be gathered to thy side,
By those, who, in their turn, shall follow them.

11

8. So live, that when thy summons comes to join
The innumerable caravan that moves
To the pale realms of shade, where each shall take
His chamber in the silent halls of death,
Thou go not like the quarry-slave at night,
Scourged to his dungeon, but, sustained and soothed
By an unfaltering trust, approach thy grave,
Like one who wraps the drapery of his couch
About him, and lies down to pleasant dreams."

————◆————

CXVIII.—THE CHURCH-YARD.

KARAMISIN.

(*Two Voices from the Grave.*)

First Voice.   How frightful the grave! how deserted and drear!
With the howls of the storm-wind, the creaks of the bier,
And the white bones all clattering together!

Second Voice.   How peaceful the grave! its quiet how deep!
Its zephyrs breathe calmly, and soft is its sleep,
And flow'rets perfume it with ether.

First Voice.   There, riots the blood-crested worm on the dead,
And the yellow skull serves the foul toad for a bed,
And snakes in the nettle-weeds hiss.

Second Voice.   How lovely, how sweet the repose of the tomb!
No tempests are there; but the nightingales come,
And sing their sweet chorus of bliss.

First Voice.   The ravens of night flap their wings o'er the grave:
'Tis the vulture's abode: 'tis the wolf's dreary cave,
Where they tear up the dead with their fangs.

Second Voice.   There, the cony, at evening, disports with his love,
Or rests on the sod; while the turtles above
Repose on the bough that o'erhangs.

First Voice.   There, darkness and dampness, with poisonous breath,
And loathsome decay, fill the dwelling of death:
The trees are all barren and bare.

Second Voice.   O! soft are the breezes that play round the tomb,
And sweet, with the violet's wafted perfume,
With lilies and jessamine fair.

First Voice.   The pilgrim, who reaches this valley of tears,
Would fain hurry by; and, with trembling and fears,
He is launched on the wreck-covered river.

Second Voice. Here, the traveller, worn with life's pilgrimage dreary,
Lays down his rude staff, like one that is weary,
And sweetly reposes forever.

CXIX.—JEPHTHAH'S DAUGHTER.

WILLIS.

1. SHE stood before her father's gorgeous tent,
To listen for his coming. I have thought,
A brother's and a sister's love was much.
I know a brother's is, for I have loved
A trusting sister ; and I know how broke
The heart may be with its own tenderness.
But the affection of a delicate child
For a fond father, gushing as it does
With the sweet springs of life, and living on
Through all earth's changes,
Must be holier ! The wind-bore on
The leaden tramp of thousands. Clarion notes
Rang sharply on the ear at intervals ;
And the low, mingled din of mighty hosts,
Returning from the battle, poured from far,
Like the deep murmur of a restless sea.

2. Jephthah led his warriors on
Through Mizpeh's streets. His helm was proudly set,
And his stern lip curled slightly, as if praise
Were for the hero's scorn. His step was firm,
But free as India's leopard ; and his mail,
Whose shekels none in Israel might bear,
Was lighter than a tassel on his frame.
His crest was Judah's kingliest, and the look
Of his dark, lofty eye
Might quell a lion. He led on ; but thoughts
Seemed gathering round which troubled him. The veins
Upon his forehead were distinctly seen ;
And his proud lip was painfully compressed.
He trod less firmly ; and his restless eye
Glanced forward frequently, as if some ill
He dared not meet, were there. His home was near,
And men were thronging, with that strange delight
They have in human passions, to observe
The struggle of his feelings with his pride.
He gazed intensely forward.

3.   A moment more,
And he had reached his home ; when lo ! there sprang
One with a bounding footstep, and a brow
Like light, to meet him. Oh ! how beautiful !
Her dark eye flashing like a sun-lit gem,
And her luxuriant hair, 'twas like the sweep
Of a swift wing in visions. He stood still,
As if the sight had withered him. She threw
Her arms about his neck : he heeded not.
She called him "Father," but he answered not.
She stood and gazed upon him. Was he wroth ?
There was no anger in that blood-shot eye.
Had sickness seized him ? She unclasped his helm,
And laid her white hand gently on his brow.
The touch aroused him. He raised up his hands,
And spoke the name of God in agony.
She knew that he was stricken then, and rushed
Again into his arms, and with a flood
Of tears she could not stay, she sobbed a prayer
That he would tell her of his wretchedness.
He told her, and a momentary flush
Shot o'er her countenance ; and then, the soul
Of Jephthah's daughter wakened, and she stood
Calmly and nobly up, and said, " 'Tis well ;
And I will die ! " And when the sun had set,
Then she was dead—but not by violence,

CXX.—FRANCE AND THE UNITED STATES.

GEORGE WASHINGTON.

1. BORN, Sir, in a land of liberty, having early learned its value, having engaged in a perilous conflict to defend it, having, in a word, devoted the best years of my life to secure its permanent establishment in my own country,— my anxious recollections, my sympathetic feelings, and my best wishes, are irresistibly excited, whensoever, in any country, I see an oppressed Nation unfurl the banners of freedom. But, above all, the events of the French Revolution have produced the deepest solicitude, as well as the highest admiration.

2. To call your nation brave, were to pronounce but

common praise. Wonderful People! Ages to come will read with astonishment the history of your brilliant exploits! I rejoice that the period of your toils and of your immense sacrifices is approaching. I rejoice that the interesting revolutionary movements of so many years have issued in the formation of a Constitution designed to give permanency to the great object for which you have contended.

3. I rejoice that liberty, which you have so long embraced with enthusiasm,—liberty, of which you have been the invincible defenders,—now finds an asylum in the bosom of a regularly organized Government;—a Government, which, being formed to secure the happiness of the French People, corresponds with the ardent wishes of my heart, while it gratifies the pride of every citizen of the United States, by its resemblance to his own. On these glorious events, accept, Sir, my sincere congratulations.

4. In delivering to you these sentiments, I express not my own feelings only, but those of my fellow-citizens, in relation to the commencement, the progress, and the issue, of the French Revolution; and they will cordially join with me in purest wishes to the Supreme Being, that the citizens of our sister Republic, our magnanimous allies, may soon enjoy in peace that liberty which they have purchased at so great a price, and all the happiness which liberty can bestow.

5. I receive, Sir, with lively sensibility, the symbol of the triumphs and of the enfranchisement of your Nation, the colors of France, which you have now presented to the United States. The transaction will be announced to Congress; and the colors will be deposited with those archives of the United States which are at once the evidences and the memorials of their freedom and independence. May these be perpetual! And may the friendship of the two Republics be commensurate with their existence!

CXXI.—MARMION TAKING LEAVE OF DOUGLAS.

Sir Walter Scott.

1. THE train from out the castle drew ;
But Marmion stopped to bid adieu :—
   "Though something I might 'plain," he said,
   "Of cold respect to stranger guest,
Sent hither by your King's behest,
   While in Tantallon's towers I stayed,—
Part we in friendship from your land,
And, noble Earl, receive my hand."

2. But Douglas round him drew his cloak,
Folded his arms, and thus he spoke :—
   "My manors, halls and bowers, shall still
Be open, at my sovereign's will,
To each one whom he lists, howe'er
Unmeet to be the owner's peer.
My castles are my King's alone,
From turret to foundation-stone ;—
The *hand* of Douglas is his own ;
And never shall in friendly grasp
The hand of such as Marmion clasp ! "

3. Burned Marmion's swarthy cheek like fire,
And shook his very frame for ire,
   And—" This to me ! " he said :
   "An'twere not for thy hoary beard,
Such hand as Marmion's had not spared
   To cleave the Douglas' head !
And first I tell thee, haughty Peer,
He who does England's message here,
Although the meanest in her state,
May well, proud Angus, be thy mate !
And, Douglas, more I tell thee here,
   Even in thy pitch of pride,
Here, in thy hold, thy vassals near
(Nay, never look upon your Lord,
And lay your hands upon your sword !),
   I tell thee, thou'rt defied !
And if thou saidst I am not peer
To any lord in Scotland here,
Lowland or Highland, far or near,
   Lord Angus, thou hast lied ! "

4. On the Earl's cheek the flush of rage
O'ercame the ashen hue of age :
Fierce he broke forth :—" And darest thou, then,
To beard the lion in his den,—
   The Douglas in his hall ?
And hopest thou hence unscathed to go ?
No, by Saint Bride of Bothwell, no !
Up drawbridge, grooms !—what, warder, ho !
  Let the portcullis fall."

5. Lord Marmion turned,—well was his need,—
And dashed the rowels in his steed ;
Like arrow through the archway sprung,
The ponderous gate behind him rung :
To pass, there was such scanty room,
The bars, descending, razed his plume.
The steed along the drawbridge flies,
Just as it trembled on the rise :
Not lighter does the swallow skim
Along the smooth lake's level brim ;
And when Lord Marmion reached his band,
He halts, and turns with clenched hand,
A shout of loud defiance pours,
And shakes his gauntlet at the towers !

CXXII.—THE DEATH OF MARMION.

SCOTT.

1. AND soon straight up the hill there rode
   Two horsemen, drenched with gore,
And in their arms, a helpless load,
   A wounded knight they bore.
His hand still strained the broken brand,
His arms were smeared with blood and sand :
Dragged from among the horses' feet,
With dinted shield and helmet beat,
The falcon-crest and plumage gone,—
Can that be haughty Marmion ?

2. Young Blount his armor did unlace,
And, gazing on his ghastly face,
   Said—" By Saint George, he's gone !
The spear-wound has our master sped ;

And see the deep cut on his head!
  Good-night to Marmion!"
"Unnurtured Blount! thy brawling cease:
He opes his eyes," said Eustace, "peace!"
When, doffed his casque, he felt free air,
Around 'gan Marmion wildly stare:

3. "Where's Harry Blount? Fitz Eustace, where?
Linger ye here, ye hearts of hare?
Redeem my pennon!—charge again!
Cry, 'Marmion to the rescue!'—Vain!
Last of my race, on battle-plain
· That shout shall ne'er be heard again!
Must I bid twice?—hence, varlets! fly;
Leave Marmion here alone—to die."

4. With fruitless labor, Clara bound,
And strove to stanch the gushing wound.
The war, that for a space did fail,
Now, trebly thundering, swelled the gale,
  And "Stanley!" was the cry;
A light on Marmion's visage spread,
  And fired his glazing eye;
With dying hand, above his head
He shook the fragment of his blade,
  And shouted, "Victory!"
"Charge, Chester, charge! On, Stanley, on!"
Were the last words of Marmion.

CXXIII.—MAUD MULLER.

WHITTIER.

1. MAUD MULLER, on a summer's day,
Raked the meadow sweet with hay.
Beneath her torn hat glowed the wealth
Of simple beauty and rustic health.
Singing, she wrought, and her merry glee
The mock-bird echoed from his tree.

2. But when she glanced to the far-off town,
White from its hill-slope looking down,
The sweet song died, and a vague unrest
And a nameless longing filled her breast—
A wish, that she hardly dared to own,
For something better than she had known.

3. The Judge rode slowly down the lane,
Smoothing his horse's chestnut mane.
He drew his bridle in the shade
Of the apple-trees, to greet the maid,
And ask a draught from the spring that flowed
Through the meadow, across the road.

4. She stooped where the cool spring bubbled up,
And filled for him her small tin-cup,
And blushed as she gave it, looking down
On her feet so bare, and her tattered gown.
"Thanks!" said the Judge: "a sweeter draught
From a fairer hand was never quaffed." ·

5. He spoke of the grass, and flowers, and trees,
Of the singing-birds and the humming bees;
Then talked of the haying, and wondered whether
The cloud in the west would bring foul weather.
And Maud forgot her brier-torn gown,
And her graceful ankles, bare and brown,
And listened, while a pleased surprise
Looked from her long-lashed hazel eyes.
At last, like one who for delay
Seeks a vain excuse, he rode away.

6. Maud Muller looked and sighed: "Ah me!
That I the Judge's bride might be!
He would dress me up in silks so fine,
And praise and toast me at his wine.
My father should wear a broadcloth coat,
My brother should sail a painted boat.
I'd dress my mother so grand and gay,
And the baby should have a new toy each day.
And I'd feed the hungry and clothe the poor,
And all should bless me who left our door."

7. The Judge looked back as he climbed the hill,
And saw Maud Muller standing still:
"A form more fair, a face more sweet,
Ne'er hath it been my lot to meet.
And her modest answer and graceful air
Show her wise and good as she is fair.
Would she were mine, and I to-day,
Like her, a harvester of hay:
No doubtful balance of rights and wrongs,
Nor weary lawyers with endless tongues,

11*

But low of cattle and song of birds,
And health, and quiet, and loving words."

8. But he thought of his sister, proud and cold,
And his mother, vain of her rank and gold.
So, closing his heart, the Judge rode on,
And Maud was left in the field alone.
But the lawyers smiled that afternoon,
When he hummed in court an old love-tune;
And the young girl mused beside the well,
Till the rain on the unraked clover fell.

9. He wedded a wife of richest dower,
Who lived for fashion, as he for power.
Yet oft, in his marble hearth's bright glow,
He watched a picture come and go;
And sweet Maud Muller's hazel eyes
Looked out in their innocent surprise.

10. Oft, when the wine in his glass was red,
He longed for the wayside well instead;
And closed his eyes on his garnished rooms,
To dream of meadows and clover blooms;
And the proud man sighed with a secret pain,—
"Ah, that I were free again!
Free as when I rode that day
Where the barefoot maiden raked the hay."

11. She wedded a man unlearned and poor,
And many children played round her door.
But care and sorrow, and childbirth pain,
Left their traces on heart and brain.
And oft, when the summer's sun shone hot
On the new-mown hay in the meadow lot,
And she heard the little spring-brook fall
Over the roadside, through the wall,
In the shade of the apple-tree again
She saw a rider draw his rein,
And, gazing down with timid grace,
She felt his pleased eyes read her face.

12. Sometimes her narrow kitchen walls
Stretched away into stately halls:
The weary wheel to a spinet turned,
The tallow candle an astral burned;
And for him who sat by the chimney lug,
Dozing and grumbling o'er pipe and mug,

A manly form at her side she saw,
And joy was duty, and love was law.
Then she took up her burden of life again,
Saying only, " It might have been."

13. Alas for maiden, alas for Judge,
For rich repiner and household drudge !
God pity them both ! and pity us all,
Who vainly the dreams of youth recall ;
For all sad words of tongue or pen,
The saddest are these : " IT MIGHT HAVE BEEN ! "
Ah, well ! for us all some sweet hope lies
Deeply buried from human eyes ;
And in the hereafter, angels may
Roll the stone from its grave away.

CXXIV.—ON RECOGNIZING THE INDEPENDENCE OF
GREECE, 1824.

CLAY.

1. ARE we so low, so base, so despicable, that we may
not express our horror, articulate our detestation, of the
most brutal and atrocious war that ever stained earth, or
shocked high Heaven, with the ferocious deeds of a brutal
soldiery, set on by the clergy and followers of a fanatical
and inimical religion, rioting in excess of blood and butch-
ery, at the mere details of which the heart sickens ? If
the great mass of Christendom can look coolly and calmly
on, while all this is perpetrated on a Christian People, in
their own vicinity, in their very presence, let us, at least,
show that, in this distant extremity, there is still some sensibility and sympathy for Christian wrongs and sufferings ;
that there are still feelings which can kindle into indignation at the oppression of a People endeared to us by every
ancient recollection, and every modern tie. But, Sir, it is
not first and chiefly for Greece that I wish to see this measure adopted.

2. It will give them but little aid,—that aid purely of
a moral kind. It is, indeed, soothing and solacing, in distress, to hear the accents of a friendly voice. We know

this as a People. But, Sir, it is principally and mainly for America herself, for the credit and character of our common country, that I hope to see this resolution pass : it is for our own unsullied name that I feel. What appearance, Sir, on the page of history, would a record like this make : —" In the month of January, in the year of our Lord and Saviour 1824, while all European Christendom beheld with cold, unfeeling apathy the unexampled wrongs and inexpressible misery of Christian Greece, a proposition was made in the Congress of the United States,—almost the sole, the last, the greatest repository of human hope and of human freedom, the representatives of a Nation capable of bringing into the field a million of bayonets,—while the freemen of that Nation were spontaneously expressing its deep-toned feeling, its fervent prayer for Grecian success : while the whole Continent was rising, by one simultaneous motion, solemnly and anxiously supplicating and invoking the aid of Heaven to spare Greece, and to invigorate her arms : while temples and senate-houses were all resounding with one burst of generous sympathy ;—in the year of our Lord and Saviour,—that Saviour alike of Christian Greece and of us,—a proposition was offered in the American Congress, to send a messenger to Greece, to inquire into her state and condition, with an expression of our good wishes and our sympathies ;—and it was rejected ! "

3. Go home, if you dare,—go home, if you can,—to your constituents, and tell them that you voted it down ! Meet, if you dare, the appalling countenances of those who sent you here, and tell them that you shrank from the declaration of your own sentiments : that, you cannot tell how, but that some unknown dread, some indescribable apprehension, some indefinable danger, affrighted you : that the spectres of cimeters, and crowns, and crescents, gleamed before you, and alarmed you ; and, that you suppressed all the noble feelings prompted by religion, by liberty, by National Independence, and by humanity ! I cannot bring myself to believe that such will be the feeling of a majority of this House.

CXXV.—MEN ALWAYS FIT FOR FREEDOM.

T. B. MACAULAY.

1. THERE is only one cure for the evils which newly-acquired freedom produces,—and that cure is freedom! When a prisoner leaves his cell, he cannot bear the light of day: he is unable to discriminate colors, or recognize faces; but the remedy is not to remand him into his dungeon, but to accustom him to the rays of the sun. The blaze of truth and liberty may at first dazzle and bewilder Nations which have become half blind in the house of bondage; but let them gaze on, and they will soon be able to bear it.

2. In a few years men learn to reason: the extreme violence of opinion subsides: hostile theories correct each other: the scattered elements of truth cease to conflict, and begin to coalesce; and, at length, a system of justice and order is educed out of the chaos. Many politicians of our time are in the habit of laying it down as a self-evident proposition, that no People ought to be free till they are fit to use their freedom. The maxim is worthy of the fool in the old story, who resolved not to go into the water till he had learned to swim! If men are to wait for liberty till they become wise and good in slavery, they may, indeed, wait forever!

CXXVI.—RAIN ON THE ROOF.

COATES KINNEY.

1. WHEN the humid showers gather over all the starry spheres,
   And the melancholy darkness gently weeps in rainy tears,
   'Tis a joy to press the pillow of a cottage chamber bed,
   And listen to the patter of the soft rain overhead.

2. Every tinkle on the shingles has an echo in the heart,
   And a thousand dreary fancies into busy being start;
   And a thousand recollections weave their bright hues into woof,
   As I listen to the patter of the soft rain on the roof.

3. There in fancy comes my mother, as she used to years agone,
   To survey the infant sleepers ere she left them till the dawn.

I can see her bending o'er me, as I listen to the strain
Which is played upon the shingles by the patter of the rain.

4. Then my little seraph sister, with her wings and waving hair,
And her bright-eyed, cherub brother—a serene, angelic pair—
Glide around my wakeful pillow with their praise or mild reproof,
As I listen to the murmur of the soft rain on the roof.

5. And another comes to thrill me with her eyes' delicious blue.
I forget, as gazing on her, that her heart was all untrue :
I remember that I loved her as I ne'er may love again,
And my heart's quick pulses vibrate to the patter of the rain.

6. There is naught in art's bravuras that can work with such a spell,
In the spirit's pure, deep fountains, whence the holy passions swell,
As that melody of nature—that subdued, subduing strain,
Which is played upon the shingles by the patter of the rain !

CXXVII.—THE SHIPWRECK.

Byron.

1. At half-past eight o'clock, booms, hen-coops, spars,
And all things, for a chance, had been cast loose,
That still could keep afloat the struggling tars ;
For yet they strove, although of no great use.
There was no light in heaven but a few stars :
The boats put off, o'ercrowded with their crews :
She gave a heel, and then a lurch to port,
And going down head-foremost—sunk, in short.

2. Then rose from sea to sky the wild farewell ; .
Then shrieked the timid, and stood still the brave ;
Then some leaped overboard, with dreadful yell,
As eager to anticipate their grave ;
And the sea yawned around her like a hell ;
And down she sucked with her the whirling wave,
Like one who grapples with his enemy,
And strives to strangle him before he die.

3. And first a universal shriek there rushed,
Louder than the loud ocean, like a crash
Of echoing thunder ; and then all was hushed,
Save the wild wind and the remorseless dash
Of billows ; but at intervals there gushed,
Accompanied with a convulsive splash,
A solitary shriek : the bubbling cry
Of some strong swimmer in his agony.

CXXVIII.—FORCE OF HABIT.

CHARLES A. WILEY.

1. In the Arctic ocean near the coast of Norway is situated the famous Maelstrom or whirlpool. Many are the goodly ships that have been caught in its circling power, and plunged into the depths below. On a fine spring morning, near the shore opposite, are gathered a company of peasants. The winter and the long night have passed away; and, in accordance with their ancient custom, they are holding a greeting to the return of the sunlight, and the verdure of spring. Under a green shade are spread, in abundance, all the luxuries their pleasant homes could afford. In the grove at one side are heard the strains of music, and the light step of the dance.

2. At the shore lies a beautiful boat, and a party near are preparing for a ride. Soon all things are in readiness, and, amid the cheers of their companions on shore, they push gayly away. The day is beautiful, and they row on, and on. Weary, at length, they drop their oars to rest; but they perceive their boat to be still moving. Somewhat surprised,—soon it occurs to them that they are under the influence of the whirlpool.

3. Moving slowly and without an effort—presently faster, at length the boat glides along with a movement far more delightful than with oars. Their friends from the shore perceive the boat moving, and see no working of the oars,—it flashes upon *their* minds—they are evidently within the circles of the maelstrom. When the boat comes near they call to them, " Beware of the whirlpool ! " But they laugh at fear,—they are too happy to think of returning: " When we see there is danger then we will return." Oh, that some good angel would come with warning unto them, " Unless ye *now* turn back ye *cannot* be saved." Like as the voice of God comes to the soul of the impenitent, " Unless ye mend your ways ye cannot be saved."

4. The boat is now going at a fearful rate; but, deceived by the moving waters, they are unconscious of its rapidity.

They hear the hollow rumbling at the whirlpool's centre. The voices from the shore are no longer audible, but every effort is being used to warn them of their danger. They now, for the first time, become conscious of their situation, and head the boat towards shore. But, like a leaf in the autumn gale, she quivers under the power of the whirlpool. Fear drives them to frenzy! Two of the strongest seize the oars, and ply them with all their strength, and the boat moves towards the shore. With *joy* they cherish hope! and some, for the first time in all their lives, *now* give *thanks* to God,—that they are *saved*. But, suddenly, CRASH! goes an oar! and such a shriek goes up from that ill-fated band, as can only be heard when a spirit lost drops into perdition!

5. The boat whirls again into its death-marked channel and skips on with the speed of the wind. The roar at the centre grinds on their ears, like the grating of prison doors on the ears of the doomed. Clearer, more deafening is that dreadful roar, as nearer and still nearer the vessel approaches the centre! then, whirling for a moment on that awful brink, she plunges with her freight of human .souls into that dreadful yawning hollow, where their bodies shall lie in their watery graves till the sea gives up its dead!

6. And so, every year, aye, every month, thousands, passing along in the boat of life, enter almost unaware the fatal circles of the wine-cup. And, notwithstanding the earnest voices of anxious friends, "Beware of the gutter! of the grave! of hell!" they continue their course until the "force of habit" overpowers them; and, cursing and shrieking, they whirl for a time on the crater of the maelstrom, and are plunged below!

CXXIX.—POETICAL AND PROSE SELECTIONS.

1.—FROM GOLDEN LEGEND.

1. THE Life which is, and that which is to come,
   Suspended hang in such nice equipoise

A breath disturbs the balance; and that scale
In which we throw our hearts preponderates,
And the other, like an empty one, flies up,
And is accounted vanity and air!

2.—FROM LONGFELLOW.

1. IN ancient records it is stated
  That, whenever an evil deed is done,
  Another devil is created
  To scourge and torment the offending one!
  But evil is only good perverted,
  And Lucifer, the Bearer of Light,
  But an angel fallen and deserted,
  Thrust from his Father's house with a curse
  Into the black and endless night.

3.—COUNT DE CABRA.

1. A GENTLEMAN who assisted the Count de Cabra in putting on his armor before the battle, perceiving him tremble, asked what could cause this emotion in a man of such known bravery? The Count answered: " My flesh trembles at the danger into which my soul will lead it."

4.—AN ENEMY'S GIFT.

1. WHEN the Crusaders under King Richard, of England, defeated the Saracens, the sultan, seeing his troops fly, asked what was the number of the Christians who were making all this slaughter? He was told that it was only King Richard and his men, and they were all afoot. " Then," said the Sultan, " God forbid that such a noble fellow as King Richard should march on foot," and sent him a noble charger. The messenger took it, and said: " Sir, the Sultan sends you this charger, in order that you may not be on foot." The King was cunning as his enemy, and ordered one of his squires to mount the horse, in order to try him. The squire did so ; but the animal was fiery, and he could not hold him : he set off at full speed to the Sultan's pavilion. The Sultan expected he had got King

Richard, and was not a little mortified to discover his mistake.

5.—The Power of Love.

Shakspeare.

1. But love, first learned in a lady's eyes,
   Lives not alone immured in the brain ;
   But with the motion of all elements,
   Courses as swift as thought in every power ;
   And gives to every power a double power,
   Above their functions and their offices.
   It adds a precious seeing to the eye :
   A lover's eyes will gaze an eagle blind ;
   A lover's ear will hear the lowest sound,
   When the suspicious head of theft is stopped :
   Love's feeling is more soft, and sensible,
   Than are the tender horns of cockled snails :
   Love's tongue proves dainty Bacchus gross in taste ;
   For valor, is not love a Hercules,
   Still climbing trees in the Hesperides?
   Subtle as sphinx, as sweet and musical
   As bright Apollo's lute, strung with his hair ;
   And, when love speaks, the voice of all the gods,
   Makes heaven drowsy with the harmony.
   Never durst poet touch a pen to write,
   Until his ink were tempered with love's sighs :
   O, then his lines would ravish savage ears,
   And plant in tyrants mild humility.

6.—Imperishability of Great Examples.

Edward Everett.

1. To be cold and breathless,—to feel not and speak not,—this is not the end of existence to the men who have breathed their spirits into the institutions of their country, who have stamped their characters on the pillars of the age, who have poured their hearts' blood into the channels of the public prosperity. Tell me, ye who tread the sods of yon sacred height, is Warren dead? Can you not still see him, not pale and prostrate, the blood of his gallant heart pouring out of his ghastly wound, but moving resplendent over the field of honor, with the rose of Heaven upon his cheek, and the fire of liberty in his eye?

2. Tell me, ye who make your pious pilgrimage to the shades of Vernon, is Washington, indeed, shut up in that cold and narrow house? That which made these men, and men like these, cannot die. The hand that traced the charter of Independence is, indeed, motionless; the eloquent lips that sustained it are hushed; but the lofty spirits that conceived, resolved, and maintained it, and which alone, to such men, "make it life to live," these cannot expire:

> "These shall resist the empire of decay,
> When time is o'er, and worlds·have passed away:
> Cold in the dust the perished heart may lie,
> But that which warmed it once can never die."

7.—VICE.

POPE.

1. VICE is a monster of so frightful mien,
   As, to be hated, needs but to be seen;
   But, seen too oft, familiar with her face,
   We first endure, then pity, then embrace.

8.—FROM HIAWATHA'S WOOING.

LONGFELLOW.

1. AND the ancient arrow maker
   Turned again unto his labor,
   Sat down by his sunny doorway,
   Murmuring to himself, and saying:
   "Thus it is our daughters leave us,
   Those we love, and those who love us!
   Just when they have learned to help us,
   When we are old and lean upon them,
   Comes a youth with flaunting feathers,
   With his flute of reed, a stranger
   Wanders piping through the village,
   Beckons to the fairest maiden,
   And she follows where he leads her,
   Leaving all things for the stranger!"

9.—THE LUNATIC, THE LOVER, AND THE POET.

SHAKSPEARE.

1. THE lunatic, the lover, and the poet
   Are of imagination all compact.
   One sees more devils than vast hell can hold;

That is the madman : the lover, all as frantic,
Sees Helen's beauty in a brow of Egypt:
The poet's eye, in a fine phrenzy rolling,
Doth glance from heaven to earth, from earth to heaven ;
And, as imagination bodies forth
The forms of things unknown, the poet's pen
Turns them to shapes, and gives to airy nothing
A local habitation and a name.

CXXX.—LA FAYETTE'S LAST VISIT TO AMERICA.
J. T. HEADLEY.

1. AGAIN, in his old age,* La Fayette determined to
look on the young Republic that had escaped the disasters
which had overwhelmed France. When his plans were
made known, our government offered to place a national
vessel at his disposal; but he declined accepting it, and embarked at Havre in a merchantman, and arrived at New
York, August 15, 1824. His reception in this country, and
triumphal march through it, is one of the most remarkable
events in the history of the world. Such gratitude and unbounded affection were never before received by a man
from a foreign nation.

2. As he passed from Staten Island to New York, the
bay was covered with gay barges decorated with streamers ;
and when the beautiful fleet shoved away, the bands struck
up, "Where can one better be, than in the bosom of his
family?" Never did this favorite French air seem so appropriate,—not even when the shattered Old Guard closed
sternly around its Emperor, and sang it amid the fire of the
enemy's guns,—as when a free people thus chanted it
around the venerable La Fayette.

3. As he touched the shore, the thunder of cannon
shook the city,—old soldiers rushed weeping into his arms ;
and "WELCOME LA FAYETTE!" waved from every banner,
rung from every trumpet, and was caught up by every

---

* La Fayette was sixty-seven years of age at the time of his last visit to America.

voice, till " WELCOME, WELCOME! " rose and fell in deafening shouts from the assembled thousands. During the four days he remained in the city, it was one constant jubilee ; and when he left for Boston, all along his route, the people rose to welcome him.

4. He traveled every night till twelve o'clock, and watch-fires were kept burning on the hill-tops, along his line of progress. Blazing through the darkness, they outshone the torches that heralded him : while in the distance the pealing bells from every church spire, announced his coming. The same enthusiastic joy awaited him at Boston ; and when he returned to New York, the city was wilder than ever with excitement.

5. In Castle-Garden there was a splendid illumination in honor of him : the bridge leading to it was surmounted by a pyramid sixty feet high, with a blazing star at the top, from the center of which flashed the name of LA FAYETTE. The planks were covered with carpets, and trees and flowers innumerable lined the passage. Over the entrance was a triumphal arch of flowers,—huge columns arose from the area, supporting arches of flowers, and flags, and statues. As he entered this wilderness of beauty, the bands struck up, " *See the conquering hero comes,*" and shouts shook the edifice to its foundation.

6. He had scarcely taken his seat in a splendid marquee prepared for his reception, when the curtain before the gallery, in front of him, lifted,—and there was a beautiful transparency, representing La Grange, with its grounds and towers, and beneath it, " *This is his home.*" Nothing could be more touching and affectionate than this device ; and as La Fayette's eye fell upon it, a tear was seen to gather there, and his lip to quiver with feeling.

7. Thus the people received the "people's friend." From New York he went to Albany and Troy, and one long shout of welcome rolled the length of the Hudson, as he floated up the noble stream. After visiting other cities, and receiving similar demonstrations of gratitude, he turned

his steps toward Mount Vernon, to visit the tomb of Washington. The thunder of cannon announced his arrival at the consecrated ground, calling to his mind the time when he had seen that now lifeless chieftain, move through the tumult of battle.

8. Wishing no one to witness his emotions, as he stood beside the ashes of his friend, he descended alone into the vault. With trembling steps, and uncovered head, he passed down to the tomb. The secrets of that meeting of the living with the dead, no one knows; but when the aged veteran came forth again, his face was covered with tears. He then took his son and secretary by the hand, and led them into the vault. He could not speak,— his bursting heart was too full for utterance, and he mutely pointed to the coffin of Washington. They knelt reverently beside it, then rising threw themselves into La Fayette's arms, and burst into tears. It was a touching scene, there in the silent vault, and worthy the noble sleeper.

9. Thence he went to Yorktown, and then proceeded South, passed through all the principal cities to New Orleans, and thence up the Mississippi to Cincinnati and across to Pittsburg. Wherever he went the entire nation rose to do him homage. " Honor to La Fayette," " Welcome to La Fayette, the nation's guest," and such like exclamations had met him at every step. Flowers were strewed along his pathway : his carriage detached from the horses, and drawn by the enthusiastic crowd, along ranks of grateful freemen who rent the heavens with their acclamations. Melted to tears by these demonstrations of love, he had moved like a father amid his children, scattering blessings wherever he went.

10. One of his last acts in this country, was to lay the corner-stone of the Bunker Hill Monument. It was fit that he, the last survivor of the major-generals of the American Revolution, should consecrate the first block in that grand structure. Amid the silent attention of fifty thousand spectators, this aged veteran, and friend of Washington, with

uncovered head, performed the imposing ceremonies, and, "LONG LIVE LA FAYETTE," swelled up from the top of Bunker Hill.

CXXXI.—ADVERTISEMENT OF A LOST DAY.

MRS. SIGOURNEY.

1. Lost! lost! lost!
   A gem of countless price,
   Cut from the living rock,
   And graved in Paradise.
   Set round with three times eight
   Large diamonds, clear and bright,
   And each with sixty smaller ones,
   All changeful as the light.

2. Lost,—where the thoughtless throng
   In fashion's mazes wind,
   Where trilleth folly's song,
   Leaving a sting behind:
   Yet to my hand 'twas given
   A golden harp to buy,
   Such as the white-robed choir attune
   To deathless minstrelsy.

3. Lost! lost! lost!
   I feel all search is vain:
   That gem of countless cost
   Can ne'er be mine again:
   I offer no reward,
   For till these heart-strings sever,
   I know that Heaven-intrusted gift
   Is reft away forever.

4. But when the sea and land,
   Like burning scroll have fled,
   I'll see it in His hand,
   Who judgeth quick and dead;
   And when of scathe and loss,
   That man can ne'er repair,
   The dread inquiry meets my soul,
   What shall it answer there?

CXXXII.—CATO'S SOLILOQUY ON IMMORTALITY.

ADDISON.

1. IT must be so.—Plato, thou reasonest well,
Else whence this pleasing hope, this fond desire,
This longing after immortality?
Or whence this secret dread, and inward horror,
Of falling into naught? Why shrinks the soul
Back on herself, and startles at destruction?
'Tis the divinity that stirs within us,
'Tis Heaven itself, that points out an hereafter,
And intimates eternity to man.

2. Eternity!—thou pleasing, dreadful thought!
Through what variety of untried being,
Through what new scenes and changes must we pass!
The wide, the unbounded prospect lies before me;
But shadows, clouds and darkness, rest upon it.
Here will I hold. If there's a Power above us,—
And that there is, all Nature cries aloud
Through all her works,—He must delight in virtue;
And that which He delights in must be happy.
But when? or where? This world was made for Cæsar.
I'm weary of conjectures,—this must end 'em.

3. Thus am I doubly armed. My death and life,
My bane and antidote, are both before me.
This in a moment brings me to my end;
But this informs me I shall never die.
The soul, secure in her existence, smiles
At the drawn dagger, and defies its point.
The stars shall fade away, the sun himself
Grow dim with age, and Nature sink in years,
But thou shalt flourish in immortal youth,
Unhurt amid the war of elements,
The wreck of matter, and the crush of worlds.

CXXXIII.—CATILINE TO HIS FRIENDS, AFTER FAILING IN HIS ELECTION TO THE CONSULSHIP.

REV. GEORGE CROLY.

1. ARE there not times, Patricians, when great States
Rush to their ruin? Rome is no more like Rome,
Than a foul dungeon's like the glorious sky.

What is she now ?   Degenerate, gross, defiled,
The tainted haunt, the gorged receptacle,
Of every slave and vagabond of earth :
A mighty grave that Luxury has dug,
To rid the other realms of pestilence !
   Ye wait to hail me Consul?
Consul ! Look on me,—on this brow,—these hands,
Look on this bosom, black with early wounds :
Have I not served the State from boyhood up,
Scattered my blood for her, labored for, loved her ?
I had no chance : wherefore should *I* be Consul ?
No.   Cicero still is master of the crowd.
Why not ?   He's made for them, and they for him,
They want a sycophant, and *he* wants slaves.
Well, let him have them !

2.   Patricians !   They have pushed me to the gulf,
I have worn down my heart, wasted my means,
Humbled my birth, bartered my ancient name,
For the rank favor of the senseless mass,
That frets and festers in your Commonwealth,—
And now—
The very men with whom I walked through life,
Nay, till within this hour, in all the bonds
Of courtesy and high companionship,
This day, as if the Heavens had stamped me black,
Turned on their heel, just at the point of fate,
Left me a mockery in the rabble's midst,
And followed their Plebeian Consul, Cicero !
This was the day to which I looked through life,
And it has failed me—vanished from my grasp,
Like air !

3.   Roman no more !   The rabble of the streets
Have seen me humbled : slaves may gibe at me,
For all the ills
That chance or nature lays upon our heads,
In chance or nature there is found a cure !
But *self*-abasement is beyond all cure !
The brand is here, burned in the living flesh,
That bears its mark to the grave ; that dagger's plunged
Into the central pulses of the heart :
The act is the mind's suicide, for which
There is no after health, no hope, no pardon !

12

CXXXIV.—CATILINE'S DEFIANCE.

REV. GEORGE CROLY.

1.   CONSCRIPT FATHERS!
I do not rise to waste the night in words:
Let that Plebeian talk: 'tis not *my* trade;
But *here* I stand for right,—let him show *proofs*,—
For Roman right; though none, it seems, dare stand
To take their share with me. Ay, cluster there!
Cling to your master, judges, Romans, *slaves!*
His charge is false;—I dare him to his *proofs*.
You have my answer. Let my actions speak!

2.   But this I will avow, that I *have* scorned,
And still do scorn, to hide my sense of wrong!
Who brands me on the forehead, breaks my sword,
Or lays the bloody scourge upon my back,
Wrongs me not half so much as he who shuts
The gates of honor on me,—turning out
The Roman from his birthright; and, for what?
                              [*Looking round him.*
To fling your offices to every slave!
Vipers, that creep where man disdains to climb,
And, having wound their loathsome track to the top,
Of this huge, mouldering monument of Rome,
Hang hissing at the nobler men below!
    Come, consecrated Lictors, from your thrones;
                              [*To the Senate.*
Fling down your sceptres: take the rod and axe,
And make the murder as you make the law!

3.   "Banished from Rome!" What's banished, but set free
From daily contact of the things I loathe?
"Tried and convicted traitor!" Who says this?
Who'll prove it, at his peril, on my head?
"Banished!" I thank you for't. It breaks my chain!
I held some slack allegiance till this hour;
But *now* my sword's my own. Smile on, my Lords!
I scorn to count what feelings, withered hopes,
Strong provocations, bitter, burning wrongs,
I have within my heart's hot cells shut up,
To leave you to your lazy dignities.
But here I stand and scoff you! here, I fling
Hatred and full defiance in your face!
Your Consul's merciful.—For this, all thanks.
He *dares* not touch a hair of Catiline!

4.   "Traitor!" I go; but, I *return.* This—trial!
Here I devote your Senate! I've had wrongs
To stir a fever in the blood of age,
Or make the infant's sinews strong as steel.
This day's the birth of sorrow! 'This hour's work
Will breed proscriptions! Look to your hearths, my Lords!
For there, henceforth, shall sit, for household gods,
Shapes hot from Tartarus!—all shames and crimes
Wan Treachery, with his thirsty dagger drawn:
Suspicion, poisoning his brother's cup:
Naked Rebellion, with the torch and axe,
Making his wild sport of your blazing Thrones;
Till Anarchy comes down on you like Night,
And Massacre seals Rome's eternal grave.

5.   I go; but not to leap the gulf alone.
I go; but, when I come, 't will be the burst
Of ocean in the earthquake,—rolling back
In swift and mountainous ruin. Fare you well:
You build my funeral-pile; but your best blood
Shall quench its flame! Back, slaves!   [*To the Lictors.*]
I will return.

----◆----

CXXXV.—ADDRESS OF BLACK HAWK TO GENERAL STREET.

1. You have taken me prisoner, with all my warriors. I am much grieved; for I expected, if I did not defeat you, to hold out much longer, and give you more trouble, before I surrendered. I tried hard to bring you into ambush, but your last General understood Indian fighting. I determined to rush on you, and fight you face to face. I fought hard. But your guns were well aimed. The bullets flew like birds in the air, and whizzed by our ears like the wind through the trees in winter. My warriors fell around me: it begun to look dismal. I saw my evil day at hand. The sun rose dim on us in the morning, and at night it sank in a dark cloud, and looked like a ball of fire. That was the last sun that shone on Black Hawk. His heart is dead, and no longer beats quick in his bosom. He is now a prisoner to the white men: they will do with him as they

wish. But he can stand torture, and is not afraid of death. He is no coward. Black Hawk is an Indian.

2. He has done nothing for which an Indian ought to be ashamed. He has fought for his countrymen, against white men, who came, year after year, to cheat them, and take away their lands. You know the cause of our making war. It is known to all white men. They ought to be ashamed of it. The white men despise the Indians, and drive them from their homes. They smile in the face of the poor Indian, to cheat him : they shake him by the hand, to gain his confidence, to make him drunk, and to deceive him. We told them to let us alone, and keep away from us ; but they followed on and beset our paths, and they coiled themselves among us like the snake. They poisoned us by their touch. We were not safe. We lived in danger. We looked up to the Great Spirit. We went to our father. We were encouraged. His great council gave us fair words and big promises ; but we got no satisfaction : things were growing worse. There were no deer in the forest. The opossum and beaver were fled. The springs were drying up, and our squaws and papooses without victuals to keep them from starving.

3. We called a great council, and built a large fire. The spirit of our fathers arose, and spoke to us to avenge our wrongs or die. We set up the war-whoop, and dug up the tomahawk : our knives were ready, and the heart of Black Hawk swelled high in his bosom, when he led his warriors to battle. He is satisfied. He will go to the world of spirits contented. He has done his duty. His father will meet him there, and commend him. Black Hawk is a true Indian, and disdains to cry like a woman. He feels for his wife, his children, and his friends. But he does not care for himself. He cares for the Nation and the Indians. They will suffer. He laments their fate. Farewell, my Nation ! Black Hawk tried to save you, and avenge your wrongs. He drank the blood of some of the whites. He has been taken prisoner, and his plans are

crushed. He can do no more. He is near his end. His sun is setting, and he will rise no more. Farewell to Black Hawk!

------♦------

CXXXVI.—WILLIAM TELL AMONG THE MOUNTAINS.

J. S. KNOWLES.

1.   YE crags and peaks, I'm with you once again!
I hold to you the hands you first beheld,
To show they still are free. Methinks I hear
A spirit in your echoes answer me,
And bid your tenant welcome to his home
Again!—O sacred forms, how proud you look!
How high you lift your heads into the sky!
How huge you are! how mighty, and how free!
Ye are the things that tower, that shine,—whose smile
Makes glad, whose frown is terrible, whose forms,
Robed or unrobed, do all the impress wear
Of awe divine.

2.   Ye guards of liberty,
I'm with you once again!—I call to you
With all my voice!—I hold my hands to you,
To show they still are free. I rush to you
As though I could embrace you!
  Scaling yonder peak,
I saw an eagle wheeling near its brow
O'er the abyss: his broad-expanded wings
Lay calm and motionless upon the air,
As if he floated there without their aid,
By the sole act of his unlorded will
That buoyed him proudly up.

3.   Instinctively
I bent my bow; yet kept he rounding still
His airy circle, as in the delight
Of measuring the ample range beneath
And round about: absorbed, he heeded not
The death that threatened him. I could not shoot!—
'T was liberty!—I turned my bow aside,
And let him soar away!

------♦------

CXXXVII.—MOUNT TABOR.

J. T. HEADLEY.

1. FORTY-SEVEN years ago, a form was seen standing on Mount Tabor, with which the world has since become familiar. It was a bright spring morning, and as he sat on his steed in the clear sunlight, his eye rested on a scene in the vale below, which was sublime and appalling enough to quicken the pulsations of the calmest heart. That form was NAPOLEON BONAPARTE; and the scene before him, the fierce and terrible "BATTLE OF MOUNT TABOR."

2. From Nazareth, where the Saviour once trod, KLEBER had marched with three thousand French soldiers forth into the plain, when lo! at the foot of Mount Tabor he saw the whole Turkish army, drawn up in order of battle. Fifteen thousand infantry and twelve thousand splendid cavalry moved down in majestic strength on this band of three thousand French. Kleber had scarcely time to throw his handful of men into squares, with the cannon at the angles, before those twelve thousand horse, making the earth smoke and thunder as they came, burst in a headlong gallop upon them.

3. But round those steady squares rolled a fierce devouring fire, emptying the saddles of those wild horsemen with frightful rapidity, and strewing the earth with the bodies of riders and steeds together. Again and again did those splendid squadrons wheel, re-form and charge with deafening shouts, while their uplifted and flashing cimeters gleamed like a forest of steel through the smoke of battle; but that same wasting fire received them, till those squares seemed bound by a girdle of flame, so rapid and constant were the discharges. Before their certain and deadly aim, as they stood fighting for existence, the charging squadrons fell so fast that a rampart of dead bodies was soon formed around them. Behind this embankment of dead men and horses, this band of warriors stood and fought for six dreadful hours, and was still steadily thinning the ranks of the

enemy, when Napoleon debouched with a single division on Mount Tabor, and turned his eye below.

4. What a scene met his gaze! The whole plain was filled with marching columns and charging squadrons of wildly galloping steeds, while the thunder of cannon and fierce rattle of musketry, amid which now and then was heard the blast of thousands of trumpets, and strains of martial music filled the air. The smoke of battle was rolling furiously over the hosts, and all was confusion and chaos in his sight. Amid the twenty-seven thousand Turks that crowded the plain, and enveloped their enemy like a cloud, and amid the incessant discharge of artillery and musketry, Napoleon could tell where his own brave troops were struggling, only by the steady simultaneous volleys which showed how discipline was contending with the wild valor of overpowering numbers. The constant flashes from behind that rampart of dead bodies, were like spots of flame on the tumultuous and chaotic field.

5. Napoleon descended from Mount Tabor with his little band, while a single twelve-pounder, fired from the hights, told the wearied Kleber that he was rushing to the rescue. Then for the first time he took the offensive, and pouring his enthusiastic followers on the foe, carried death and terror over the field. Thrown into confusion, and trampled under foot, that mighty army rolled turbulently back toward the Jordan, where Murat was anxiously waiting to mingle in the fight. Dashing with his cavalry among the disordered ranks, he sabered them down without mercy, and raged like a lion amid the prey. This chivalric and romantic warrior declared that the remembrance of the scenes that once transpired on Mount Tabor, and on these thrice consecrated spots, came to him in the hottest of the fight, and nerved him with ten-fold courage. As the sun went down over the plains of Palestine, and twilight shed its dim ray over the rent, and trodden, and dead-covered field, a sulphurous cloud hung around the summit of Mount Tabor. The smoke of battle had settled there where once

the cloud of glory rested, while groans, and shrieks, and cries, rent the air. Nazareth, Jordan, and Mount Tabor! what spots for battle-fields!

---------◆---------

CXXXVIII.—MOUNT TABOR.—Continued.

J. T. Headley.

1. Roll back eighteen centuries, and again view that Mount. The day is bright and beautiful, as on the day of battle, and the same rich oriental landscape is smiling in the same sun. There is Nazareth, with its busy population, —the same Nazareth, from which Kleber marched his army; and there is Jordan, rolling its bright waters along, —the same Jordan, along whose banks charged the glittering squadrons of Murat's cavalry; and there is Mount Tabor,—the same, on which Bonaparte stood with his cannon; and the same beautiful plain where rolled the smoke of battle, and struggled thirty thousand men in mortal combat.

2. But how different is the scene that is passing there. The Son of God stands on that hight, and casts his eye over the quiet valley, through which Jordan winds its silvery current. Three friends are beside Him. They have walked together up the toilsome way, and now they stand, mere specks on the distant summit. Far away to the north-west, shines the blue Mediterranean: all around is the great plain of Esdraelon and Galilee: eastward the lake of Tiberias dots the landscape, while Mount Carmel lifts its naked summit in the distance.

3. But the glorious landscape at their feet is forgotten in a sublimer scene that is passing before them. The son of Mary—the carpenter of Nazareth—the wanderer, with whom they have travelled on foot many a weary league, in all the intimacy of companions and friends, begins to change before their eyes. Over his garments is spreading a strange light, steadily brightening into intenser beauty,

till that form glows with such splendor that it seems to waver to and fro, and dissolve in the still radiance.

4. The three astonished friends gaze on it in speechless admiration, then turn to that familiar face. But lo! a greater change has passed over it. That sad and solemn countenance which has been so often seen stooping over the couch of the dying, entering the door of the hut of poverty, passing through the streets of Jerusalem, and pausing by the weary way-side—aye, bedewed with the tears of pity, —now burns like the sun in his mid-day splendor. Meekness has given way to majesty,—sadness, to dazzling glory, —the look of pity, to the grandeur of a God.

5. The still radiance of Heaven sits on that serene brow, and all around that divine form flows an atmosphere of strange and wondrous beauty. Heaven has poured its brightness over that consecrated spot, and on the beams of light, which glitter there, Moses and Elias have descended, and, wrapped in the same shining vestments, stand beside him. Wonder follows wonder, for those three glittering forms are talking with each other, and amid the thrilling accents are heard the words, "Mount Olivet," "Calvary!" —"the agony and the death of the crucifixion!"

6. No wonder a sudden fear came over Peter, that paralyzed his tongue, and crushed him to the earth, when, in the midst of his speech, he saw a cloud descend like a falling star from heaven, and, bright and dazzling, balance itself over those forms of light, while from its bright foldings came a voice, saying, "This is my beloved Son, in whom I am well pleased, hear ye Him!" How long the vision lasted we can not tell; but all that night did Jesus, with his friends, stay on that lonely mountain. Of the conversation that passed between them there, we know nothing; but little sleep, we imagine, visited their eyes that night; and as they sat on the high summit, and watched the stars, as they rose one after another above the horizon, and gazed on the moon as she poured her light over the dim and darkened landscape, words were spoken, that

12*

seemed born of Heaven, and truths never to be forgotten were uttered in the ears of the subdued and reverent disciples.

7. O, how different is Heaven and earth! Can there be a stronger contrast than the BATTLE and TRANSFIGURA-TION of Mount Tabor? One shudders to think of Bonaparte and the Son of God on the same mountain,—one with his wasting cannon by his side, and the other with Moses and Elias just from Heaven. But no after desecration can destroy the first consecration of Mount Tabor; for, surrounded with the glory of Heaven, and honored with the wondrous scene of the TRANSFIGURATION, it stands a SACRED MOUNTAIN on the earth.

CXXXIX.—REFLECTIONS FROM THE SUMMIT OF AN EGYPTIAN PYRAMID.

1. THRONED on the sepulcher of mighty kings,
   Whose dust in solemn silence sleeps below,
Till that great day, when sublunary things
   Shall pass away, e'en as the April bow
Fades from the gazer's eyes, and leaves no trace
Of its bright colors, or its former place:

2. I gaze in sadness o'er the scenery wild:
   On scattered groups of palms, and seas of sand:
On the wide desert, and the desert's child:
   On ruins made by Time's destructive hand:
On temples, towers, and columns now laid low,—
A land of crime, of tyranny, and woe.

3. O Egypt! Egypt! how art thou debased!
   A Moslem slave upon Busiris' throne!
And all thy splendid monuments defaced!
   Long, long beneath his iron rod shall groan
Thy hapless children: thou hast had thy day,
And all thy glories now have passed away.

4. O! could thy princely dead rise from their graves,
   And view with me the changes Time has wrought,—
A land of ruins, and a race of slaves,
   Where wisdom flourished, and where sages taught,

A scene of desolation, mental night!—
How would they shrink with horror from the sight!

5. Ancient of days! nurse of fair science, arts!
   All that refines and elevates mankind!
Where are thy palaces, and where thy marts,
   Thy glorious cities, and thy men of mind?
Forever gone!—the very names they bore,
The sites they occupied, are now no more.

6. But why lament, since such must ever be
   The fate of human greatness, human pride?
E'en those who mourn the loudest over thee,
   Are drifting headlong down the rapid tide
That sweeps, resistless, to the yawning grave,
All that is great and good, or wise and brave.

7. E'en thou, proud fabric! whence I now survey
   Scenes so afflicting to the feeling heart,
Despite thy giant strength, must sink the prey
   Of hoary age, and all thy fame depart;
In vain thy head, aspiring, scales the sky:
Prostrate in dust that lofty head must lie.

8. The soul alone,—the precious boon of Heaven,—
   Can fearless brave of time and fate the rage,
When to thy deep foundations thou art riven,
   Yea, Egypt! blotted from th' historic page,
She shall survive, shall ever, ever bloom,
In radiant youth, triumphant o'er the tomb.

CXL.—ROMANTIC STORY.

1. THERE is a cavern in the island of Hoonga, one of
the Tonga islands, in the South Pacific Ocean, which can
only be entered by diving into the sea, and which has no
other light, than that which is reflected from the bottom
of the water. A young chief discovered it accidentally,
while diving after a turtle, and the use which he made of
his discovery, will probably be sung in more than one
European language, so beautifully is it adapted for a tale
in verse.

2. There was a tyrannical governor at Vavaoo, against

whom one of the chiefs formed a plan of insurrection. It was betrayed, and the chief, with all his family and kin, was ordered to be destroyed. He had a beautiful daughter, betrothed to a chief of high rank, and she also was included in the sentence. The youth who had found the cavern, and had kept the secret to himself, loved this damsel. He told her the danger in time, and persuaded her to trust to him. They got into a canoe : the place of her retreat was described to her on the way to it,—these women swim like mermaids,—she dived after him, and rose in the cavern. In the widest part it is about fifty feet: its medium hight being about the same, and it is hung with sta lactites.

3. Here, he brought her the choicest food, the finest clothing, mats for her bed, and sandal oil to perfume herself with. Here, he visited her as often as was consistent with prudence, and here, as may be imagined, this Tonga Leander, wooed and won the maid, whom, to make the interest complete, he had long loved in secret, when he had no hope. Meantime he prepared, with all his dependents, male and female, to emigrate in secret to the Fiji islands.

4. The intention was so well concealed, that they embarked in safety, and his people asked him, at the point of their departure, if he would not take with him a Tonga wife ; and, accordingly, to their great astonishment, having steered close to the rock, he desired them to wait while he went into the sea to fetch her, jumped overboard, and just as they were beginning to be seriously alarmed at his long disappearance, he rose with his mistress from the water. This story is not deficient in that which all such stories should have, to be perfectly delightful—a fortunate conclusion. The party remained at the Fijis till the oppressor died, and then returned to Vavaoo, where they enjoyed a long and happy life.

CXLI.—THE PHILOSOPHER'S SCALES.

JANE TAYLOR.

1. A MONK, when his rites sacerdotal were o'er,
In the depth of his cell with his stone-covered floor,
Resigning to thought his chimerical brain,
Once formed the contrivance we now shall explain;
But whether by magic's or alchomy's powers,
We know not,—indeed, 'tis no business of ours.
Perhaps, it was only by patience and care,
At last, that he brought his invention to bear;
In youth 'twas projected, but years stole away,
And ére 'twas complete, he was wrinkled and gray;
But success is secure, unless energy fails;
And, at length, he produced the philosopher's scales.

2. "What were they?" you ask,—you shall presently see:
These scales were not made to weigh sugar and tea,—
O no; for such properties wondrous had they,
That qualities, feelings, and thoughts, they could weigh:
Together with articles small or immense,
From mountains or planets, to atoms of sense.
Naught was there so bulky, but there it would lay,
And naught so ethereal, but there it would stay,
And naught so reluctant, but in it must go:
All which some examples more clearly will show.

3. The first thing he weighed was the head of Voltaire,
Which retained all the wit that had ever been there:
As a weight he threw in a torn scrap of a leaf,
Containing the prayer of the penitent thief:
When the skull rose aloft with so sudden a spell,
That it bounced like a ball on the roof of the cell.
One time, he put in Alexander the Great,
With a garment that Dorcas had made, for a weight,
And, though clad in armor from sandals to crown,
The hero rose up, and the garment went down.

4. A long row of alms-houses, amply endowed
By a well esteemed Pharisoe, busy and proud,
Next loaded one scale: while the other was prest
By those mites the poor widow dropt into the chest:
Up flew the endowment, not weighing an ounce,
And down, down the farthing-worth came with a bounce.
By further experiments, (no matter how,)
He found that ten chariots weighed less than one plow;

A sword with gilt trapping rose up in the scale,
Though balanced by only a ten-penny nail :
A shield and a helmet, a buckler and spear,
Weighed less than a widow's uncrystallized tear.

5. A lord and a lady went up at full sail,
When a bee chanced to light on the opposite scale :
Ten doctors, ten lawyers, two courtiers, one earl,
Ten counselors' wigs, full of powder and curl,
All heaped in one balance and swinging from thence,
Weighed less than a few grains of candor and sense :
A first water diamond, with brilliants begirt,
Than one good potato, just washed from the dirt :
Yet not mountains of silver and gold could suffice,
One pearl to outweigh, 'twas the pearl of great price.

6. Last of all, the whole world was bowled in at the grate,
With the soul of a beggar to serve for a weight,
When the former sprang up with so strong a rebuff,
That it made a vast rent and escaped at the roof;
When, balanced in air, it ascended on high,
And sailed up aloft, a balloon in the sky :
While the scale with the soul in't so mightily fell,
That it jerked the philosopher out of his cell.

CXLII.—THE THREE WARNINGS.

Mrs. Thrale.

1. The tree of deepest root is found
    Least willing still to quit the ground :
    'Twas therefore said, by ancient sages,
      That love of life increased with years,
    So much, that in our latter stages,
    When pains grow sharp and sickness rages,
      The greatest love of life appears.
    This great affection to believe,
    Which all confess, but few perceive,
    If old assertions can't prevail,
    Be pleased to hear a modern tale.

2. When sports went round, and all were gay,
    On neighbor Dobson's wedding-day :
    Death called aside the jocund groom
    With him into another room ;

And looking grave, "You must," says he,
" Quit your sweet bride, and come with me."
" With you ! and quit my Susan's side ?
With you ? " the hapless bridegroom cried :
" Young as I am, 'tis monstrous hard !
Besides, in truth, I'm not prepared."

3. What more he urged, I have not heard :
    His reasons could not well be stronger :
So Death the poor delinquent spared,
    And left to live a little longer.
Yet calling up a serious look,
His hour-glass trembled, while he spoke ;
" Neighbor," he said, " farewell : no more
Shall Death disturb your mirthful hour,
And further, to avoid all blame
Of cruelty upon my name,
To give you time for preparation,
And fit you for your future station,
Three several warnings you shall have,
Before you're summoned to the grave :
Willing, for once, I'll quit my prey,
 - And grant a kind reprieve :
In hopes you'll have no more to say,
But when I call again this way,
Well pleased the world will leave."
To these conditions both consented,
And parted perfectly contented.

4. What next the hero of our tale befell,
    How long he lived, how wise, how well,
    It boots not, that the muse should tell :
He plowed, he sowed, he bought, he sold,
Nor once perceived his growing old,
    Nor thought of Death as near :
His friends not false, his wife no shrew,
Many his gains, his children few,
    He passed his hours in peace :
But, while he viewed his wealth increase,
While thus along life's dusty road,
The beaten track, content, he trod,
Old Time, whose haste no mortal spares,
Uncalled, unheeded, unawares,
    Brought on his eightieth year.

5. And now, one night, in musing mood
   As all alone he sat,
   The unwelcome messenger of Fate
   Once more before him stood.
   Half killed with wonder and surprise,
   " So soon returned ! " old Dobson cries.
   " So *soon* d'ye call it ? " Death replies :
   " Surely, my friend, you're but in jest :
   Since I was here before,
   'Tis six and thirty years at least,
   And you are now four-score."
   " So much the worse ! " the clown rejoined :
   " To spare the aged would be kind :
   Besides, you promised me *three warnings*,
   Which I have looked for, nights and mornings ! "

6. " I know," cries Death, " that at the best,
   I seldom am a welcome guest ;
   But don't be captious, friend : at least,
   I little thought that you'd be able
   To stump about your farm and stable,
   Your years have run to a great length,
   Yet still you seem to have your strength."
   " Hold ! " says the farmer, " not so fast !
   I have been lame, these four years past."
   " And no great wonder," Death replies :
   " However, you still keep your eyes ;
   And surely, sir, to see one's friends,
   For legs and arms would make amends."
   " Perhaps," says Dobson, " so it might,
   But latterly I've lost my sight."
   " This is a shocking story, faith ;
   But there's some comfort still," says Death :
   " Each strives your sadness to amuse :
   I warrant you hear all the news."
   " There's none," cries he, " and if there were,
   I've grown so deaf, I could not hear."

7. " Nay then," the specter stern rejoined,
   " These are unpardonable yearnings :
   If you are lame, and deaf, and blind,
   You've *had* your *three* sufficient warnings :
   So, come along ! no more we'll part : "
   He said, and touched him with his dart.

And now, old Dobson, turning pale,
Yields to his fate—so ends my tale.

———◆———

CXLIII.—THE PILOT—A THRILLING INCIDENT.

JOHN B. GOUGH.

1. JOHN MAYNARD was well known in the lake district as a God-fearing, honest and intelligent pilot. He was pilot on a steamboat from Detroit to Buffalo, one summer afternoon—at that time those steamers seldom carried boats—smoke was seen ascending from below, and the captain called out:

" Simpson, go below and see what the matter is down there."

Simpson came up with his face pale as ashes, and said, " Captain, the ship is on fire."

Then " Fire! fire! fire! " on shipboard.

All hands were called up. Buckets of water were dashed on the fire, but in vain. There were large quantities of rosin and tar on board, and it was found useless to attempt to save the ship.

2. The passengers rushed forward and inquired of the pilot:

" How far are we from Buffalo ? "

" Seven miles."

" How long before we can reach there ? "

" Three-quarters of an hour at our present rate of steam."

" Is there any danger ? "

" Danger, here—see the smoke bursting out—go forward if you would save your lives."

Passengers and crew, men, women and children, crowded the forward part of the ship. John Maynard stood at the helm. The flames burst forth in a sheet of fire: clouds of smoke arose.

3. The captain cried out through his trumpet:

" John Maynard! "

" Aye, aye, sir! "

" Are you at the helm ? "

" Aye, aye, sir ! "

" How does she head ? "

" South-east by east, sir."

" Head her south-east and run her on shore," said the captain.

Nearer, nearer, yet nearer, she approached the shore. Again the captain cried out :

" John Maynard ! "

The response came feebly this time, " Aye, aye, sir ! "

" Can you hold on five minutes longer, John ? " he said.

" By God's help, I will."

The old man's hair was scorched from the scalp, one hand disabled, his knee upon the stanchion, and his teeth set, with his other hand upon the wheel, he stood firm as a rock. He beached the ship : every man, woman, and child was saved, as John Maynard dropped, and his spirit took its flight to its God.

CXLIV.—TWENTY YEARS AGO.

1. I'VE wandered to the village, Tom : I've sat beneath the tree,
Upon the school house play-ground, which sheltered you and me ;
But none were there to greet me, Tom, and few were left to know,
That played with us upon the green, some twenty years ago.

2. The grass was just as green, Tom, bare-footed boys at play,
Were sporting just as we did then, with spirits just as gay ;
But " Master " sleeps upon the hill, which, coated o'er with snow,
Afforded us a sliding place just twenty years ago.

3. The school house has altered some—the benches are replaced
By new ones, very like the same our pen-knives had defaced ;
But the same old bricks are in the wall—the bell swings to and fro,
Its music just the same, dear Tom, 'twas twenty years ago.

4. The boys were playing some old game, beneath that same old tree :
I do forget the name just now—you've played the same with me—
On that same spot, 'twas played with knives, by throwing so and so :
The leader had a task to do—there twenty years ago.

5. The river's running just as still, the willows on its side,
Are larger than they were, Tom : the stream appears less wide :
But the grape-vine swing is ruined now, where once we played the beau,
And swung our sweet-hearts, " pretty girls," just twenty years ago.

6. The spring that bubbled 'neath the hill, close by the spreading beech,
Is very low—'twas once so high, that we could almost reach ;
And kneeling down to get a drink, dear Tom, I startled so,
To see how much I've changed since twenty years ago.

7. Near by the spring, upon an elm, you know I cut your name,
Your sweet-heart's just beneath it, Tom, and you did mine the same :
Some heartless wretch has peeled the bark, 'twas dying sure but slow,
Just as that one, whose name you cut, died twenty years ago.

8. My lids have long been dry, Tom, but tears came in my eyes :
I thought of her I loved so well, those early broken ties :
I visited the old church-yard, and took some flowers to strew
Upon the graves of those we loved, some twenty years ago.

9. Some are in the church-yard laid—some sleep beneath the sea ;
But few are left of our old class, excepting you and me ;
And when our time shall come, Tom, and we are called to go,
I hope they'll lay us where we played just twenty years ago.

———————◆———————

CXLV.—THE RAVEN.
EDGAR A. POE.

1. ONCE upon a midnight dreary, while I pondered, weak and weary,
Over many a quaint and curious volume of forgotten lore :
While I nodded, nearly napping, suddenly there came a tapping,
As of some one gently rapping, rapping at my chamber-door.
" 'Tis some visitor," I mutter'd, " tapping at my chamber-door—
Only this, and nothing more."

2. Ah, distinctly I remember, it was in the bleak December,
And each separate dying ember wrought its ghost upon the floor.
Eagerly I wished the morrow : vainly I had sought to borrow
From my books surcease of sorrow—sorrow for the lost Lenore—
For the rare and radiant maiden whom the angels named Lenore—
Nameless here forevermore.

3. And the silken, sad, uncertain rustling of each purple curtain,
Thrill'd me—fill'd me with fantastic terrors never felt before :
So that now, to still the beating of my heart, I stood repeating,
" 'Tis some visitor entreating entrance at my chamber-door :

Some late visitor entreating entrance at my chamber-door :
· That it is, and nothing more."

4. Presently my soul grew stronger : hesitating then no longer,
" Sir," said I, " or Madam, truly your forgiveness I implore ;
But the fact is, I was napping, and so gently you came rapping,
And so faintly you came tapping, tapping at my chamber-door,
That I scarce was sure I heard you "—here I open'd wide the door :
Darkness there, and nothing more.

5. Deep into that darkness peering, long I stood there, wondering, fearing,
Doubting, dreaming dreams no mortal ever dared to dream before ;
But the silence was unbroken, and the darkness gave no token,
And the only word there spoken was the whisper'd word " Lenore ! "
This *I* whisper'd, and an echo murmur'd back the word " LENORE ! "
Merely this, and nothing more.

6. Back into the chamber turning, all my soul within me burning,
Soon again I heard a tapping, something louder than before.
" Surely," said I, " surely that is something at my window-lattice :
Let me see then what thereat is, and this mystery explore,—
Let my heart be still a moment, and this mystery explore ; —
'Tis the wind, and nothing more."

7. Open then I flung the shutter, when, with many a flirt and flutter,
In there stepp'd a stately raven of the saintly days of yore.
Not the least obeisance made he : not an instant stopp'd or stay'd he ;
But, with mien of lord or lady, perched above my chamber-door,—
Perch'd upon a bust of Pallas, just above my chamber-door—
Perch'd, and sat, and nothing more.

8. Then this ebony bird beguiling my sad fancy into smiling,
By the grave and stern decorum of the countenance it wore,
" Though thy crest be shorn and shaven, thou," I said, " art sure no
craven :
Ghastly, grim, and ancient raven, wandering from the nightly shore,
Tell me what thy lordly name is on the Night's Plutonian shore ? "
Quoth the raven, " Nevermore ! "

9. Much I marvel'd this ungainly fowl to hear discourse so plainly,
Though its answer little meaning—little relevancy bore ;
For we cannot help agreeing that no living human being
Ever yet was bless'd with seeing bird above his chamber-door—
Bird or beast upon the sculptured bust above his chamber-door,
With such name as " Nevermore ! "

10. But the raven sitting lonely on the placid bust, spoke only
That one word, as if his soul in that one word he did outpour.

Nothing further then he utter'd—not a feather then he flutter'd—
Till I scarcely more than mutter'd, "Other friends have flown before—
On the morrow *he* will leave me, as my hopes have flown before."
Then the bird said, "Nevermore!"

11. Startled at the stillness broken by reply so aptly spoken,
"Doubtless," said I, " what it utters is its only stock and store,
Caught from some unhappy master, whom unmerciful disaster
Follow'd fast and followed faster, till his song one burden bore,—
Till the dirges of his hope that melancholy burden bore,
Of 'Nevermore—nevermore!'"

12. But the raven still beguiling all my sad soul into smiling,
Straight I wheeled a cushion'd seat in front of bird, and bust, and door,
Then, upon the velvet sinking, I betook myself to linking
Fancy unto fancy, thinking what this ominous bird of yore—
What this grim, ungainly, ghastly, gaunt, and ominous bird of yore
Meant in croaking "Nevermore!"

13. This I sat engaged in guessing, but no syllable expressing
To the fowl, whose fiery eyes now burned into my bosom's core:
This and more I sat divining, with my head at ease reclining
On the cushion's velvet lining that the lamp-light gloated o'er,
But whose velvet violet lining, with the lamp-light gloating o'er,
She shall press—ah! nevermore!

14. Then methought the air grew denser, perfumed from an unseen censer
Swung by seraphim, whose foot-falls tinkled on the tufted floor.
"Wretch," I cried, "thy God hath lent thee—by these angels he hath
sent thee
Respite—respite and nepenthe from thy memories of Lenore!
Quaff, oh quaff this kind nepenthe, and forget this lost Lenore!"
Quoth the raven, "Nevermore!"

15. "Prophet!" said I, "thing of evil!—prophet still, if bird or devil!
Whether tempter sent, or whether tempest toss'd thee here ashore,
Desolate, yet all undaunted, on this desert land enchanted—
On this home by Horror haunted—tell me truly, I implore—
Is there—*is* there balm in Gilead?—tell me—tell me, I implore!"
Quoth the raven, "Nevermore!"

16. "Prophet!" said I, "thing of evil!—prophet still, if bird or devil!
By that heaven that bends above us—by that God we both adore,
Tell this soul with sorrow laden, if, within the distant Aidenn,
It shall clasp a sainted maiden, whom the angels name Lenore:
Clasp a fair and radiant maiden, whom the angels name Lenore!"
Quoth the raven, "Nevermore!"

17. "Be that word our sign of parting, bird or fiend!" I shrieked up-
    starting—
    "Get thee back into the tempest and the Night's Plutonian shore!
    Leave no black plume as a token of that lie thy soul hath spoken!
    Leave my loneliness unbroken!—quit the bust above my door!
    Take thy beak from out my heart, and take thy form from off my door!"
        Quoth the raven, "Nevermore!"

18. And the raven, never flitting, still is sitting, still is sitting
    On the pallid bust of Pallas, just above my chamber door;
    And his eyes have all the seeming of a demon that is dreaming,
    And the lamp-light o'er him streaming throws his shadow on the floor;
    And my soul from out that shadow that lies floating on the floor,
        Shall be lifted—NEVERMORE!

CXLVI.—MAJESTY AND SUPREMACY OF THE SCRIPTURES CONFESSED BY A SKEPTIC.

ROUSSEAU.

1. I WILL confess that the majesty of the Scriptures, strikes me with admiration, as the purity of the Gospel hath its influence on my heart. Peruse the works of our philosophers with all their pomp of diction. How mean, how contemptible are they, compared with the Scriptures! Is it possible that a book, at once so simple and sublime, should be merely the work of man? Is it possible that the sacred personage, whose history it contains, should be himself a mere man? Do we find that he assumed the tone of an enthusiast or ambitious sectary?

2. What sweetness, what purity in his manner! What an affecting gracefulness in his delivery! What sublimity in his maxims! What profound wisdom in his discourses! What presence of mind, what subtlety, what truth in his replies. How great the command over his passions! Where is the man, where the philosopher, who could so live, and so die, without weakness, and without ostentation? When Plato described his imaginary good man, loaded with all the shame of guilt, yet meriting the high-est rewards of virtue, he describes exactly the character of JESUS CHRIST.

3. What prepossession, what blindness must it be, to compare the son of SOPHRONISCUS to the son of Mary! What an infinite disproportion there is between them! SOCRATES, dying without pain or ignominy, easily supported his character to the last; and if his death, however easy, had not crowned his life, it might have been doubted whether SOCRATES, with all his wisdom, was any thing more than a vain sophist. He invented, it is said, the theory of morals. Others, however, had before put them in practice: he had only to say, therefore, what they had done, and reduce their examples to precepts.

4. ARISTIDES had been *just* before Socrates defined justice: LEONIDAS had given up his life for his country, before Socrates declared patriotism to be a duty: the Spartans were a sober people, before Socrates recommended sobriety: before he had even defined virtue, Greece abounded in virtuous men. But where could JESUS learn, among his competitors, that pure and sublime morality, of which he only hath given us both precept and example? The greatest wisdom was made known among the most bigoted fanaticism, and the simplicity of the most heroic virtues, did honor to the vilest people on earth.

5. The death of Socrates, peaceably philosophizing with his friends, appears the most agreeable that could be wished for; that of JESUS, expiring in the midst of agonizing pains, abused, insulted, and accused by a whole nation, is the most horrible that could be feared. Socrates, in receiving the cup of poison, blessed indeed the weeping executioner who administered it; but JESUS, in the midst of excruciating torments, prayed for his merciless tormentors. Yes, if the life and death of Socrates were those of a sage, the life and death of JESUS are those of a GOD.

6. Shall we suppose the evangelic history a mere fiction? Indeed, it bears not the marks of fiction; on the contrary, the history of Socrates, which nobody presumes to doubt, is not so well attested as that of JESUS CHRIST. Such a supposition, in fact, only shifts the difficulty with-

out obviating it;—it is more inconceivable that a number
of persons should agree to write such a history, than that
one only should furnish the subject of it. The Jewish
authors were incapable of the diction, and strangers to the
morality contained in the Gospel, the marks of whose truth
are so striking and inimitable, that the inventor would be
a more astonishing character than the hero.

———————◆———————

CXLVII.—FIFTY YEARS AGO.

W. D. GALLAGHER.

1. A SONG for the early times out west,
    And our green old forest home,
   Whose pleasant memories freshly yet
    Across the bosom come :
   A song for the free and gladsome life
    In those early days we led,
   With a teeming soil beneath our feet,
    And a smiling heaven o'erhead !
   Oh, the waves of life danced merrily,
    And had a joyous flow,
   In the days when we were pioneers,
    Fifty years ago !

2. The hunt, the shot, the glorious chase,
    The captured elk or deer :
   The camp, the big bright fire, and then
    The rich and wholesome cheer :
   The sweet, sound sleep, at dead of night,
    By our camp-fire blazing high—
   Unbroken by the wolf's long howl,
    And the panther springing by.
   Oh, merrily passed the time, despite
    Our wily Indian foe,
   In the days when we were pioneers,
    Fifty years ago !

3. We shunned not labor; when 'twas due
    We wrought with right good will ;
   And for the home we won for them,
    Our children bless us still.
   We lived not hermit lives ; but oft
    In social converse met ;

And fires of love were kindled then,
  That burn on warmly yet.
Oh, pleasantly the stream of life
  Pursued its constant flow,
In the days when we were pioneers,
  Fifty years ago !

4. We felt that we were fellow-men :
  We felt we were a band
Sustained here in the wilderness,
  By Heaven's upholding hand.
And when the solemn Sabbath came,
  We gathered in the wood,
And lifted up our hearts in prayer
  To God, the only Good.
Our temples then were earth and sky :
  None others did we know,
In the days when we were pioneers,
  Fifty years ago.

5. Our forest life was rough and rude,
  And dangers closed us round,
But here, amid the green old trees,
  Freedom we sought and found.
Oft through our dwellings wintry blasts
  Would rush with shriek and moan :
We cared not—though they were but frail,
  We felt they were our own !
Oh, free and manly lives we led,
  'Mid verdure or 'mid snow,
In the days when we were pioneers,
  Fifty years ago.

6. But now our course of life is short ;
  And as, from day to day,
We're walking on with halting step,
  And fainting by the way,
Another land, more bright than this,
  To our dim sight appears,
And on our way to it we'll soon
  Again be pioneers !
And while we linger, we may all
  A backward glance still throw
To the days when we were pioneers,
  Fifty years ago.

13

CXLVIII.—THE VOICE OF WISDOM.

POLLOK.

1. WISDOM took up her harp, and stood in place
Of frequent concourse—stood in every gate,
By every way, and walked in every street;
And, lifting up her voice, proclaimed : " Be wise,
Ye fools ! be of an understanding heart.
Forsake the wicked : come not near his house :
Pass by : make haste : depart, and turn away.
Me follow—me, whose days are pleasantness,
Whose paths are peace, whose end is perfect joy."

2. The Seasons came and went, and went and came,
To teach men gratitude, and as they passed,
Gave warning of the lapse of time, that else
Had stolen unheeded by. The gentle flowers
Retired, and, stooping o'er the wilderness,
Talked of humility, and peace, and love.
The Dews came down unseen at evening-tide,
And silently their bounties shed, to teach
Mankind's unostentatious charity.

3. With arm in arm the Forest rose on high,
And lesson gave of brotherly regard.
And, on the rugged mountain-brow exposed,—
Bearing the blast alone,—the ancient oak
Stood, lifting high his mighty arm, and still
To courage in distress exhorted loud.
The flocks, the herds, the birds, the streams, the breeze,
Attuned the heart to melody and love.

4. Mercy stood in the cloud, with eye that wept
Essential love ; and from her glorious bow,
Bending to kiss the earth in token of peace,
With her own lips, her gracious lips, which God
Of sweetest accent made, she whispered still,
She wispered to Revenge :—" Forgive, forgive ! "

5. The Sun rejoicing round the earth, announced
Daily the wisdom, power, and love of God.
The Moon awoke, and from her maiden face,
Shedding her cloudy locks, looked meekly forth,
And with her virgin stars walked in the heavens,
Walked nightly there, conversing as she walked,
Of purity, and holiness, and God.

6. In dreams and visions, Sleep instructed much.
Day uttered speech to day, and night to night
Taught knowledge : silence had a tongue : the grave,
The darkness, and the lonely waste, had each
A tongue that ever said—" Man ! think of God !
Think of thyself! think of eternity ! "
Fear God, the thunders said : fear God, the waves :
Fear God, the lightning of the storm replied :
Fear God, deep loudly answered back to deep.

CXLIX.—LOOK ALOFT.

J. LAWRENCE.

1. In the tempest of life, when the wave and the gale
Are around and above, if thy footing should fail,—
If thine eye should grow dim, and thy caution depart,—
" Look aloft," and be firm, and be fearless of heart.

2. If the friend who embraced in prosperity's glow,
With a smile for each joy, and a tear for each woe,
Should betray thee when sorrows, like clouds, are arrayed,
' Look aloft " to the friendship which never shall fade.

3. Should the visions which hope spreads in light to thine eye,
Like the tints of the rainbow, but brighten to fly,
Then turn, and, through tears of repentant regret,
" Look aloft " to the Sun that is never to set.

4. Should they who are nearest and dearest thy heart,—
Thy friends and companions,—in sorrow depart,
" Look aloft " from the darkness and dust of the tomb,
To that soil where " affection is ever in bloom."

5. And, O ! when Death comes in his terrors, to cast
His fears on the future, his pall on the past,
In that moment of darkness, with hope in thy heart,
And a smile in thine eye, " LOOK ALOFT," and depart.

CL.—THE LIGHT OF HOME.

MRS. HALE.

1. My boy, thou wilt dream the world is fair,
And thy spirit will sigh to roam ;
And thou must go—but *never*, when there,
Forget the light of home.

2. Though pleasure may smile with a ray more bright,
    It dazzles to lead astray:
    Like the meteor's flash, 'twill deepen the night,
    When thou treadest the lonely way.

3. But the hearth of home has a constant flame,
    And pure as vestal fire:
    'Twill burn, 'twill burn forever the same,
    For nature feeds the pyre.

4. The sea of ambition is tempest-tost,
    And thy hopes may vanish like foam;
    But when sails are shiver'd, and rudder lost,
    Then look to the light of home.

5. And there, like a star through the midnight cloud,
    Thou shalt see the beacon bright;
    For never, till shining on thy shroud,
    Can be quenched its holy light.

6. The sun of fame, 'twill gild the name,
    But the heart ne'er felt its ray;
    And fashion's smiles, that rich ones claim,
    Are but beams of a wintry day.

7. And how cold and dim those beams must be,
    Should life's wretched wanderer come!
    But, my boy, when the world is dark to thee,
    Then turn to the light of home.

CLI.—MY FATHER'S AT THE HELM.

1. THE curling waves with awful roar,
    A gallant bark assailed,
    And pallid fear's distracting power,
    O'er all on board prevailed,—
    Save one, the captain's darling child,
    Who steadfast viewed the storm,
    And fearless with composure smiled,
    At danger's threat'ning form.

2. "And fear'st thou not," a seaman cried,
    "While terrors overwhelm?"
    "Why should I fear?" the boy replied:
    "My father's at the helm."

Thus when our worldly hopes are reft
  Our earthly comforts gone,
We still have one sure anchor left,—
  God helps, and He alone.

3.   He to our cries will lend an ear,
  He gives our pangs relief:
He turns to smiles each trembling tear
  To joy each torturing grief.
Then turn to Him, 'mid terrors wild,
  When sorrows overwhelm,
Remembering, like the fearless child,
  Our Father's at the helm.

------◆------

CLII.—MARCO BOZZARIS.

FITZ-GREENE HALLECK.

1. At midnight in his guarded tent,
  The Turk was dreaming of the hour,
When Greece, her knee in suppliance bent,
  Should tremble at his power:
In dreams, through camp and court, he bore
The trophies of a conqueror:
  In dreams, his song of triumph heard:
Then wore his monarch's signet ring:
Then pressed that monarch's throne,—a king;
As wild his thoughts, and gay of wing,
  As Eden's garden bird.

2. An hour passed on,—the Turk awoke;—
  That bright dream was his last:
He woke—to hear his sentries shriek:
  "To ARMS! they *come!* the GREEK! the GREEK!"
He woke to die 'midst flame and smoke,
And shout, and groan, and saber-stroke,
  And death-shots falling thick and fast
As lightnings from the mountain cloud;
And heard, with voice as trumpet loud,
  Bozzaris cheer his band;—
"Strike—till the last armed foe expires!
Strike—for your altars and your fires!
Strike—for the green graves of your sires!
  GOD, and your native land!"

3. They fought, like brave men, long and well:
    They piled the ground with Moslem slain:
They conquered; but Bozzaris fell,
    Bleeding at every vein.
His few surviving comrades saw
His smile, when rang their proud hurrah,
    And the red field was won:
Then saw in death his eyelids close
Calmly, as to a night's repose,
    Like flowers at set of sun.

4. Come to the bridal chamber, Death!
    Come to the mother's when she feels
For the first time her first-born's breath:
    Come when the blessed seals
That close the pestilence, are broke,
And crowded cities, wail its stroke:
Come in Consumption's ghastly form,
The earthquake shock, the ocean storm:
Come when the heart beats high and warm.
    With banquet-song and dance, and wine,—
And *thou* art terrible—the tear,
The groan, the knell, the pall, the bier,
And all we know, or dream, or fear,
    Of agony, are thine.

5. But to the Hero, when his sword
    Has won the battle for the free,
Thy voice sounds like a prophet's word,
And in its hollow tones are heard
    The thanks of millions yet to be.
Bozzaris, with the storied brave
    Greece nurtured in her glory's time,
Rest thee: there is no prouder grave,
    Even in her own proud clime.
We tell thy doom without a sigh;
For thou art Freedom's now, and Fame's—
One of the few, the immortal names,
    That were not born to die!

CLIII.—THE PEN AND THE PRESS.

1. YOUNG GENIUS walked out by the mountain and streams,
Entranced by the power of his own pleasant dreams,

Till the silent—the wayward—the wandering thing
Found a plume that had fallen from a passing bird's wing:
Exulting and proud, like a boy at his play,
He bore the new prize to his dwelling away,
He gazed for a while on its beauties, and then
He cut it, and shaped it, and called it—a PEN.

2. But its magical use he discovered not yet,
Till he dipp'd its bright lips in a fountain of jet;
And O! what a glorious thing it became,
For it spoke to the world in a language of flame:
While its master wrote on like a being inspired,
Till the hearts of the millions were melted or fired;—
It came as a boon and a blessing to men,
The peaceful—the pure—the victorious PEN!

3. Young Genius went forth on his rambles once more,
The vast sinless caverns of earth to explore!
He searched the rude rock, and with rapture he found
A substance unknown, which he brought from the ground:
He fused it with fire, and rejoiced in the change,
As he molded the ore into characters strange,
Till his thoughts and his efforts were crown'd with success:
For an engine uprose, and he call'd it—the PRESS.

4. The Pen and the Press, blest alliance! combin'd
To soften the heart and enlighten the mind;
For that to the treasures of knowledge gave birth,
And this sent them forth to the ends of the earth:
Their battles for truth were triumphant indeed,
And the rod of the tyrant was snapp'd like a reed:
They were made to exalt us—to teach us to bless
Those invincible brothers—the PEN AND THE PRESS!

CLIV.—THE BOYS.

OLIVER W. HOLMES.

This selection was addressed to the class of 1829, in Harvard College,
some thirty years after their graduation. The author, who retains the
freshness and joyousness of youth, addresses his classmates as "boys."

1. HAS there any old fellow got mixed with the boys?
If there has, take him out, without making a noise.
Hang the almanac's cheat and the catalogue's spite!
Old Time is a liar! we're twenty to-night!

2. We're twenty! We're twenty! Who says we are more?
He's tipsy,—young jackanapes!—show him the door!
" Gray temples at twenty " ?—Yes! *white* if we please :
Where the snow-flakes fall thickest there's nothing can freeze!

3. Was it snowing I spoke of? Excuse the mistake!
Look close,—you will see not a sign of a flake !
We want some new garlands for those we have shed,
And these are white roses in place of the red.

4. We've a trick, we young fellows, you may have been told,
Of talking (in public) as if we were old :
That boy we call "Doctor," and this we call "Judge":
It's a neat little fiction,—of course it's all fudge.

5. That fellow's the "Speaker," the one on the right:
" Mr. Mayor," my young one, how are you to-night?
That's our "Member of Congress," we say when we chaff:
There's the " Reverend "—what's his name?—don't make me laugh.

6. That boy with the grave mathematical look
Made believe he had written a wonderful book,
And the Royal Society thought it was *true !*
So they chose him right in,—a good joke it was too!

7. There's a boy, we pretend, with a three-decker brain,
That could harness a team with a logical chain;
When he spoke for our manhood in syllabled fire,
We called him " The Justice," but now he's the " Squire."

8. And there's a nice youngster of excellent pith :
Fate tried to conceal him by naming him Smith ;
But he shouted a song for the brave and the free,—
Just read on his medal, " My country," "of thee " !

9. You hear that boy laughing? You think he's all fun ;
But the angels laugh, too, at the good he has done:
The children laugh loud as they troop to his call,
And the poor man that knows him laughs loudest of all !

10. Yes, we're boys,—always playing with tongue or with pen ;
And I sometimes have asked, Shall we ever be men ?
Shall we always be youthful, and laughing, and gay,
Till the last dear companion drops smiling away?

11. Then here's to our boyhood, its gold and its gray !
The stars of its winter, the dews of its May !
And when we have done with our life-lasting toys,
Dear Father, take care of Thy children, THE BOYS !

CLV.—ASPIRATIONS OF THE HEAVEN-BORN SPIRIT.

MRS. HEMANS

1. WHEN the young Eagle with exulting eye,
Has learned to dare the splendor of the sky,
And leave the Alps beneath him in his course,
To bathe his crest in morn's empyreal source;
Will his free wing, from that majestic hight,
Descend to follow some wild meteor's light,
Which, far below, with evanescent fire,
Shines to elude, and dazzles to expire?

2. No! still through clouds he wings his upward way,
And proudly claims his heritage of day!
And shall the spirit, on whose ardent gaze
The day-spring from on high hath poured its blaze,
Turn from that pure effulgence, to the beam
Of earth-born light, that sheds a treacherous gleam.
Luring the wanderer, from the star of faith?
To the deep valley of the shades of death?
What bright exchange, what treasure shall be given,
For the high birthright of its hope in Heaven?

———◆———

CLVI.—THE UNION OF THE STATES.

EDMUND RANDOLPH.

1. I HAVE labored for the continuance of the union—
the rock of our salvation. I believe that as sure as there
is a God in heaven, our safety, our political happiness, and
existence, depend on the "UNION OF THE STATES;" and
that, without this union, the people of this and other States,
will undergo the unspeakable calamities which discord,
faction, turbulence, war, and bloodshed, have produced in
other countries. The American spirit ought to be mixed
with American pride—pride to see the union magnificently
triumph.

2. Let it not be recorded of America, that, after having
performed the most gallant exploits, after having overcome
the most astonishing difficulties, and after having gained
the admiration of the world by their incomparable valor
and policy, they lost their acquired reputation,—their

13*

national consequence and happiness,—by their own indis-
cretion. Let no future historian inform posterity that they
wanted wisdom and virtue to concur in any regular, effi-
cient government. Should any writer, doomed to so disagreeable a task, feel the indignation of an honest historian,
he would reprehend and recriminate our folly with equal
severity and justice.

3. Catch the present moment: seize it with avidity and
eagerness; for it may be lost, never to be regained. If the
union be now lost, I fear it will remain so forever. When
I maturely weigh the advantages of the union, and the
dreadful consequences of its dissolution : when I see safety
on my right, and destruction on my left: when I behold
respectability and happiness acquired by the one, but annihilated by the other, I can not hesitate to decide in favor
of the UNION.

———◆———

CLVII.—TO THE REVOLUTIONARY VETERANS.

DANIEL WEBSTER.

[At the laying of the corner-stone of the Bunker Hill Monument, June 17,
1825.]

1. WE hold still among us some of those who were active agents in the scenes of 1775, and who are now here,
from every quarter of New England, to visit once more,
and under circumstances so affecting,—I had almost said so
overwhelming,—this renowned theatre of their courage and
patriotism. Venerable men! you have come down to us
from a former generation. Heaven has bounteously lengthened out your lives, that you might behold this joyous day.
You are now, where you stood, fifty years ago, this very
hour, with your brothers, and your neighbors, shoulder to
shoulder, in the strife for your country.

2. Behold, how altered. The same heavens are indeed
over your heads: the same ocean rolls at your feet; but all
else how changed! You hear now no roar of hostile cannon, you see now no mixed volumes of smoke and flame

rising from burning Charlestown. The ground strewed with the dead and the dying: the impetuous charge : the steady and successful repulse : the loud call to repeated assault: the summoning of all that is manly to repeated resistance, a thousand bosoms freely and fearlessly bared in an instant to whatever of terror there may be in war and death ;—all these you have witnessed, but you witness them no more. All is peace.

3. The heights of yonder metropolis, its towers and roofs, which you then saw filled with wives and children and countrymen in distress and terror, and looking with unutterable emotions for the issue of the combat, have presented you to-day with the sight of its whole happy population come out to welcome and greet you with an universal jubilee. All is peace ; and God has granted you this sight of your country's happiness, ere you slumber in the grave forever.

4. But, alas ! you are not all here. Time and the sword have thinned your ranks. Prescott, Putnam, Stark, Brooks, Read, Pomeroy, Bridge !—our eyes seek for you in vain amidst this broken band. But let us not too much grieve, that you have met the common fate of men. You lived to see your country's independence established, and to sheathe your swords from war. On the light of Liberty, you saw arise the light of Peace, like

> " Another morn
> Risen on mid-noon ; "—

and the sky on which you closed your eyes was cloudless.

5. But—ah !—him ! the first great martyr in this great cause ! Him ! the premature victim of his own self-devoting heart ! Him ! the head of our civil counsels, and the destined leader of our military bands, whom nothing brought hither but the unquenchable fire of his own spirit ! Him ! cut off by Providence in the hour of overwhelming anxiety and thick gloom : failing, ere he saw the star of his country rise : pouring out his generous blood, like water, before he knew whether it would fertilize a land of freedom or of

bondage!—how shall I struggle with the emotions that stifle the utterance of thy name! Our poor work may perish, but thine shall endure! This monument may moulder away: the solid ground it rests upon may sink down to a level with the sea;.but thy memory shall not fail! Wheresoever among men a heart shall be found that beats to the transports of patriotism and liberty, its aspirations shall be to claim kindred with thy spirit!

6. Veterans! you are the remnant of many a well-fought field. You bring with you marks of honor from Trenton and Monmouth, from Yorktown, Camden, Bennington, and Saratoga. Veterans of half a century! when, in your youthful days, you put everything at hazard in your country's cause, good as that cause was, and sanguine as youth is, still your fondest hopes did not stretch onward to an hour like this. Look abroad into this lovely land, which your young valor defended, and mark the happiness with which it is filled: yea, look abroad into the whole earth, and see what a name you have contributed to give to your country, and what a praise you have added to freedom, and then rejoice in the sympathy and gratitude which beam upon your last days from the improved condition of mankind.

———◆———

CLVIII.—PLEASURES OF HOPE.

THOMAS CAMPBELL,

1. At summer's eve, when heaven's aërial bow
   Spans, with bright arch, the glittering hills below,
   Why to yon mountain turns the musing eye,
   Whose sun-bright summit mingles with the sky?
   Why do these hills of shadowy tint appear
   More sweet than all the landscape smiling near?
   'Tis distance lends enchantment to the view,
   And robes the mountain with its azure hue.

2. Thus, with delight, we linger to survey
   The promised joys of life's unmeasured way;
   Thus, from afar, each dim-discovered scene
   More pleasing seems than all the past hath been;

And every form that fancy can repair
From dark oblivion, glows divinely there.

3. What potent spirit guides the raptured eye
To pierce the shades of dim futurity?
Can Wisdom lend, with all her boasted power,
The pledge of joys' anticipated hour?
•Or, if she holds an image to the view,
'Tis nature pictured too severely true.
With thee, sweet Hope, resides the heavenly light,
That pours remotest rapture on the sight:
Thine is the charm of life's bewildered way,
That calls each slumbering passion into play.

4. Eternal Hope! when yonder spheres sublime
Pealed their first notes to sound the march of Time,
Thy joyous youth began,—but not to fade.
When all the sister planets have decayed:
When, wrapt in fire, the realms of ether glow,
And Heaven's last thunder shakes the world below,
Thou, undismayed, shalt o'er the ruins smile,
And light thy torch at Nature's funeral pile.

———————◆———————

CLIX.—PRESIDENT LINCOLN'S LAST INAUGURAL ADDRESS.

1. FELLOW-COUNTRYMEN :—On the occasion correspond-
ing to this, four years ago, all thoughts were anxiously
directed to an impending civil war. All dreaded it—all
sought to avert it. While the Inaugural Address was being delivered from this place, devoted altogether to *saving*
the Union without war, insurgent agents were in this city
seeking to *destroy* it without war—seeking to dissolve the
Union, and divide effects, by negotiation. Both parties
deprecated war; but one of them would *make* war rather
than let the nation survive; and the other would *accept*
war rather than let it perish; and the war came.

2. One-eighth of the whole population were colored
slaves—not distributed generally over the Union, but local-
ized over the southern part of it. These slaves constituted
a peculiar and powerful interest. All knew that this interest was, somehow, the cause of the war. To strengthen,

perpetuate, and extend this interest was the object for which the insurgents would rend the Union, even by war: while the Government claimed no right to do more than restrict the territorial enlargement of it. Neither anticipated that the *cause* of the conflict might cease with, or even before. the conflict itself should cease. Each looked . for an easier triumph, and a result less fundamental and astounding. Both read the same Bible, and pray to the same God; and each invokes His aid against the other. It may seem strange that any men could dare to ask a just God's assistance in wringing their bread from the sweat of other men's faces; but let us judge not, that we be not judged. The prayers of both could not be answered —that of neither has been answered fully.

3. The Almighty has His own purposes. " Woe unto the world because of offenses! for it must be that offenses come; but woe to that man by whom the offense cometh." If we shall suppose that American slavery is one of those offenses which, having continued through His appointed time. He now wills to remove, and that He gives to both North and South this terrible war. as the woe due to those by whom the offense came, shall we discern therein any departure from those divine attributes which the believers in a living God always ascribe to Him? Fondly do we hope—fervently do we pray—that this mighty scourge of war may speedily pass away.

4. Yet, if God wills that it continue until all the wealth piled by the bond man's two hundred and fifty years of unrequited toil shall be sunk, and until every drop of blood drawn with the lash shall be paid with another drawn with the sword, as was said three thousand years ago, so still it must be said, " The judgments of the Lord are true and righteous altogether." With malice toward none: with charity for all: with firmness in the right, as God gives us to see the right, let us strive on to finish the work we are in: to bind up the nation's wounds: to care for him who shall have borne the battle, and for his widow and orphan:

—to do all which may achieve and cherish a just and lasting peace among ourselves, and with all nations.

CLX.—ANNIVERSARY OF THE EMANCIPATION PROCLAMATION.

1. Fling the flags out, grand and glorious,
    Red with blood of battles won,
 Over rebel bands victorious,
    Let them greet the rising sun.
 On the land and on the ocean
    Let the banners blossom out,
 While the guns with grim devotion
    Thunder Freedom's anthem-shout.

2. Gone the gloom of wrong and error,
    Broken the oppressor's ban :
 Gone is Slavery's reign of terror,
    Freedom is the right of man.
 Labor's mighty diapason
    Fills the land from sea to sea :
 On our banners we emblazon
    Man forever more is free !

3. On the mountain, in the valley,
    Raise aloft the stripes and stars :
 Let the sons of labor rally,
    Mightier in their strength than Mars !
 Architect of every nation,
    Labor is the only king,
 Working out in lowly station
    Nobler deeds than poets sing.

CLXI.—THE GRAVE OF LINCOLN.
EDNA DEAN PROCTOR.

1. Now must the storied Potomac
    Laurels forever divide :
 Now to the Sangamon fameless
    Give of its century's pride ;—
 Sangamon, stream of the prairies,
    Placidly westward that flows,
 Far in whose city of silence
    Calm he has sought his repose.

Over our Washington's river
Sunrise beams rosy and fair:
Sunset on Sangamon fairer,—
Father and martyr lies there.

2. Kings under pyramids slumber,
Sealed in the Libyan sands:
Princes in gorgeous cathedrals,
Decked with the spoil of the lands:
Kinglier, princelier sleeps he,
Couched 'mid the prairies serene,
Only the turf and the willow
Him and God's heaven between:
Temple nor column to cumber
Verdure and bloom of the sod,—
So, in the vale by Beth-peor,
Moses was buried of God.

3. Break into blossom, O prairies!
Snowy and golden and red:
Peers of the Palestine lilies
Heap for your Glorious Dead!
Roses as fair as of Sharon,
Branches as stately as palm,
Odors as rich as the spices,—
Cassia and aloes and balm,—
Mary, the loved, and Salome,
All with a gracious accord,
Ere the first glow of the morning,
Brought to the tomb of the Lord.

4. Wind of the West! breathe around him
Soft as the saddened air's sigh,
When, to the summit of Pisgah,
Moses had journeyed to die:
Clear as its anthem that floated
Wide o'er the Moabite plain,
Low, with the wail of the people,
Blending its burdened refrain.
Rarer, O wind! and diviner—
Sweet as the breeze that went by,
When, over Olivet's mountain,
Jesus was lost in the sky.

5. Not for thy sheaves nor savannas
Crown we thee, proud Illinois!

Here in his grave is thy grandeur,
  Born of his sorrow thy joy.
Only the tomb by Mount Zion,
  Hewn for the Lord, do we hold
Dearer than his in thy prairies,
  Girdled with harvests of gold !
Still for the world, through the ages,
  Wreathing with glory his brow,
He shall be liberty's savior,—
  Freedom's Jerusalem thou !

CLXII.—OVER THE RIVER.

NANCY A. W. PRIEST.

1. OVER the river they beckon to me—
    Loved ones who've crossed to the further side :
  The gleam of the snowy robes I see,
    But their voices are drowned in the rushing tide.
  There's one, with ringlets of sunny gold,
    And eyes, the reflection of heaven's own blue :
  He crossed in the twilight, gray and cold,
    And the pale mist hid him from mortal view.
  We saw not the angels that met him there :
    The gates of the city we could not see ;—
  Over the river, over the river,
    My brother stands waiting to welcome me !

2. Over the river the boatman pale
    Carried another—the household pet :
  Her brown curls waved in the gentle gale—
    Darling Minnie ! I see her yet !
  She crossed on her bosom her dimpled hands,
    And fearlessly entered the phantom bark :
  We watched it glide from the silver sands,
    And all our sunshine grew strangely dark.
  We know she is safe on the further side,
    Where all the ransomed and angels be ;—
  Over the river, the mystic river,
    My childhood's idol is waiting for me !

3. For none return from those quiet shores,
    Who cross with the boatman cold and pale :
  We hear the dip of the golden oars,
    And catch a gleam of the snowy sail,

And, lo! they have passed from our yearning hearts:
    They cross the stream, and are gone for aye:
We may not sunder the veil apart
    That hides from our vision the gates of day:
We only know that their bark no more
    May sail with us o'er life's stormy sea:
Yet, somewhere, I know, on the unseen shore,
    They watch and beckon and wait for me!

4. And I sit and think, when the sunset's gold
    Is flushing river and hill and shore,
I shall one day stand by the water cold,
    And list for the sound of the boatman's oar:
I shall watch for a gleam of the flapping sail:
I shall hear the boat as it gains the strand:
I shall pass from sight with the boatman pale,
    To the better shore of the spirit land:
I shall know the loved who have gone before,
    And joyfully sweet shall the meeting be,
When over the river, the peaceful river,
    The angel of death shall carry me!

CLXIII.—THE BAYONET CHARGE.

NATHAN D. URNER.

1. Not a sound, not a breath!
    And as still as death,
As we stand on the steep in our bayonet's shine:
    All is tumult below—
    Surging friend, surging foe;
But, not a hair's breadth moves our adamant line—
    Waiting so grimly.
    The battle smoke lifts
    From the valley, and drifts
Round the hill where we stand, like a pall for the world;
    And a gleam now and then
    Shows the billows of men,
In whose black, boiling surge we are soon to be hurled,
    Redly and dimly.
    There's the word! "Ready all!"

2. See the serried points fall—
The grim horizontal so bright and so bare!

Then the other word—Ha!
We are moving! Huzza!
We snuff the burnt powder, we plunge in the glare,
Rushing to glory!
Down the hill, up the glen,
O'er the bodies of men.
Then on with a cheer, to the roaring redoubt!
Why stumble so, Ned?
No answer: he's dead!
And there's Dutch Peter down, with his life leaping out,
Crimson and gory!

3. On! on! Do not think
Of the falling; but drink
Of the mad, living cataract torrent of war!
On! on! let them feel
The cold vengeance of steel!
Catch the Captain—he's hit! 'Tis a scratch—nothing more!
Forward forever!
Huzza! Here's a trench!
In and out of it! Wrench
From the jaws of the cannon the guerdon of Fame!
Charge! charge! with a yell
Like the shriek of a shell—
O'er the abatis, on through the curtain of flame!
Back again! Never!

4. The rampart! 'Tis crossed—
It is ours! It is lost!
No—another dash now and the glacis is won!
Huzza! What a dust!
Hew them down. Cut and thrust!
A T-i-g-a-r! brave lads, for the red work is done—
Victory! Victory!

CLXIV.—THE BRIDGE OF SIGHS.
THOMAS HOOD.

1. ONE more unfortunate,
Weary of breath,
Rashly importunate,
Gone to her death!
Take her up tenderly,
Lift her with care!

Fashioned so slenderly—
Young, and so fair !

2. Look at her garments,
Clinging like cerements,
While the wave constantly
   Drips from her clothing :
Take her up instantly,
   Loving, not loathing !

3. Touch her not scornfully !
Think of her mournfully,
   Gently and humanly—
Not of the stains of her,
All that remains of her
   Now is pure womanly.

4. Make no deep scrutiny,
Into her mutiny,
   Rash and undutiful :
Past all dishonor,
Death has left on her
   Only the beautiful.

5. Still, for all slips of hers—
   One of Eve's family—
Wipe those poor lips of hers,
   Oozing so clammily.
Loop up her tresses
   Escaped from the comb—
Her fair auburn tresses—
While wonderment guesses,
   Where was her home ?

6. Who was her father ?
Who was her mother ?
Had she a sister ?
Had she a brother ?
Or was there a dearer one
Still, and a nearer one
   Yet, than all other ?

7. Alas ! for the rarity
Of Christian charity
   Under the sun !
Oh ! it was pitiful !

Near a whole city full,
   Home she had none.

8. Sisterly, brotherly,
   Fatherly, motherly
      Feelings had changed—
   Love, by harsh evidence,
   Thrown from its eminence;
   Even God's providence
      Seeming estranged.

9. Where the lamps quiver
   So far in the river,
      With many a light
   From window and casement,
   From garret to basement,
   She stood, with amazement,
      Houseless by night.

10. The bleak wind of March
      Made.her tremble and shiver;
   But not the dark arch,
      Or the black, flowing river:
   Mad from life's history,
   Glad to death's mystery,
      Swift to be hurled—
   Anywhere—anywhere
      Out of the world!

11. In she plunged boldly—
   No matter how coldly
      The rough river ran—
   Over the brink of it!
   Picture it—think of it!
      Dissolute Man!
   Lave in it, drink of it,
      Then, if you can!—
   Take her up tenderly,
      Lift her with care!
   Fashioned so slenderly,
      Young, and so fair.

12. Ere her limbs, frigidly,
   Stiffen too rigidly,
      Decently, kindly,
   Smooth and compose them;

And her eyes, close them,
   Staring so blindly !

13. Dreadfully staring
   Through muddy impurity,
As when with the daring
Last look of despairing
   Fixed on futurity.

14. Perishing gloomily,
Spurred by contumely,
Cold inhumanity,
Burning insanity,
   Into her rest !
Cross her hands humbly,
As if praying dumbly,
   Over her breast !
Owning her weakness,
   Her evil behavior,
And leaving with meekness
   Her sins to her Saviour !

CLXV.—THE HEART'S CHARITY.

E. Cook.

1. A RICH man walked abroad one day,
And a poor man walked the self-same way,
When a pale and starving face came by,
With a pallid lip and a hopeless eye ;
And that starving face presumed to stand
And ask for bread from the rich man's hand.
But the rich man sullenly looked askance,
With a gathering frown and a doubtful glance :
" I have nothing," said he, " to give to you,
Nor any such rogue of a canting crew ; "
And he fastened his pocket, and on he went,
With his soul untouched and his conscience content.

2. Now this great owner of golden store
Had built a church not long before ;
As noble a fane as man could raise,
And the world had given him thanks and praise ;
And all who beheld it lavished fame
On his Christian gift and godly name.

3. The poor man passed, and the white lips dared
   To ask of him if a mite could be spared :
   He stood for a moment, but not to pause
   On the truth of the tale, or the parish laws :
   He was seeking to give—though it was but small,
   For a penny, a single penny was all,
   But he gave it with a kindly word,
   While the warmest pulse in his heart was stirred.
   'Twas a tiny seed his charity shed,
   But the white lips got a taste of bread,
   And the beggar's blessing hallowed the crust
   That came like a spring in the desert dust.

4. The rich man and the poor man died,
   As all of us must ; and they both were tried
   At the sacred judgment-seat above,
   For their thoughts of evil and deeds of love.
   The balance of justice *there* was true,
   And fairly bestowed what fairly was due :
   And the two fresh comers at heaven's gate
   Stood waiting to learn their eternal fate.

5. The recording angel told of things
   That fitted them both with kindred wings ;
   But as they stood in the crystal light,
   The plumes of the rich man grew less bright.
   The angels knew by that shadowy sign
   That the poor man's work had been most divine,
   And they brought the unerring scales to see
   Where the rich man's falling off could be.

6. Full many deeds did the angels weigh,
   But the balance kept an even sway,
   And at last the church endowment laid
   With its thousands promised and thousands paid,
   With the thanks of prelates by its side,
   In the stately words of pious pride ;
   And it weighed so much that the angels stood
   To see how the poor man could balance such good.

7. A cherub came and took his place
   By the empty scale, with a radiant grace,
   And he dropped the penny that had fed
   White starving lips with a crust of bread :
   The church endowment went up with the beam,

And the whisper of the great Supreme,
As he beckoned the poor man to his throne,
Was heard in this immortal tone :
. " Blessed are they who from great gain
Give thousands with a reasoning brain,
But holier still shall be his part
Who gives one coin with a pitying heart ! "

CLXVI.—THE LOST STEAMSHIP.

FITZ-JAMES O'BRIEN.

1. " Ho, there ! fisherman, hold your hand !
    Tell me what is that far away—
There, where over the Isle of Sand
    Hangs the mist-cloud sullen and gray ?
See ! it rocks with a ghastly life,
    Raising and rolling through clouds of spray,
Right in the midst of the breakers' strife—
    Tell me, what is it, Fisherman, pray ? "

2. " That, good sir, was a steamer, stout
    As ever paddled around Cape Race,
And many's the wild and stormy bout
    She had with the winds in that self-same place ;
But her time had come ; and at ten o'clock
    Last night she struck on that lonesome shore,
And her sides were gnawed by the hidden rock,
    And at dawn this morning she was no more."

3. " Come, as you seem to know, good man,
    The terrible fate of this gallant ship,
Tell me all about her that you can,—
    And here's my flask to moisten your lip
Tell me how many she had on board—
    Wives and husbands, and lovers true—
How did it fare with her human hoard,
    Lost she many or lost she few ? "

4. " Master, I may not drink of your flask,
    Already too moist I feel my lip ;
But I'm ready to do what else you ask,
    And spin you my yarn about the ship :
'Twas ten o'clock, as I said, last night,
    When she struck the breakers and went ashore,

And scarce had broken the morning's light
    Than she sank in twelve feet of water, or more.

5. " But long ere this they knew their doom,
    And the Captain called all hands to prayer ;
And solemnly over the ocean's boom
    The orisons rose on the troubled air.
And round about the vessel there rose
    Tall plumes of spray as white as snow,
Like angels in their ascension clothes,
    Waiting for those who prayed below.

6. " So those three hundred people clung
    As well as they could to spar and rope ;
With a word of prayer upon every tongue,
    Nor on any face a glimmer of hope.
But there was no blubbering weak and wild—
    Of tearful faces I saw but one,
A rough old salt, who cried like a child,
    And not for himself, but the Captain's son.

7. " The Captain stood on the quarter-deck,
    Firm but pale, with trumpet in hand,
Sometimes he looked on the breaking wreck,
    Sometimes he sadly looked on land.
And often he smiled to cheer the crew—
    But, Lord ! the smile was terrible grim—
'Till over the quarter a huge sea flew,
    And that was the last they saw of him.

8. " I saw one young fellow, with his bride,
    Standing amidship upon the wreck :
His face was white as the boiling tide,
    And *she* was clinging about his neck.
And I saw them try to say good-bye,
    But neither could hear the other speak :
So they floated away through the sea to die—
    Shoulder to shoulder, and cheek to cheek.

9. " And there was a child, but eight at best,
    Who went his way in a sea we shipped,
All the while holding upon his breast
    A little pet parrot whose wings were clipped.
And as the boy and the bird went by,
    Swinging away on a tall wave's crest,
They were grappled by a man with a drowning cry,
    And together the three went down to rest.

14

10. " And so the crew went one by one,
    Some with gladness, and few with fear :
Cold and hardship such work had done
    That few seemed frightened when death was near.
Thus every soul on board went down—
    Sailor and passenger, little and great :
The last that sank was a man of my town,
    A capital swimmer—the second mate."

11. " Now, lonely Fisherman, who are you,
    That say you saw this terrible wreck ?
How do I know what you say is true,
    When every mortal was swept from the deck ?
Where were you in that hour of death ?
    How do you know what you relate ? "
His answer came in an under-breath—
    " Master, I was the second mate ! "

CLXVII.—THE VAGABONDS.

TROWBRIDGE.

1. WE are two travelers, Roger and I.
    Roger's my dog.—Come here, you scamp !
Jump for the gentlemen,—mind your eye !
    Over the table,—look out for the lamp !—
The rogue is growing a little old :
    Five years we've tramped through wind and weather,
And slept out-doors when nights were cold,
    And ate and drank—and starved—together.

2. We've learned what comfort is, I tell you!
    A bed on the floor, a bit of rosin,
A fire to thaw our thumbs, (poor fellow !
    The paw he holds up there 's been frozen,)
Plenty of catgut for my fiddle,
    (This out-door business is bad for strings,)
Then a few nice buckwheats hot from the griddle
    And Roger and I set up for kings!

3. No, thank ye, sir,—I never drink :
    Roger and I are exceedingly moral—
Aren't we, Roger ?—See him wink !—
    Well, something hot, then,—we won't quarrel.
He's thirsty, too,—see him nod his head ?
    What a pity, sir, that dogs can't talk !

He understands every word that's said,—
And he knows good milk from water-and-chalk.

4. The truth is, sir, now I reflect,
I've been so sadly given to grog,
I wonder I've not lost the respect
(Here's to you, sir!) even of my dog.
But he sticks by, through thick and thin;
And this old coat, with its empty pockets,
And rags that smell of tobacco and gin,
He'll follow while he has eyes in his sockets.

5. There isn't another creature living
Would do it, and prove, through every disaster,
So fond, so faithful, and so forgiving,
To such a miserable, thankless master!
No, sir!—see him wag his tail and grin!
By George! it makes my old eyes water!
That is, there's something in this gin
That chokes a fellow. But no matter!

6. We'll have some music, if you're willing,
And Roger (hem! what a plague a cough is, sir!)
Shall march a little.—Start, you villain!
Stand straight! 'Bout face! Salute your officer!
Put up that paw! Dress! Take your rifle!
(Some dogs have arms, you see!) Now hold your
Cap while the gentlemen give a trifle,
To aid a poor, old, patriot soldier!

7. March! Halt! Now show how the rebel shakes,
When he stands up to hear his sentence.
Now tell us how many drams it takes
To honor a jolly new acquaintance.
Five yelps,—that's five: he's mighty knowing!
The night's before us, fill the glasses!—
Quick, sir! I'm ill,—my brain is going!—
Some brandy,—thank you,—there!—it passes!

8. Why not reform? That's easily said;
But I've gone through such wretched treatment,
Sometimes forgetting the taste of bread,
And scarce remembering what meat meant,
That my poor stomach's past reform;
And there are times when, mad with thinking,
I'd sell out heaven for something warm
To prop a horrible inward sinking.

9.   Is there a way to forget to think?
     At your age, sir, home, fortune, friends,
     A dear girl's love,—but I took to drink;—
     The same old story: you know how it ends.
     If you could have seen these classic features,—
       You need'nt laugh, sir: they were not then
     Such a burning libel on God's creatures:
       I was one of your handsome men!

10.   If you had seen me, so fair and young,
       Whose head was happy on this breast!
     If you could have heard the song I sung
       When the wine went round, you would'nt have guessed
     That ever I, sir, should be straying
       From door to door, with fiddle and dog,
     Ragged and penniless, and playing
       To you to-night for a glass of grog!

11.   She's married since,—a parson's wife:
       'Twas better for her that we should part,—
     Better the soberest, prosiest life
       Than a blasted home and a broken heart.
     I have seen her? Once: I was weak and spent
       On a dusty road: a carriage stopped:
     But little she dreamed, as on she went,
       Who kissed the coin that her fingers dropped!

12.   You've set me talking, sir: I'm sorry:
       It makes me wild to think of the change!
     What do you care for a beggar's story?
       Is it amusing? you find it strange?
     I had a mother so proud of me!
       'Twas well she died before—Do you know
     If the happy spirits in heaven can see
       The ruin and wretchedness here below?

13.   Another glass, and strong, to deaden
       This pain: then Roger and I will start.
     I wonder, has he such a lumpish, leaden,
       Aching thing, in place of a heart?
     He is sad sometimes, and would weep, if he could,
       No doubt, remembering things that were,—
     A virtuous kennel, with plenty of food,
       And himself a sober, respectable cur.

14.   I'm better now: that glass was warming.—
       You rascal! limber your lazy feet!

We must be fiddling and performing
  For supper and bed, or starve in the street.
Not a very gay life to lead, you think ?
  But soon we shall go where lodgings are free,
And the sleepers need neither victuals nor drink :
  The sooner, the better for Roger and me !

———————◆———————

CLXVIII.—COMMENCEMENT MORALITIES.

1. It is an unpleasant peculiarity of the present period that we think so much about thinking. The President of a College, when he takes leave of a little flock of just fledged Bachelors, tells them that they must be sure to go on cultivating their minds : that intellectual progress alone is consistent with true happiness : that they must be faithful to the Republic and to themselves : that he wishes them abundant prosperity and a great deal of taste. The Bachelors then pack up their goods and go out for a pilgrimage over "the hot sands of this wilderness of a world," each one bearing a parchment certificate that he has studied to the acceptance of his Faculty for four years, Greek, Latin, Mathematics, Natural and Moral and Intellectual Philosophy, with other small side branches of learning. Many of the young gentlemen so dismissed are full of rather indefinite aspirations and poetical purposes. Most of them are of an ingenuous spirit, and mean to be honorable, industrious, and successful. They are going out to the Battle of Life—for so they call it—and propose to be good soldiers. There is an immensity of preparation—what shall we say of the performance ?

2. There is something pathetic in the consideration that so many must fall and fail, must die by the wayside, must waste mind and lose heart in the struggle—so many of these poor boys now starting with the morning light upon their unwrinkled brows! For of all failures in this world of disappointment, there is none so melancholy as that of the intellectual man missing the prize of success through

feebleness of will or the perversity of fate, and suffering ten-fold more than wretches of a less sensitive nature. But the world moves on in its career of business or of pleasure, mindful for the most part only of its own affairs, and thinking it does enough if it bestows a momentary sigh upon the private tragedy of which every day brings a new one. A newspaper, consecrated to the practical bustle of affairs, can do no more.

3. We believe that we have read about ten thousand sermons, addresses, lectures, and speeches, be the same more or less, upon " The Duties of the Scholar in the Nineteenth Century." At any rate, we have read more of them than we propose ever to read again. The best of them are but respectable repetitions. The Bachelor of Arts is " to woo solitude as a bride." He is to give his days and nights to high philosophy. He is to be virtuous. He is to be truthful. He is to be patriotic. After hearing this he goes away: he forgets his Greek and Latin as soon as possible: he opens a broker's office in Wall-st., or a cotton mill in Lowell: he practices law and discards his virtue: he turns politician and has no use for it: he preaches without it ; or he becomes a member of Congress, and finds " high philosophy " a drug ! If he ever talks about it again, it is only once a year at the Commencement dinner.

4. Of purely professional scholars we have hardly a hundred in the whole land, and most of these are engaged in teaching—the mill-horses, if we may say so, of classical routine. The rest of the Bachelors are doing something better—they are making money ! Now, if the President of a College should say to his departing pupils, " My young friends, be sure and make money ! " what a clamor would fill the academic shades ! With what celerity would that respectable S. T. D. be expelled from his office, even although he couched the obnoxious sentiment in Latin, and said :

>   "——quærenda pecunia primum est ;
> Virtus post nummos ! "

But we do not see why he should not say it, when we all mean it and do it, with our whole heart, and mind, and strength.

5. And pray what should be the business of a College but to prepare young gentlemen for the business of life ? Then why should we not have Professorships of Stock Broking ? Chairs devoted to the art and mystery of cornering a stock ? Teachers of the science of bamboozling a jury and of driving a coach and horses through the flaws of an indictment ? Lecturers on the pure mathematics of Number One ? Good, hard-headed, practical Doctors of the Main Chance, with appropriate and necessary text-books ? If it is to come to that at last, why not in the beginning ? Questions like these bring us out of the salt fog of our cynicism into a grateful and sunny recognition of what the Colleges have done for us, and may, with all their faults, still do for us. This is a very imperfect world : it is " prone and obedient," as Sallust has it, " to the appetites ;" and colleges, like churches, are perpetual protests against complete surrender to the temporal and the mechanical. They are a confession of faith which it is better to gabble unconsciously than not to say at all.

6. When a man who can hardly read English, dies, and leaves $50,000 to endow a Hebrew chair, he acknowledges duly by hand and seal that there is something better than bulling or bearing stock. He would have scoffed at Parson Adams if he had met him with Æschylus in his pocket in Wall-st. ; but as the roar of that seething thoroughfare grows faint in his dying ears, he bethinks him that it will be a very good thing to have poor boys taught Greek. These are miracles, but we have had too many of them to disbelieve in them altogether. Most of our seats of polite learning, owe their existence to the liberality of departed shop-keepers. Hundreds of churches are under like obligations. A mutation of the hide and tallow market may give the languishing Chinese mission a new lease of life. So Colleges are to be cultured and endowed, and honorably mentioned in last wills and testaments, if for no other rea-

son than for proof that Poor Richard was right, and that "learning *is* better than house or lands." All the world, in a muzzy sort of way, feels and acknowledges this.

7. On the other hand, what Wealth does for Learning, is amply and generously repaid, both by the new paths of enterprise and emolument which cultivation opens, and by respectable methods of expending money which refinement establishes. Mr. Astor would never have thought of establishing his great library, if there had not been so many little ones in the country. One never knows in what form the planted seed will spring up. Harvard College generates picture galleries in New-York, and Yale may have something to do with the Academy of Music. The beginning of all newspaper success, is in the dame-school where the alphabet is taught. The great operations of the banks are first scrawled upon a boy's slate. It is not the ignorant money-changer who is intolerable, but the money-changer who is ignorant of the wretchedness of ignorance. The main educational idea of this age is that of diffusion: that of a past age, concentration. We may have fewer great scholars than lived, and pored, and endlessly wrote in monastic times: but what we have gained is a sufficiency of knowledge, so that no man need be miserable through ignorance. In the promotion of this, Colleges do their part, especially in keeping up a high standard; and the multiplication of universities only shows an advance in the ambition and intelligence of the masses. For this, whatever may be collegiate shortcomings, let us be grateful.

CLXIX.—THE MISER.

CUTTER.

1. An old man sat by a fireless hearth,
   Though the night was dark and chill,
And mournfully over the frozen earth
   The wind sobbed loud and shrill.
His locks were gray, and his eyes were gray,
   And dim, but not with tears;

And his skeleton form had wasted away
  With penury, more than years.

2. A rush-light was casting its fitful glare
  O'er the damp and dingy walls,
Where the lizard hath made his slimy lair,
  And the venomous spider crawls;
But the meanest thing in this lonesome room
  Was the miser worn and bare,
Where he sat like a ghost in an empty tomb,
  On his broken and only chair.

3. He had bolted the window and barred the door,
  And every nook had scanned;
And felt the fastening o'er and o'er,
  With his cold and skinny hand;
And yet he sat gazing intently round,
  And trembled with silent fear,
And startled and shuddered at every sound
  That fell on his coward ear.

4. "Ha! ha!" laughed the miser: "I'm safe at last,
  From this night so cold and drear,
From the drenching rain and driving blast,
  With my gold and treasures here.
I am cold and wet with the icy rain,
  And my health is bad, 'tis true;
Yet if I should light that fire again,
  It would cost me a cent or two.

5. But I'll take a sip of the precious wine:
  It will banish my cold and fears:
It was given long since by a friend of mine—
  I have kept it for many years."
So he drew a flask from a mouldy nook,
  And drank of its ruby tide;
And his eyes grew bright with each draught he took,
  And his bosom swelled with pride.

6. "Let me see: let me see!" said the miser then,
  "'Tis some sixty years or more
Since the happy hour when I began
  To heap up the glittering store;
And well have I sped with my anxious toil,
  As my crowded chest will show:
I've more than would ransom a kingdom's spoil,
  Or an emperor could bestow."
14*

7. He turned to an old worm-eaten chest,
  And cautiously raised the lid,
  And then it shone like the clouds of the west,
  With the sun in their splendor hid;
  And gem after gem, in precious store,
  Are raised with exulting smile;
  And he counted and counted them o'er and o'er,
  In many a glittering pile.

8. Why comes the flush to his pallid brow,
  While his eyes like his diamonds shine?
  Why writhes he thus in such torture now?
  What was there in the wine?
  He strove his lonely seat to gain:
  To crawl to his nest he tried;
  But finding his efforts all in vain,
  He clasped his gold, and—*died.*

CLXX.—THE WRECK OF THE ARCTIC.

H. W. BEECHER.

1. IT was autumn. Hundreds had wended their way from pilgrimages: from Rome and its treasures of dead arts, and its glory of living nature: from the sides of the Switzer's mountains, from the capitals of various nations: all saying in their hearts, we will wait for the September gales to have done with their equinoctial fury, and then we will embark: we will slide across the appeased ocean, and in the gorgeous month of October, we will greet our longed-for native land, and our heart-loved homes. And so the throng streamed along from Berlin, from•Paris, from the Orient, converging upon London, still hastening toward their welcome ship, and narrowing every day the circles of engagements and preparations.

2. They crowded aboard. Never had the Arctic borne such a host of passengers, nor passengers so nearly related to so many of us. The hour was come. The signal-ball fell at Greenwich. It was noon also at Liverpool. The anchors were weighed: the great hull swayed to the current: the national colors streamed aboard, as if them-

selves instinct with life and national sympathy. The bell strikes: the wheels revolve: the signal gun beats its echoes in upon every structure along the shore, and the Arctic glides joyfully forth from the Mersey, and turns her prow to the winding channel, and begins her homeward run.

3. The pilot stood at the wheel, and men saw him. Death sat upon the prow, and no eye beheld him. Whoever stood at the wheel in all that voyage, Death was the pilot that steered the craft, and and no one knew it. He neither revealed his presence nor whispered his errand. And so hope was effulgent, and lithe gayety disported itself, and joy was with every guest. Amid all the inconveniences of the voyage, there was that which hushed every murmur—home is not far away,—and every morning it was one night nearer home, and at evening one day nearer home! Eight days had passed. They beheld that distant bank of mist that forever haunts the vast shallows of Newfoundland. Boldly they made it, and plunging in, its pliant wreaths wrapped them about. They shall never emerge. The last sunlight has flashed from that deck. The last voyage done to ship and passengers.

4. At noon there came noiselessly stealing from the north that fated instrument of destruction. In that mysterious shroud, that vast atmosphere of mist, both steamers were holding their way with rushing prow and roaring wheels, but invisible. At a league's distance, but unconscious, and at nearer approach unwarned: within hail, and bearing right toward each other, unseen, unfelt, till in a moment more, emerging from the gray mist, the ill-omened Vesta dealt her deadly blow to the Arctic. The death blow was scarcely felt along that mighty hull. She neither reeled nor shivered. Neither commander nor officers deemed that they had suffered harm.

5. Prompt upon humanity, the brave Luce (let his name be ever spoken with admiration and respect) ordered away his boat with the first officer, to inquire if the stranger had suffered harm. As Gourley went over the ship's

side, Oh, that some good angel had called to the brave commander in the words of Paul on a like occasion, " except these abide in the ship ye cannot be saved." They departed, and with them the hope of the ship, for now the waters, gaining upon the hold and rising up upon the fires, revealed the mortal blow. Oh, had now that stern, brave mate, Gourley, been on deck, whom the sailors were wont to mind—had he stood to execute efficiently the commander's will,—we may believe that we should not have to blush for the cowardice and recreancy of the crew, nor weep for the untimely dead.

6. But, apparently, each subordinate officer lost all presence of mind, then courage, and so honor. In a wild scramble, that ignoble mob of firemen, engineers, waiters, and crew, rushed for the boats, and abandoned the helpless women, children, and men to the mercy of the deep! Four hours there were from the catastrophe of the collision to the catastrophe of sinking! Oh, what a burial was here! not as when one is borne from his home, among weeping throngs, and gently carried to the green fields, and laid peacefully beneath the turf and the flowers. No priest stood to pronounce a burial service. It was an ocean grave. The mists alone shrouded the burial place. No spade prepared the grave, nor sexton filled up the hallowed earth. Down, down, down they sank, and the quick returning waters smoothed out every ripple, and left the sea as if it had not been.

--------◆--------

CLXXI.—THE FIRST PREDICTED ECLIPSE.

MITCHELL.

1. To those who have given but little attention to the subject, even in our own day, with all the aids of modern science, the prediction of an eclipse seems sufficiently mysterious and unintelligible. How, then, it was possible, thousands of years ago, to accomplish the same great

object, without any just views of the structure of the system, seems utterly incredible.

2. Follow, in imagination, this bold interrogator of the skies to his solitary mountain summit;—withdrawn from the world, surrounded by his mysterious circles, there to watch and ponder through the long nights of many, many years. But hope cheers him on, and smooths his rugged path-way. Dark and deep as is his problem, he sternly grapples with it, and resolves never to give over till victory crowns his efforts. Long and patiently did the astronomer wait and watch. Each eclipse is duly observed, and its attendant circumstances are recorded, when, at last, the darkness begins to give way, and a ray of light breaks in upon his mind.

3. He finds that no eclipse of the sun ever occurs unless the new moon is in the act of crossing the sun's track. Here is a grand discovery. He now holds the key which will unlock the dread mystery. Reaching forward with piercing intellectual vigor, he at last finds a new moon which occurs precisely at the computed time of her passage across the sun's track. Here he makes his stand, and announces to the startled inhabitants of the world that on the day of the occurrence of that new moon the sun shall expire in a dark eclipse. Bold prediction!—mysterious prophet!—With what scorn must the unthinking world have received this solemn declaration.

4. How slowly do the moons roll away; and with what intense anxiety does the stern philosopher await the coming of that day which should crown him with victory, or dash him to the ground in ruin and disgrace! Time to him moves on leaden wings: day after day, and at last hour after hour, roll heavily away. The last night is gone,—the moon has disappeared from his eagle gaze in her approach to the sun, and the dawn of the eventful day breaks in beauty on a slumbering world. This daring man, stern in his faith, climbs alone to his rocky home, and greets the sun as he rises and mounts the heavens, scattering brightness and glory in his path.

5. Beneath him is spread out the populous city, already teeming with life and activity. The busy morning hum rises on the still air, and reaches the watching place of the solitary astronomer. The thousands below him, uncon-scious of his intense anxiety, buoyant with life, joyously pursue their rounds of business,—their cycles of amusement. The sun slowly climbs the heavens, round, and bright, and full-orbed. The lone tenant of the mountain top almost begins to waver in the sternness of his faith, as the morning hours roll away.

6. But the time of his triumph, long delayed, at length begins to dawn: a pale and sickly hue creeps over the face of nature. The sun has reached his highest point, but his splendor is dimmed, his light is feeble. At last it comes! Blackness is eating away his round disc,—onward with slow but steady pace the dark veil moves, blacker than a thousand nights,—the gloom deepens,—the ghastly hue of death covers the universe,—the last ray is gone, and horror reigns. A wail of terror fills the murky air,—the clangor of brazen trumpets resounds,—an agony of despair dashes the stricken millions to the ground, while that lone man, erect on his rocky summit, with arms outstretched to heaven, pours forth the grateful gushings of his heart to God, who had crowned his efforts with triumphant victory.

---◆---

CLXXII.—LARVÆ.

B. F. TAYLOR.

1. My little maiden of four years old,
    (No myth, but a genuine child is she,
    With her bronze brown eyes and her curls of gold,)
    Came quite in disgust one day to me:

2. Rubbing her shoulders with rosy palm,
    As the loathsome touch seemed yet to thrill her,
    She cried, "Oh, mother, I found on my arm
    A horrible, crawling, caterpillar."

3. And with mischievous smile she scarce could smother,
    Yet a glance in its daring half awed and shy,

She added, "While they were about it mother,
I wish they'd just finished the butterfly."

4. They were words to the thought of the soul that turns,
From the coarser form of a partial growth :
Reproaching the infinite patience that yearns
With an unknown glory to crown them both.

5. Ah! look thou largely with lenient eyes
On what so beside thee may creep and cling,
For the possible beauty that underlies
The passing phase of the meanest thing.

.6. What if God's great angels, whose waiting love
Beholdeth our pitiful life below,
From the holy height of the Heaven above,
Couldn't bear with the worm till the wings should grow.

CLXXIII.—A BAYONET CHARGE.

1. THERE was a bayonet charge. Let those who wish
to know the sublimest moment in the physical existence of
man, look at a division when the order is given to hurl it,
silently and stealthily, but sternly and steadily into the
jaws of destruction, whence-it can escape only by breaking
the very teeth of the death which threatens it. It is not
mere bull-dog daring that is then aroused : it is more than
passionate blood which at the word leaps through the veins
with such hot impetuosity that toughly corded nerves and
brawny muscles quiver under the fresh life impulse.

2. It is spirit—soul that gushes up warm and eager from
the heart, and pours through the old blood channels with
such vivifying tumult that the dark, dull, venous clots rush
along as bright and sparkling as if their foaming were the
mantles of new fermented wine. It is the capacity for
high and glorious things—for suffering, daring and death :
which latent before, and felt as but faint and fragmentary,
now spring into omnipotent and full-statured existence.

3. You do not know what they are—the capabilities of
life—you, of the North, who tread your little daily rounds,
in and out, and have no ambition beyond the bounds of

wealth and ease : you are dreaming, all of you. Let me strap a knapsack on you instead of a journal, give you a pistol for a pen, and put a bayonet into your hands, which before held a yard stick. Now, stand in the ranks, and wait for the word. It comes, " Charge Bayonets." " Off! and God be with you! Fight your way stoutly! it is for your life! Fight it unflinchingly! it is for your honor! If you fall, the glory of the cause and the sublimity of this scene will brighten your eye in spite of the death glaze, and hold high your hopes, even when life is ebbing. If you pass through you are a man forever—a man on a large scale of character—a man of intensity and concentrated force, a man who has more than glimpses into the magnificent possibilities of the spirit within him."

4. Such are the men of *Huntgleman's* corps d'armes who escaped the chances of their glorious charge. They have lived ages in moments : they have passed through the most terrible ordeal that can test the stuff of manhood; and they have recompense beyond gold or emolument,— self-asserted honor and a deep insight of life; for was it not bordered closely and terribly with death : the men were by no means fresh when they were submitted to this trial : they had fought through a greater part of a most fatiguing day : they were tired to verge of exhaustion : they had been without provision, and worse than all an intolerable thirst consumed them : hungry, thirsty, dirty, every thing but dispirited. In the eyes of the world, they would have been justified in treating the order as a mistake, whether intentional or unintentional.

5. They had been forced back by the sheer weight of overwhelming numbers : new forces had been constantly hurried upon them, and it was but madness to refuse the chances of meeting reinforcements in the rear. The awful crash of the battle was still around them. A superior artillery was hurling havoc into their ranks. Musketry was increasing its deadly volleys, and there began to be symptoms of a flanking movement, and cross-fire. It was under

such circumstances that Huntgleman ceased fire. It made
a decided difference in the noise of the field: the diminu-
tion of sound was almost a hush, though the enemy was
blazing away as rapidly as ever : it is the guns immediately
about that fills our ears. For an instant the great line
wavered: this suspense was horrible, it must be filled with
acts of some kind! mortal men cannot stand it! for God's
sake let the great gap of inaction be crammed with death if
nothing else! "Steady, men." A resumption of the
line; but also an increase of the adverse firing.

6. Again a wave. "Steady, steady, men." Aye, brawl
till you are hoarse, brave captains, but these seconds are
centuries : you must give these men something to do : you
must steady them by action. And here comes enough :
aids gallop down with orders that bring every musket to
its most threatening position. Then the cheering words
of the commanders as they dash down the lines. Then a
mild waving of swords by the shoulder straps, as the final
word is given and the column starts forward. Slowly, at
first, and rather lamely: joints stiff with fatigue; but as
the distance from the foe is shortened, the pace is quick-
ened. Faster, and faster moves that steadily advancing
column, till on a run like a deer, with leaps and shouts
like savage creatures, they hurl themselves right into the
midst of the expectant foe! What passed there no man
can tell. They are not more silent who fell with death
sealed lips than are those who came out unharmed: the
excitement is too great for memory to hold any ground:
all faculties are swept away in one wild thirst for blood.

CLXXIV.—KOSSUTH'S FIRST SPEECH IN AMERICA.

Louis Kossuth.

1. FREEDOM AND HOME! what heavenly music in those
two words! Alas, I have no home ; and the freedom of
my people is down-trodden. Young Giant of Free America,
do not tell me that thy shores are an asylum to the op-

pressed, and a home to the homeless exile. An asylum it is, but all the blessings of your glorious country, can they drown into oblivion the longing of the heart, and the fond desires for our native land ?

2. My beloved native land! thy very sufferings make thee but dearer to my heart: thy bleeding image dwells with me when I wake, as it rests with me in the short moments of my restless sleep. It has accompanied me over the waves. It will accompany me when I go back to fight over again the battles of thy freedom once more. I have no idea but thee : I have no feeling but thee. Even here, with this prodigious view of greatness, freedom, and happiness, which spreads before my astonished eyes, my thoughts are wandering toward home; and when I look over these thousands of thousands before me, the happy inheritance of yonder freedom for which your fathers fought and bled, and when I turn to you, citizens, to bow before the majesty of the United States, and to thank the people of New York for their generous share in my liberation, and for the unparalleled honor of this reception, I see, out of the very midst of this great assemblage, rise the bleeding image of Hungary, looking to you with anxiety whether there be in the lustre of your eyes a ray of hope for her: whether there be in the thunder of your hurrahs a trumpet call of resurrection.

3. If there were no such ray of hope in your eyes, and no such trumpet call in your cheers, then woe to Europe's oppressed nations. They will stand alone in the hour of need. Less fortunate than you were, they will meet no brother's hand to help them in the approaching gigantic struggle against the leagued despots of the world; and woe also to me. I will feel no joy even here, and the days of my stay here will turn out to be lost to my fatherland, —lost at the very time when every moment is teeming in the decision of Europe's destiny.

4. Gentlemen, I have to thank the people, Congress and Government of the United States, for my liberation from

captivity. Human tongue has no words to express the bliss which I felt when I,—the down-trodden Hungary's wandering chief—saw the glorious flag of the stripes and stars fluttering over my head,—when I first bowed before it with deep respect, when I saw around me the gallant officers and the crew of the Mississippi frigate, the most of them the worthiest representatives of true American principles, American greatness, American generosity; and to think that it was not a mere chance which cast the star-spangled banner around me, but that it was your protecting will: to see a powerful vessel of America coming to far Asia, to break the chains by which the mightiest despots of Europe fettered the activity of an exiled Magyar, whose very name disturbed the proud security of their sleep: to feel restored by such a protection, and in such a way, to freedom, and by freedom to activity, you may be well aware of what I have felt, and still feel, at the remembrance of this proud moment of my life.

5. Others spoke, you acted, and I was free! You acted; and at this act of yours, tyrants trembled: humanity shouted with joy: the down-trodden people of Magyars—the down-trodden, but not broken, raised his head with resolution and with hope, and the brilliancy of your stars was greeted by Europe's oppressed nations as the morning star of rising liberty. Now, gentlemen, you must be aware how boundless the gratitude must be which I feel for you. You have restored me to life, because restored to activity; and should my life, by the blessings of the Almighty, still prove useful to my fatherland and to humanity, it will be your merit, it will be your work. May you and your glorious country be blessed for it.

CLXXV.—CLOISTER LIFE.

DONALD G. MITCHELL.

1. THE class in advance, you study curiously; and are quite amazed at the precocity of certain youths belonging

to it, who are apparently about your own age. The Juniors you look upon with a quiet reverence for their aplomb, and dignity of character; and look forward with intense yearnings, to the time when you, too, shall be admitted freely to the precincts of the Philosophical chamber, and to the very steep benches of the Laboratory. This last seems, from occasional peeps through the blinds, a most mysterious building. The chimneys, recesses, vats, and cisterns,—to say nothing of certain galvanic communications, which you are told, traverse the whole building, in a way capable of killing a rat, at an incredible remove from the bland professor,—utterly fatigue your wonder! You humbly trust (though you have doubts upon the point) that you will have the capacity to grasp it all, when once you shall have arrived to the dignity of a Junior.

2. As for the Seniors, your admiration for them is utterly boundless. In one or two individual instances, it is true, it has been broken down, by an unfortunate squabble, with thick-set fellows in the Chapel aisle. A person who sits not far before you at prayers, and whose name you seek out very early, bears a strong resemblance to some portrait of Dr. Johnson: you have very much the same kind of respect for him, that you feel for the great lexicographer; and do not for a moment doubt his capacity to compile a dictionary equal if not superior to Johnson's.

3. Another man with very bushy, black hair, and an easy look of importance, carries a large cane; and is represented to you, as an astonishing scholar, and speaker. You do not doubt it: his very air proclaims it. You think of him, as presently (say four or five years hence) astounding the United States Senate with his eloquence. And when once you have heard him in debate, with that ineffable gesture of his, you absolutely languish in your admiration for him; and you describe his speaking to your country friends, as very little inferior, if any, to Mr. Burke's.

4. Beside this one, are some half dozen others, among whom the question of superiority is, you understand, strong-

ly mooted. It puzzles you to think, what an avalanche of talent will fall upon the country, at the graduation of those seniors! You will find, however, that the country bears such inundations of college talent, with a remarkable degree of equanimity. It is quite wonderful how all the Burkes, and Scotts, and Peels, among college seniors, do quietly disappear, as a man gets on in life.

CLXXVI.—CLOISTER LIFE.—Continued.

DONALD G. MITCHELL.

1. As for any degree of fellowship with such giants, as college seniors, it is an honor hardly to be thought of. But you have a classmate—I will call him Dalton,—who is very intimate with a dashing senior : they room near each other outside the college. You quite envy Dalton, and you come to know him well. He says that you are not a " green one,"—that you have " cut your eye teeth : " in return for which complimentary opinions, you entertain a strong friendship for Dalton.

2. He is a " fast " fellow, as the senior calls him ; and it is a proud thing to happen at their rooms occasionally, and to match yourself for an hour or two (with the windows darkened) against a senior at " old sledge." It is quite " the thing," as Dalton says, to meet a senior familiarly in the street. Sometimes you go, after Dalton has taught you " the ropes," to have a cosy sit-down over oysters and champagne :—to which the senior lends himself, with the pleasantest condescension in the world.

3. You are not altogether used to hard drinking ; but this you conceal, (as most young fellows do,) by drinking a great deal. You have a dim recollection of certain circumstances, very unimportant, yet very vividly impressed on your mind, which occurred on one of these occasions. The oysters were exceedingly fine, and the champagne — exquisite. You have a recollection of something being said, toward the end of the first bottle, of Xenophon, and of the senior's saying in his playful way,—" Oh, d——n

Xenophon!" You remember Dalton laughed at this; and you laughed—for company.

4. You remember that you thought, and Dalton thought, and the senior thought—by a singular coincidence, that the second bottle of champagne was better even than the first. You have a dim remembrance of the senior's saying very loudly, "Clarence—(calling you by your family name) is no spooney;" and drinking a bumper with you in confirmation of the remark. You remember that Dalton broke out into a song, and that for a time you joined in the chorus: you think the senior called you to order for repeating the chorus, in the wrong place. You think the lights burned with remarkable brilliancy; and you remember that a remark of yours to that effect, met with very much such a response from the senior, as he had before employed with reference to Xenophon. You have a confused idea of calling Dalton—Xenophon.

5. You think the meeting broke up with a chorus; and that somebody—you cannot tell who—broke two or three glasses. You remember questioning yourself very seriously, as to whether you were or were not, tipsy. You think you decided you were not, but—*might* be. You have a confused recollection of leaning upon some one, or something, going to your room: this sense of a *desire to lean*, you think, was very strong. You remember of being horribly afflicted with the idea of having tried your night key at your tutor's door, instead of your own room: you remember further a hot stove,—made certain indeed, by a large blister which appeared on your hand, next day.

6. You think of throwing off your clothes, by one or two spasmodic efforts, leaning in the intervals, against the bed-post. There is a recollection of an uncommon dizziness afterward, as if your body was very quiet, and your head gyrating with strange velocity, and a kind of centrifugal action, all about the room, and the college, and indeed the whole town. You think that you felt uncontrollable nausea after this, followed by positive sickness :—

which waked your chum, who thought you very incoherent, and feared derangement. A dismal state of lassitude follows, broken by the college clock striking three, and by very rambling reflections upon champagne, Xenophon, " Captain Dick," Madge, and the old deacon who clinched his wig in the church.

7. The next morning—(ah, how vexatious that all our follies are followed by a—" next morning!") you wake with a parched mouth, and a torturing thirst: the sun is shining broadly into your reeking chamber. Prayers and recitations are long ago over; and you see, through the door, in the outer room, that hard faced chum, with his Lexicon, and Livy, open before him, working out with all the earnestness of his iron purpose, the steady steps toward preferment and success.

HUMOROUS.

CLXXVII.—THE GOUTY MERCHANT AND THE STRANGER.

1. In Broadstreet building, (on a winter night,)
Snug by his parlor-fire, a gouty wight
Sat all alone, with one hand rubbing
His feet, rolled up in fleecy hose,
With t'other he'd beneath his nose
The Public Ledger, in whose columns grubbing,
    He noted all the sales of hops,
    Ships, shops, and slops:
Gum, galls, and groceries: ginger, gin,
Tar, tallow, turmeric, turpentine, and tin:
When lo! a decent personage in black,
Entered and most politely said—
    " Your footman, sir, has gone his nightly track
    To the King's Head,
And left your door ajar, which I
Observed in passing by;
    And thought it neighborly to give you notice."

2. " Ten thousand thanks : how very few do get,
   In time of danger,
   Such kind attentions from a stranger !
   Assuredly, that fellow's throat is
   Doomed to a final drop at Newgate :
   He knows, too, (the unconscionable elf,)
   That there's no soul at home except myself."
       " Indeed," replied the stranger (looking grave),
       " Then he's a double knave :   ·
   He knows that rogues and thieves by scores
   Nightly beset unguarded doors ;
   And see, how easily might one
       Of these domestic foes,
       Even beneath your very nose,
   Perform his knavish tricks :
   Enter your room, as I have done,
   Blow out your candles—thus—and thus—,
   Pocket your silver candlesticks,
       And—walk off—thus "—
   So said, so done : he made no more remark,
       Nor waited for replies,
       But marched off with his prize,
   Leaving the gouty merchant in the dark.

CLXXVIII.—THE HEIGHT OF THE RIDICULOUS.

OLIVER WENDELL HOLMES.

1. I WROTE some lines once on a time
       In wondrous merry mood,
   And thought, as usual, men would say
       They were exceeding good.
   They were so queer, so very queer,
       I laughed as I would die :
   Albeit, in the general way,
       A sober man am I.

2. I called my servant, and he came :
       How kind it was of him,
   To mind a slender man like me,
       He of the mighty limb !
   " These to the printer" I exclaimed,
       And, in my humorous way,

I added (as a trifling jest),
  " There'll be the devil to pay."

3. He took the paper, and I watched,
    And saw him peep within :
  At the first line he read, his face
    Was all upon the grin.
  He read the next : the grin grew broad,
    And shot from ear to ear :
  He read the third : a chuckling noise
    I now began to hear.

4. The fourth, he broke into a roar :
    The fifth, his waistband split :
  The sixth, he burst five buttons off,
    And tumbled in a fit.
  Ten days and nights, with sleepless eye,
    I watched that wretched man,
  And since, I never dare to write
    As funny as I can.

CLXXIX.—THE MUSIC GRINDERS.

OLIVER WENDELL HOLMES.

1. THERE are three ways in which men take
    One's money from his purse,
  And very hard it is to tell
    Which of the three is worse ;
  But all of them are bad enough
    To make a body curse.

2. You're riding out some pleasant day,
    And counting up your gains :
  A fellow jumps from out a bush,
    And takes your horse's reins,
  Another hints some words about
    A bullet in your brains.

3. Perhaps you're going out to dine,—
    Some filthy creature begs
  You'll hear about the cannon-ball
    That carried off his pegs,
  And says it is a dreadful thing
    For men to lose their legs.

15

4. He tells you of his starving wife,
   His children to be fed,
Poor little, lovely innocents,
   All clamorous for bread ;
And so you kindly help to put
   A bachelor to bed. ˙

5. You're sitting on your window-seat,
   Beneath a cloudless moon :
You hear a sound that seems to wear
   The semblance of a tune,
As if a broken fife should strive
   To drown a cracked bassoon.

6. And nearer, nearer still, the tide
   Of music seems to come,
There's something like a human voice,
   And something like a drum :
You sit in speechless agony,
   Until your ear is numb.

7. You think they are crusaders, sent
   From some infernal clime,
To pluck the eyes of Sentiment,
   And dock the tail of Rhyme,
To crack the voice of Melody,
   And break the legs of Time.

8. But hark ! the air again is still, ·
   The music all is ground,
And silence, like a poultice, comes
   To heal the blows of sound :
It cannot be,—it is,—it is,—
   A hat is going round.

9. No ! Pay the dentist when he leaves
   A fracture in your jaw,
And pay the owner of the bear,
   That stunned you with his paw,
And buy the lobster that has had
   Your knuckles in his claw.

10. But if you are a portly man,
   Put on your fiercest frown,
And talk about a constable
   To turn them out of town ;

Then close your sentence with an oath,
And shut the window down !

11. And if you are a slender man,
Not big enough for that,
Or, if you cannot make a speech,
Because you are a flat,
Go very quietly and drop
A button in the hat !

CLXXX.—SAM WELLER'S VALENTINE.
CHARLES DICKENS.

1. "I've done now," said Sam, with slight embarrassment: "I've been a writin'."

"So I see," replied Mr. Weller. "Not to any young 'ooman, I hope, Sammy."

"Why, it's no use a sayin' it ain't," replied Sam. "It's a walentine."

"A what!" exclaimed Mr. Weller, apparently horror-stricken by the word.

"A walentine," replied Sam.

2. "Samivel, Samivel," said Mr. Weller, in reproachful accents, "I didn't think you'd ha' done it. Arter the warnin' you've had o' your father's wicious propensities, arter all I've said to you upon this here wery subject: arter actiwally seein' and bein' in the company o' our own mother-in-law, vich I should ha' thought was a moral lesson as no man could ever ha' forgotten to his dyin' day ! I didn't think you'd ha' done it, Sammy, I didn't think you'd ha' done it." These reflections were too much for the good old man. He raised Sam's tumbler to his lips and drank off the contents.

3. "Wot's the matter now ?" said Sam.

"Nev'r mind, Sammy," replied Mr. Weller, "it'll be a wery agonizin' trial to me at my time of life, but I'm pretty tough, that's vun consolation, as the wery old turkey remarked ven the farmer said he wos afeerd he should be obliged to kill him, for the London market."

" Wot'll be a trial ? " inquired Sam.

" To see you married, Sammy—to see you a deluded wictim, and thinkin' in your innocence that it's all wery capital," replied Mr. Weller. " It's a dreadful trial to a father's feelin's, that 'ere, Sammy."

" Nonsense," said Sam, " I ain't a goin' to get married, don't you fret yourself about that : I know you're a judge o' these things. Order in your pipe, and I'll read you the letter—there."

4. Sam dipped his pen into the ink to be ready for any corrections, and began with a very theatrical air—

" ' Lovely ———' "

" Stop," said Mr. Weller, ringing the bell. " A double glass o' the inwariable, my dear."

" Very well, sir," replied the girl : who with great quickness appeared, vanished, returned, and disappeared.

" They seem to know your ways here," observed Sam.

"Yes," replied his father, " I've been here before, in my time. Go on, Sammy."

" ' Lovely creetur','' repeated Sam.

" 'Taint in poetry, is it ? " interposed the father.

" No, no," replied Sam.

5. " Wery glad to hear it," said Mr. Weller. " Poetry's unnat'ral : no man ever talked in poetry 'cept a beadle on boxin' day, or Warren's blackin' or Rowland's oil, or some of them low fellows : never you let yourself down to talk poetry, my boy. Begin again, Sammy."

Mr. Weller resumed his pipe with critical solemnity, and Sam once more commenced and read as follows :

" ' Lovely creetur i feel myself a damned ' "—

" That ain't proper," said Mr. Weller, taking his pipe from his mouth.

6. " No : it ain't damned," observed Sam, holding the letter up to the light, " it's ' shamed,' there's a blot there— ' I feel myself ashamed.' "

" Wery good," said Mr. Weller. " Go on."

" ' Feel myself ashamed, and completely cir—.' I forget wot this here word is," said Sam, scratching his head with the pen, in vain attempts to remember.

" Why don't you look at it, then ? " inquired Mr. Weller.

" So I *am* a lookin' at it," replied Sam, " but there's another blot : here's a ' c,' and a ' i,' and a ' d.' "

" Circumwented, p'rhaps," suggested Mr. Weller.

" No, it ain't that," said Sam, " circumscribed, that's it."

" That ain't as good a word as circumwented, Sammy," said Mr. Weller, gravely.

" Think not ? " said Sam.

" Nothin' like it," replied his father.

" But don't you think it means more ? " inquired Sam.

" Vell, p'rhaps it's a more tenderer word," said Mr. Weller, after a few moments' reflection. " Go on, Sammy."

7. " ' Feel myself ashamed and completely circum-scribed in a dressin' of you, for you *are* a nice gal and nothin' but it.' "

" That's a wery pretty sentiment," said the elder Mr. Weller, removing his pipe to make way for the remark.

" Yes, I think it's rayther good," observed Sam, highly flattered.

" Wot I like in that 'ere style of writin'," said the elder Mr. Weller, " is, that there ain't no callin' names in it,— no Wenuses, nor nothin' o' that kind : wot's the good o' callin' a young 'ooman a Wenus or a angel, Sammy ? "

" Ah ! what, indeed ? " replied Sam.

" You might jist as vell call her a griffin, or a unicorn, or a king's arms at once, which is wery well known to be a col-lection o' fabulous animals," added Mr. Weller.

" Just as well," replied Sam.

" Drive on, Sammy," said Mr. Weller.

Sam complied with the request, and proceeded as fol-lows : his father continuing to smoke with a mixed ex-pression of wisdom and complacency, which was particu-larly edifying.

" ' Afore I see you I thought all women was alike.' "

"So they are," observed the elder Mr. Weller, parenthetically.

8. "'But now,'" continued Sam, "'now I find what a reg'lar soft-headed, ink-red'lous turnip I must ha' been, for there ain't nobody like you, though *I* like you better than nothin' at all.' I thought it best to make that rayther strong," said Sam, looking up.

Mr. Weller nodded approvingly, and Sam resumed.

"'So I take the privilidge of the day, Mary, my dear —as the gen'lem'n in difficulties did, ven he valked out of a Sunday,—to tell you that the first and only time I see you your likeness was took on my hart in much quicker time and brighter colors than ever a likeness was taken by the profeel macheen (wich p'rhaps you may have heerd on Mary my dear), altho' it *does* finish a portrait and put the frame and glass on complete with a hook at the end to hang it up by, and all in two minutes and a quarter.'"

"I am afeerd that werges on the poetical, Sammy," said Mr. Weller, dubiously.

"No it don't," replied Sam, reading on very quickly, to avoid contesting the point.

9. "Except of me Mary my dear as your walentine, and think over what I've said. My dear Mary I will now conclude.' That's all," said Sam.

"That's rayther a sudden pull up, ain't it, Sammy?" inquired Mr. Weller.

"Not a bit on it," said Sam: "she'll vish there wos more, and that's the great art o' letter writin'."

"Well," said Mr. Weller, "there's somethin' in that; and I wish your mother-in-law 'ud only conduct her conwersation on the same gen-teel principle. Ain't you a goin' to sign it?"

"That's the difficulty," said Sam: "I don't know what *to* sign it?"

"Sign it—Veller," said the oldest surviving proprietor of that name.

" Won't do," said Sam. " Never sign a walentine with your-own name."

" Sign it ' Pickvick,' then," said Mr. Weller: "it's a wery good name, and a easy one to spell."

" The wery thing," said Sam. "I *could* end with a werse: what do you think?"

" I don't like it, Sam," rejoined Mr. Weller. "I never know'd a respectable coachman as wrote poetry, 'cept one, as made an affectin' copy o' werses the night afore he wos hung for a highway robbery; and *he* wos only a Camber-vell man, so even that's no rule."

But Sam was not to be dissuaded from the poetical idea that had occurred to him, so he signed the letter—

" Your love-sick
Pickwick."

CLXXXI.—THE DEACON'S MASTERPIECE: OR, THE WONDER-FUL " ONE-HOSS SHAY."

OLIVER WENDELL HOLMES.

1. HAVE you heard of the wonderful one-hoss shay,
That was built in such a logical way
It ran a hundred years to a day,
And then, of a sudden, it—ah, but stay,
I'll tell you what happened without delay,
Scaring the parson into fits,
Frightening people out of their wits,—
Have you ever heard of that, I say?

2. Seventeen hundred and fifty-five,
Georgius Secundus was then alive,—
Snuffy old drone from the German hive.
That was the year when Lisbon town
Saw the earth open and gulp her down,
And Braddock's army was done so brown,
Left without a scalp to its crown.
It was on the terrible Earthquake-day
That the Deacon finished the one-hoss shay.

3. Now in building of chaises, I tell you what,
There is always *somewhere* a weakest spot,—

In hub, tire, felloe, in spring or thill,
In panel, or crossbar, or floor, or sill,
In screw, bolt, thoroughbrace,—lurking still,
Find it somewhere you must and will,—
Above or below, or within or without,—
And that's the reason, beyond a doubt,
A chaise *breaks down*, but doesn't *wear out*.
But the Deacon swore (as deacons do,
With an " I dew vum," or an " I tell *yeou* "),
He would build one shay to beat the taown
'n' the kcounty 'n' all the kentry raoun' :
It should be so built that it *couldn'* break daown :
—" Fur," said the Deacon, " 't's mighty plain
Thut the weakes' place mus' stan' the strain ;
'n' the way t' fix it, uz I maintain,
                    Is only jest
T' make that place uz strong uz the rest."

4. So the Deacon inquired of the village folk
Where he could find the strongest oak,
That couldn't be split nor bent nor broke,—
That was for spokes and floor and sills :
He sent for lancewood to make the thills :
The crossbars were ash, from the straightest trees :
The panels of white-wood, that cuts like cheese,
But lasts like iron for things like these :
The hubs of logs from the " Settler's ellum,"—
Last of its timber,—they couldn't sell 'em,
Never an ax had seen their chips,
And the wedges flew from between their lips,
Their blunt ends frizzled like celery-tips :
Step and prop-iron, bolt and screw,   •
Spring, tire, axle, and linchpin too,
Steel of the finest, bright and blue :
Thoroughbrace bison-skin, thick and wide :
Boot, top, dasher, from tough old hide
Found in the vat when the tanner died.
That was the way he " put her through."
" There ! " said the Deacon, " naow she'll dew ! "

5. Do ! I tell you, I rather guess
She was a wonder, and nothing less !
Colts grew horses, beards turned gray,
Deacon and deaconess dropped away,

Children and grandchildren—where were they?
But there stood the stout old one-hoss shay
As fresh as on Lisbon-Earthquake-day!

6. EIGHTEEN HUNDRED:—it came and found
The Deacon's masterpiece strong and sound.
Eighteen hundred increased by ten:
"Hahnsum kerridge " they called it then.
Eighteen hundred and twenty came:
Running as usual: much the same.
Thirty and forty at last arrive,
.And then come fifty, and FIFTY-FIVE.

7. FIRST OF NOVEMBER,—the Earth-quake day.
There are traces of age in the one-hoss shay,
A general flavor of mild decay,
But nothing local, as one may say.
There couldn't be,—for the Deacon's art
Had made it so like in every part
That there wasn't a chance for one to start.
For the wheels were just as strong as the thills,
And the floor was just as strong as the sills,
And the panels just as strong as the floor,
And the whippletree neither less nor more,
And the back-crossbar as strong as the fore,
And the spring and axle and hub *encore*.
And yet, *as a whole*, it is past a doubt
In another hour it will be *worn out!*

8. First of November, 'Fifty-five!
This morning the parson takes a drive.
Now, small boys, get out of the way!
Here comes the wonderful one-hoss shay,
Drawn by a rat-tailed, ewe-necked bay.
" Huddup! " said the parson.—Off went they.

9. The parson was working his Sunday's text:
Had got to *fifthly*, and stopped perplexed
At what the—Moses—was coming next.
All at once the horse stood still,
Close by the meet'r.'-house on the hill.
—First a shiver, and then a thrill,
Then something decidedly like a spill,—
And the parson was sitting upon a rock,
At half-past nine by the meet'n'-house clock,—

Just the hour of the Earthquake shock!—
What do you think the parson found,
When he got up and stared around?
The poor old chaise in a heap or mound,
As if it had been to the mill and ground!
You see, of course, if you're not a dunce,
How it went to pieces all at once,—
All at once, and nothing first,
Just as bubbles do when they burst.
End of the wonderful one-hoss shay.
Logic is logic. That's all I say.

CLXXXII.—MRS. CAUDLE'S CURTAIN LECTURE ON UMBRELLAS.

DOUGLAS JERROLD.

1. THAT's the third umbrella gone since Christmas. *What were you to do?* Why, let him go home in the rain, to be sure. I'm very certain there was nothing about *him* that could spoil. Take cold, indeed! He doesn't look like one of the sort to take cold. Besides, he'd have better taken cold than take our only umbrella. Do you hear the rain, Mr. Caudle? I say, do you hear the rain? And as I'm alive, if it isn't St. Swithin's day! Do you hear it against the windows? Nonsense: you don't impose upon me. You can't be asleep with such a shower as that? Do you hear it, I say? Oh, you *do* hear it! Well, that's a pretty flood, I think, to last for six weeks; and no stirring all the time out of the house. Pooh! don't think me a fool, Mr. Caudle. Don't insult me. *He* return the umbrella! Any body would think you were born yesterday. As if any body ever *did* return an umbrella! There—do you hear it? Worse and worse! Cats and dogs, and for six weeks—always six weeks. And no umbrella!

2. But I know why you lent the umbrella. Oh, yes: I know very well. I was going out to tea at dear mother's to-morrow—you knew that; and you did it on purpose. Don't tell me: you hate me to go there, and take every mean advantage to hinder me. But don't you think it,

Mr. Caudle. No, Sir ; if it comes down in buckets-full, I'll go all the more. No; and I won't have a cab. Where do you think the money's to come from? You've got nice high notions at that club of yours. A cab, indeed! Cost me sixteen pence at least—sixteen pence! two-and-eight-pence, for there's back again. Cabs, indeed! I should like to know who's to pay for 'em : I can't pay for 'em, and I am sure you can't, if you go on as you do: throwing away your property, and beggaring your children—buying umbrellas!

3. Do you hear the rain, Mr. Caudle? I say, do you hear it? But I don't care—I'll go to mother's to-morrow : I will; and what's more, I'll walk every step of the way, —and you know that will give me my death. Don't call me a foolish woman, it's you that's the foolish man. Ugh! I do look forward with dread for to-morrow! How I am to go to mother's I'm sure I can't tell. But if I die, I'll do it. No, Sir : I won't borrow an umbrella. No ; and you shan't buy one. Now, Mr. Caudle, only listen to this: if you bring home another umbrella, I'll throw it in the street. I'll have my own umbrella, or none at all.

4. Ha! and it was only last week I had a new nozzle put to that umbrella. I'm sure, if I'd have known as much as I do now, it might have gone without one for me. Paying for new nozzles, for other people to laugh at you. Oh, it's all very well for you—you can go to sleep. You've no thought of your poor patient wife, and your own dear children. You think of nothing but umbrellas! Men, in-deed!—call themselves lords of the creation!—pretty lords, when they can't even take care of an umbrella!

----------◆----------

CLXXXIII.—SCENES FROM PICKWICK.—*The Dilemma.*

DICKENS.

1. MR. PICKWICK'S apartments in Goswell street, al-though on a limited scale, were not only of a very neat and comfortable description, but peculiarly adapted for the res-

idence of a man of his genius and observation. His sitting-room was the first floor front, his bed-room was the second floor front ; and thus, whether he was sitting at his desk in the parlor, or standing before the dressing-glass in his dormitory, he had an equal opportunity of contemplating human nature in all the numerous phases it exhibits, in that not more populous than popular thoroughfare.

2. His landlady, Mrs. Bardell—the relict and sole executrix of a deceased custom-house officer—was a comely woman of bustling manners and agreeable appearance, with a natural genius for cooking, improved by study and long practice into an exquisite talent. There were no children, no servants, no fowls. The only other inmates of the house were a large man and a small boy : the first a lodger, the second a production of Mrs. Bardell's. The large man was always at home precisely at ten o'clock at night, at which hour he regularly condensed himself into the limits of a dwarfish French bedstead in the back parlor ; and the infantine sports and gymnastic exercises of Master Bardell were exclusively confined to the neighboring pavements and gutters. Cleanliness and quiet reigned throughout the house ; and in it Mr. Pickwick's will was law.

3. To any one acquainted with these points of the domestic economy of the establishment, and conversant with the admirable regulation of Mr. Pickwick's mind, his appearance and behavior, on the morning previous to that which had been fixed upon for the journey to Eatansvill, would have been most mysterious and unaccountable. He paced the room to and fro with hurried steps, popped his head out of the window at intervals of about three minutes each, constantly referred to his watch, and exhibited many other manifestations of impatience, very unusual with him. It was evident that something of great importance was in contemplation ; but what that something was, not even Mrs. Bardell herself had been enabled to discover.

4. " Mrs. Bardell," said Mr. Pickwick, at last, as that amiable female approached the termination of a prolonged

dusting of the apartment. "Sir," said Mrs. Bardell. "Your little boy is a very long time gone." "Why, it's a good long way to the Borough, sir," remonstrated Mrs. Bardell. "Ah," said Mr. Pickwick, "very true : so it is." Mr. Pickwick relapsed into silence, and Mrs. Bardell resumed her dusting.

5. "Mrs. Bardell," said Mr. Pickwick, at the expiration of a few minutes. "Sir," said Mrs. Bardell again. "Do you think it's a much greater expense to keep two people, than to keep one?" "La, Mr. Pickwick," said Mrs. Bardell, coloring up to the very border of her cap, as she fancied she observed a species of matrimonial twinkle in the eyes of her lodger : "La, Mr. Pickwick, what a question!" "Well, but *do* you?" inquired Mr. Pickwick. "That depends," said Mrs. Bardell, approaching the duster very near to Mr. Pickwick's elbow, which was planted on the table : "that depends a good deal upon the person, you know, Mr. Pickwick; and whether it's a saving and careful person, sir." "That's very true," said Mr. Pickwick; "but the person I have in my eye (here he looked very hard at Mrs. Bardell) I think possesses these qualities; and has, moreover, a considerable knowledge of the world, and a great deal of sharpness, Mrs. Bardell; which may be of material use to me."

6. "La, Mr. Pickwick," said Mrs. Bardell : the crimson rising to her cap-border again. "I do," said Mr. Pickwick, growing energetic, as was his wont in speaking of a subject which interested him. "I do, indeed; and to tell you the truth, Mrs. Bardell, I have made up my mind." "Dear me, sir," exclaimed Mrs. Bardell. "You'll think it not very strange now," said the amiable Mr. Pickwick, with a good-humored glance at his companion, "that I never consulted you about this matter, and never mentioned it, till I sent your little boy out this morning—eh?"

7. Mrs. Bardell could only reply by a look. She had long worshipped Mr. Pickwick at a distance, but here she was, all at once, raised to a pinnacle to which her wildest

and most extravagant hopes had never dared to aspire.
Mr. Pickwick was going to propose—a deliberate plan, too
—sent her little boy to the Borough, to get him out of the
way—how thoughtful—how considerate!—" Well," said
Mr. Pickwick, " what do you think?"   " Oh, Mr. Pickwick," said Mrs. Bardell, trembling with agitation, " you're
very kind, sir."   " It will save you a great deal of trouble,
won't it ?" said Mr. Pickwick.   " Oh, I never thought any
thing of the trouble, sir," replied Mrs. Bardell; " and of
course, I should take more trouble to please you then than
ever; but it is so kind of you, Mr. Pickwick, to have so
much consideration for my loneliness."

8. " Ah to be sure," said Mr. Pickwick: " I never
thought of that. When I am in town, you'll always have
somebody to sit with you. To be sure, so you will." " I'm
sure I ought to be a very happy woman," said Mrs. Bardell.
" And your little boy—" said Mr. Pickwick. " Bless his
heart," interposed Mrs. Bardell, with a maternal sob. " He,
too, will have a companion," resumed Mr. Pickwick, " a
lively one, who'll teach him, I'll be bound, more tricks in a
week, than he would ever learn in a year." And Mr.
Pickwick smiled placidly.

9. " Oh you dear—" said Mrs. Bardell. Mr. Pickwick
started. " Oh you kind, good, playful dear," said Mrs.
Bardell; and without more ado, she rose from her chair,
and flung her arms round Mr. Pickwick's neck, with a cataract of tears, and a chorus of sobs. " Bless my soul," cried
the astonished Mr. Pickwick;—" Mrs. Bardell, my good
woman—dear me, what a situation—pray consider. Mrs.
Bardell, don't—if any body should come—" " Oh, let them
come," exclaimed Mrs. Bardell, frantically: " I'll never
leave you—dear, kind, good, soul ;" and, with these words,
Mrs. Bardell clung the tighter.

10. " Mercy upon me," said Mr. Pickwick, struggling
violently, " I hear somebody coming up the stairs. Don't,
don't, there's a good creature, don't." But entreaty and
remonstrance were alike unavailing: for Mrs. Bardell had

fainted in Mr. Pickwick's arms; and before he could gain time to deposit her on a chair, Master Bardell entered the room, ushering in Mr. Tupman, Mr. Winkle, and Mr. Snodgrass. Mr. Pickwick was struck motionless and speechless. He stood with his lovely burden in his arms, gazing vacantly on the countenances of his friends, without the slightest attempt at recognition or explanation. They, in their turn, stared at him; and Master Bardell, in his turn, stared at every body.

11. The astonishment of the Pickwickians was so absorbing, and the perplexity of Mr. Pickwick was so extreme, that they might have remained in exactly the same relative situation until the suspended animation of the lady was restored, had it not been for a most beautiful and touching expression of filial affection on the part of her youthful son. Clad in a tight suit of corduroy, spangled with brass buttons of a very considerable size, he at first stood at the door astounded and uncertain; but by degrees, the impression that his mother must have suffered some personal damage, pervaded his partially developed mind, and considering Mr. Pickwick the aggressor, he set up an appalling and semi-earthly kind of howling, and butting forward, with his head, commenced assailing that immortal gentleman about the back and legs, with such blows and pinches as the strength of his arm, and the violence of his excitement allowed.

12. "Take this little villain away," said the agonized Mr. Pickwick, "he's mad." "What *is* the matter?" said the three tongue-tied Pickwickians. "I don't know," replied Mr. Pickwick, pettishly. "Take away the boy—(here Mr. Winkle carried the interesting boy, screaming and struggling, to the farther end of the apartment). Now help me to lead this woman down stairs." "Oh, I'm better now," said Mrs. Bardell, faintly. "Let me lead you down stairs," said the ever gallant Mr. Tupman. "Thank you, sir—thank you:" exclaimed Mrs. Bardell, hysterically. And down stairs she was led accordingly, accompanied by her affectionate son.

13. " I cannot conceive "—said Mr. Pickwick, when his
friend returned—" I cannot conceive what has been the
matter with that woman. I had merely announced to her
my intention of keeping a man-servant, when she fell into
the extraordinary paroxysm in which you found her. Very
extraordinary thing." "Very," said his three friends.
" Placed me in such an extremely awkward situation," continued Mr. Pickwick. "Very :" was the reply of his followers, as they coughed slightly, and looked dubiously at
each other.

14. This behavior was not lost on Mr. Pickwick. He
remarked their incredulity. They evidently suspected him.
—"There is a man in the passage, now," said Mr. Tupman.
" It's the man that I spoke to you about," said Mr. Pickwick,
" I sent for him to the Borough this morning. Have the
goodness to call him up, Snodgrass."

CLXXXIV.—SCENES FROM PICKWICK.—*Speech of Sergeant Buzfuz.*
DICKENS.

1. You heard from my learned friend, Gentlemen of the
Jury, that this is an action for a breach of promise of marriage, at which the damages are laid at fifteen hundred
pounds. The plaintiff, Gentlemen, is a widow : yes, Gentlemen, a widow. The late Mr. Bardell, some time before
his death, became the father, Gentlemen, of a little boy.
With this little boy, the only pledge of her departed excise-
man, Mrs. Bardell shrunk from the world and courted the
retirement and tranquillity of Goswell street ; and here she
placed in her front parlor-window a written placard, bearing this inscription,—" APARTMENTS FURNISHED FOR A SIN-
GLE GENTLEMEN. INQUIRE WITHIN."

2. Mrs. Bardell's opinions of the opposite sex, Gentlemen, were derived from a long contemplation of the inestimable qualities of her lost husband. She had no fear,—
she had no distrust,—all was confidence and reliance. "Mr.
Bardell," said the widow, "was a man of honor,—Mr.

Bardell was a man of his word,—Mr. Bardell was no de-
ceiver,—Mr. Bardell was once a single gentleman himself:
to single gentlemen I look for protection, for assistance, for
comfort, and consolation: in single gentlemen I shall perpetually see something to remind me of what Mr. Bardell
was, when he first won my young and untried affections:
to a single gentleman, then, shall my lodgings be let."

3. Actuated by this beautiful and touching impulse
(among the best impulses of our imperfect nature, Gentle-
tlemen), the lonely and desolate widow dried her tears,
furnished her first floor, caught her innocent boy to her
maternal bosom, and put the bill up in her parlor-window.
Did it remain there long? No. The serpent was on the
watch, the train was laid, the mine was preparing, the sap-
per and miner was at work! Before the bill had been in
the parlor-window three days,—three days, Gentlemen,—a
being, erect upon two legs, and bearing all the outward
semblance of a man, and not of a monster, knocked at the
door of Mrs. Bardell's house! He inquired within: he
took the lodgings; and on the very next day he entered
into possession of them. This man was Pickwick,—Pickwick, the defendant!

4. Of this man I will say little. The subject presents
but few attractions; and I, Gentlemen, am not the man,
nor are you, Gentlemen, the men, to delight in the contemplation of revolting heartlessness, and of systematic villainy. I say systematic villainy, Gentlemen; and when I
say systematic villainy, let me tell the defendant Pickwick,
if he be in court, as I am informed he is, that it would have
been more decent in him, more becoming, if he had stopped
away. Let me tell him, further, that a counsel, in the discharge of his duty, is neither to be intimidated, nor bullied,
nor put down; and that any attempt to do either the one
or the other will recoil on the head of the attempter, be he
plaintiff or be he defendant, be his name Pickwick, or
Noakes, or Stoakes, or Stiles, or Brown, or Thompson.

5. I shall show you, Gentlemen, that for two years

Pickwick continued to reside constantly, and without interruption or intermission, at Mrs. Bardell's house. I shall show you that Mrs. Bardell, during the whole of that time, waited on him, attended to his comforts, cooked his meals, looked out his linen for the washerwoman when it went abroad, darned, aired, and prepared it for wear when it came home, and, in short, enjoyed his fullest trust and confidence. I shall show you that, on many occasions, he gave half-pence, and on some occasions even sixpence, to her little boy. I shall prove to you, that on one occasion, when he returned from the country, he distinctly and in terms offered her marriage,—previously, however, taking special care that there should be no witnesses to their solemn contract; and I am in a situation to prove to you, on the testimony of three of his own friends,—most unwilling witnesses, Gentlemen—most unwilling witnesses,—that on that morning he was discovered by them holding the plaintiff in his arms, and soothing her agitation by his caresses and endearments.

6. And now, Gentlemen, but one word more. Two letters have passed between these parties,—letters that must be viewed with a cautious and suspicious eye,—letters that were evidently intended, at the time, by Pickwick, to mislead and delude any third parties into whose hands they might fall. Let me read the first:—"Garraway's, twelve o'clock.—Dear Mrs. B.—Chops and Tomato sauce. Yours, Pickwick." Gentlemen, what does this mean? Chops and Tomato sauce! Yours, Pickwick! Chops! Gracious heavens! And Tomato sauce! Gentlemen, is the happiness of a sensitive and confiding female to be trifled away by such shallow artifices as these?

7. The next has no date whatever, which is in itself suspicious:—"Dear Mrs. B., I shall not be at home tomorrow. Slow coach." And then follows this very remarkable expression,—"Don't trouble yourself about the warming-pan." The warming-pan! Why, Gentlemen, who *does* trouble himself about a warming-pan? Why is Mrs. Bar-

dell so earnestly entreated not to agitate herself about this warming-pan, unless (as is no doubt the case) it is a mere cover for hidden fire—a mere substitute for some endearing word or promise, agreeably to a preconcerted system of correspondence, artfully contrived by Pickwick with a view to his contemplated desertion? And what does this allusion to the slow coach mean? For aught I know, it may be a reference to Pickwick himself, who has most unquestionably been a criminally slow coach during the whole of this transaction, but whose speed will now be unexpectedly accelerated, and whose wheels, Gentlemen, as he will find to his cost, will very soon be greased by you!

8. But enough of this, Gentlemen. It is difficult to smile with an aching heart. My client's hopes and prospects are ruined, and it is no figure of speech to say that her occupation is gone indeed. The bill is down; but there is no tenant! Eligible single gentlemen pass and repass; but there is no invitation for them to inquire within, or without! All is gloom and silence in the house: even the voice of the child is hushed: his infant sports are disregarded, when his mother weeps.

9. But Pickwick, Gentlemen, Pickwick, the ruthless destroyer of this domestic oasis in the desert of Goswell street,—Pickwick, who has choked up the well, and thrown ashes on the sward,—Pickwick, who comes before you to-day with his heartless tomato-sauce and warming-pans,— Pickwick still rears his head with unblushing effrontery, and gazes without a sigh on the ruin he has made! Damages, Gentlemen, heavy damages, is the only punishment with which you can visit him,—the only recompense you can award to my client! And for those damages she now appeals to an enlightened, a high-minded, a right-feeling, a conscientious, a dispassionate, a sympathizing, a contemplative Jury of her civilized countrymen!

CLXXXV.—SCENES FROM PICKWICK.—*Sam Weller as Witness.*

DICKENS.

1. "WHAT's your name, sir?" inquired the judge. "Sam Weller, my lord," replied that gentleman. "Do you spell it with a 'V' or a 'W?'" inquired the judge. "That depends upon the taste and fancy of the speller, my lord," replied Sam : "I never had occasion to spell it more than once or twice in my life, but I spells it with a 'V.'" Here a voice in the gallery exclaimed aloud,—"Quite right, too, Samivel : quite right. Spell it wid a *we*, my lord, spell it wid a *we*." "Who is that that dares to address the court?" said the little judge looking up ;—"Usher!" "Yes, my lord!" "Bring that person here instantly." "Yes, my lord."

2. But, as the usher didn't *find* the person, he didn't *bring* him ; and, after a great commotion, all the people who had got up to look for the culprit, sat down again. The little judge turned to the witness as soon as his indignation would allow him to speak, and said—"Do you know who that was, sir?" "I rather suspect it was my father, my lord," replied Sam. "Do you see him here now?" said the judge. "No, I don't, my lord," replied Sam, staring right up into the lantern in the roof of the court. "If you could have pointed him out, I would have committed him instantly," said the judge. Sam bowed his acknowledgments, and turned with unimpaired cheerfulness of countenance toward Sergeant Buzfuz.

3. "Now, Mr. Weller," said Sergeant Buzfuz. "Now, sir," replied Sam. "I believe you are in the service of Mr. Pickwick, the defendant in this case. Speak up, if you please, Mr. Weller." "I mean to speak up, sir," replied Sam. "I am in the service o' that 'ere gen'l'man, and a wery good service it is." "Little to do, and plenty to get, I suppose?" said Sergeant Buzfuz, with jocularity. "Oh, quite enough to get, sir, as the soldier said ven they ordered him three hundred and fifty lashes," replied Sam. "You must not tell us what the soldier or any other man said,

sir," interposed the judge: "it's not evidence." "Wery good, my lord," replied Sam.

4. "Do you recollect any thing particular happening on the morning when you were first engaged by the defendant, eh, Mr. Weller?" said Sergeant Buzfuz. "Yes, I do, sir," replied Sam. "Have the goodness to tell the jury what it was." "I had a reg'lar new fit out o' clothes that mornin', gen'l'men of the jury," said Sam, "and that was a *wery* particler and uncommon circumstance vith me in those days."

5. Hereupon there was a general laugh; and the little judge, looking with an angry countenance over his desk, said,—"You had better be careful, sir." "So Mr. Pickwick said at the time, my lord," replied Sam, "and I was wery careful o' that 'ere suit 'o clothes: wery careful, indeed, my lord." The judge looked sternly at Sam for full two minutes, but Sam's features were so perfectly calm and serene that he said nothing, and motioned Sergeant Buzfuz to proceed.

6. "Do you mean to tell me, Mr. Weller," said Sergeant Buzfuz, folding his arms emphatically, and turning half round to the jury, as if in mute assurance he would bother the witness yet—"Do you mean to tell me, Mr. Weller, that you saw nothing of this fainting on the part of the plaintiff in the arms of the defendant, which you have heard described by the witnesses?" "Certainly not," replied Sam. "I was in the passage till they called me up, and then the old lady was not there."

7. "Now attend, Mr. Weller," said Sergeant Buzfuz, dipping a large pen into the inkstand before him, for the purpose of frightening Sam with a show of taking down his answer, "you were in the passage and yet saw nothing of what was going forward. Have you a pair of eyes, Mr. Weller?" "Yes, I have a pair of eyes," replied Sam, "and that's just it. If they wos a pair o' patent double million magnifyin' gas microscopes of hextra power, p'raps I might be able to see through a flight o' stairs and a deal door; but bein' only eyes, you see, my wision's limited."

8. At this answer, which was delivered without the slightest appearance of irritation, and with the most complete simplicity and equanimity of manner, the spectators tittered, the little judge smiled, and Sergeant Buzfuz looked particularly foolish. After 'a short consultation with Dodson and Fogg, the learned sergeant again turned to Sam, and said, with a painful effort to conceal his vexation,—"Now, Mr. Weller, I'll ask you a question on another point, if you please." "If you please, sir," rejoined Sam, with the utmost good-humor.

9. "Do you remember going up to Mrs. Bardell's house, one night in November last?" "Oh, yes: wery well." "Oh, you *do* remember that, Mr. Weller," said Sergeant Buzfuz, recovering his spirits, "I thought we should get at something at last." "I rather thought that, too, sir," replied Sam; and at this the spectators tittered again. "Well: I suppose you went up to have a little talk about this trial—eh, Mr. Weller?" said Sergeant Buzfuz, looking knowingly at the jury. "I went up to pay the rent; but we *did* get a talking about the trial," replied Sam. "Oh, you did get a talking about the trial," said Sergeant Buzfuz, brightening up with the anticipation of some important discovery. "Now what passed about the trial: will you have the goodness to tell us, Mr. Weller?"

10. "Vith all the pleasure in my life, sir," replied Sam. "Arter a few unimportant observations from the two wirtuous females as has been examined here to-day, the ladies gets into a wery great state o' admiration at the honorable conduct of Mr. Dodson and Fogg—them two gen'l'men as is sittin' near you now." This, of course, drew general attention to Dodson and Fogg, who looked as virtuous as possible. "The attorneys for the plaintiff," said Mr. Sergeant Buzfuz: "well, they spoke in high praise of the honorable conduct of Messrs. Dodson and Fogg, the attorneys for the plaintiff, did they?" "Yes," said Sam; "they said what a wery gen'rous thing it was o' them to have taken up the case on spec, and to charge

nothin' at all for costs, unless they got 'em out of Mr. Pickwick."

11. At this very unexpected reply, the spectators tittered again, and Dodson and Fogg, turning very red, leaned over to Sergeant Buzfuz, and in a hurried manner whispered something in his ear. "You are quite right," said Sergeant Buzfuz aloud, with affected composure. "It's perfectly useless, my lord, attempting to get at any evidence through the impenetrable stupidity of this witness. I will not trouble the court by asking him any more questions. Stand down, sir."

12. "Would any other gen'l'man like to ask me any thin'?" inquired Sam, taking up his hat, and looking round most deliberately. "Not I, Mr. Weller, thank you," said Sergeant Snubbin, laughing. "You may go down, sir," said Buzfuz, waving his hand impatiently. Sam went down accordingly, after doing Messrs. Dobson and Fogg's case as much harm as he conveniently could, and saying just as little respecting Mr. Pickwick as might be, which was precisely the object he had in view all along.

CLXXXVI.—RULES FOR PRESERVING HEALTH.

I SEE there is a fellow who calls himself Dr. Hall, and who publishes a *Journal of Health*, in which he gives a good many ridiculous rules which he says will preserve the health. I haven't much confidence in this fellow, for he is a doctor, and it is naturally against his interest to publish rules that will keep people healthy. I believe he has designs on the community and only wants to shatter and break up their constitutions. As for his rules, I can beat them myself, if I try, and I herewith do so. If these are accurately followed they will do as much good as old man Hall's, any time.

1st. Never hang yourself out of an open window when you go to bed at night. The attraction of gravitation is always powerful during the nocturnal hours, and it may draw you violently against the pavement, and tear your night shirt.

2d. Always avoid drafts—on yourself—unless endorsed by a man with lots of " soap."

3d. In cold weather always wear thick, warm clothing about your body. If you haven't money enough to buy it, attend an inextinguishable conflagration in the vicinity of a first-class clothing shop.

4th. If you wear spectacles avoid going into any fire-men's riots that may be transpiring. The reason of this is, that in addition to having your feelings hurt, you will very likely get more glass in your eyes than you had outside.

5th. If you are quite a small baby be careful that there are no pins in your clothes, and always take a drink of milk punch out of a bottle with a gum thing on the muzzle, before you get into your cradle.

6th. In eating raw oysters always peel the shells off before swallowing. The shells are indigestible and are apt to lay on the stomach.

7th. Never sleep more than nine in a bed, even in a country hotel where a Political Convention is being held. It is apt to produce a nightmare if any of the party kick in their sleep. This is especially the case when they go to bed with their boots on.

8th. Abstain entirely from alcoholic drinks. The best way to do that is not to drink any alcohol.

9th. Never travel on railroad trains. Many persons have died quite unexpectedly by this imprudence.

10th. Never jab butcher knives, steel forks, and such things into your vitals : it is very unwholesome.

11th. Always come in when it rains, and if a rattlesnake bites you in the leg cut it off, unless you wear false calves or a wooden leg. In that case just untie it and take it off.

I don't say that fellows who follow these instructions will never die and let their friends enjoy a ride to the cemetery, but you won't get choked off in the bloom of your youth and beauty.

By the way, isn't it odd that as soon as death overtakes us, man *undertakes* us? It is. It is.

* * *

CLXXXVII.—A MAIDEN'S "PSALM OF LIFE."

1. Tell me not in idle jingle,
  " Marriage is an empty dream ! "
  For the girl is dead that's single,
  And girls are not what they seem.

2. Life is real !   Life is earnest !
  Single blessedness a fib !
  "Man thou art, to man returnest !"
  Has been spoken of the rib.

3. Not enjoyment, and not sorrow,
  Is our destined end or way ;
  But to act that each to-morrow
  Finds us nearer marriage day.

4. Life is long, and youth is fleeting,
  And our hearts, though light and gay.
  Still like pleasant drums are beating
  Wedding marches all the way.

5. In the world's broad field of battle,
  In the bivouac of life,
  Be not like dumb driven cattle !
  Be a heroine—a wife !——

6. Trust no future, howe'er pleasant,
  Let the dead past bury its dead !
  Act—act to the living Present !
  Heart within and hope ahead !

7. Lives of married folks remind us
  We can live our lives as well,
  And, departing, leave behind us
  Such examples as shall " tell."

8. Such example that another,
  Wasting time in idle sport,
  A forlorn, unmarried brother,
  Seeing, shall take heart and court.

9. Let us, then be up and doing,
  With a heart on triumph set ;

16

Still contriving, still pursuing,
And each one a husband get.

CLXXXVIII.—JOSH BILLINGS ON "GONGS."

1. Josh Billings relateth his first experience with the gong, thusly: I kan never holi eradicate from my memory the sound ove the first gong I ever herd. I was settin on the frunt step of a tavurn in the sity of Bufferlow, pensively smokin. The sun was goin to bed, and the hevins fur and near was a blushin at the performance. The Ery Kanal with its golden waters was on its way to Albany, and I was perusin the line botes a floatin bi, and thinking of Italy (wher I uste to live) and gondolers and gallus wimmin. Mi entire sole, was, az it were, in a swet—i wanted to klimb—i felt grate, I aktually gru. There are things in this life not tu be trifled with: there are times when a man brakes luce from hisself, when he sees spiruts, when he kin almost tuch the mune, and feels az if he could fil both hans with the stars of hevin, and almost swear he was a bank president—that's what ailed me.

2. But the koarse ov tru luv never did run smuthe, (this is Shakespere's opinyun tu, I and he often thunk thru ⅟ quil)—jist az I waz duin mi best—dummer, dummer, spat, bang, beller, crash, roar, jam, dummer, rip, whang, roar, menjus, rally, jump, I struck the center of the sidewalk, with anuther I klared the gutter, and with another I struck the middle of the street, snortin like an injun pony at a band uv musick. I gazed in despair at the tavurn, and mi heart waz swelled up as big as a outdore uven, mi teeth were as loose as a string of bedes. I thot all the crockery in the tavurn had fell down. I thot of fenomenons. I thot of Gabril and hiz horn. I was jist on the pint of thinkin sumthin else when the landlord kum to the front step uv the tavurn, holdin by a string, the bottom of a brass kittle. He kawled me gentli with his hand. I went slola and slola up to him, he kammed my fearz, he

said it was a gong. I saw the kussed thing : he said supper
waz reddy.

———————◆———————

CLXXXIX.—SPEECH OF THE HOOSIER.

1. Mr. Speeker: I hail from the wild-fire district, State
of Indiana, continent of North America. I am indebted
for the high and extinguished honor, which I now enjoy, to
the most humane and disarming constitency, that can be
scared up in all the diggins of the mighty west. Why sir,
if a man of parts makes his apperance among them, it beats
all natur, what a meeking kindness they take to him.

2. Finely sir, lastly says they to me " Swackerhammer "
says they, (my name is Swackerhammer, Nathan Swackerhammer,) " Swackerhammer " says they, " You are a man
of parts, and you must go to congress." I carculate not
says I, but sure enough, here I are ; and sir, I should deserve to be catawamptiously chawed up, if I did not embrace this proud occasion, to express to them the lofty
depths of my gratitude.

3. I will sing their praises as long as the waters of the
broad Mississippi shall kiss its pebbled shore ; as long as
the bright and beautiful rainbow displays its gorgeous tints
across the heavens' blue arch ; as long as the roaring
tempest sweeps in awful majesty over the face of the terrified earth : yes, as long, Mr. Speeker, as long as a goose
can stand on one foot.

4. When I first took my seat upon this floor, and beheld
the dazzling lustre of this spacious hall, the absteneous and
emaciating dignity of this Assembly, and heard the strains
of divine eloquence which played like the winged lightning
around us, I felt as contamnacious as a pair of new greeced
boots, and no more thought of trying to make a speech
here, than of plucking bright honors from the pale-faced
moon, or drinking a cup of sour buttermilk with a fly in it.
But now I go it with a perfect looseness.

5. There seems to be a cutanhereous disposition on the part.of members from the South, and East to down upon us from the West, with a contempt more lofty and letanacious, than that of Col. Webb of the regular army for Common Marshal, before his bullet made his calf blat. Do the gentlemen suppose that we don't know the difference between a halk and a handsaw? or a shot gun and sixteen dollars in cash? We pretend to have no more learning sir than we could get of a winter's evening, out of an old spelling book by the light of a pine knot. But as for native intellect and genuine whale hogerine we raise no name for it; and if there is any man here, Mr. Speeker, who presumes to say, that Nathan Swackerhammer aint in his sphere: that he aint the complete yellow flower of the forest: that he cant whip his weight in wild cats: that he aint got the fastest hoss, the prettiest sister, the ugliest dog in all the universe, shiver my timbers if I don't make a spread eagle of him, quicker than you can say "whaw" with your mouth stretched from ear to ear.

6. It are a fair principle, Mr. Speeker, to render unto Cæsar the things that are Cæsar's, and unto Mrs. Cæsar the things that are hers, and unto us of the West the things that are our'n. Them things, Mr. Speeker, we have sworn by the glorious triumph of New Orleans: by the genius of our free institutions: by the indomitable spirit of our Anglo-Saxon Fathers, we will achieve, or else take our hats and go home, and butter our brains and put our heads to soak. I intend, sir, before I take my seat, to halt into the affairs of this government, like a thirty-two pound shot: to perpetuate the planks of the ship of state, like a gridiron; and scatter the solemn mysteries, like chickens before a sparrow halk.

7. Whatever I discourse worthy of praise I shall illumine with the glittering rays of approbation, until it shines like fiery Apollo in his middle prime: like sparkling gems in kingly diamonds: like bear's eyes in a cornfield by moonlight; or a tin six-pence in a bowl of hot greece. What-

ever I detect of iniquity and composition, I shall pour out
my vial of wrath upon it, with the writhing power of the
Sirocco: I shall hurl the fulminating words of denunciation
upon it, like thunderbolts from the arm of omnipotent Jove.
I shall hammer it, as it were, upon a cobblers lap-stone,
until it becomes as soft as a baked apple, and vanishes like
roasted meat before a hungry niggar.   The doctrine that
to the spoils belong the victors, assumes the noble passion
of my soul, and makes my mouth water enough to run a
tread-mill—I go for it sled length.

8. It is one of the principles of the Declaration of Independence, and according to Scripture, which says, " Blessed
be nothing, for a poor man is a reproach to any people,"—
I am in favor of dividing the proceeds of public lands
among the people, until every man's sheep kines are full
of pretentions; and taxes are annihilated, like a musquetoe
under the fist of Davy Crocket:—which would you rather.
Mr. Speeker, it is more blessid to receive than to give.
The veto power are a power, Mr. Speeker, which o'ershad-
dows congress and the government, like a dark cloud
laden with the blossoms of destruction.   It conveys dismay
into the hearts of widdows and orphants: it makes up the
stormy view of popular indignation; and showers abroad
cart loads of the suds of dissolution as thick as autumn
leaves in the valleys; as pebbles upon the sea shore; or
cucumber bugs in a cabbage garden.

9. Captain Taylor, sir, has resumed the responsibility,
and John, Mr. Botts has promised to head him.   Yes, sir,
the immortal Botts, destined, by heaven, to rid his country
of a " Cataline " or kill a hoss.   He is a goin' to head him,
sir, cause why, cause he aint got any head of his own.
That noble and last speeker, a nation proud and jealous of
the blessing.   Push forward illustrious Botts! let not your
step falter! let not your firm purpose yield! hold fast in
your present grasp the blazing sword of pestilence, and
when you strike let its chivalrous edge enter his jugular!
as the fierce thunderbolt raises the gnarled oak: as the

swift winged swallow cleaves the liquid air : as the gilded arrow glides from the quiver of remorseless cupid ; or a little niggar runs when a big dog's arter him.

10. Then with conquering hand above your head, shake the fragment of your blade and shout, "I too have killed a hog." My voice is still for war,—war to the knife. Whatever aint, aint right : Glory, Honor, Democracy, Vox Populi, Vox Dei. John Bull with his right of seccsh' and his South Carolina, have been rearing and tearing up the turf, and shaking his horns, and Brother Jonithan brawling, "Git out you tarnal critter" long enough. The fountains of patriotism is exausted. Blood must be let. Gentlemen may cry peace : I have no objections sir, providing we can fight for it, if we can't have it without.

11. But as to knocking under to John Bull in any way you can fix it, shiver my timbers, if I can stand it any longer. Hatspur says, "Cry Haddock, and let slip the "dogs of war." them's my sentiments exactly. Sodom and Gomorrow, wild fire and blazing cat-tails, why stand ye here idle. Why if you are all afraid of him, the State of Indiana will take the war by the job ; for we are half hoss, half alligatur, and half filled with earthquake ; and if we leave hide or hair of his, then call it "great cry and little wool," as the devil said when he sheared the hog. Thats all : I'm done. And now, Mr. Speeker, as they say in the theatre, my performances have completed.

CXC.—VARIETIES.

1.—An Elysium.

1. Some "feller," with a hankering after an elysium, "sighs his soul away" in the following poetic effusion :

"Oh is there not a happy land—
    A land beyond the seas—
    Where pot-pie smokes in roundless lakes,
    And dumplings grow on trees :

> Where ginger bread is found in sticks,
>   And ' smearcase ' by the ton,
> And when you do a job of work,
>   You get the ' ready John ? '
> Where Nature's lessons may be read,
>   In every bubbling brook,
> Where bumble bees don't sting a chap,
>   And mully cows don't hook ? "

2.—A New Reading.

1. In a boarding-school not far from Boston the rector was accustomed to require the smaller boys to read every evening, before going to bed, a chapter of the New Testament—each a verse. One of the boys, who prided himself on his elocutionary ability, and frequently neglected orthography for emphasis, had fall to him one evening the verse : " And Herod *laid* hold on John." Rising gracefully, and mistaking the *l* in the third word for an *s*, he thundered out : " And Herod *said*, hold on, John ! "

3.—A Polite Man.

1. Indeed, my friends, far better it would seem
> Were you to choose the opposite extreme :
> Like one " Down East " who an umbrella took
> And from the rain gave shelter to a duck :
> Who to a limping dog once lent his arm,
> And to a setting hen said, " Don't rise, ma'am ; "
> Nor e'er to lifeless things respect did lack—
> Said always to a chair, " Excuse my back ; "
> " Excuse my curiosity," he said to books ;
> And to the looking-glass, " Excuse my looks."

4.—Why Diggest Thou ?

1. " Old man, for whom diggest thou this grave ? "
>   I asked as I walked along ;
> For I saw in the heart of London streets
>   A dark and busy throng.
> 'Twas a strange, wild deed, but a wilder wish
>   Of the parted soul, to lie,
> 'Mid the troubled numbers of living men
>   Who would pass him idly by.

So I said, "For whom diggest thou this grave,
    In the heart of London town?"
And the deep-toned voice of the digger replied—
    "We're laying a gas-pipe down."

5.—JOSH BILLINGS ON BUMBLE BEES.

1. THE Bumble Bee iz one ov naturs sekrets. They probably have a destiny tew fill, and are probably necessary, if a fellow only knew how. They liv apart from the rest ov mankind, in little circles, numbering about 75 or 80 souls. They are born about haying time, and are different from enny bug I kno ov : they are the biggest when they are fust born. They resemble sum men in this respekt. Their principle bizziness iz making poor honey, but they don't make enny to sell.

2. Boys sumtimes rob them ov a whole summers work; but thare iz one thing about a bumbel bee that boys alwuz watch cluss and that iz their *helm*. I had rather not have awl the bumbel bee honey·thare iz between here and the city of Jerusalem, than to have a bumbel bee hit me with his helm, when he cums round sudden. They are different from other war vessels : the helm alwuz minds the bumble bee.

———◆———

CXCI.—DRAMATIC STYLES.

BLACKWOOD'S MAG.

1. IN dramatic writing, the difference between the Grecian and Roman styles is very great. When you deal with a Greek subject, you must be very devout, and have unbounded reverence for Diana of the Ephesians. You must also believe in the second sight, and be as solemn, calm, and passionless, as the ghost of Hamlet's father. Never descend to the slightest familiarity, nor lay off the stilts for a moment; and, far from calling a spade a spade, call it

    That sharp instrument
    With which the Theban husbandman lays bare
    The breast of our great mother.

2. The Roman, on the other hand, may occasionally be jocular, but always warlike. One is like a miracle-play in church;—the other, a tableau vivant in a camp. If a Greek has occasion to ask his sweetheart "if her mother knows she's out," and "if she has sold her mangle yet," he says:

> *Menestheus.* Cleanthe!
>
> *Cleanthe.* My Lord!
>
> *Men.* Your mother,—your kind, excellent mother,—
> She who hung o'er your couch in infancy,
> And felt within her heart the joyous pride
> Of having such a daughter,—does she know,
> Sweetest Cleanthe! that you've left the shade
> Of the maternal walls?
>
> *Cle.* She does, my Lord.
>
> *Men.* And,—but I scarce can ask the question,—when
> I last beheld her, 'gainst the whitened wall
> Stood a strong engine, flat, and broad, and heavy:
> Its entrail stones, and moved on mighty rollers,
> Rendering the crisped web as smooth and soft
> As whitest snow.—That engine, sweet Cleanthe,
> Fit pedestal for household deity,—
> Lares and old Penates;—has she 't still?
> Or for gold bribes has she disposed of it?
> I fain would know;—pray tell me, is it sold?

The Roman goes quicker to work:

> Tell me, my Julia, does your mother know
> You're out? and has she sold her mangle yet!

3. The Composite, or Elizabethan, has a smack of both:

> *Conradin.* Ha! Celia here! Come hither, pretty one.
> Thou hast a mother, child?
>
> *Celia.* Most people have, Sir.
>
> *Con.* I' faith thou'rt sharp,—thou hast a biting wit;—
> But does this mother,—this epitome
> Of what all other people are possessed of,—
> Knows she thou'rt out, and gadding?
>
> *Cel.* No, not gadding!
> Out, sir: she knows I'm out.
>
> *Con.* She had a mangle:
> Faith, 'twas a huge machine, and smoothed the web

16*

Like snow. I've seen it oft : it was, indeed,
A right good mangle.
    Cel. Then thou'rt not in thought
To buy it, else thou would not praise it so.
    Con. A parlous child ! keen as the cold North wind,
Yet like as Zephyrs. No, no : I'd not buy it ;
But has she sold it, child ?

CXCII.—FUSS AT FIRES.

1. It having been announced to me, my young friends, that you were about forming a fire-company, I have called you together to give you such directions as long experience in a first-quality engine company qualifies me to communicate. The moment you hear an alarm of fire, scream like a pair of panthers. Run any way, except the right way—for the furthest way round is the nearest way to the fire. If you happen to run on the top of a wood-pile, so much the better : you can then get a good view of the neighborhood. If a light breaks on your view, "break" for it immediately ; but be sure you don't jump into a bow window. Keep yelling, all the time ; and, if you can't make night hideous enough yourself, kick all the dogs you come across, and set them yelling, too. A brace of cats dragged up stairs by the tail would be a " powerful auxiliary." When you reach the scene of the fire, do all you can to convert it into a scene of destruction. Tear down all the fences in the vicinity. If it be a chimney on fire, throw salt down it ; or, if you can't do that, perhaps the best plan would be to jerk off the pump-handle and pound it down. Don't forget to yell, all the while, as it will have a prodigious effect in frightening off the fire. The louder the better, of course ; and the more ladies in the vicinity, the greater necessity for " doing it brown."

2. Should the roof begin to smoke, get to work in good earnest, and make any man " smoke " that interrupts you. If it is summer, and there are fruit-trees in the lot,

cut them down, to prevent the fire from roasting the apples. Don't forget to yell! Should the stable be threatened, carry out the cow-chains. Never mind the horse—he'll be alive and kicking; and if his legs don't do their duty, let them pay for the roast. Ditto as to the hogs—let them save their own bacon, or smoke for it. When the roof begins to burn, get a crow-bar and pry away the stone steps; or, if the steps be of wood, procure an axe and chop them up. Next, cut away the wash-boards in the basement story; and, if that don't stop the flames, let the chair-boards on the first floor share a similar fate. Should the "devouring element" still pursue the "even tenor of its way," you had better ascend to the second story. Pitch out the pitchers, and tumble out the tumblers. Yell all the time!

3. If you find a baby abed, fling it into the second story window of the house across the way; but let the kitten carefully down in a work-basket. Then draw out the bureau drawers, and empty their contents out of the back window: telling some body below to upset the slop-barrel and rain-water hogshead at the same time. Of course, you will attend to the mirror. The further it can be thrown, the more pieces will be made. If any body objects, smash it over his head. Do not, under any circumstances, drop the tongs down from the second story: the fall might break its legs, and render the poor thing a cripple for life. Set it straddle of your shoulders, and carry it down carefully. Pile the bed-clothes carefully on the floor, and throw the crockery out of the window. By the time you will have attended to all these things, the fire will certainly be arrested, or the building be burnt down. In either case, your services will be no longer needed; and, of course, you require no further directions, except at all times to keep up a yell.

CXCIII.—BOARDING-SCHOOL BREAKFAST.

CHARLES DICKENS.

1. MR. SQUEERS had before him a small measure of coffee, a plate of hot toast, and a cold round of beef; but he was at that moment intent on preparing breakfast for the little boys.

"This is twopenn'orth of milk, is it, waiter?" said Mr. Squeers, looking down into a large blue mug, and slanting it gently so as to get an accurate view of the quantity of fluid contained in it.

"That's twopenn'orth, Sir," replied the waiter.

"What a rare article milk is, to be sure, in London," said Mr. Squeers, with a sigh. "Just fill that mug up with lukewarm water, William, will you?"

"To the wery top, Sir?" inquired the waiter. "Why, the milk will be drownded."

"Never you mind that," replied Mr. Squeers. "Serve it right for being so dear. You ordered that thick bread and butter for three, did you?"

"Coming directly, Sir."

"You needn't hurry yourself," said Squeers; "there's plenty of time. Conquer your passions, boys, and don't be eager after vittles." As he uttered this moral precept, Mr. Squeers took a large bite out of the cold beef, and recognized Nicholas.

"Sit down, Mr. Nickleby," said Squeers. "Here we are, a breakfasting, you see."

2. Nicholas did *not* see that any one was breakfasting except Mr. Squeers; but he bowed with all becoming reverence, and looked as cheerful as he could.

"Oh! that's the milk and water, is it, William?" said Squeers. "Very good: don't forget the bread and butter presently."

At this fresh mention of the bread and butter, the five little boys looked very eager, and followed the waiter out with their eyes: meanwhile Mr. Squeers tasted the milk and water.

" Ah ! " said that gentleman, smacking his lips, "here's richness ! Think of the many beggars and orphans in the streets that would be glad of this, little boys ! A shocking thing hunger is, isn't it, Mr. Nickleby ? "

" Very shocking, Sir," said Nicholas.

" When I say number one," pursued Mr. Squeers, putting the mug before the children, " the boy on the left hand nearest the window may take a drink ; and when I say number two the boy next him will go in, and so till we come to number five, which is the last boy. Are you ready ? "

" Yes, Sir," cried all the boys, with great eagerness.

3. " That's right," said Squeers, calmly getting on with his breakfast : " keep ready till I tell you to begin. Subdue your appetites, my dears, and you've conquered human natur. This is the way we inculcate strength of mind, Mr. Nickleby," said the schoolmaster, turning to Nicholas, and speaking with his mouth very full of beef and toast.

" Thank God for a good breakfast," said Squeers, when he had finished. " Number one may take a drink."

Number one seized the mug ravenously, and had just drunk enough to make him wish for more, when Mr. Squeers gave the signal for number two, who gave up at the same interesting moment to number three, and the process was repeated till the milk and water terminated with number five.

" And now," said the schoolmaster, dividing the bread and butter for three into as many portions as there were children, " you had better look sharp with your breakfast, for the horn will blow in a minute or two, and then every boy leaves off."

Permission being thus given to fall to, the boys began to eat voraciously, and in desperate haste, while the schoolmaster (who was in high good-humor after his meal) picked his teeth with a fork and looked smilingly on.

CXCIV.—MRS. CAUDLE'S LECTURE ON SHIRT-BUTTONS.

DOUGLAS JERROLD.

1. THERE, Mr. Caudle, I hope you're in a little better temper than you were this morning. There, you needn't begin to whistle : people don't come to bed to whistle. But it's like you : I can't speak, that you don't try to insult me. Once, I used to say you were the best creature living : now, you get quite a fiend. *Do* let you rest? No, I won't let you rest. It's the only time I have to talk to you, and you *shall* hear me. I'm put upon all day long : it's very hard if I can't speak a word at night ; and it isn't often I open my mouth, goodness knows !

2. Because *once* in your lifetime your shirt wanted a button, you must almost swear the roof off the house. You *didn't* swear? Ha, Mr. Caudle! you don't know what you do when you're in a passion. You were not in a passion, weren't you ? Well, then I don't know what a passion is ; and I think I ought by this time. I've lived long enough with you, Mr. Caudle, to know that.

3. It's a pity you haven't something worse to complain of than a button off your shirt. If you'd *some* wives, you would, I know. I'm sure I'm never without a needle-and-thread in my hand ; what with you and the children, I'm made a perfect slave of. And what's my thanks? Why, if once in your life a button's off your shirt—what do you say ? I say once, Mr. Caudle ; or twice or three times, at most. I'm sure, Caudle, no man's buttons in the world are better looked after than yours. I only wish I'd kept the shirts you had when you were first married ! I should like to know where were you buttons then ?

4. Yes, it is worth talking of ! But that's how you always try to put me down. You fly into a rage, and then, if I only try to speak, you won't hear me. That's how you men always will have all the talk to yourselves : a poor woman isn't allowed to get a word in. A nice notion you have of a wife, to suppose she's nothing to think of but her husband's buttons. A pretty notion, indeed,

you have of marriage. Ha! if poor women only knew
what they had to go through! What with buttons, and
one thing and another! They'd never tie themselves up
to the best man in the world, I'm sure. What would they
do, Mr. Caudle?—Why, do much better without you, I'm
certain.

5. And it's my belief, after all, that the button wasn't
off the shirt: it's my belief that you pulled it off, that you
might have something to talk about. Oh, you're aggra-
vating enough, when you like, for any thing! All I know
is, it's very odd that the button should be off the shirt;
for I'm sure no woman's a greater slave to her husband's
buttons than I am. I only say it's very odd.

6. However, there's one comfort: it can't last long.
I'm worn to death with your temper, and sha'n't trouble
you a great while. Ha, you may laugh! And I dare say
you would laugh! I've no doubt of it! That's your love:
that's your feeling! I know that I'm sinking every day,
though I say nothing about it. And when I'm gone, we
shall see how your second wife will look after your buttons! You'll find out the difference, then. Yes, Caudle,
you'll think of me, then; for then, I hope, you'll never
have a blessed button to your back.

CXCV.—LEGEND OF LAKE SARATOGA.

JOHN G. SAXE.

1. A LADY stands beside the silver lake:
   "What," said the Mohawk, "would'st thou have me do?"
"Across the water, Sir, be pleased to take
   Me and my children in thy bark canoe."

2. "Ah!" said the Chief, "thou knowest not, I think,
   The legend of the lake—hast ever heard
That in its wave the stoutest boat will sink,
   If any passenger shall speak a word?"

3. "Full well we know the Indian's strange belief,"
   The lady answered, with a civil smile;

"But take us o'er the water, mighty chief:
In rigid silence we will sit the while."

4. Thus they embarked, but ere the little boat
Was half across the lake, the woman gave
Her tongue its wonted play!—but still they float,
And pass in safety o'er the utmost wave!

5. Safe on the shore, the warrior looked amazed,
Despite the stoic calmness of his race:
No word he spoke, but long the Indian gazed
In moody silence on the woman's face.

6. "What think you now?" the lady gayly said:
"Safely to land your frail canoe is brought!
No harm, you see, has touched a single head:
So superstition ever comes to naught!"

7. Smiling, the Mohawk said, "Our safety shows
That God is merciful to old and young:
Thanks unto the Great Spirit!—well he knows
The pale-faced woman cannot hold her tongue!"

CXCVI.—ODE TO MY NEW BONNET.

1. Soft triangle of straw and lace
That curves around my blushing face
With such a coy, bewitching grace,
No mortal man would dream your place
Was on my head.

2. Your airy touch can scarcely press
The shape from curl or flowing tress,
So light, so next to nothingness,
You surely could not well be less
And be a bonnet.

3. A bit of straw adorned with leather,
A yard of lace, a spray of heather,
Some bugles and a tossing feather,
These trifles shaken altogether—
Thus were you made.

4. No cape with starchy netting lined,
No buckram crown projects behind;
But streamers flutter in the wind,

There flows, in silken mesh confined,
    My waterfall.

5. Yet most your dainty form I prize,
    As sweeping back above mine eyes
    It lets the drinkled hillock rise,
    Where underneath in ambush lies
        My pair of mice.

6. But when rough Autumn winds sweep past,
    And all your laces shake aghast,
    Then can you shield me from the blast,
    And round my neck a shelter cast
        To keep me warm ?

7. Alas, a summer friend are you,
    And only kind while skies are blue :
    I long have known the saying true—
    Old friends are better than the new
        When trouble comes.

8. So ere the dog-day heats be fled
    Let me your flimsy glories spread ;
    For soon as Winter whistles dread
    I'll tie once more about my head
        My old scoop bonnet.

CXCVII.—POETRY NOW-A-DAYS.

1. How very absurd is half the stuff
        Called " Poetry," now-a-days !
    The " Stanzas," and " Epics," and " Odes," are enough
    To put every lover of rhyme in a huff,
        And disgust the old hens with their " lays."

2. There's one sighing for " wings to soar o'er the sea,"
        And " bask in some distant clime,"
    Without ever thinking how " sore " he'd be,
    After flying away on such a spree,
        With nothing to eat, the meantime.

3. Another insists on being a " bird,"
        To " fly to his lady-love's bower,"
    When he knows that the " lady " to whom he referred
    Don't own such a thing ; for (upon my word)
    In a " yaller " brick house, up in story the third,
        She's living this very hour.

4. One asks but "a cave in some forest dell,
  Away from the cold world's strife."
Now, the woods in fine weather are all very well,
But give him a six weeks' "rainy spell,"
And he'll soon "cave in" in his forest cell,
  And be sick enough of the life.

5. Another one wants his "love to go
  And roam o'er the dark blue sea : "
Perhaps he don't think, if there "comes on a blow,"
That they'd both be sea-sick down below,
  And a wretched pair they'd be.

6. Another young man would like to die
  "When the roses bloom in spring."
Just let him get sick, and he'll change his cry :
His "passing away" is "all in my eye ; "
Of "dreamless sleeps" he gets quite shy :
  It isn't exactly the thing.

7. Another would "die and be laid in a dell,
  Beneath some murmuring rill."
Now, in poetry's jingle, it's nice to tell ;
But a nasty, wet place !—so why not as well
Have a nice, dry grave on the hill ?

8. One "loves "—how he loves !—" the glittering foam
  And the mad waves' angry strife."
Just take the young genius who wrote the pome,
Where the "billows dash and the sea-birds roam,"
And he'd give all he had to be safely at home :
  He'd stay there the rest of his life.

9. Another young "heart-broken " calls on his " own,
  To cheer him with one sweet smile ; "
Then he follows it up in a love-sick tone,
With his "bosom pangs : " (if the truth was known,)
It isn't the "love " that causes his moan,
  But a superabundance of "bile."

CXCVIII.—ALL TIPSY BUT ME.

1. Out of the tavern I've just stepped to-night—
Street ! you are caught in a very bad plight :
Right hand and left hand are both out of place—
Street, you are drunk : 'tis a very clear case.

2. Moon! 'tis a very queer figure you cut:
   One eye is staring while t'other is shut—
   Tipsy, I see, and you're greatly to blame:
   Old as you are, 'tis a horrible shame.

3. Then the street lamps—what a scandalous sight!
   None of them soberly standing upright:
   Rocking and staggering—why, on my word,
   Each of those lamps is as drunk as a lord.

4. All is confusion! now isn't it odd?
   Nothing is sober that I see abroad:
   Sure it were rash with this crew to remain:
   . Better go into the tavern again.

CXCIX.—A MODEST WIT.

1. A SUPERCILIOUS nabob of the east—
   Haughty, being great—purse-proud, being rich,
   A governor, or general, at the least,
   I have forgotten which—
   Had in his family an humble youth,
   Who went from England in his patron's suite,
   An unassuming boy, and in truth
   A lad of decent parts, and good repute.

2. This youth had sense and spirit;
   But yet, with all his sense,
   Excessive diffidence
   Obscured his merit.

3. One day, at table, flushed with pride and wine,
   His honor, proudly free, severely merry,
   Conceived it would be vastly fine
   To crack a joke upon his secretary.

4. "Young man," he said, "by what art, craft or trade,
   Did your good father gain a livelihood?"—
   "He was a saddler, sir," Modestus said,
   "And in his time was reckoned good."

5. "A saddler, eh! and taught you Greek,
   Instead of teaching you to sew!
   Pray, why did not your father make
   A saddler, sir, of you?"

6. Each parasite, then, as in duty bound,
The joke applauded, and the laugh went round.
At length Modestus, bowing low,
Said, (craving pardon, if too free he made,)
"Sir, by your leave I fain would know
Your father's trade!"

7. "My father's trade! Bless me, that's too bad!
My father's trade? Why, blockhead, are you mad?
My father, sir, did never stoop so low—
He was a gentleman, I'd have you know."

8. "Excuse the liberty I take,"
Modestus said, with archness on his brow, •
"Pray, why did not your father make
A gentleman of you?"

———————◆———————

CC.—THE JESTER CONDEMNED TO DEATH.

HORACE SMITH.

1. ONE of the Kings of Scanderoon, a royal jester, had in his train a gross buffoon, who used to pester the court with tricks inopportune, venting on the highest folks his scurvy pleasantries and hoaxes. It needs some sense to play the fool: which wholesome rule occurred not to our jacanapes, who consequently found his freaks lead to innumerable scrapes, and quite as many kicks and tweaks: which only made him faster try the patience of his master.

2. Some sin, at last, beyond all measure, incurred the desperate displeasure of his serene and raging Highness. Whether the wag had twitched his beard, which he was bound to have revered, or had intruded on the shyness of the seraglio, or let fly an epigram at royalty, none knows —his sin was an occult one; but records tell us that the Sultan, meaning to terrify the knave, exclaimed, " 'Tis time to stop that breath! Thy doom is sealed, presumptuous slave! Thou stand'st condemned to death! Silence, base rebel! no replying. But such is my indulgence still, that, of my own free grace and will, I leave to thee the mode of dying." "Your royal will be done: 'tis just,"

replied the wretch, and kissed the dust: " since, my last
moments to assuage, your majesty's humane decree has
deigned to leave the choice to me, I'll die, so please you,
of old age ! "

———————◆———————

CCI.—PARODY,—THE OLD OAKEN BUCKET.

1. How dear to my heart are the scenes of my childhood,
    When fond recollection presents them to view !
The cheese-press, the goose-pond, the pigs in the wild-wood,
    And every old stump that my infancy knew.
The big linkum-basswood, with wide-spreading shadow:
    The horses that grazed where my grandmother fell:
The sheep on the mountain, the calves in the meadow,
    And all the young kittens we drowned in the well—
The meek little kittens, the milk-loving kittens,
The poor little kittens, we drowned in the well.

2. I remember with pleasure my grandfather's goggles,
    Which rode so majestic astraddle his nose ;
And the harness, oft mended with tow-string and "toggles,"
    That belonged to old Dolly, now free from her woes.
And fresh in my heart is the long maple wood-pile,
    Where often I've worked with beetle and wedge,
Striving to whack up enough to last for a good while,
    And grumbling because my old ax had no edge.
And there was the kitchen, and pump that stood nigh it,
    Where we sucked up the drink through a quill in the spout,
And the hooks where we hung up the pumpkin to dry it ;
    And the old cider pitcher, "no doing without : "
The brown earthen pitcher, the nozzle-cracked pitcher,
The pain-easing pitcher, "no doing without."

3. And there was the school-house, away from each dwelling,
    Where school-ma'ams would govern with absolute sway:
Who taught me my "'rithmetic," reading, and spelling,
    And " whaled me like blazes " about every day !
I remember the ladder that swung in the passage,
    Which led to the loft in the peak of the house :
Where my grandmother hung up her " pumpkin and sausage,"
    To keep them away from the rat and the mouse.
But now, far removed from that nook of creation,
    Emotions of grief big as tea-kettles swell,

When Fancy rides back to my old habitation,
And thinks of the kittens we drowned in the well—
The meek little kittens, the milk-loving kittens,
The poor little kittens, we drowned in the well.

DIALOGUES.

CCII.—SCENE FROM THE LADY OF LYONS.

LYTTON.

[Claude Melnotte, who had received many indignities to his slighted love, from Pauline, married her under the false appearance of an Italian prince. He afterward repents: makes proper amends; and, impelled by affection, and a noble ambition, conquers a position, and becomes, in fact, her husband.]

MELNOTTE'S *cottage*—WIDOW *bustling about. · A table spread for supper.*

WIDOW. So—I think that looks very neat. He sent me a line, so blotted that I can scarcely read it, to say he would be here almost immediately. She must have loved him well indeed, to have forgotten his birth; for though he was introduced to her in disguise, he is too honorable not to have revealed to her the artifice which her love only could forgive. Well, I do not wonder at it; for though my son is not a prince, he ought to be one, and that's almost as good. [*Knock at the door.*] Ah! here they are. [*Enter* MELNOTTE *and* PAULINE.]

Widow. Oh, my boy—the pride of my heart!—welcome, welcome! I beg pardon, Ma'am, but I do love him so!

Pauline. Good woman, I really—Why, Prince, what is this?—does the old woman know you? Oh, I guess you have done her some service. Another proof of your kind heart, is it not?

Melnotte. Of my kind heart, ay!

Pauline. So you know the prince?

Widow. Know him, Madame?—Ah, I begin to fear it is you who know him not!

Pauline. Do you think she is mad? Can we stay here, my lord? I think there is something very wild about her.

Melnotte. Madame, I—No, I can not tell her! My knees knock together: what a coward is a man who has lost his honor! Speak to her—speak to her—[*to his mother*]—tell her that—O Heaven, that I were dead!

Pauline. How confused he looks!—this strange place—this woman—what can it mean? I half suspect—Who are you, Madame?—who are you? Can't you speak? are you struck dumb?

Widow. Claude, you have not deceived her?—Ah, shame upon you! I thought that, before you went to the altar, she was to have known all?

Pauline. All! what? My blood freezes in my veins!

Widow. Poor lady!—dare I tell her, Claude? [MELNOTTE *makes a sign of assent.*] Know you not then, Madame, that this young man is of poor though honest parents? Know you not that you are wedded to my son, Claude Melnotte?

Pauline. Your son! hold! hold! do not speak to me—[*approaches* MELNOTTE *and lays her hand on his arm.*] Is this a jest? Is it? I know it is: only speak—one word—one look—one smile. I can not believe— I, who loved thee so—I can not believe that thou art such a—No, I will not wrong thee by a harsh word.—Speak!

Melnotte. Leave us—have pity on her, on me: leave us.

Widow. O Claude! that I should live to see thee bowed by shame! thee, of whom I was so proud! [*Exit* WIDOW.

Pauline. Her son! her son!

Melnotte. Now, lady, hear me.

Pauline. Hear thee?
Ay, speak. Her son! have fiends a parent? Speak,
That thou mayst silence curses—Speak!

Melnotte. No, curse me:
Thy curse would blast me less than thy forgiveness.

Pauline. [*laughing wildly.*] "This is thy palace, where the perfumed light
Steals through the mist of alabaster lamps,
And every air is heavy with the sighs
Of orange-groves, and music from sweet lutes,
And murmurs of low fountains, that gush forth
I' the midst of roses!" Dost thou like the picture?
THIS is my bridal home, and THOU my bridegroom!
O fool!—O dupe!—O wretch!—I see it all—
The by-word and the jeer of every tongue
In Lyons! Hast thou in thy heart one touch
Of human kindness? If thou hast, why, kill me,
And save thy wife from madness. No, it can not,
It can not be! this is some horrid dream:
I shall wake soon. [*Touching him.*] Art flesh? art man? or but
The shadows seen in sleep?—It is too real.
What have I done to thee—how sinned against thee,
That thou shouldst crush me thus?

Melnotte. Pauline! by pride
Angels have fallen ere thy time: by pride—
That sole alloy of thy most lovely mold—

The evil spirit of a bitter love,
And a revengeful heart, had power upon thee.
From my first years, my soul was filled with thee:
I saw thee, midst the flowers the lowly boy
Tended, unmarked by thee—a spirit of bloom,
And joy, and freshness, as if Spring itself
Were made a living thing, and wore thy shape!
I saw thee! and the passionate heart of man
Entered the breast of the wild-dreaming boy;
And from that hour I grew—what to the last
I shall be—thine adorer! Well! this love,
Vain, frantic, guilty, if thou wilt, became
A fountain of ambition and bright hope:
I thought of tales that by the winter hearth
Old gossips tell—how maidens, sprung from kings,
Have stooped from their high sphere: how Love, like Death,
Levels all ranks, and lays the shepherd's crook
Beside the scepter. Thus I made my home
In the soft palace of a fairy Future!
My father died; and I, the peasant-born,
Was my own lord. Then did I seek to rise
Out of the prison of my mean estate;
And, with such jewels as the exploring Mind
Brings from the caves of Knowledge, buy my ransom
From those twin jailers of the daring heart—
Low Birth and iron Fortune. The bright image,
Glassed in my soul, took all the hues of glory,
And lured me on to those inspiring toils
By which man masters man! For thee I grew
A midnight student o'er the dreams of sages:
For thee I sought to borrow from each Grace,
And every Muse, such attributes as lend
Ideal charms to Love. I thought of thee,
And passion taught me Poesy—of thee,
And on the painter's canvas grew the life
Of beauty!—Art became the shadow
Of the dear star-light of thy haunting eyes!
Men called me vain—some mad: I heeded not,
But still toiled on—hoped on—for it was sweet,
If not to win, to feel more worthy thee!
Pauline. Has he a magic to exorcise hate?
Melnotte. At last, in one mad hour, I dared to pour
The thoughts that burst their channels into song,

And sent them to thee,—such a tribute, lady,
As beauty rarely scorns, even from the meanest.
The name—appended by the burning heart
That longed to show its idol what bright things
It had created—yea, the enthusiast's name
That should have been thy triumph, was thy scorn!
That very hour,—when passion, turned to wrath,
Resembled hatred most—when thy disdain
Made my whole soul a chaos,—in that hour
The tempters found me a revengeful tool
For their revenge! Thou hadst trampled on the worm—
It turned and stung thee!
    Pauline.   Love, Sir, hath no sting. _
What was the slight of a poor powerless girl
To the deep wrong of this most vile revenge?
Oh, how I loved this man!—a serf!—a slave!
    Melnotte. Hold, lady!—No, not slave! Despair is free.
I will not tell thee of the throes—the struggles—
The anguish—the remorse. No—let it pass!
And let me come to such most poor atonement
Yet in my power. Pauline!—   [*Approaching her with great
                    emotion, and about to take her hand.*

    Pauline.   No, touch me not!
I know my fate. You are, by law, my tyrant;
And I—O Heaven!—a peasant's wife! I'll work,
Toil, drudge: do what thou wilt; but touch me not:
Let my wrongs make me sacred!
    Melnotte.   Do not fear me.
Thou dost not know me, Madame: at the altar
My vengeance ceased—my guilty oath expired!
Henceforth, no image of some marble saint,
Niched in cathedral's aisles, is hallowed more
From the rude hand of sacrilegious wrong.
I am thy husband—nay, thou need'st not shudder;—
Here, at thy feet, I lay a husband's rights.
A marriage thus unholy—unfulfilled—
A bond of fraud—is, by the laws of France,
Made void and null. To-night, then, sleep—in peace.
To-morrow, pure and virgin as this morn
I bore thee, bathed in blushes, from the altar,
Thy father's arms shall take thee to thy home.
The law shall do thee justice, and restore
Thy right to bless another with thy love.
    17

And when thou art happy, and hast half forgot
Him who so loved—so wronged thee, think at least
Heaven left some remnant of the angel still
In that poor peasant's nature!—Ho! my mother!
Enter WIDOW.
Conduct this lady (she is not my wife—
She is our guest, our honored guest, my mother!)
To the poor chamber where the sleep of virtue
Never beneath my father's roof
E'en villains dared to mar! Now, lady, now,
I think thou wilt believe me. Go, my mother!
Widow. She is not thy wife!
Melnotte.   Hush! hush! for mercy sake:
Speak not, but go.   [WIDOW *ascends the stairs :* PAULINE
                               follows weeping—turns to look back.
Melnotte [*sinking down.*] All angels bless and guard her!

------◆------

CCIII.—THE SENSITIVE AUTHOR.
R. B. SHERIDAN.

[In this dialogue from "The Critic, or a Tragedy Rehearsed," Sheridan caricatured the peculiarities of Richard Cumberland, a vain and sensitive, but good man, a writer of several plays, who died in 1811.]

*Characters—*DANGLE, SNEER, SIR FRETFUL PLAGIARY.

Dangle. Ah, my dear friend! We were just speaking of your tragedy. Admirable, Sir Fretful, admirable!

Sneer. You never did anything beyond it, Sir Fretful, never in your life.

Sir F. Sincerely then,—do you like the piece?

Sneer. Wonderfully!

Sir F. But come now, there must be something that you think might be mended, hey?—Mr. Dangle, has nothing struck you?

Dan. Why, faith, it is but an ungracious thing, for the most part, to——

Sir F. With most authors it is just so indeed : they are in general strangely tenacious! But, for my part, I am never so well pleased as when a judicious critic points out any defect in me; for what is the purpose of showing a work to a friend, if you don't mean to profit by his opinion?

Sneer. Very true. Why, then, though I seriously admire the piece upon the whole, yet there is one small objection; which, if you'll give me leave, I'll mention.

Sir F. Sir, you can't oblige me more.

Sneer. I think it wants incident.

Sir F. You surprise me!—wants incident?

Sneer. Yes: I own, I think the incidents are too few.

Sir F. Believe me, Mr. Sneer, there is no person for whose judgment I have a more implicit deference. But I protest to you, Mr. Sneer, I am only apprehensive that the incidents are too crowded. My dear Dangle, how does it strike you?

Dan. Really, I can't agree with my friend Sneer. I think the plot quite sufficient; and the first four acts by many degrees the best I ever read or saw in my life. If I might venture to suggest anything, it is that the interest rather falls off in the fifth.

Sir F. Rises, I believe, you mean, sir——

Dan. No: I don't upon my word.

Sir F. Yes, yes, you do, upon my word,—it certainly don't fall off, I assure you. No, no, it don't fall off.

Dan. Well, Sir Fretful, I wish you may be able to get rid as easily of the newspaper criticisms as you do of ours.

Sir F. The newspapers!—Sir, they are the most villainous—licentious—abominable—infernal—Not that I ever read them! No! I make it a rule never to look into a newspaper.

Dan. You are quite right,—for it certainly must hurt an author of delicate feelings to see the liberties they take.

Sir F. No!—quite the contrary: their abuse is, in fact, the best panegyric—I like it of all things. An author's reputation is only in danger from their support.

Sneer. Why, that's true,—and that attack now on you the other day——

Sir F. What? where?

Dan. Ay, you mean in a paper of Thursday: it was completely ill-natured, to be sure.

Sir F. O, so much the better—Ha! ha! ha!—I wouldn't have it otherwise.

Dan. Certainly, it's only to be laughed at: for——

Sir F. You don't happen to recollect what the fellow said, do you?

Sneer. Pray, Dangle—Sir Fretful seems a little anxious——

Sir F. O no!—anxious,—not I,—not the least. I—But one may as well hear, you know.

Dan. Sneer, do you recollect?—[*Aside to* Sneer.] Make out something.

Sneer. [*Aside to* Dangle.] I will. [*Aloud.*] Yes, yes, I remember perfectly.

Sir F. Well, and pray now—not that it signifies—what might the gentleman say?

Sneer. Why, he roundly asserts that you have not the slightest invention or original genius whatever; though you are the greatest traducer of all other authors living.

Sir F. Ha! ha! ha! Very good!

Sneer. That, as to comedy, you have not one idea of your own, he believes, even in your commonplace-book, where stray jokes and pilfered witticisms are kept with as much method as the ledger of the Lost and Stolen Office.

Sir F. Ha! ha! ha! Very pleasant!

Sneer. Nay, that you are so unlucky as not to have the skill even to steal with taste; but that you glean from the refuse of obscure volumes, where more judicious plagiarists have been before you; so that the body of your work is a composition of dregs and sediments,—like a bad tavern's worst wine.

Sir F. Ha! ha!

Sneer. In your more serious efforts, he says, your bombast would be less intolerable, if the thoughts were ever suited to the expression; but the homeliness of the sentiment stares through the fantastic encumbrance of its fine language, like a clown in one of the new uniforms!

Sir F. Ha! ha!

Sneer. That your occasional tropes and flowers suit the general coarseness of your style, as tambour sprigs would a ground of linsey-wolsey; while your imitations of Shakspeare resemble the mimicry of Falstaff's Page, and are about as near the standard of the original.

Sir F. Ha!

Sneer. In short, that even the finest passages you steal are of no service to you; for the poverty of your own language prevents their assimilating; so that they lie on the surface like lumps of marl on a barren moor, encumbering what it is not in their power to fertilize!

Sir F. [*After great agitation.*] Now, another person would be vexed at this.

Sneer. Oh! but I wouldn't have told you, only to divert you.

Sir F. I know it—I am diverted—Ha! ha! ha!—not the least invention!—Ha! ha! ha! very good! very good!

Sneer. Yes—no genius! Ha! ha! ha!

Dan. A severe rogue! ha! ha! But you are quite right, Sir Fretful, never to read such nonsense. You are quite right.

Sir F. To be sure—for, if there is any thing to one's praise, it is a foolish vanity to be gratified at it; and if it is abuse,—why, one is always sure to hear of it from one good-natured friend or another!

CCIV.—FROM NOLENS VOLENS.

HALL.

[Sir Christopher is an elderly gentleman, who has a son at college, against whom he is much enraged for having fallen prematurely in love. Quiz, under the assumed name of "Blackletter," personates a professor of languages, having come for the purpose of pacifying Sir Christopher, and thus to obtain money for the son.]

ENTER SIR CHRISTOPHER AND QUIZ.

Sir Christopher. And so, friend Blackletter, you are just come from college?

Quiz. Yes, sir.

Sir Ch. Ah, Mr. Blackletter, I once loved the name of a college, until my son proved so worthless.

Quiz. In the name of all the literati, what do you mean ? You fond of books, and not bless your stars in giving you such a son !

Sir Ch. Ah, sir, he was once a youth of promise.—But do you know him ?

Quiz. What! Frederick Classic ?—Ay, that I do— heaven be praised !

Sir Ch. I tell you, Mr. Blackletter, he is wonderfully changed.

Quiz. And a lucky change for him. What, I suppose he was once a wild young fellow ?

Sir Ch. No, sir, you don't understand me, or I don't you. I tell you, he neglects his studies, and is foolishly in love, for which I shall certainly cut him off with a shilling.

Quiz. You surprise me, sir. I must beg leave to unde- ceive you : you are either out of your senses, or some wicked enemy of his has, undoubtedly, done him this in- jury. Why, sir, he is in love, I grant you, but it is only with his book. He hardly allows himself time to eat ; and as for sleep, he scarcely takes two hours in the twenty-four. [*Aside.*] This is a thumper ; for the dog has not looked into a book these six months, to my certain knowledge.

Sir Ch. I have received a letter from farmer Down- right this very day, who tells me he has received a letter from him, containing proposals for his daughter.

Quiz. This is very strange. I left him at college as close to his books as—oh, oh—I believe I can solve this mystery, and much to your satisfaction.

Sir Ch. I should be happy indeed if you could.

Quiz. Oh, as plain as that two and three are five. 'Tis, thus : an envious fellow, a rival of your son's—a fellow who has not as much sense in his whole corporation, as your son has in his little finger—yes, I heard this very fellow order- ing a messenger to farmer Downright, with a letter ; and this is, no doubt, the very one. Why, sir, your son will certainly surpass the Admirable Crichton. Sir Isaac Newton will be a perfect automaton compared with him; and the sages of antiquity, if resuscitated, would hang their heads in despair.

Sir Ch. Is it possible that my son is now at college, making these great improvements?

Quiz. Ay, that he is, sir.

Sir Ch. [*Rubbing his hands.*] Oh, the dear fellow, the dear fellow!

Quiz. Sir, you may turn to any part of Homer, and repeat one line—he will take it up, and by dint of memory, continue repeating to the end of the book.

Sir Ch. Well, well, well. I find I was doing him great injustice: however, I'll make him ample amends—oh, the dear fellow, the dear fellow, the dear fellow—[*With great joy*]—he will be immortalized; and so shall I, for if I had not cherished the boy's genius in embryo, he would never have soared above mediocrity.

Quiz. True, sir.

Sir Ch. I cannot but think what superlative pleasure I shall have, when my son has got his education. No other man's in England shall be comparative with it—of that I am positive. Why, sir, the moderns are such dull, plodding, senseless barbarians, that a man of learning is as hard to be found, as the unicorn.

Quiz. 'Tis much to be regretted, sir; but such is the lamentable fact.

Sir Ch. Even the shepherds, in days of yore, spoke their mother tongue in Latin; and now, hic, hæc, hoc, is as little understood as the language of the moon.

Quiz. Your son, sir, will be a phenomenon, depend upon it.

Sir Ch. So much the better, so much the better. I expected soon to have been in the vocative, for, you know, you found me in the accusative case, and that's very near it—ha! ha! ha!

Quiz. You have reason to be merry, sir, I promise you.

Sir Ch. I have, indeed. Well, I shall leave off interjections, and promote an amicable conjunction with the dear fellow. Oh! we shall never think of addressing each other in plain English—no, no, we will converse in the pure classical language of the ancients. You remember the Eclogues of Virgil, Mr. Blackletter?

Quiz. Oh, yes, sir, perfectly : have 'em at my fingers' ends. [*Aside.*] Not a bit of a one did I ever hear of in my life.

Sir Ch. How sweetly the first of them begins!

Quiz. Very sweetly, indeed, sir. [*Aside.*] I heartily wish he would change the subject.

Sir Ch. "Tytere, tu patulæ recubans:" faith, 'tis more musical than fifty hand-organs.

Quiz. [*Aside.*] I had rather hear a jew's-harp.

Sir Ch. Talking of music, though—the Greek is the language for that.

Quiz. Truly is it.

Sir Ch. Even the conjugations of the verbs far excel the finest sonata of Pleyel or Handel—for instance, "tupto, tupso, tetupha "—can any thing be more musical?

Quiz. Nothing—" stoop low, stoop so, stoop too far."

Sir Ch. Ha! ha! ha! " stoop too far!" that's a good one.

Quiz. [*Aside.*] Faith, I have stooped too far. All's over now, by Jupiter.

Sir Ch. Ha! ha! ha! a plaguy good pun, Mr. Blackletter.

Quiz. Tolerable. [*Aside.*] I am well out of that scrape, however.

Sir Ch. Pray, sir, which of the classics is your favorite?

Quiz. Why, sir, Mr. Frederick Classic, I think—he is so great a scholar—

Sir Ch. Po, po, you don't understand me. I mean, which of the Latin classics do you admire most?

Quiz. [*Aside.*] Hang it! what shall I say now.

[*Aloud.*] The Latin classics? · Oh really, sir, I admire them all so much, it is difficult to say.

Sir Ch. Virgil is my favorite. How very expressive is his description of the unconquerable passion of Queen Dido, where he says, "haret lateri lethalis arundo." Is not that very expressive?

Quiz. Very expressive, indeed, sir. [*Aside.*] I wish we were forty miles asunder. I shall never be able to hold out much longer, at this rate.

Sir Ch. And Ovid is not without his charms.

Quiz. He is not indeed, sir.

Sir Ch. And what a dear, enchanting fellow, Horace is!

Quiz. Wonderfully so!

Sir Ch. Pray, what do you think of Xenophon?

Quiz. [*Aside.*] Who the plague is he, I wonder. [*Aloud.*] Xenophon! oh, I think he unquestionably wrote good Latin, sir.

Sir Ch. Good Latin, man!—he wrote Greek—good Greek, you meant.

Quiz. True, sir, I did. Latin, indeed! [*In great confusion.*] I meant Greek—did I say Latin? I really meant Greek. [*Aside.*] In fact, I don't know what I mean myself.

Sir Ch. Oh! Mr. Blackletter, I have been trying a long time to remember the name of one of Achilles's horses, but I can't for my life think of it—you doubtless can tell me.

Quiz. O yes, his name was—but which of them do you mean!—What was he called?

Sir Ch. What was he called? Why, that's the very thing I wanted to know. The one I allude to was born of the Harpy Celæno. I can't for the blood of me, tell it.

Quiz. [*Aside.*] Faith! if I can either. [*Aloud.*] Born of the Harpy—oh! his name was—[*striking his forehead.*] Gracious! I forget it now. His name was,—was,—was,—Pshaw, 'tis as familiar to me as my A, B, C.

Sir Ch. Oh! I remember—'twas Xanthus, Xanthus—I

17*

remember now—'twas Xanthus—plague o' the name—
that's it.

Quiz. Egad! so 'tis. " Thankus, Thankus "—that's it
—strange I could not remember it. [*Aside.*] 'Twould
have been stranger if I had.

Sir Ch. You seem at times a little absent, Mr. Blackletter.

Quiz. [*Aside.*] Absent! I wish I was absent altogether.

Sir Ch. We shall not disagree about learning, sir. I
discover you are a man, not only of profound learning, but
correct taste.

Quiz. [*Aside.*] I am glad you have found that out, for
I never should. I came here to quiz the old fellow, and
he'll quiz me, I fear. [*Aloud.*] O, by-the-by, I have been
so confused—I mean, so confounded : pshaw ! so much
engrossed with the contemplation of the Latin classics, I
had almost forgot to give you a letter from your son.

Sir Ch. Bless me, sir! why did you delay that pleasure so long ?

Quiz. I beg pardon, sir, here 'tis. [*Gives a letter.*]

Sir Ch. [*Puts on his spectacles and reads.*] " To Miss
Clara."

Quiz. No, no, no—that's not it—here 'tis. [*Takes the
letter, and gives him another.*]

Sir Ch. What, are you the bearer of love epistles, too,
Mr. Blackletter ?

Quiz. [*Aside.*] What a horrid blunder. [*Aloud.*] Oh,
no, sir, that letter is from a female cousin at a boarding-
school, to Miss Clara Upright,—no, Downright. That's
the name.

Sir Ch. Truly, she writes a good masculine fist. Well,
let me see what my boy has to say. [*Reads.*]

" Dear Father,—There is a famous Greek manuscript
just come to light. I must have it. The price is about a
thousand dollars. Send me the money by the bearer." Short
and sweet. There's a letter for you, in the true Lacedæ-

monian style—laconic. Well, the boy shall have it, were it ten times as much. I should like to see this Greek manuscript. Pray, sir, did you ever see it ?

Quiz. I can't say I ever did, sir. [*Aside.*] This is the only truth I have been able to edge in, yet.

Sir Ch. I'll just send to my bankers for the money. In the mean time, we will adjourn to my library. I have been much puzzled with an obscure passage in Livy—we must lay our heads together for a solution. But I am sorry you are addicted to such absence of mind, at times.

Quiz. 'Tis a misfortune, sir ; but I am addicted to a greater than that, at times.

Sir Ch. Ah! what's that?

Quiz. I am sometimes addicted to an absence of body.

Sir Ch. As how?

Quiz. Why thus, sir. [*Takes up his hat and stick, and walks off.*]

Sir Ch. Ha, ha, ha,—that's an absence of body, sure enough—an absence of body with a vengeance! A very merry fellow this. He will be back for the money, I suppose, presently. He is, at all events, a very modest man, not fond of expressing his opinion—but that's a mark of merit.

———◆———

CCV.—GIL BLAS AND THE OLD ARCHBISHOP.

LA SAGE.

Archbishop. Well, young man, what is your business with me ?

Gil Blas. I am the young man whom your nephew, Don Fernando, was pleased to mention to you.

Arch. Oh! you are the person, then, of whom he spoke so handsomely. I engage you in my service, and consider you a valuable acquisition. From the specimens he showed me of your powers, you must be pretty well acquainted with the Greek and Latin authors. It is very evident your education has not been neglected. I am satisfied with your handwriting, and still more with your understanding. I thank my nephew, Don Fernando, for having given me such an able young man, whom I consider a rich acquisition. You transcribe so well, you must certainly understand grammar. Tell me, ingenuously, my friend, did you find nothing that shocked you in writing over the homily I sent you on trial,—some neglect, perhaps, in style, or some improper term ?

Gil B. Oh! sir, I am not learned enough to make critical observations; and if I was, I am persuaded the works of your grace would escape my censure.

Arch. Young man, you are disposed to flatter; but tell me, which parts of it did you think most strikingly beautiful.

Gil B. If, where all was excellent, any parts were particularly so, I should say they were the personification of hope, and the description of a good man's death.

Arch. I see you have a delicate knowledge of the truly beautiful. This is what I call having taste and sentiment. Gil Blas, henceforth give thyself no uneasiness about thy fortune, I will take care of that. I love thee, and as a proof of my affection, I will make thee my confidant: yes, my child, thou shalt be the repository of my most secret thoughts. Listen with attention to what I am going to say. My chief pleasure consists in preaching, and the Lord gives a blessing to my homilies, but I confess my weakness. The honor of being thought a perfect orator has charmed my imagination: my performances are thought equally nervous and delicate; but I would of all things avoid the fault of good authors, who write too long. Wherefore, my dear Gil Blas, one thing that I exact of thy zeal, is, whenever thou shalt perceive my pen smack of old age, and my genius flag, don't fail to advertise me of it, for I don't trust to my own judgment, which may be seduced by self-love. That observation must proceed from a disinterested understanding, and I make choice of thine, which I know is good, and am resolved to stand by thy decision.

Gil B. Thank heaven, sir, that time is far off. Besides, a genius like that of your grace, will preserve its vigor much better than any other ; or, to speak more justly, will be always the same. I look upon you as another Cardinal Ximenes, whose superior genius, instead of being weakened, seemed to acquire new strength by age.

Arch. No flattery, friend : I know I am liable to sink all at once. People at my age begin to feel infirmities, and the infirmities of the body often affect the understanding. I repeat it to thee again, Gil Blas, as soon as thou shalt judge mine in the least impaired, be sure to give me notice. And be not afraid of speaking freely and sincerely, for I shall receive thy advice as a mark of thy affection.

Gil B. Your grace may always depend upon my fidelity.

Arch. I know thy sincerity, Gil Blas ; and now tell me plainly, hast thou not heard the people make some remarks upon my late homilies ?

Gil B. Your homilies have always been admired, but it seems to me that the last did not appear to have had so powerful an effect upon the audience as former ones.

Arch. How, sir, has it met with any Aristarchus ?

Gil B. No, sir, by no means, such works as yours are not to be criticised : everybody is charmed with them. Nevertheless, since you have laid your injunctions upon me to be free and sincere, I will take the liberty to tell you that your last discourse, in my judgment, has not altogether the energy of your other performances. Did you not think so, sir, yourself ?

Arch. So, then, Gil Blas, this piece is not to your taste ?

Gil B. I don't say so, sir : I think it excellent, although a little inferior to your other works.

Arch. I understand you : you think I flag, don't you ? Come, be plain : you believe it is time for me to think of retiring.

Gil B. I should not have been so bold as to speak so freely, if your grace had not commanded me : I do no

more, therefore, than obey you; and I most humbly beg
that you will not be offended at my freedom.

Arch. God forbid! God forbid that I should find
fault with it. I don't at all take it ill that you should speak
your sentiments, it is your sentiment itself, only, that I
find bad. I have been most egregiously deceived in your
narrow understanding.

Gil B. Your grace will pardon me for obeying—

Arch. Say no more, my child, you are yet too raw to
make proper distinctions. Be it known to you, I never
composed a better homily than that which you disapprove;
for, my genius, thank Heaven, hath, as yet, lost nothing
of its vigor: henceforth I will make a better choice of a
confidant. Go! go, Mr. Gil Blas, and tell my treasurer to
give you a hundred ducats, and may Heaven conduct you
with that sum. Adieu, Mr. Gil Blas! I wish you all manner of prosperity, with a little more taste.

———————◆———————

CCVI.—CONVERSATIONS AFTER MARRIAGE.

From "THE SCHOOL FOR SCANDAL."

R. B. SHERIDAN.

PART FIRST.

Enter LADY TEAZLE *and* SIR PETER.

Sir Peter. Lady Teazle, Lady Teazle, I'll not bear it!

Lady Teazle. Sir Peter, Sir Peter, you may bear it or
not, as you please; but I ought to have my own way in
every thing; and what's more, I will too. What! though
I was educated in the country, I know very well that
women of fashion in London are accountable to nobody
after they are married.

Sir P. Very well, ma'am, very well—so a husband is
to have no influence, no authority?

Lady T. Authority! No, to be sure :—if you wanted
authority over me, you should have adopted me, and not
married me : I am sure you were old enough.

Sir P. Old enough!—ay—there it is. 'Well, well, Lady Teazle, though my life may be made unhappy by your temper, I'll not be ruined by your extravagance.

Lady T. My extravagance! I'm sure I'm not more extravagant than a woman ought to be.

Sir P. No, no, madam, you shall throw away no more sums on such unmeaning luxury. 'Slife! to spend as much to furnish your dressing-room with flowers in winter as would suffice to turn the Pantheon into a green-house.

Lady T. Lord, Sir Peter, am I to blame, because flowers are dear in cold weather? You should find fault with the climate, and not with me. For my part, I'm sure, I wish it was spring all the year round, and that roses grew under our feet!

Sir P. Zounds! madam—if you had been born to this, I shouldn't wonder at your talking thus; but you forget what your situation was when I married you.

Lady T. No, no, I don't: 'twas a very disagreeable one, or I should never have married you.

Sir P. Yes, yes, madam, you were then in somewhat a humbler style,—the daughter of a plain country squire. Recollect, Lady Teazle, when I saw you first sitting at your tambor, in a pretty figured linen gown, with a bunch of keys at your side: your hair combed smooth over a roll, and your apartment hung round with fruits in worsted of your own working.

Lady T. Oh yes! I remember it very well, and a curious life I led,—my daily occupation to inspect the dairy, superintend the poultry, make extracts from the family receipt-book, and comb my aunt Deborah's lap dog.

Sir P. Yes, yes, ma'am, 'twas so indeed.

Lady T. And then, you know, my evening amusements;—to draw patterns for ruffles, which I had not materials to make up: to play Pope Joan with the curate: to read a novel to my aunt; or to be stuck down to an old spinet to strum my father to sleep after a fox-chase. [*Crosses, L.*]

Sir P. I am glad you have so good a memory. Yes, madam, these were the recreations I took you from; but now you must have your coach—*vis-à-vis*—and three powdered footmen before your chair; and, in the summer, a pair of white cats to draw you to Kensington Gardens. No recollection, I suppose, when you were content to ride double, behind the butler, on a docked coach-horse.

Lady T. No—I never did that: I deny the butler and the coach-horse.

Sir P. This, madam, was your situation; and what have I done for you? I have made you a woman of fashion, of fortune, of rank: in short, I have made you my wife.

Lady T. Well, then; and there is but one thing more you can make me add to the obligation, and that is—

Sir P. My widow, I suppose?

Lady T. Hem! hem!

Sir P. I thank you, madam; but don't flatter yourself; for though your ill conduct may disturb my peace of mind, it shall never break my heart, I promise you: however, I am equally obliged to you for the hint. [*Crosses, L.*]

Lady T. Then why will you endeavor to make yourself so disagreeable to me, and thwart me in every little elegant expense?

Sir P. 'Slife, madam, I say, had you any of these little elegant expenses when you married me?

Lady. T. Lud, Sir Peter! would you have me.be out of the fashion?

Sir P. The fashion, indeed! What had you to do with the fashion before you married me?

Lady T. For my part, I should think you would like to have your wife thought a woman of taste.

Sir P. Ay: there again—taste. Zounds! madam, you had no taste when you married me!

Lady T. That's very true indeed, Sir Peter; and after having married you, I should never pretend to taste again, I allow. But now, Sir Peter, since we have finished our daily jangle, I presume I may go to my engagement at Lady Sneerwell's.

Sir P. Ay, there's another precious circumstance—a charming set of acquaintance you have made there.

Lady T. Nay, Sir Peter, they are all people of rank and fortune, and remarkably tenacious of reputation.

Sir P. Yes, egad, they are tenacious of reputation with a vengeance; for they don't choose anybody should have a character but themselves!—Such a crew! Ah! many a wretch has rid on a hurdle who has done less mischief than these utterers of forged tales, coiners of scandal, and clippers of reputation.

Lady T. What! would you restrain the freedom of speech ?

Sir P. Ah! they have made you just as bad as any one of the society.

Lady T. Why, I believe I do bear a part with a tolerable grace.

Sir P. Grace, indeed!

Lady P. But I vow I bear no malice against the people I abuse. When I say an ill-natured thing, 'tis out of pure good-humor; and I take it for granted, they deal exactly in the same manner with me. But, Sir Peter, you know you promised to come to Lady Sneerwell's too.

Sir P. Well, well, I'll call in just to look after my own character.

Lady T. Then indeed you must make haste after me, or you'll be too late. So, good-by to you. [*Exit* LADY TEAZLE.

Sir P. So—I have gained much by my intended expostulation: yet, with what a charming air she contradicts every thing I say, and how pleasingly she shows her contempt for my authority! Well, though I can't make her love me, there is great satisfaction in quarreling with her; and I think she never appears to such advantage, as when she is doing everything in her power to plague me.

CCVII.—CONVERSATIONS AFTER MARRIAGE.

PART SECOND.

Lady Teazle. Lud! Sir Peter, I hope you haven't been quarreling with Maria? It is not using me well to be ill-humored when I am not by.

Sir Peter. Ah! Lady Teazle, you might have the power to make me good-humored at all times.

Lady T. I am sure I wish I had; for I want you to be in a charming sweet temper at this moment. Do be good-humored now, and let me have two hundred pounds, will you?

Sir P. Two hundred pounds! What, ain't I to be in a good-humor without paying for it? But speak to me thus, and i' faith there's nothing I could refuse you. You shall have it [*gives her notes*]; but seal me a bond of repayment.

Lady T. Oh no: there—my note of hand will do as well.
[*Offering her hand.*

Sir P. And you shall no longer reproach me with not giving you an independent settlement. I mean shortly to surprise you:—but shall we always live thus, hey?

Lady T. If you please. I'm sure I don't care how soon we leave off quarreling, provided you'll own you were tired first.

Sir P. Well: then let our future contest be, who shall be most obliging.

Lady T. I assure you, Sir Peter, good-nature becomes you: you look now as you did before we were married, when you used to walk with me under the elms, and tell me stories of what a gallant you were in your youth, and chuck me under the chin, you would; and ask me if I thought I could love an old fellow, who would deny me nothing—didn't you?

Sir P. Yes, yes, and you were kind and attentive—

Lady T. Ay, so I was, and would always take your part when my acquaintance used to abuse you, and turn you into ridicule.

Sir P. Indeed!

Lady T. Ay; and when my cousin Sophy has called you a stiff, peevish old bachelor, and laughed at me for thinking of marrying one who might be my father, I have always defended you, and said, I didn't think you so ugly by any means.

Sir P. Thank you.

Lady T. And I dared say you'd make a very good sort of a husband.

Sir P. And you prophesied right; and we shall now be the happiest couple—

Lady T. And never differ again?

Sir P. No, never!—though at the same time, indeed, my dear Lady Teazle, you must watch your temper very seriously; for in all our little quarrels, my dear, if you recollect, my love, you always begin first.

Lady T. I beg your pardon, my dear Sir Peter; indeed, you always gave the provocation.

Sir P. Now see, my angel! take care—contradicting isn't the way to keep friends.

Lady T. Then don't you begin it, my love.

Sir P. There, now! you—you are going on. You don't perceive, my life, that you are just doing the very thing which you know always makes me angry.

Lady T. Nay, you know if you will be angry without any reason, my dear—

Sir P. There! now you want to quarrel again.

Lady T. No, I am sure I don't; but if you will be so peevish—

Sir P. There now! who begins first?

Lady T. Why you, to be sure. I said nothing—but there's no bearing your temper.

Sir P. No, no, madam: the fault's in your own temper.

Lady T. Ay, you are just what my cousin Sophy said you would be.

Sir P. Your cousin Sophy is a forward, impertinent gipsy.

Lady T. You are a great bear, I'm sure, to abuse my relations.

Sir P. Now may all the plagues of marriage be doubled on me, if ever I try to be friends with you any more.

Lady T. So much the better.

Sir P. No, no, madam: 'tis evident you never cared a pin for me, and I was a madman to marry you—a pert, rural coquette, that had refused half the honest squires in the neighborhood.

Lady T. And I am sure I was a fool to marry you—an old dangling bachelor, who was single at fifty, only because he never could meet with any one who would have him.

[*Crosses L.*

Sir P. Ay, ay, madam; but you were pleased enough to listen to me: you never had such an óffer before.

Lady T. No! didn't I refuse Sir Tivy Terrier, who everybody said would have been a bettèr match? for his estate is just as good as yours, and he has broke his neck since we have been married. [*Crosses R.*

Sir P. I have done with you, madam! You are an unfeeling, ungrateful—but there's an end of every thing. I believe you capable of every thing that is bad. Yes, madam, I now believe the reports relative to you and Charles, madam. Yes, madam, *you* and Charles are—not without grounds.

Lady T. Take care, Sir Peter! you had better not insinuate any such thing! I'll not be suspected without cause, I promise you.

Sir P. Very well, madam! very well! A separate maintenance as soon as you please! Yes, madam, or a divorce!—I'll make an example of myself for the benefit of all old bachelors.

Lady T. Agreed! agreed! And now, my dear Sir Peter, we are of a mind once more, we may be the happiest couple—and never differ again, you know—ha! ha! ha! Well, you are going to be in a passion, I see, and I shall only interrupt you; so, bye-bye. [*Exit* LADY TEAZLE.

Sir P. Plagues and tortures! Can't I make her angry either? Oh, I am the most miserable fellow! But I'll not bear her presuming to keep her temper: no! she may break my heart, but she sha'n't keep her temper. [*Exit.*

CCIX.—FROM THE LADY OF THE LAKE.

SCOTT.

Characters—KING JAMES, RODERIC DHU.

Scene.—A rock, with a watch-fire burning near it. A Scotch Highlander, Roderic Dhu, wrapped in his tartan, is discovered sleeping by it.

[*Enter King James in a warrior's garb.*]

Roderic. [*Grasping his sword and springing on his feet.*] Thy name and purpose, Saxon?—Stand!

James. A stranger.

Rod. What dost thou require?

James. Rest and a guide, and food and fire.
My life's beset, my path is lost,
The gale has chilled my limbs with frost.

Rod. Art thou a friend to Roderic?

James. No.

Rod. Thou dost not call thyself his foe?

James. I dare, to him and all the band
He brings to aid his murderous hand.

Rod. Bold words! But, though the beast of game
The privilege of chase may claim:
Though space and law the stag we lend,
Ere hound we slip, or bow we bend,
Who ever cared where, how, or when
The prowling fox was trapped or slain?
Thus treacherous scouts,—yet sure they lie,
Who say thou comest a secret spy.

James. They do, by Heaven! Come Roderic Dhu,
And of his clan the boldest two,
And, let me but till morning rest,
I'll write the falsehood on their crest.

Rod. If by the blaze I mark aright,
Thou bearest the belt and spur of knight.

James. Then by these tokens mayst thou know
Each proud oppressor's mortal foe.

Rod. Enough, enough: sit down and share
A soldier's couch, a soldier's fare.

[*They sit down and eat together, and in a few minutes the soldier continues the conversation.*]

Rod. Stranger, I am to Roderic Dhu,
A clansman born, a kinsman true:
Each word against his honor spoke,
Demands of me avenging stroke.
It rests with me to wind my horn,
Thou art with numbers overborne:
It rests with me, here, brand to brand,
Worn as thou art, to bid thee stand;
But not for clan, nor kindred's cause,
Will I depart from honor's laws.
To assail a wearied man were shame,
And Stranger is a holy name.
Guidance and rest, and food and fire,
In vain he never must require.
Myself will guide thee on the way,
Through watch and ward till break of day,
As far as Coilantogle ford;
From thence thy warrant is thy sword.
    James. I take thy courtesy, by Heaven,
As freely as 'tis nobly given.
    Rod. Why seek these wilds, traversed by few,
Without a pass from Roderic Dhu?
    James. Brave man, my pass, in danger tried,
Hangs in my belt, and by my side.
Yet sooth to tell, though naught I dread,
I dreamed not now to claim its aid.
When here but three days since I came,
Bewildered in pursuit of game
All seemed as peaceful and as still,
As the mist slumbering on yon hill.
Thy dangerous chief was then afar,
Nor soon expected back from war;
Thus said, at least, my mountain guide,
Though deep, perchance, the villain lied.
    Rod. Yet, why a second venture try?
    James. A warrior, thou, and ask me why?
Perhaps I sought to drive away
The lazy hours of peaceful day:
Slight cause will then suffice to guide
A knight's free footsteps far and wide:
A falcon flown, a greyhound strayed,

The merry glance of mountain maid:
Or, if a path be dangerous known,
The danger's self is lure alone.

    Rod. Thy secret keep: I urge thee not,
Yet, ere again you sought this spot,
Say, heard you not of lowland war, –
Against Clan Alpine raised by Mar?

    James. No, by my word; of bands prepared
To guard King James's sports I heard;
Nor doubt I aught, but, when they hear
This muster of the Mountaineer,
Their pennons will abroad be flung,
Which else in Doune had peaceful hung.

    Rod. Free be they flung! for we are loath
Their silken folds should feed the moth.
Free be they flung! as free shall wave
Clan Alpine's pine in banner brave.
But, stranger, peaceful since you came,
Bewildered in the mountain game,
Whence the bold boast, by which we know
Vich Alpine's vowed and mortal foe?

    James. Warrior, but yester morn, I knew
Naught of thy chieftain, Roderic Dhu,
Save as an outlawed, desperate man,
The chief of a rebellious clan,
Who in the regent's court and sight,
With ruffian dagger stabbed a knight.
Yet this alone should from his part
Sever each true and loyal heart.

    Rod. [*Frowning, and both rising hastily.*]
And heardst thou why he drew his blade?
Heardst thou, that shameful word, and blow
Brought Roderic's vengeance on his foe?
What recked the chieftain, if he stood
On highland heath or Holy Rood?
He rights such wrong where it is given,
Though it were in the court of heaven.

    James. Still it was outrage: yet, 'tis true,
Not then claimed sovereignty his due:
The young king, mewed in Stirling tower,
Was stranger to respect and power.
But then thy chieftain's robber life,
Winning mean prey by causeless strife,

Wrenching from ruined lowland swain
His flocks and harvest reared in vain—
Methinks a soul like thine, should scorn
The spoils from such foul conflict borne.
   Rod. Saxon, from yonder mountain high,
I marked thee send delighted eye,
O'er waving fields and pastures green,
With gentle slopes, and groves between :
These fertile plains, that softened vale,
Were once the birthright of the Gael.
The Saxons came with iron hand,
And from our fathers reft the land.
Where dwell we now ? see rudely swell
Crag over crag, and fell o'er fell.
Ask we this savage hill we tread,
For fattened steer, or household bread :
Ask we for flocks these shingles dry,
And well the mountain might reply :
" To you, as to your sires of yore,
Belong the target and claymore !
I give you shelter in my breast,
Your own good blades must do the rest."
Pent in this fortress of the north,
Thinkst thou we will not sally forth
To spoil the spoiler as we may,
And from the robber rend the prey ?
Ay, by my soul ! while on yon plain
The Saxon rears one shock of grain :
While of ten thousand herds, there strays
But one along yon river's maze—
The Gael, of plain and river heir,
Shall, with strong hand, redeem his share.
Where live the mountain chiefs, who hold
That plundering lowland field and fold,
Is aught but retribution due ?—
Seek other cause 'gainst Roderic Dhu.
   James.   And if I sought,
Thinks thou no other could be brought ?
What deem ye, of my path waylaid,
My life given o'er to ambuscade ?
   Rod. As a reward to rashness due :
Hadst thou sent warning fair and true,
Free hadst thou been to come and go :

But secret path marks secret foe.

James. Well, let it pass; nor will I now
Fresh cause of enmity avow,
To chafe thy mood and cloud thy brow.
Enough, I am by promise tied
To match me with this man of pride.
Twice have I sought Clan Alpine's glen
In peace; but, when I come again,
I come with banner, brand, and bow,
As leader seeks his mortal foe.
For love-lorn swain in lady's bower,
Ne'er panted for the appointed hour,
As I, until before me stand
This rebel chieftain and his band.

 Rod. Have then thy wish. [*He whistles, and soldiers rush in on all
 sides.*] How sayest thou now?
These are Clan Alpine's warriors true;
And, Saxon, I AM RODERIC DHU. [*King James starts back a little, then
 draws his sword and places his back against the rock.*]
 James. Come one, come all! this rock shall fly
From its firm base, as soon as I. [*Roderic waves his hand, and the soldiers
 Rod. Fear not, nay, that I need not say,   [*retire.*
But doubt not aught from mine array.
Thou art my guest, I pledged my word
As far as Coilantogle ford.
So move we on: I only meant
To show the reed on which you leant,
Deeming this path you might pursue
Without a pass from Roderic Dhu.
Bold Saxon! to his promise just,
Vich Alpine shall discharge his trust.
This murderous chief, this ruthless man,
This head of a rebellious clan,
Will lead thee safe through watch and ward
Far past Clan Alpine's outmost guard;
Then man to man, and steel to steel,
A chieftain's vengeance thou shalt feel.

 James. I ne'er delayed
When foeman bade me draw my blade;
Nay, more, brave chief, I vowed thy death:
Yet sure thy fair and generous faith,
And my deep debt for life preserved,
A better meed have well deserved:

18

Can naught but blood our feud atone?
Are there no means?

   Rod. No, stranger, none!

   James. Nay, first to James at Stirling go.
When, if thou wilt be still his foe,
Or if the king shall not agree
To grant thee grace and favor free,
I plight mine honor, oath, and word,
That to thy native holds restored,
With each advantage shalt thou stand,
That aids thee now to guard thy land.

   Rod. Thy rash presumption now shall rue
The homage named to Roderic Dhu.
He yields not, he, to man nor fate—
Thou add'st but fuel to my hate!
My clansmen's wrongs demand revenge
Not yet prepared! by Heaven! I change
My thought, and hold thy valor light
As that of some vain carpet knight,
Who ill deserved my courteous care,
And whose best boast is but to wear
A braid of his fair lady's hair. [*Pointing to a braid on James' breast.*]

   James. I thank thee, Roderic, for the word:
It nerves my heart, it steels my sword.
I had it from a frantic maid,
By thee dishonored and betrayed;
And I have sworn the braid to stain
In the best blood that warms thy vein.
Now, truce, farewell! and ruth, begone!
I heed not that my strength is worn—
Thy word's restor'd; and if thou wilt,
We try this quarrel, hilt to hilt.

———◆———

CCX.—NOTHING IN IT.

CHARLES MATTHEWS.

Leech. But you don't laugh, Coldstream! Come, man, be amused, for once in your life!—you don't laugh.

Sir Charles. O, yes, I do. You mistake: I laughed twice, distinctly,—only, the fact is, I'm bored to death!

Leech. Bored? What! after such a feast as that you

have given us? Look at me,—I'm inspired! I'm a King at this moment, and all the world is at my feet!

Sir C. My dear Leech, you began life late. You are a young fellow,—forty-five,—and have the world yet before you. I started at thirteen, lived quick, and exhausted the whole round of pleasure before I was thirty. I tried every thing, heard every thing, done every thing, know every thing; and here I am, a man of thirty-three, literally used up—completely *blasé!*

Leech. Nonsense, man!—used up, indeed!—with your wealth, with your twenty estates in the sunniest spots in England,—not to mention that Utopia, within four walls, in the *Rue de Provence,* in Paris.

Sir C. I am dead with *ennui!*

Leech. Ennui! poor Crœsus!

Sir C. Crœsus!—no, I'm no Crœsus! My father,—you've seen his portrait, good old fellow!—he certainly did leave me a little matter of twelve thousand pounds a year; but, after all—

Leech. O, come!—

Sir C. O, I don't complain of it.

Leech. I should think not.

Sir C. O, no: there are some people who can manage to do on less,—on credit.

Leech. I know several. My dear Coldstream, you should try change of scene.

Sir C. I have tried it;—what's the use?

Leech. But I'd gallop all over Europe.

Sir C. I have;—there's nothing in it.

Leech. Nothing in all Europe?

Sir C. Nothing!—O, dear, yes! I remember, at one time, I did, somehow, go about a good deal.

Leech. You should go to Switzerland.

Sir C. I have been. Nothing there,—people say so much about every thing. There certainly were a few glaciers, some monks, and large dogs, and thick ankles, and bad wine, and Mont Blanc: yes, and there was ice on the top, too ; but I prefer the ice at Gunter's,—less trouble, and more in it.

Leech. Then, if Switzerland wouldn't do, I'd try Italy.

Sir C. My dear Leech, I've tried it over and over again,—and what then ?

Leech. Did not Rome inspire you ?

Sir C. O, believe me, Tom, a most horrible hole ! People talk so much about these things. There's the Coloseum now ;—round, very round,—a goodish ruin enough ; but I was diappointed with it. Capitol,—tolerable high ; and St. Peter's,—marble, and mosaics, and fountains,—dome certainly not badly scooped ; but there was nothing in it.

· *Leech.* Come, Coldstream, you must admit we have nothing like St. Peter's in London.

Sir C. No, because we don't want it ; but, if we wanted such a thing, of course we should have it. A dozen gentlemen meet, pass resolutions, institute, and in twelve months it would be run up : nay, if that were all, we'd buy St. Peter's itself, and have it sent over.

Leech. Ha, ha ! well said,—you're quite right. What say you to beautiful Naples ?

Sir C. Not bad,—excellent watermelons, and goodish opera : they took me up Vesuvius,—a horrid bore ! It smoked a good deal, certainly, but altogether a wretched mountain ;—saw the crater—looked down, but there was nothing in it.

Leech. But the bay ? ·

Sir C. Inferior to Dublin !

Leech. The Campagna ?

Sir C. A swamp !

Leech. Greece ?

Sir C. A morass !

Leech. Athens ?

Sir C. A bad Edinburgh !

Leech. Egypt ?

Sir C. A desert !

Leech. The Pyramids?

Sir C. Humbugs!—nothing in any of them! You bore me. Is it possible that you cannot invent something that would make my blood boil in my veins,—my hair stand on end,—my heart beat,—my pulse rise;—that would produce an excitement—an emotion—a sensation—a palpitation—but, no!—

Leech. I've an idea!

Sir C. You? What is it?

Leech. Marry!

Sir C. Hum!—well, not bad. There's novelty about the notion: it never did strike me to—O, but, no: I should be bored with the exertion of choosing. If a wife, now, could be had like a dinner—for ordering.

Leech. She can, by you. Take the first woman that comes: on my life, she'll not refuse twelve thousand pounds a year.

Sir C. Come, I don't dislike the project: I almost feel something like a sensation coming. I haven't felt so excited for some time: it's a novel enjoyment—a surprise. I'll try it.

CCXI.—THE WEATHERCOCK.

J. T. ALLINGHAM.

Old Fickle. What reputation, what honor, what profit can accrue to you from such conduct as yours? One moment you tell me you are going to become the greatest musician in the world, and straight you fill my house with fiddlers.

Tristram Fickle. I am clear out of that scrape now, sir.

Old F. Then, from a fiddler, you are metamorphosed into a philosopher; and, for the noise of drums, trumpets and hautboys, you substitute a vile jargon, more unintelligible than was ever heard at the tower of Babel.

Tri. You are right, sir. I have found out that philosophy is folly: so I have cut the philosophers of all sects, from Plato and Aristotle down to the puzzlers of modern date.

Old F. How much had I to pay the cooper, the other day, for barrelling you up in a large tub, when you resolved to live like Diogenes ?

Tri. You should not have paid him any thing, sir ; for the tub would not hold. You see the contents are run out.

Old F. No jesting, sir ! this is no laughing matter. Your follies have tired me out. I verily believe you have taken the whole round of arts and sciences in a month, and have been of fifty different minds in half an hour.

Tri. And, by that, shown the versatility of my genius.

Old F. Don't tell me of versatility, sir ! Let me see a little steadiness. You have never yet been constant to any thing but extravagance.

Tri. Yes, sir,—one thing more.

Old F. What is that, sir ?

Tri. Affection for you. However my head may have wandered, my heart has always been constantly attached to the kindest of parents ; and, from this moment, I am resolved to lay my follies aside, and pursue that line of conduct which will be most pleasing to the best of fathers and of friends.

Old F. Well said, my boy,—well said ! You make me happy, indeed ! [*Patting him on the shoulder.*] Now, then, my dear Tristram, let me know what you really mean to do.

Tri. To study the law—

Old F. The law !

Tri. I am most resolutely bent on following that profession.

Old F. No !

Tri. Absolutely and irrevocably fixed.

Old F. Better and better ! I am overjoyed. Why, 'tis the very thing I wished. Now I am happy ! [*Tristram makes gestures as if speaking.*] See how his mind is engaged !

Tri. Gentlemen of the Jury—

Old F. Why, Tristram!

Tri. This is a cause—

Old F. O, my dear boy! I forgive you all your tricks. I see something about you now that I can depend on. [*Tristram continues making gestures.*]

Tri. I am for the plaintiff in this cause—

Old F. Bravo! bravo! Excellent boy! I'll go and order your books, directly!

Tri. 'Tis done, sir.

Old F. What, already!

Tri. I ordered twelve square feet of books, when I first thought of embracing the arduous profession of the law.

Old F. What, do you mean to read by the foot?

Tri. By the foot, sir: that is the only way to become a solid lawyer.

Old F. Twelve square feet of learning! Well—

Tri. I have likewise sent for a barber—

Old F. A barber! What, is he to teach you to shave close?

Tri. He is to shave one-half of my head, sir.

Old F. You will excuse me if I cannot perfectly understand what that has to do with the study of the law.

Tri. Did you never hear of Demosthenes, sir, the Athenian orator? He had half his head shaved, and locked himself up in a coal-cellar.

Old F. Ah, he was perfectly right to lock himself up, after having undergone such an operation as that. He certainly would have made rather an odd figure abroad.

Tri. I think I see him now, awaking the dormant patriotism of his countrymen,—lightning in his eye, and thunder in his voice: he pours forth a torrent of eloquence, resistless in its force: the throne of Philip trembles while he speaks: he denounces, and indignation fills the bosom of his hearers: he exposes the impending danger, and every one sees impending ruin: he threatens the tyrant,—

they grasp their swords: he calls for vengeance,—their thirsty weapons glitter in the air, and thousands reverberate the cry! One soul animates a nation, and that soul is the soul of the orator!

Old F. O, what a figure he will make on the King's Bench! But, come, I will tell you now what my plan is, and then you will see how happily this determination of yours will further it. You have [*Tristram makes extravagant gestures, as if speaking*] often heard me speak of my friend Briefwit, the barrister—

Tri. Who is against me in this cause—

Old F. He is a most learned lawyer—

Tri. But, as I have justice on my side—

Old F. Zounds! he doesn't hear a word I say! Why, Tristram!

Tri. I beg your pardon, sir: I was prosecuting my studies.

Old F. Now, attend—

Tri. As my learned friend observes— Go on, sir: I am all attention.

Old F. Well, my friend the counsellor—

Tri. Say learned friend, if you please, sir. We gentlemen of the law always—

Old F. Well, well,—my learned friend—

Tri. A black patch!

Old F. Will you listen, and be silent?

Tri. I am as mute as a judge.

Old F. My friend, I say, has a ward who is very handsome, and who has a very handsome fortune. She would make you a charming wife.

Tri. This is an action—

Old F. Now, I have hitherto been afraid to introduce you to my friend, the barrister, because I thought your lightness and his gravity—

Tri. Might be plaintiff and defendant.

Old F. But now you are grown serious and steady, and have resolved to pursue his profession, I will shortly bring you together: you will obtain his good opinion, and all the rest follows, of course.

Tri. A verdict in my favor.

Old F. You marry and sit down, happy for life.

Tri. In the King's Bench.

Old F. Bravo! Ha, ha, ha! But now run to your study—run to your study, my dear Tristram, and I'll go and call upon the counsellor.

Tri. I remove by *habeas corpus.*

Old F. Pray have the goodness to make haste, then. [*Hurrying him off.*]

Tri. Gentlemen of the Jury, this is a cause— [*Exit.*]

Old F. The inimitable boy! I am now the happiest father living. What genius he has! He'll be lord chancellor, one day or other, I dare be sworn. I am sure he has talents! O, how I long to see him at the bar!

CCXII.—FROM BRUTUS.

PAYNE.

Characters.—Brutus, Centurion, Valerius, Titus, Collatinus, Lictors, Guards, People.

SCENE 1.—A Street in Rome.

[*Enter Brutus and Collatinus, as consuls, followed by lictors, guards, and people.*]

Brutus. You judge me rightly, friends. The purpled robe
The curule chair, the lictor's keen-edged axe,
Rejoice not Brutus—'tis his country's freedom:
When once that freedom shall be firmly rooted,
Then, with redoubled pleasure, will your consul
Exchange the splendid miseries of power,
For the calm comforts of a happy home.
[*Enter Centurion.*]

Centurion. Health to Brutus!
Shame and confusion to the foes of Rome!

Bru. Now, without preface, soldier, to your business.

Cent. As I kept watch at the Quirinal gate,
Ere break of day, an armed company
Burst on a sudden through the barrier guard,

18*

Pushing their course for Ardea. Straight alarmed,
I wheeled my cohort round, and charged them home :
Sharp was the conflict for a while, and doubtful,
Till, on the seizure of Tarquinia's person,
A young patrician——
    Bru. Hah ! patrician ?
    Cent. Such
His dress bespoke him, though to me unknown.
    Bru. Proceed !—what more ?
    Cent. The lady being taken,
This youth, the life and leader of the band,
His sword high waving in the act to strike,
Dropt his uplifted weapon, and at once
Yielded himself my prisoner. Oh, Valerius,
What have I said, that thus the consul changes ?
    Bru. Why do you pause ? Go on.
    Cent. Their leader seized,
The rest surrendered. Him, a settled gloom
Possesses wholly ; nor, as I believe,
Hath a word passed his lips, to all my questions
Still obstinately shut.
    Bru. Set him before us.   [*Exit Centurion.*]
    Valerius. Oh, my brave friend, horror invades my heart.
    Bru. Silence ! Be calm.
    Val. I know thy soul,
A compound of all excellence, and pray
The mighty gods to put thee to no trial
Beyond a mortal bearing.
    Bru. No, they will not—
Nay, be secure, they cannot. Pray thee, friend,
Look out, and if the worst that can befall me
Be verified, turn back.
Thou canst excuse this weakness,
Being thyself a father.   [*Valerius returns.*]
Since it must be so,
Do your great pleasure, gods ! Now, now it comes !
        [*Enter Titus, guarded.*]
    Titus. My father,—give me present death, ye powers !
    Cent. What have I done ! art thou the son of Brutus ?
    Tit. No—Brutus scorns to father such a son !
Oh, venerable judge, wilt thou not speak ?
Turn not away : hither direct thine eyes,
And look upon this sorrow-stricken form.

Then to thine own great heart remit my plea,
And doom as nature dictates.

Val. Peace, you'll anger him—
Be silent and await! Oh, suffering mercy,
Plead in a father's heart, and speak for nature !

Bru. Come hither, Collatinus. The deep wound
You suffered in the loss of your Lucretia,
Demanded more than fortitude to bear :
I saw your agony—I felt your woe—

Collatinus. You more than felt it : you revenged it, too.

Bru. But ah, my brother consul, your Lucretia
Fell nobly, as a Roman spirit should.
She fell a model of transcendant virtue.

Col. My mind misgives. What dost thou aim at, Brutus?

Bru. [*Almost overpowered.*]   That youth, my Titus, was my age's
        hope :
I loved him more than language can express :
I thought him born to dignify the world.

Col. My heart bleeds for you—he may yet be saved—

Bru. [*Firmly.*] Consul, for Rome I live, not for myself.
I dare not trust my firmness in this crisis,
Warring against every thing my soul holds dear !
Therefore return without me to the Senate—
I ought not now to take a seat among them—
Haply my presence might restrain their justice.
Look that these traitors meet their trial straight,
And then despatch a messenger to tell me
How the wise fathers have disposed of——go !

Tit. A word for pity's sake. Before thy feet,
Humbled in soul, thy son and prisoner kneels.
Love is my plea : a father is my judge :
Nature my advocate ! I can no more :
If these will not appease a parent's heart,
Strike through them all, and lodge thy vengeance here !

Bru. Break off! I will not, cannot hear thee further.
The affliction nature hath imposed on Brutus,
Brutus will suffer as he may.
Lictors, secure your prisoner. Point your axes
To the Senate. On !

        [*Exeunt all but Brutus. After a pause of restless agony,*]
Like a lost, guilty wretch, I look around
And start at every footstep, lest it bring
The fatal news of my poor son's conviction !

Oh, Rome, thou little knowest—no more. It comes.

[*Enter Valerius.*]

Val. My friend, the Senate hath to thee transferred
The right of judgment on thy son's offense.

Bru. To me?

Val. To thee alone.

Bru. What of the rest?

Val. Their sentence is already passed :
Even now, perhaps, the lictor's dreaded hand
Cuts off their forfeit lives.

Bru. Sayst thou the Senate have to me referred
The fate of Titus?

Val. Such is their sovereign will.
They think you merit this distinguished honor.
A father's grief deserves to be revered :
Rome will approve whatever you decree.

Bru. And is his guilt established beyond doubt?

Val. Too clearly.

Bru. [*With a burst of tears.*] Oh, ye gods! ye gods!
[*Collecting himself.*] Valerius!

Val. What wouldst thou, noble Roman?

Bru. 'Tis said thou hast pulled down thine house, Valerius,
The stately pile that with such cost was reared.

Val. I have; but what doth Brutus thence infer?

Bru. It was a goodly structure: I remember
How fondly you surveyed its rising grandeur.
With what a—fatherly—delight you summoned
Each grace and ornament, that might enrich
The—child—of your creation—till it swelled
To an imperial size, and overpeered
The petty citizens, that humbly dwelt
Under its lofty walls, in huts and hovels,
Like emmets at the foot of towering Etna :
Then, noble Roman, then, with patriot zeal,
Dear as it was, and valued, you condemned
And leveled the proud pile ; and, in return,
Were by your grateful countrymen surnamed,
And shall to all posterity descend,—
Poplicola.

Val. Yes, Brutus, I conceive
The awful aim and drift of thy discourse—
But I conjure thee, pause! thou art a father.

Bru. I am a Roman consul. What, my friend,

Shall no one but Valerius love his country
Dearer than house, or property, or children?
Now, follow me;—and in the face of heaven—
See, see, good Valerius, if Brutus
Feel not for Rome as warmly as Poplicola. [*Exeunt.*]

SCENE 2.—Interior of a Temple.

[*Brutus seated on the tribunal.*]

Bru. Romans, the blood which hath been shed this day
Hath been shed wisely. Traitors, who conspire
Against mature societies, may urge
Their acts as bold and daring; and though villains,
Yet they are manly villains—but to stab
The cradled innocent, as these have done,—
To strike their country in the mother-pangs,
And direct the dagger
To freedom's infant throat,—is a deed so black,
That my foiled tongue refuses it a name. [*A pause.*]
There is one criminal still left for judgment.
Let him approach. [*Enter Titus, guarded.*]
Pris-on-er—[*The voice of Brutus falters, and is choked, and he ex-
claims, with violent emotion,*]
Romans! forgive this agony of grief—
My heart is bursting—nature must have way—
I will perform all that a Roman should—
I cannot feel less than a father ought: [*He becomes more calm.*]
Well, Titus, speak—how is it with thee now?
Tell me, my son, art thou prepared to die?

Tit. Father! I call the powers of heaven to witness,
Titus dares die, when you have so decreed.
The gods will have me.

Bru. They will, my Titus;
Nor heaven, nor earth can have it otherwise.
The violated genius of thy country
Rears its sad head, and passes sentence on thee!
It seems as if thy fate were pre-ordained
To fix the reeling spirits of the people,
And settle the loose liberty of Rome.
'Tis fixed;—oh, therefore, let not fancy cheat thee!
So fixed thy death, that 'tis not in the power
Of mortal man to save thee from the axe.

Tit. The axe! Oh, heavens!—then must I fall so basely?
What, shall I perish like a common felon?

Bru. How else do traitors suffer? Nay, Titus, more :
I must myself behold thee meet this shame of death,—
With all thy hopes and all thy youth upon thee,—
See thy head taken by the common axe.
All,—if the gods can hold me to my purpose,—
Without a groan, without one pitying tear.
    Tit. Die like a felon ?—ha ! a common felon !—
But I deserve it all :—yet here I fail :
This ignominy quite unmans me !
Oh, Brutus, Brutus ! must I call you father,
Yet have no token of your tenderness,
No sign of mercy ? not even leave to fall
As noble Romans fall, by my own sword ?
Father, why should you make my heart suspect
That all your late compassion was dissembled ?
How can I think that you did ever love me ?
    Bru. Think that I love thee by my present passion,
By these unmanly tears, these earthquakes here,
These sighs, that strain the very strings of life :
Let these convince you that no other cause
Could force a father thus to wrong his nature.
    Tit. Oh, hold, thou violated majesty !
I now submit with calmness to my fate.
Come forth, ye executioners of justice—
Come, take my life,—and give it to my country !
    Bru. Embrace thy wretched father. May the gods
Arm thee with patience in this awful hour.
The sovereign magistrate of injured Rome,
Bound by his high authority, condemns
A crime thy father's bleeding heart forgives.
Go—meet thy death with a more manly courage
Than grief now suffers me to show in parting ;
And, while she punishes, let Rome admire thee !
No more ! Farewell ! eternally farewell !
    Tit. Oh, Brutus ! oh, my father !
Farewell, forever.
    Bru. Forever.
Lictors, attend !—conduct your prisoner forth !
    Val. [*Rapidly and anxiously.*] Whither ?
        [*All the characters bending forward with great anxiety.*]
    Bru. To death ! [*All start.*] When you do reach the spot,
My hand shall wave the signal for the act.
Then let the trumpet's sound proclaim it done !

[*Titus is conducted out by the lictors.*]
Poor youth! thy pilgrimage is at an end!
A few sad steps have brought thee to the brink
Of that tremendous precipice, whose depth
No thought of man can fathom.   Justice now
Demands her victim!   A little moment
And I am childless.—One effort, and 'tis past—

[*Waves his hand.*]
Justice is satisfied, and Rome is free.   [*Brutus falls.*]

CCXIII.—THE YOUNG POETS.

FRED AND HARRY.

[Or, by altering a few words, KATE and LIZZIE.]

Harry. Fred, have you written your composition?

Fred. No, I can't write poetry, and the teacher says he will take nothing else, you know.   Besides, I don't like the subject.   I should as soon think of writing a poem upon an old apron, as upon Industry.

H. There is not much room for imagination, but I'll tell you what, we can put our heads together, and write a poem between us.   You know there's the Ant and the Sluggard, we can bring that in.

F. Good, good, so we can.   Well, now start us with the first line.

H. No, you may do that.   It is easier to begin, because I must match your rhyme, you know.

F. Well, how will this do?
     " An ant upon an ant-hill sot."

H. Sot, Fred, why a sot is a drunkard.

F. Well, then,
     " An ant upon an aut-hill sat."

H. That is a good line, but what in the world would an industrious ant be sitting on an ant-hill for?

F. To rest herself, to be sure.   Come, now match my line, will you.
     " An ant upon an ant-hill sot—sat."
     " I wonder what she can be at."

You must account for her being seated, you know, for you seated her.

F. How will it do to say,—

"She thought of this and then of that."

H. She must have been a wonderful ant to do so ; but, no matter, here is another line,—

"And then, as lazy as a cat,"

F. How do you know a cat is lazy ? and *who* is lazy as a cat ?

H. Who ever knew a cat to do any work, unless watching for dinner is called work. But you interrupted me, or you would have known *who* was lazy. Hark!

"And then, as lazy as a cat,
A sluggard came to have some chat."

F. Good. Now for a dialogue. We must imagine the scene before we can describe it.

H. Well, there's the ant sitting flat, and there's the sluggard standing. Good. Now the ant, being a female, and, of course the greatest talker, would begin.

"O sluggard, said the ant, consider!"

F. That will never do, Harry: there's nothing on earth to rhyme with consider but *widder.*

H. Well, who knows but she was a *widder.* She was an *Aunt,* wasn't she ? Then she was a woman; and as *widders* work hard to keep their babies from starving, she must have been a *widder.*

F. That'll do, and we can put the explanation in a note. Now, suppose we say,—

ı "Sluggard, said the ant, consider,
I'm a poor, industrious widder."

H. Good, now push on, and finish her speech.

F. No, it is your turn.

H. Well, how will it do to make her say,

"And now you may depend upon it,"

F. Depend upon what ? Gracious, Harry, there's nothing to rhyme with *on it* but *bonnet,* and what has an ant to do with a bonnet ?

H. Poh, that is easily got over. You see this is per-

sonification, and she has a right to wear a bonnet, but there
is no need of it, for, I propose to make her say,—

> "And now you may depend upon it,
> Sure as my head's without a bonnet,"

F. (*Solemnly.*) Is not that an oath, Harry?

H. An oath? no, she don't swear by her bonnet, for she
hasn't any. Suppose we make her say next,

> "Until you learn to work and labor,"

F. That'll never do. What can you get to rhyme with
labor?

H. There's tabor.

F. It is not to be supposed the hard working ant ever
played.

H. Well then, take *sabre.*

F. Much less did she fight. Besides, *work* and *labor* is
what the teacher calls tortuology, or something else: the
words mean the same thing.

H. Don't stand for trifles. Go on, Fred.

F. I've caught a grand rhyme, hark!

> "Until you learn to work and labor,
> As I have done ever since I was a little babe uh!"

H. Your line is too long, Fred: you must cut off both
the feet of your baby, or the line will limp dreadfully.

F. Better have the line limp than the baby. So go on
and let the baby alone. What else does the widder say to
the sluggard?

> "Until you learn to work and labor,
> As I have done ever since I was a little babe uh!"

H. Now, we go on,—

> "You never can be rich or wise,
> Which with mankind the same thing is."

F. O, Harry, *is* can never rhyme with *wise,* and, besides,
to be rich and to be wise don't mean the same thing.

H. Yes they do. All the ant ever did was to hoard
up; and all the sluggard had to do was to consider her
ways. So, you see, there's scripture for it, and wealth must
be wisdom, for who ever heard of a poor man being wise.

F. Well, it is time for the sluggard to say something now. Suppose we say,—

"The sluggard yawned and raised his head,"

H. Better say *scratched* his head, that is more natural for a sluggard.

F. Very well, so be it.

"The sluggard yawned and scratched his head,"

H. Well, are you going to make him reform or not? because every thing depends upon the cat-a-cata something, what is it?

F. Catastrophe, I suppose you mean; but I have a line that dodges the reform question, and leaves the field open for my successors.

"The sluggard yawned and scratched his head,
And no reply for some time made."

There now, go it, and make him say something smart.

H. He's too lazy to be smart. *You* must tell what he said, and I will only say,—

"Then, yawning, as if his under jaw
Would never close up as before,—

What did he say? now wind it up in style.

F. "He stared the widder in the face,
And said, Old pismire, go to grass!"

[*From Fowle's Hundred Dialogues.*]

CCXIV.—THE RIGHTEOUS JUDGE.—Merchant of Venice.

Duke, Judge, Shylock, the Jew, Antonio, the merchant, Bassanio, and Gratiano, merchant's friends.

[*Enter Judge.*]

Duke. You are welcome: take your place.
Are you acquainted with the difference
That holds this present question in the court?

Judge. I am informed thoroughly of the cause:
Which is the merchant here, and which the Jew?

D. Antonio and old Shylock, both stand forth.

J. Is your name Shylock?

Shylock. Shylock is my name.

J. Of a strange nature is the suit you follow:
Yet in such rule, that the Venetian law
Cannot impugn you, as you do proceed.—
You stand within his danger, do you not?   (*To Antonio.*)
   Antonio. Ay, so he says.
   J. Do you confess the bond?
   A. I do.
   J. Then must the Jew be merciful.
   S. On what compulsion must I? tell me that?
   J. The quality of mercy is not strained:
It droppeth as the gentle rain from heaven
Upon the place beneath: it is twice blessed:
It blesseth him that gives, and him that takes:
'Tis mightiest in the mightiest. It becomes
The throned monarch better than his crown:
His sceptre shows the force of temporal power,
The attribute to awe and majesty,
Wherein doth sit the dread and fear of kings;
But mercy is above this sceptred sway,
It is enthroned in the hearts of kings,
It is an attribute to God himself;
And earthly power doth then show likest God's
When mercy seasons justice. Therefore, Jew,
Though justice be thy plea, consider this,—
That, in the course of justice, none of us
Should see salvation. We do pray for mercy;
And that same prayer doth teach us all to render
The deeds of mercy. I have spoke thus much,
To mitigate the justice of thy plea;
Which if thou follow, this strict court of Venice
Must needs give sentence 'gainst the merchant there.
   S. My deeds upon my head! I crave the law,
The penalty and forfeit of my bond.
   J. Is he not able to discharge the money?
   Bassanio. Yes: here I tender it for him in the court:
Yea, twice the sum: if that will not suffice,
I will be bound to pay it ten times o'er,
On forfeit of my hands, my head, my heart:
If this will not suffice, it must appear
That malice bears down truth. And I beseech you,
Wrest once the law to your authority:
To do a great right, do a little wrong;
And curb this cruel demon of his will.

J. It must not be : there is no power in Venice
Can alter a decree established :
'Twill be recorded for a precedent :
And many an error, by the same example,
Will rush into the state : it cannot be.

S. A Daniel come to judgment! yea, a Daniel !—
O wise young judge, how do I honor thee !

J. I pray you let me look upon the bond.

S. Here 'tis, most reverend doctor, here it is.

J. Shylock, there's thrice thy money offered thee.

S. An oath, an oath, I have an oath in heaven :
Shall I lay perjury upon my soul?
No, not for Venice.

J. Why, this bond is forfeit;
And lawfully by this the Jew may claim
A pound of flesh to be by him cut off
Nearest the merchant's heart.   Be merciful :
Take thrice thy money : bid me tear the bond.

S. When it is paid according to the tenor.
It doth appear you are a worthy judge ;
You know the law, your exposition
Hath been most sound : I charge you, by the law,
Whereof you are a well deserving pillar,
Proceed to judgment : by my soul I swear,
There is no power in the tongue of man
To alter me.   I stay here on my bond.

A. Most heartily do I beseech the court
To give the judgment.

J. Why, then, thus it is.
You must prepare your bosom for his knife.

S. O noble judge !   O excellent young man !

J. For the intent and purpose of the law
Hath full relation to the penalty,
Which here appeareth due upon the bond.

S. 'Tis very true : O wise and upright judge
How much more elder art thou than thy looks !

J. Therefore, lay bare your bosom.

S. Ay, his breast:
So says the bond.   Doth it not, noble judge ?
Nearest his heart, those are the very words.

J. It is so.   Are there balance here to weigh
The flesh ?

S. I have them ready.

J. Have by some surgeon, Shylock, on your charge,
To stop his wounds, lest he do bleed to death.
    S. Is it so nominated in the bond?
    J. It is not so expressed; but what of that?
'Twere good you do so much for charity.
    S. I cannot find it: 'tis not in the bond.
We trifle time: I pray thee, pursue sentence.
    J. A pound of that same merchant's flesh is thine:
The court awards it, and the law doth give it.
    S. Most rightful judge!
    J. And you must cut this flesh from off his breast:
The law allows it, and the court awards it.
    S. Most learned judge!—A sentence: come, prepare!
                         (Approaches Antonio.)
    J. Tarry a little;—there is something else.
This bond doth give thee here no jot of blood:
The words expressly are, a pound of flesh:
Take then thy bond, take thou thy pound of flesh;
But, in the cutting it, if thou dost shed
One drop of Christian blood, thy lands and goods
Are, by the laws of Venice, confiscate
Unto the state of Venice.
    Gratiano. O upright judge!—Mark, Jew: O learned judge!
    S. Is that the law?
    J. Thyself shalt see the act:
For as thou urgest justice, be assured,
Thou shalt have justice, more than thou desirest.
    G. O learned judge!—Mark, Jew: a learned judge!
    S. I take this offer, then;—pay the bond thrice;
And let the Christian go.
    B. Here is the money.
    J. Soft:
The Jew shall have all justice:—soft!—no haste:—
He shall have nothing but the penalty.
    G. O Jew! an upright judge, a learned judge!
    J. Therefore, prepare thee to cut off the flesh.
Shed thou no blood; nor cut thou less, nor more,
But just a pound of flesh; if thou tak'st more,
Or less, than a just pound,—be it but so much
As makes it light, or heavy, in the substance,
Or the division of the twentieth part
Of one poor scruple; nay, if the scale do turn
But in the estimation of a hair,—
Thou diest, and all thy goods are confiscate.

G. A second Daniel, a Daniel, Jew !

J. Why doth the Jew pause? take thy forfeiture.

S. Give the principal and let me go.

B. I have it ready for thee: here it is.

J. He hath refused it in the open court:
He shall have merely justice and his bond.

G. A Daniel, still say I: a second Daniel !
I thank thee, Jew, for teaching me that word.

S. Shall I not have barely my principal ?

J. Thou shalt have nothing but the forfeiture,
To be so taken at thy peril.   Tarry, Jew :
The law hath yet another hold on you.
It is enacted in the laws of Venice,—
If it be proved against an alien,
That by direct, or indirect attempts,
He seek the life of any citizen,
The party 'gainst the which he doth contrive
Shall seize one half his goods: the other half
Comes to the privy coffer of the state ;
And the offender's life lies in the mercy
Of the duke only, 'gainst all other voice.
In which predicament, I say, thou standest :
Down, therefore, and beg mercy of the duke.

CCXV.—THE QUACK.

SCENE—The Inn.

Enter HOSTESS, *followed by* LAMPEDO, *a Quack Doctor.*

Hostess. Nay, nay : another fortnight.

Lampedo. It can't be.
The man's as well as I am : have some mercy !
He hath been here almost three weeks already.

Host. Well, then a week.

Lamp. We may detain him a week.   [*with a drawn sword.*
    [*Enter* BALTHAZAR, *the patient, from behind, in his night-gown,*
You talk now like a reasonable hostess,
That sometimes has a reckoning with her conscience.

Host. He still believes he has an inward bruise.

Lamp. I would to heaven he had ! or that he'd slipp'd
His shoulder-blade, or broke a leg or two,
(Not that I bear his person any malice,)
Or lux'd an arm, or even sprained his ankle !

Host. Ay, broken any thing except his neck.

Lamp. However, for a week I'll manage him :
Though he had the constitution of a horse.
A farrier shall prescribe for him.

Balthazar. [*Aside.*] A farrier !

Lamp. To-morrow, we phlebotomize again :
Next day, my new invented, patent draught ;
Then, I have some pills prepared :
On Thursday, we throw in the bark : on Friday——

Balth. [*Coming forward.*] Well, sir, on Friday—what on Friday ?
Come, proceed.

Lamp. Discovered !

Host. Mercy, noble sir !   } *They fall on their knees.*
Lamp. We crave your mercy ! }

Balth. On your knees ? 'tis well !
Pray, for your time is short.

Host. Nay, do not kill us.

Balth. You have been tried, condemn'd, and only wait
For execution. Which shall I begin with ?

Lamp. The lady, by all means, sir,

Balth. Come, prepare. [*To the hostess.*]

Host. Have pity on the weakness of my sex !

Balth. Tell me, thou quaking mountain of gross flesh,
Tell me, and in a breath, how many poisons—
If you attempt it—[*To* LAMPEDO, *who is making off.*]
                 you have cooked up for me?

Host. None, as I hope for mercy !

Balth. Is not thy wine a poison ?

Host. No, indeed, sir :
'Tis not, I own, of the first quality :
But——

Balth. What ?

Host. I always give short measure, sir.
And ease my conscience that way.

Balth. Ease your conscience !
I'll ease your conscience for you.

Host. Mercy, sir !

Balth. Rise, if thou canst, and hear me.

Host. Your commands, sir?

Balth. If, in five minutes, all things are prepared
For my departure, you may yet survive.

Host. It shall be done in less.

Balth. Away, thou lump fish !   [*Exit hostess.*

Lamp. So! now comes my turn! 'tis all over with me!
There's dagger, rope, and ratsbane in his looks!

Balth. And now, thou sketch and outline of a man!
Thou thing that hast no shadow in the sun!
Thou eel in a consumption, eldest born
Of Death on Famine! thou anatomy
Of a starved pilchard!

Lamp. I do confess my leanness.   I am spare,
And, therefore, spare me.

Balth. Why! wouldst thou not have made me
A thoroughfare, for thy whole shop to pass through?

Lamp. Man, you know, must live.

Balth. Yes: he must die, too.

Lamp. For my patients' sake—

Balth. I'll send thee to the major part of them.
The window, sir, is open: come, prepare.

Lamp. Pray, consider:
I may hurt some one in the street.

Balth. Why, then,
I'll rattle thee to pieces in a dice-box,
Or grind thee in a coffee-mill to powder,
For thou must sup with Pluto; so, make ready:
While I, with this good small-sword for a lancet,
Let thy starved spirit out, (for blood thou hast none,)
And nail thee to the wall, where thou shalt look
Like a dried beetle with a pin stuck through him.

Lamp. Consider my poor wife.

Balth. Thy wife!

Lamp. My wife, sir.

Balth. Hast thou dared think of matrimony, too?
No flesh upon thy bones, and take a wife!

Lamp. I took a wife, because I wanted flesh.
I have a wife, and three angelic babes,
Who, by those looks, are well nigh fatherless.

Balth. Well, well! you wife and children shall plead for you.
Come, come: the pills! where are the pills? produce them.

Lamp. Here is the box.

Balth. Were it Pandora's, and each single pill
Had ten diseases in it, you should take them.

Lamp. What, all?

Balth. Ay, all; and quickly too.   Come, sir, begin—that's well!
Another.

Lamp. One's a dose.

Balth. Proceed, sir.

Lamp. What will become of me?
Let me go home, and set my shop to rights,
And, like immortal Cæsar, die with decency.

Balth. Away! and thank thy lucky star I have not
Bray'd thee in thine own mortar, or exposed thee
For a large specimen of the lizard genus.

Lamp. Would I were one! for they can feed on air.

Balth. Home, sir, and be more honest.   [*Exit.*

Lamp. If I am not,
I'll be more wise, at least.   [*Exit.*]

CCXVI.—LOST REPUTATION—FROM OTHELLO.

SHAKSPEARE.

Characters—IAGO—CASSIO.

Iago. What! be you hurt, lieutenant?

Cass. Past all surgery.

Iago. Marry, heaven forbid!

Cass. Reputation! reputation! reputation! Oh I have lost my reputation! I have lost the immortal part of myself; and what remains is bestial. My reputation! Iago, my reputation—

Iago. As I am an honest man, I thought you had received some bodily wound: there is more sense in that, than in reputation. Reputation is an idle and false imposition: oft got without merit, and lost without deserving. What, man! There are ways to recover the general again: sue to him, and he is yours.

Cass. I will rather sue to be despised—Drunk! and squabble! swagger! swear! and discourse fustian with one's own shadow! Oh thou invincible spirit of wine! if thou hast no name to be known by, let us call thee, Devil.

Iago. What was he that you followed with your sword! what had he done to you?

Cass. I know not.

Iago. Is it possible?

Cass. I remember a mass of things, but nothing dis-

19

tinctly: a quarrel, but nothing wherefore: Oh, that men should put an enemy in their mouths to steal away their brains! that we should with joy, pleasance, revel, and applause, transform ourselves into beasts!

Iago. Why, but you are now well enough: how came you thus recovered?

Cass. It has pleased the devil Drunkenness, to give place to the devil Wrath. One imperfection shows me another, to make me frankly despise myself.

Iago. Come: you are too severe a moraler. As the time, place, and the condition of this country stands, I could heartily wish this had not befallen; but since it is as it is, mend it for your own good.

Cass. I will ask him for my place again: he shall tell me I am a drunkard! Had I as many mouths as Hydra, such an answer would stop them all. To be now a sensible man, by and by a fool, and presently a beast!—Every inordinate cup is unblessed, and the ingredient is a devil.

Iago. Come: come: good wine is a good familiar creature, if it be well used: exclaim no more against it;—and, good lieutenant, I think you think I love you?

Cass. I have well approved it, sir:—I drunk!

Iago. You, or any man living, may be drunk some time, man! I tell you what you shall do. Our general's wife is now the general: confess yourself freely to her: importune her help to put you in your place again. She is of so free, so kind, so apt, so blessed a disposition, she holds it a vice in her goodness, not to do more than she is requested. This broken joint between you and her husband entreat her to splinter; and my fortune against any lay worth naming, this crack of your love shall grow stronger than it was before.

Cass. You advise me well.

Iago. I protest, in the sincerity of love and honest kindness.

Cass. I think it freely; and betimes in the morning, I will beseech the virtuous Desdemona to undertake for me.

Iago. You are in the right. Good night, lieutenant.

Cass. Good night, honest Iago.

CCXVII.—THE LETTER.

LOVER.

SQUIRE EGAN, *and his new Irish servant,* ANDY.

Squire. Well, Andy: you went to the post-office, as I ordered you?

Andy. Yis, sir.

S. Well, what did you find?

A. A most imperthinent fellow, indade, sir.

S. How so?

A. Says I, as dacent like as a genthleman, "I want a letther, sir, if you plase." "Who do you want it for?" said the posth-masther as ye call him. "I want a letther, sir, if you plase," said I. "And whom do you want it for?" said he again. "And what's that to you?" said I.

S. You blockhead, what did he say to that?

A. He laughed at me, sir, and said he could not tell what letther to give me unless I tould him the direction.

S. Well, you told him then, did you?

A. "The directions I got," said I, "was to get a letther here—that's the directions." "Who gave you the directions?" says he. "The masther," said I. "And who's your masther?" said he. "What consarn is that o' yours'?" said I.

S. Did he break your head, then?

A. No, sir. "Why, you stupid rascal," said he, "if you don't tell me his name, how can I give you his letther?" "You could give it if you liked," said I: "only you are fond of axing impident questions, because you think I'm simple." "Get out o' this!" said he. "Your masther must be as great a goose as yourself, to send such a missinger."

S. Well, how did you save my honor, Andy?

A. "Bad luck to your impidence!" said I. "Is it

Squire Egan you dare to say goose to?" "O, Squire Egan's your masther?" said he. "Yis," says I. "Have you any thing to say agin it?"

S. You got the letter, then, did you?

A. "Here's a letther for the Squire," says he. "You are to pay me eleven pence posthage." "What 'ud I pay 'leven pence for?" said I. "For *posthage*," says he. "Didn't I see you give that gentleman a letther for fourpence, this blessed minit?" said I: "and a bigger letther than this? Do you think I'm a fool?" says I. "Here's a fourpence for you—and give me the letther."

S. I wonder he did not break your skull, and let some light into it.

A. "Go along, you stupid thafe!" says he, because I would not let him *chate* your honor.

S. Well, well: give me the letter.

A. I haven't it, sir. He wouldn't give it to me, sir.

S. Who wouldn't give it to you?

A. That old *chate* beyent in the town.

S. Didn't you pay him what he asked?

A. Arrah, sir, why would I let you be chated, when he was selling them before my face for fourpence apace?

S. Go back, you scoundrel, or I'll horsewhip you!

A. He'll murther me, if I say another word to him about the letther: he swore he would.

S. I'll do it, if he don't, if you are not back in less than half an hour. [*Exit.*]

A. O that the like of me should be murthered for defending the charrackther of my masther! It's not I'll go to *dale* with that bloody *chate* again. I'll off to Dublin, and let the letther rot on his dirty hands, bad luck to him!

CCXVIII.—THE WILL.

Characters.—SWIPES, *a brewer:* CURRIE, *a saddler:* FRANK MILLINGTON, *and* SQUIRE DRAWL.

Swipes. A sober occasion, this, brother Currie. Who would have thought the old lady was so near her end?

Currie. Ah! we must all die, brother Swipes; and those who live longest, outlive the most.

Swipes. True, true; but since we must die and leave our earthly possessions, it is well that the law takes such good care of us. Had the old lady her senses when she departed?

Cur. Perfectly, perfectly. Squire Drawl told me she read every word of the will aloud, and never signed her name better.

Swipes. Had you any hint from the Squire, what disposition she made of her property?

Cur. Not a whisper: the Squire is as close as an underground tomb: but one of the witnesses hinted to me, that she had cut off her graceless nephew, Frank, without a shilling.

Swipes. Has she, good soul, has she? You know I come in, then, in right of my wife.

Cur. And I in my own right; and this is no doubt the reason why we have been called to hear the reading of the will. Squire Drawl knows how things should be done, though he is as air-tight as one of your beer-barrels. But here comes the young reprobate. He must be present, as a matter of course, you know. [*Enter* FRANK MILLINGTON.] Your servant, young gentleman. So your benefactress has left you, at last.

Swipes. It is a painful thing to part with old and good friends, Mr. Millington.

Frank. It is so, sir; but I could bear her loss better, had I not so often been ungrateful for her kindness. She was my only friend, and I knew not her value.

Cur. It is too late to repent, Master Millington. You will now have a chance to earn your own bread.

Swipes. Ay, ay, by the sweat of your brow, as better people are obliged to. You would make a fine brewer's boy, if you were not too old.

Cur. Ay, or a saddler's lackey, if held with a tight rein.

Frank. Gentlemen, your remarks imply that my aunt has treated me as I deserved. I am above your insults, and only hope you will bear your fortune as *modestly*, as I shall mine *submissively*. I shall retire. [*Going: he meets* SQUIRE DRAWL.]

Squire. Stop, stop, young man. We must have your presence. Good morning, gentlemen : you are early on the ground.

Cur. I hope the Squire is well to-day.

Squire. Pretty comfortable, for an invalid.

Swipes. I trust the damp air has not affected your lungs again.

Squire. No, I believe not. But since the heirs at law are all convened, I shall now proceed to open the last will and testament of your deceased relative, according to law.

. *Swipes.* [*While the Squire is breaking the seal.*] It is a trying thing to leave all one's possessions, Squire, in this manner.

Cur. It really makes me feel melancholy, when I look round and see every thing but the venerable owner of these goods. Well did the Preacher say, " All is vanity."

Squire. Please to be seated, gentlemen. [*He puts on his spectacles, and begins to read slowly.*] " Imprimis : whereas my nephew, Francis Millington, by his disobedience and ungrateful conduct, has shown himself unworthy of my bounty, and incapable of managing my large estate, I do hereby give and bequeath all my houses, farms, stocks, bonds, moneys, and property, both personal and real, to my dear cousins, Samuel Swipes, of Malt street, brewer, and Christopher Currie, of Fly-Court, saddler—" [*The Squire takes off his spectacles, to wipe them.*]

Swipes. Generous creature ! Kind soul ! I always loved her.

Cur. She was good, she was kind ;—and, brother Swipes, when we divide, I think I'll take the mansion-house.

Swipes. Not so fast, if you please, Mr. Currie. My wife has long had her eye upon that, and must have it.

Cur. There will be two words to that bargain, Mr. Swipes. And, besides, I ought to have the first choice. Did I not lend her a new chaise, every time she wished to ride? And who knows what influence—

Swipes. Am I not named first in her will? and did I not furnish her with my best small beer, for more than six months? and who knows—

Frank. Gentlemen, I must leave you. [*Going.*]

Squire. [*Putting on his spectacles very deliberately.*] Pray, gentlemen, keep your seats, I have not done yet. Let me see; where was I? Ay, " All my property, both personal and real, to my dear cousins, Samuel Swipes, of Malt street, brewer,"—

Swipes. Yes!

Squire. " And Christopher Currie, of Fly-Court, saddler,"—

Cur. Yes!

Squire. " To have and to hold, IN TRUST, for the sole and exclusive benefit of my nephew, Francis Millington, until he shall have attained the age of twenty-one years, by which time, I hope he will have so far reformed his evil habits, as that he may safely be intrusted with the large fortune which I hereby bequeath to him.

Swipes. What's all this? You don't mean that we are humbugged? *In trust!* How does that appear? Where is it?

Squire. There: in two words of as good old English as I ever penned.

Cur. Pretty well, too, Mr. Squire, if we must be sent for, to be made a laughing stock of. She shall pay for every ride she has had out of my chaise, I promise you.

Swipes. And for every drop of my beer. Fine times! if two sober, hard-working citizens are to be brought here, to be made the sport of a graceless profligate. But we will manage his property for him, Mr. Currie: we will make him feel that *trustees* are not to be *trifled* with.

Cur. That we will.

Squire. Not so fast, gentlemen; for the instrument is dated three years ago; and the young gentleman must be already of age, and able to take care of himself. Is it not so, Francis?

Frank. It is, your worship.

Squire. Then, gentlemen, having attended to the breaking of the seal, according to law, you are released from any further trouble about the business.

CCXIX.—GHOST SCENE FROM HAMLET.

SHAKSPEARE.

Enter HAMLET, HORATIO, *and* MARCELLUS.

Hamlet. The air bites shrewdly: it is very cold.

Horatio. It is a nipping and an eager air.

Ham. What hour now?

Hor. I think, it lacks of twelve.

Mar. No, it is struck.

Hor. Indeed? I heard it not; then it draws near the season,
Wherein the spirit held his wont to walk.

[*A flourish of trumpets, and ordnance shot off, within.*]
What does this mean, my lord?

Ham. The king doth wake to-night, and takes his rouse,
And, as he drains his draughts of Rhenish down,
The kettle-drum and trumpet thus bray out
The triumph of his pledge.

Hor. Is it a custom?

Ham. Ay, marry, is't;
But to my mind,—though I am native here,
And to the manner born,—it is a custom
More honored in the breach, than the observance.

[*Enter* GHOST.]

Hor. Look, my lord, it comes!

Ham. Angels and ministers of grace defend us!
Be thou a spirit of health, or goblin damned,
Bring with thee airs from heaven, or blasts from hell,
Be thy intents wicked, or charitable,
Thou com'st in such a questionable shape,
That I will speak to thee: I'll call thee Hamlet,
King, father, royal Dane: O, answer me:

Let me not burst in ignorance ! but tell,
Why thy canonized bones, hearsed in death,
Have burst their cerements : why the sepulcher
Wherein we saw thee quietly in-urned,
Hath oped his ponderous and marble jaws,
To cast thee up again ! What may this mean,
That thou, dead corse, again, in complete steel,
Revisit'st thus the glimpses of the moon,
Making night hideous ; and we fools of nature,
So horribly to shake our disposition,
With thoughts beyond the reaches of our souls ?
Say why is this ? wherefore ? what should we do ?

Hor. It beckons you to go away with it,
As if it some impartment did desire
To you alone.

Mar. Look, with what courteous action
It waves you to a more removed ground ;
But do not go with it.

Hor. No, by no means.

Ham. It will not speak ; then I will follow it.

Hor. Do not, my lord.

Ham. Why, what should be the fear ?
I do not set my life at a pin's fee ;
And, for my soul, what can it do to that,
Being a thing immortal, as itself ?
It waves me forth again ;—I'll follow it.

Hor. What, if it tempt you toward the flood, my lord,
Or to the dreadful summit of the cliff,
That beetles o'er his base into the sea ?
And there assume some other horrible form,
And draw you into madness ?

Ham. It waves me still :—
Go on, I'll follow thee.

Mar. You shall not go, my lord.

Ham. Hold off your hands.

Hor. Be ruled, you shall not go.

Ham. My fate cries out,
And makes each petty artery in this body
As hardy as the Nemean lion's nerve.—   [Ghost *beckons.*]
Still am I called ;—unhand me, gentlemen :—[*Breaking from them.*]
By heaven, I'll make a ghost of him that lets me :—
I say, away !—Go on, I'll follow thee.

[*Exeunt* Ghost *and* Hamlet, *followed by* Horatio *and* Marcellus.]

19*

[*Re-enter* GHOST *and* HAMLET.]

Ham. Whither wilt thou lead me ? speak, I'll go no further.

Ghost. Mark me.

Ham. I will.

Ghost. My hour is almost come,
When I to sulphurous and tormenting flames
Must render up myself.

Ham. Alas, poor ghost !

Ghost. Pity me not, but lend thy serious hearing
To what I shall unfold.

Ham. Speak, I am bound to hear.

Ghost. So art thou to revenge, when thou shalt hear.

Ham. What ?

Ghost. I am thy father's spirit :
Doomed for a certain term to walk the night,
And, for the day—confined to fast in fires,
Till the foul crimes, done in my days of nature,
Are burnt and purged away. But that I am forbid
To tell the secrets of my prison-house,
I could a tale unfold, whose lightest word
Would harrow up thy soul : freeze thy young blood :
Make thy two eyes, like stars, start from their spheres :
Thy knotted and combined locks to part,
And each particular hair to stand on end,
Like quills upon the fretful porcupine :
But this eternal blazon must not be
To ears of flesh and blood :—List,—list,—O list !—
If thou didst ever thy dear father love,——

Ham. O heaven !

Ghost. Revenge this foul and most unnatural murder.

Ham. Murder ?

Ghost. Murder most foul, as in the best it is ;
But this most foul, strange, and unnatural.

Ham. Haste me to know it ; that I, with wings as swift
As meditation, or the thoughts of love,
May sweep to my revenge.

Ghost. I find thee apt ;
And duller should'st thou be than the fat weed
That rots itself in ease on Lethe * wharf,
Would'st thou not stir in this. Now, Hamlet, hear:

---

* Lethe, a river of Africa, because the name signifies *oblivion*, was feigned to cause forgetfulness of all that was past to those who drank of its waters : oblivion : forgetfulness,

'Tis given out, that sleeping in mine orchard,
A serpent stung me : so the whole ear of Denmark
Is by a forged process of my death
Rankly abused : but know, thou noble youth,
The serpent that did sting thy father's life,
Now wears his crown.

    Ham. O, my prophetic soul ! my uncle !
    Ghost. Ay,—
With witchcraft of his wit, with traitorous gifts,
He won to his shameful love
The will of my most seeming virtuous queen :
O, Hamlet, what a falling-off was there !
From me, whose love was of that dignity,
That it went hand in hand even with the vow
I made to her in marriage ; and to decline
Upon a wretch, whose natural gifts were poor
To those of mine !—
But, soft ! methinks, I scent the morning air :
Brief let me be :—Sleeping within my orchard,
My custom always of the afternoon,
Upon my secure hour thy uncle stole,
With juice of cursed hebenon in a vial,
And in the porches of mine ears did pour
The leperous distillment : whose effect
Holds such an enmity with blood of man,
That, swift as quicksilver, it courses through
The natural gates and alleys of the body ;
And, with a sudden vigor, it doth posset
And curd, like eager droppings into milk,
The thin and wholesome blood : so did it mine :
Thus was I, sleeping, by a brother's hand,
Of life, of crown, of queen, at once dispatched :
Cut off even in the blossoms of my sin,
No reckoning made, but sent to my account
With all my imperfections on my head.

    Ham. O, horrible ! O, horrible ! most horrible !
    Ghost. If thou hast nature in thee, bear it not ;
But, howsoever thou pursu'st this act,
Taint not thy mind, nor let thy soul contrive
Against thy mother aught : leave her to heaven,
And to those thorns that in her bosom lodge,
To goad and sting her. Fare thee well at once !
The glowworm shows the matin to be near,

And 'gins to pale his ineffectual fire:
Adieu, adieu, adieu! remember me.   [*Exit.*]
    Ham. Hold, hold, my heart:
And you my sinews, grow not instant old,
But bear me stiffly up!—Remember thee !
Ay, thou poor ghost, while memory holds a seat
In this distracted globe.   Remember thee ?
Yea, from the table of my memory
I'll wipe away all trivial fond records,
All saws of books, all forms, all pressures past
That youth and observation copied there ;
And thy commandment all alone shall live
Within the book and volume of my brain,
Unmixed with baser matter : yes, by heaven,
I have sworn't.